From the diary of Miss Miranda Cheever—

8 June 1819

I am informed that certain society matrons are under the impression that Turner holds me in a romantic regard. This would be cause for great celebration, if:

1. It were true.
2. He hadn't laughed when he heard the rumor.
3. His mother hadn't shaken her head and said, "I *tried* to tell them it was impossible."
4. He hadn't responded by saying, "Miranda is certainly the least intolerable girl in London."
5. He hadn't then grinned in my direction, as if I were expected to take that as a compliment.

I laughed, of course, because he was clearly jesting, and I suppose I should be grateful he considers me a fine enough friend to tease.

But I do not wish to be his friend.

I want something so much more.

Books by
Julia Quinn

A NIGHT LIKE THIS
JUST LIKE HEAVEN
TEN THINGS I LOVE ABOUT YOU
WHAT HAPPENS IN LONDON
MR. CAVENDISH, I PRESUME
THE LOST DUKE OF WYNDHAM
THE SECRET DIARIES OF MISS MIRANDA CHEEVER
ON THE WAY TO THE WEDDING
IT'S IN HIS KISS
WHEN HE WAS WICKED
TO SIR PHILLIP, WITH LOVE
ROMANCING MISTER BRIDGERTON
AN OFFER FROM A GENTLEMAN
THE VISCOUNT WHO LOVED ME
THE DUKE AND I
HOW TO MARRY A MARQUIS
TO CATCH AN HEIRESS
BRIGHTER THAN THE SUN
EVERYTHING AND THE MOON
SPLENDID

JULIA QUINN

The Secret Diaries of Miss Miranda Cheever

AVON

An Imprint of HarperCollinsPublishers

This is a work of fiction. Names, characters, places, and incidents are products of the author's imagination or are used fictitiously and are not to be construed as real. Any resemblance to actual events, locales, organizations, or persons, living or dead, is entirely coincidental.

AVON BOOKS
An Imprint of HarperCollins*Publishers*
10 East 53rd Street
New York, New York 10022–5299

First Avon Books mass market special printing: January 2013
First Avon Books mass market printing: July 2007

Printed in the U.S.A.

10 9 8 7 6 5 4 3 2 1

For all the people who tipped well at Friendly's,
enabling me to save up for my first computer,
a Mac SE. (Sans hard drive—thanks, Dad!)

And also for Paul,
even though he has totally flaked on his promise
to turn said computer into a fishtank.

Prologue

At the age of ten, Miss Miranda Cheever showed no signs of Great Beauty. Her hair was brown—lamentably—as were her eyes; and her legs, which were uncommonly long, refused to learn anything that could be remotely called grace. Her mother often remarked that she positively loped around the house.

Unfortunately for Miranda, the society into which she was born placed great stock on female appearance. And although she was only ten, she knew that in this regard she was considered inferior to most of the other little girls who lived nearby. Children have a way of finding these things out, usually from other children.

Just such an unpleasant incident occurred at the eleventh birthday party of Lady Olivia and the Honorable Winston Bevelstoke, twin children of the Earl and Countess of Rudland. Miranda's home was quite close to Haverbreaks, the Rudlands' ancestral home near Ambleside, in the Lake District of Cumberland, and she had always shared lessons with Olivia and Winston when they were in residence. They had become quite an inseparable threesome and rarely bothered to play with the other children in the area, most of whom lived nearly an hour's ride away.

But a dozen or so times a year, and especially on birthdays, all the children of the local nobility and gentry gathered together. It was for this reason that Lady Rudland let out a most unladylike groan; eighteen urchins were gleefully tramping mud through her sitting room after the twins' party in the garden was disrupted by rain.

"You've mud on your cheek, Livvy," Miranda said, reaching out to wipe it away.

Olivia let out a dramatically weary sigh. "I'd best go to the washroom, then. I shouldn't want Mama to see me thus. She quite abhors dirt, and I quite abhor listening to her tell me how much she abhors it."

"I don't see how she will to have time to object to a little mud on your face when she's got it all over the carpet." Miranda glanced over at William Evans, who let out a war cry and cannonballed onto the sofa. She pursed her lips; otherwise, she'd smile. "And the furniture."

"All the same, I had best go do something about it."

She slipped out of the room, leaving Miranda near the doorway. Miranda watched the commotion for a minute or so, quite content to be in her usual spot as an observer, until, out of the corner of her eye, she saw someone approaching.

"What did you bring Olivia for her birthday, Miranda?"

Miranda turned to see Fiona Bennet standing before her, prettily dressed in a white frock with a pink sash. "A book," she replied. "Olivia likes to read. What did you bring?"

Fiona held up a gaily painted box tied with a silver cord. "A collection of ribbons. Silk and satin and even velvet. Do you want to see?"

"Oh, but I wouldn't want to ruin the wrapping."

Fiona shrugged. "All you need to do is untie the cord carefully. I do it every Christmas." She slipped off the cord and lifted the lid.

Miranda caught her breath. At least two dozen ribbons lay on the black velvet of the box, each exquisitely tied into a bow. "They're beautiful, Fiona. May I see one?"

Fiona narrowed her eyes.

"I haven't any mud on my hands. See?" Miranda held her hands up for inspection.

"Oh, very well."

Miranda reached down and picked up a violet ribbon. The satin felt sinfully sleek and soft in her hands. She placed the bow coquettishly against her hair. "What do you think?"

Fiona rolled her eyes. "Not violet, Miranda. Everyone knows they are for blond hair. The color practically disappears against brown. *You* certainly can't wear one."

Miranda handed the ribbon back to her. "What color suits brown hair? Green? My mama has brown hair, and I've seen her wear green ribbons."

"Green would be acceptable, I suppose. But it's better in blond hair. Everything's better in blond hair."

Miranda felt a spark of indignation rising within her. "Well, I don't know what you're going to do then, Fiona, because your hair is as brown as mine."

Fiona drew back in a huff. "It is not!"

"Is too!"

"Is not!"

Miranda leaned forward, her eyes narrowing menacingly. "You had better take a look in the mirror when you go home, Fiona, because your hair is *not* blond."

Fiona put the violet ribbon back in its case and snapped the lid shut. "Well, it used to be blond, whereas yours never was. And besides that, my hair is light brown, which everyone knows is better than dark brown. Like yours."

"There's nothing wrong with dark brown hair!" Miranda protested. But she already knew that most of England didn't agree with her.

"And," Fiona added viciously, "you've got big lips!"

Miranda's hand flew to her mouth. She knew that she was not beautiful; she knew she wasn't even considered pretty. But she'd never noticed anything wrong with her lips before. She looked up at the smirking girl. "You have freckles!" she burst out.

Fiona drew back as if slapped. "Freckles fade. Mine shall be gone before I turn eighteen. My mother puts lemon juice on them every night." She sniffed disdainfully. "But there's no remedy for you, Miranda. You're ugly."

"She is not!"

Both girls turned to see Olivia, who had returned from the washroom.

"Oh, Olivia," Fiona said. "I know you are friends with Miranda because she lives so close by and shares your lessons, but you must admit she isn't very pretty. My mama says she'll never get a husband."

Olivia's blue eyes sparkled dangerously. The Earl of Rudland's only daughter had always been loyal to a fault, and Miranda was her best friend. "Miranda will get a better husband than you, Fiona Bennet! Her father's a baronet whereas yours is a mere mister."

"Being a baronet's daughter makes little difference unless one has looks or money," Fiona recited, repeating words she had obviously heard at home. "And Miranda has neither."

"Be quiet, you silly old cow!" Olivia exclaimed, stomping her foot on the ground. "This is my birthday party, and if you can't be nice, you may leave!"

Fiona gulped. She knew better than to alienate Olivia, whose parents held the highest rank in the area. "I'm sorry, Olivia," she mumbled.

"Don't apologize to me. Apologize to Miranda."

"I'm sorry, Miranda."

Miranda stayed silent until Olivia finally kicked her. "I accept your apology," she said grudgingly.

Fiona nodded and ran off.

"I can't believe you called her a silly old cow," Miranda said.

"You must learn to stand up for yourself, Miranda."

"I was standing up for myself just fine before you came along, Livvy. I just wasn't doing it so loudly."

Olivia sighed. "Mama says I haven't an ounce of restraint or common sense."

"You don't," Miranda agreed.

"Miranda!"

"It's true, you don't. But I love you anyway."

"And I love you, too, Miranda. And don't worry about silly old Fiona. You can marry Winston when you grow up and then we'll be sisters truly."

Miranda glanced across the room and eyed Winston dubiously. He was yanking on a little girl's hair. "I don't know," she said hesitantly. "I'm not sure I would wish to marry Winston."

"Nonsense. It would be perfect. Besides, look, he just spilled punch on Fiona's dress."

Miranda grinned.

"Come with me," Olivia said, taking her hand. "I want to open my gifts. I promise I'll squeal the loudest when I get to yours."

The two girls walked back into the room, and Olivia and Winston opened their gifts. Mercifully (in Lady Rudland's opinion), they finished at four o'clock on the button, which was the time that the children were meant to go home. Not a single child was picked up by servants; an invitation to Haverbreaks was considered quite an honor, and none of the parents wanted to miss the opportunity to hobnob with the earl and countess. None of the parents besides Miranda's, that was. At five o'clock, she was still in the sitting room, assessing the birthday booty with Olivia.

"I can't imagine what has happened to your parents, Miranda," Lady Rudland said.

"Oh, I can," Miranda replied cheerfully. "Mama's gone to Scotland to visit her mama, and I'm sure Papa has forgotten about me. He often does, you know, when he's working on a manuscript. He translates from the Greek."

"I know." Lady Rudland smiled.

"*Ancient* Greek."

"I know," Lady Rudland said on a sigh. This was not the first time Sir Rupert Cheever had misplaced his daughter. "Well, you shall have to get home somehow."

"I'll go with her," Olivia suggested.

"You and Winston need to put away your new toys and write thank-you notes. If you don't do it tonight, you shan't remember who gave you what."

"But you can't send Miranda home with a servant. She'll have no one to talk to."

"I can talk to the servant," Miranda said. "I always talk to the ones at home."

"Not ours," Olivia whispered. "They're starched and silent and they always look at me disapprovingly."

"Most of the time you deserve to be looked at disapprovingly," Lady Rudland interjected, giving her daughter a loving pat on the head. "I have a treat for you, Miranda. Why don't we have Nigel bring you home?"

"Nigel!" Olivia squealed. "Miranda, you lucky duck."

Miranda raised her brows. She had never met Olivia's older brother. "All right," she said slowly. "I should like to finally meet him. You talk about him so often, Olivia."

Lady Rudland summoned a maid to fetch him. "You've never met him, Miranda? How odd. Well, I suppose he's usually only home at Christmas, and you always go to Scotland for the holiday. I had to threaten to cut him off to get him home for the twins' birthday. As it was, he wouldn't attend the party for fear that one of the mamas would try to marry him off to a ten-year-old."

"Nigel is nineteen, and he is very eligible," Olivia said matter-of-factly. "He's a viscount. And he's very handsome. He looks just like me."

"Olivia!" Lady Rudland said reprovingly.

"Well, he does, Mama. I should be very handsome if I were a boy."

"You're quite pretty as a girl, Livvy," Miranda said loyally, eyeing her friend's blond locks with just a little envy.

"So are you. Here, pick one of Fiona-cow's ribbons. I don't need them all, anyway."

Miranda smiled at her lie. Olivia was such a good friend. She looked down at the ribbons and perversely chose the violet satin. "Thank you, Livvy. I shall wear it to lessons on Monday."

"You called, Mother?"

At the sound of the deep voice, Miranda turned her face to the doorway and almost gasped. There stood quite the most splendid creature she had ever beheld. Olivia had said that Nigel was nineteen, but Miranda immediately recognized him as the man he already was. His shoulders were marvelously broad, and the rest of him was lean and firm. His hair was darker than Olivia's but still streaked with gold, attesting to time spent out in the sun. But the best part about him, Miranda immediately decided, was his eyes, which were bright, bright blue, just like Olivia's. They twinkled just as mischievously, too.

Miranda smiled. Her mother always said that one could tell a person by his eyes, and Olivia's brother had very good eyes.

"Nigel, would you please be so kind as to escort Miranda home?" Lady Rudland asked. "Her father seems to have been detained."

Miranda wondered why he winced when she said his name.

"Certainly, Mother. Olivia, did you have a good party?"

"Smashing."

"Where is Winston?"

Olivia shrugged. "He's off playing with the saber Billy Evans gave him."

"Not a real one, I hope."

"God help us if it is," Lady Rudland put in. "All right, Miranda, let's get you home. I believe your cloak is in the next room." She disappeared through the doorway and emerged a few seconds later with Miranda's serviceable brown coat.

"Shall we be off, Miranda?" The godlike creature held out his hand to her.

Miranda shrugged on her coat and placed her hand in his. Heaven!

"I will see you on Monday!" Olivia called out. "And don't worry about what Fiona said. She's just a silly old cow."

"Olivia!"

"Well, she is, Mama. I don't want to have her back."

Miranda smiled as she let Olivia's brother lead her down the hall, Olivia's and Lady Rudland's voices slowly fading away. "Thank you very much for taking me home, Nigel," she said softly.

He winced again.

"I'm—I'm sorry," she said quickly. "I ought to be calling you 'my lord,' oughtn't I? It's just that Olivia and Winston always refer to you by your given name and I—" She cast miserable eyes toward the floor. Only two minutes in his splendid company, and already she'd blundered.

He stopped and crouched down so that she could see his face. "Don't worry about the 'my lord,' Miranda. I'll tell you a secret."

Miranda's eyes widened, and she forgot to breathe.

"I despise my given name."

"That's not much of a secret, Nig— I mean, my lord, I mean, whatever you wish to be called. You wince every time your mother says it."

He smiled down at her. Something had tugged at his heart when he saw this little girl with the too-serious expression playing with his indomitable sister. She was a funny-looking little creature, but there was something quite lovable about her big, soulful brown eyes.

"What *are* you called?" Miranda asked.

He smiled at her direct manner. "Turner."

For a moment he thought she might not answer. She just stood there, utterly still save for the blinking of her eyes. And then, as if finally reaching a conclusion, she said, "That's a nice name. A bit odd, but I like it."

"Much better than Nigel, don't you think?"

Miranda nodded. "Did you choose it? I've often thought that people ought to choose their own names. I should think that most people would choose something different from what they have."

"And what would you choose?"

"I'm not certain, but not Miranda. Something plainer, I

THE SECRET DIARIES 11

think. People expect something different from a Miranda and are almost always disappointed when they meet me."

"Nonsense," Turner said briskly. "You are a perfect Miranda."

She beamed. "Thank you, Turner. May I call you that?"

"Of course. And I didn't choose it, I'm afraid. It's just a courtesy title. Viscount Turner. I've been using it in place of Nigel since I went to Eton."

"Oh. It suits you, I think."

"Thank you," he said gravely, completely entranced by this serious child. "Now, give me your hand again, and we shall be on our way."

He had held out his left hand to her. Miranda quickly moved the ribbon from her right hand to her left.

"What's that?"

"This? Oh, a ribbon. Fiona Bennet gave two dozen of them to Olivia, and Olivia said I might keep one."

Turner's eyes narrowed ever so slightly as he remembered Olivia's parting words. *Don't worry about what Fiona said.* He plucked the ribbon out of her hand. "Ribbons belong in hair, I think."

"Oh, but it doesn't match my dress," Miranda said in feeble protest. He'd already fastened it atop her head. "How does it look?" she whispered.

"Smashing."

"Really?" Her eyes widened doubtfully.

"Really. I've always thought that violet ribbons look especially nice with brown hair."

Miranda fell in love on the spot. So intense was the feeling that she quite forgot to thank him for the compliment.

"Shall we be off?" he said.

She nodded, not trusting her voice.

They made their way out of the house and to the stables. "I thought we might ride," Turner said. "It's far too nice a day for a carriage."

Miranda nodded again. It was uncommonly warm for March.

"You can take Olivia's pony. I'm sure she won't mind."

"Livvy hasn't got a pony," Miranda said, finally finding her voice. "She has a mare now. I've one at home, too. We're not babies, you know."

Turner suppressed a smile. "No, I can see that you are not. How silly of me. I wasn't thinking."

A few minutes later, their horses were saddled, and they set off on the fifteen-minute ride to the Cheever home. Miranda stayed silent for the first minute or so, too perfectly happy to spoil the moment with words.

"Did you have a good time at the party?" Turner finally asked.

"Oh, yes. Most of it was just lovely."

"Most of it?"

He saw her wince. Obviously, she hadn't meant to say so much. "Well," she said slowly, catching her lip between her teeth and then letting it go before continuing, "one of the girls said some unkind words to me."

"Oh?" He knew better than to be overly inquisitive.

And obviously, he was right, because when she spoke, she rather reminded him of his sister, staring up at him with frank eyes as her words spilled firmly from her mouth. "It was Fiona Bennet," she said, with great distaste, "and Olivia called her a silly old cow, and I must say I'm not sorry that she did."

Turner kept his expression appropriately grave. "I'm not sorry that she did, either, if Fiona said unkind things to you."

"I know I'm not pretty," Miranda burst out. "But it's dreadfully impolite to say so, not to mention downright mean."

Turner looked at her for a long moment, not exactly certain how to comfort the little girl. She wasn't beautiful, that was true, and if he tried to tell her that she was, she wouldn't believe him. But she wasn't ugly. She was just . . . rather awkward.

He was saved, however, from having to say anything by Miranda's next comment.

"It's this brown hair, I think."

He raised his brows.

"It's not at all fashionable," Miranda explained. "And neither are brown eyes. And I'm too skinny by half, and my face is too long, and I'm far too pale."

"Well, that's all true," Turner said.

Miranda turned to face him, her eyes looming large and sad in her face.

"You certainly do have brown hair and eyes. There is no use arguing that point." He tilted his head and pretended to give her a complete inspection. "You are rather thin, and your face is indeed a trifle long. And you certainly are pale."

Her lips trembled, and Turner could tease her no more.

"But as it happens," he said with a smile, "I myself prefer women with brown hair and eyes."

"You don't!"

"I do. I always have. And I like them thin and pale, as well."

Miranda eyed him suspiciously. "What about long faces?"

"Well, I must admit, I never gave the matter much thought, but I certainly don't *mind* a long face."

"Fiona Bennet said I have big lips," she said almost defiantly.

Turner bit back a smile.

She heaved a great sigh. "I never even noticed I had big lips before."

"They're not so big."

She shot him a wary glance. "You're just saying that to make me feel better."

"I do want you to feel better, but that's not why I said it. And next time Fiona Bennet says you have big lips, tell her she's wrong. You have full lips."

"What's the difference?" She looked over at him patiently, her dark eyes serious.

Turner took a breath. "Well," he stalled. "Big lips are unattractive. Full lips are not."

"Oh." That seemed to satisfy her. "Fiona has thin lips."

"Full lips are much, much better than thin lips," Turner said emphatically. He quite liked this funny little girl and wanted her to feel better.

"Why?"

Turner offered up a silent apology to the gods of etiquette and propriety before he answered, "Full lips are better for kissing."

"Oh." Miranda blushed, and then she smiled. "Good."

Turner felt absurdly pleased with himself. "Do you know what I think, Miss Miranda Cheever?"

"What?"

"I think you just need to grow into yourself." The minute he said it, he was sorry. She would surely ask him what he meant, and he had no idea how to answer her.

But the precocious little child simply tilted her head to one side as she pondered his statement. "I expect you're right," she finally said. "Just look at my legs."

A discreet cough masked the chuckle that welled up in Turner's throat. "What do you mean?"

"Well, they're far too long. Mama always says that they start at my *shoulders*."

"They appear to begin quite properly at your waist to me."

Miranda giggled. "I was speaking metaphorically."

Turner blinked. This ten-year-old had quite a vocabulary, indeed.

"What I meant," she went on, "is that my legs are all the wrong size compared to the rest of me. I think that's why I can't seem to learn how to dance. I'm forever trodding on Olivia's toes."

"On *Olivia's* toes?"

"We practice together," Miranda explained briskly. "I think that if the rest of me catches up with my legs, I won't be so clumsy. So I think you're right. I do have to grow into myself."

"Splendid," Turner said, happily aware that he had somehow managed to say exactly the right thing. "Well, we seem to have arrived."

Miranda looked up at the gray stone house that was her home. It was located right on one of the many streams that connected the lakes of the district, and one had to cross over a little cobbled bridge just to reach the front door. "Thank you very much for taking me home, Turner. I promise I'll never call you Nigel."

"Will you also promise to pinch Olivia if she calls me Nigel?"

Miranda let out a little giggle and clapped her hand to her mouth. She nodded.

Turner dismounted and then turned to the little girl and helped her down. "Do you know what I think you should do, Miranda?" he said suddenly.

"What?"

"I think you ought to keep a journal."

She blinked in surprise. "Why? Who would want to read it?"

"No one, silly. You keep it for yourself. And maybe someday after you die, your grandchildren will read it so they will know what you were like when you were young."

She tilted her head. "What if I don't have grandchildren?"

Turner impulsively reached out and tousled her hair. "You ask a lot of questions, puss."

"But what if I don't have grandchildren?"

Lord, she was persistent. "Perhaps you'll be famous." He sighed. "And the children who study about you in school will want to know about you."

Miranda shot him a doubtful look.

"Oh, very well, do you want to know why I *really* think you should keep a journal?"

She nodded.

"Because someday you're going to grow into yourself, and you will be as beautiful as you already are smart. And then you can look back into your diary and realize just how silly little girls like Fiona Bennet are. And you'll laugh when you remember that your mother said your legs started at your shoulders. And maybe you'll save a little smile for me when you remember the nice chat we had today."

Miranda looked up at him, thinking that he must be one of those Greek gods her father was always reading about. "Do you know what I think?" she whispered. "I think Olivia is very lucky to have you for a brother."

"And I think she is very lucky to have you for a friend."

Miranda's lips trembled. "I shall save a *very big* smile for you, Turner," she whispered.

He leaned down and graciously kissed the back of her hand as he would the most beautiful lady in London. "See that you do, puss." He smiled and nodded before he got on his horse, leading Olivia's mare behind him.

Miranda stared at him until he disappeared over the horizon, and then she stared for a good ten minutes more.

* * *

Later that night, Miranda wandered into her father's study. He was bent over a text, oblivious to the candle wax that was dripping onto his desk.

"Papa, how many times do I have to tell you that you need to watch the candles?" She sighed and put the candle in a proper holder.

"What? Oh, dear."

"And you need more than one. It's far too dark in here to read."

"Is it? I hadn't noticed." He blinked and then narrowed his eyes. "Isn't it past your bedtime?"

"Nanny said I could stay up an extra thirty minutes to-night."

"Did she? Well, whatever she says, then." He bent over his manuscript again, effectively dismissing her.

"Papa?"

He sighed. "What is it, Miranda?"

"Do you have an extra notebook? Like the ones you use when you're translating but before you copy out your final draft?"

"I suppose so." He opened the bottom drawer of his desk and rummaged through it. "Here we are. But what do you wish to do with it? That's a quality notebook, you know, and not cheap."

"I'm going to keep a journal."

"Are you now? Well, that's a worthy endeavor, I suppose." He handed the notebook to her.

Miranda beamed at her father's praise. "Thank you. I shall let you know when I run out of space and need another."

"All right, then. Good night, dear." He turned back to his papers.

Miranda hugged the notebook to her chest and ran up the stairs to her bedroom. She took out a pot of ink and a quill and opened the book to the first page. She wrote the date, and then, after considerable thought, wrote a single sentence. It was all that seemed necessary.

2 MARCH 1810

Today I fell in love.

Chapter 1

Nigel Bevelstoke, better known as Turner to all who cared to court his favor, knew a great many things.

He knew how to read Latin and Greek, and he knew how to seduce a woman in French and Italian.

He knew how to shoot a moving target while atop a moving horse, and he knew exactly how much he could drink before surrendering his dignity.

He could throw a punch or fence with a master, and he could do them both while reciting Shakespeare or Donne.

In short, he knew everything a gentleman ought to know, and, by all accounts, he'd excelled in every area.

People looked at him.

People looked up to him.

But nothing—not one second of his prominent and privileged life—had prepared him for this moment. And never had he felt the weight of watchful eyes so much as now, as he stepped forward and tossed a clump of dirt on the coffin of his wife.

I'm so sorry, people kept saying. *I'm so sorry. We're so sorry.*

And all the while, Turner could not help but wonder if God might smite him down, because all he could think was—

I'm not.

Ah, Leticia. He had quite a lot to thank her for.

Let's see, where to start? There was the loss of his reputation, of course. The devil only knew how many people were aware that he'd been cuckolded.

Repeatedly.

Then there was the loss of his innocence. It was difficult to recall now, but he had once given mankind the benefit of the doubt. He had, on the whole, believed the best of people—that if he treated others with honor and respect, they would do the same unto him.

And then there was the loss of his soul.

Because as he stepped back, clasping his hands stiffly behind him as he listened to the priest commit Leticia's body to the ground, he could not escape the fact that he had wished for this. He had wanted to be rid of her.

And he would not—he *did* not mourn her.

"Such a pity," someone behind him whispered.

Turner's jaw twitched. This was not a pity. It was a farce. And now he would spend the next year wearing black for a woman who had come to him carrying another man's child. She had bewitched him, teased him until he could think of nothing but the possession of her. She had said she loved him, and she had smiled with sweet innocence and delight when he had avowed his devotion and pledged his soul.

She had been his dream.

And then she had been his nightmare.

She'd lost that baby, the one that had prompted their marriage. The father had been some Italian count, or at least that's what she'd said. He was married, or unsuitable, or maybe both. Turner had been prepared to forgive her; everyone made mistakes, and hadn't he, too, wanted to seduce her before their wedding night?

But Leticia had not wanted his love. He didn't know what the hell she had wanted—power, perhaps, the heady rush of satisfaction when yet another man fell under her spell.

Turner wondered if she'd felt that when he'd succumbed. Or maybe it had just been relief. She'd been three months along by the time they married. She hadn't much time to spare.

And now here she was. Or rather, there she was. Turner wasn't precisely sure which locational pronoun was more accurate for a lifeless body in the ground.

Whichever. He was only sorry that she would spend her eternity in *his* ground, resting among the Bevelstokes of days gone by. Her stone would bear his name, and in a hundred years, someone would gaze upon the etchings in the granite and think she must have been a fine lady, and what a tragedy that she'd been taken so young.

Turner looked up at the priest. He was a youngish fellow, new to the parish and by all accounts, still convinced that he could make the world a better place.

"Ashes to ashes," the priest said, and he looked up at the man who was meant to be the bereaved widower.

Ah yes, Turner thought acerbically, *that would be me*.

"Dust to dust."

Behind him, someone actually sniffled.

And the priest, his blue eyes bright with that appallingly misplaced glimmer of sympathy, kept on talking—

"In the sure and certain hope of the Resurrection—"

Good God.

"—to eternal life."

The priest looked at Turner and actually flinched. Turner wondered what, exactly, he'd seen in his face. Nothing good, that much was clear.

There was a chorus of amens, and then the service was over. Everyone looked at the priest, and then everyone looked at Turner, and then everyone looked at the priest clasping Turner's hands in his own as he said, "She will be missed."

"Not," Turner bit off, "by me."

I can't believe he said that.

Miranda looked down at the words she'd just written. She was currently on page forty-two of her thirteenth journal, but this was the first time—the first time since that fateful day nine years earlier—that she had not a clue what to write. Even when her days were dull (and they frequently were), she managed to cobble together an entry.

In May of her fourteenth year—

Woke.
Dressed.

Ate breakfast: toast, eggs, bacon.
Read Sense and Sensibility, *authored by unknown lady.*
Hid Sense and Sensibility *from Father.*
Ate dinner: chicken, bread, cheese.
Conjugated French verbs.
Composed letter to Grandmother.
Ate supper: beefsteak, soup, pudding.
Read more Sense and Sensibility, *author's identity still unknown.*
Retired.
Slept.
Dreamed of him.

This was not to be confused with her entry of 12 November of the same year—

Woke.
Ate breakfast: Eggs, toast, ham.
Made great show of reading Greek tragedy. To no avail.
Spent much of the time staring out the window.
Ate lunch: fish, bread, peas.
Conjugated Latin verbs.
Composed letter to Grandmother.
Ate supper: roast, potatoes, pudding.
Brought tragedy to the table (book, not event).
Father did not notice.
Retired.

Slept.
Dreamed of him.

But now—now when something huge and momentous had actually occurred (which it never did) she had nothing to say except—

I can't believe he said that.

"Well, Miranda," she murmured, watching the ink dry on the tip of her quill, "you'll not achieve fame as a diarist."

"What did you say?"

Miranda snapped her diary shut. She had not realized that Olivia had entered the room.

"Nothing," she said quickly.

Olivia moved across the carpet and flopped on the bed. "What a horrible day,"

Miranda nodded, twisting in her seat so that she was facing her friend.

"I am glad you were here," Olivia said with a sigh. "Thank you for remaining for the night."

"Of course," Miranda replied. There had been no question, not when Olivia had said she'd needed her.

"What are you writing?"

Miranda looked down at the diary, only just then realizing that her hands were resting protectively across its cover. "Nothing," she said.

Olivia had been staring at the ceiling, but at that she

quirked her head in Miranda's direction. "That can't be true."

"Sadly, it is."

"Why is it sad?"

Miranda blinked. Trust Olivia to ask the most obvious questions—and the ones with the least obvious answers.

"Well," Miranda said, not precisely stalling for time—really, it was more that she was figuring it all out as she went. She moved her hands and looked down at the journal as if the answer might have magically inscribed itself onto the cover. "This all I have. It is what I am."

Olivia looked dubious. "It's a book."

"It's my life."

"Why is it," Olivia opined, "that people call *me* dramatic?"

"I'm not saying it *is* my life," Miranda said with a flash of impatience, "just that it contains it. Everything. I have written *everything* down. Since I was ten."

"Everything?"

Miranda thought about the many days she'd dutifully recorded what she'd eaten and little else. "Everything."

"I could never keep a journal."

"No."

Olivia rolled onto her side, propping her head up with her hand. "You needn't have agreed with me so quickly."

Miranda only smiled.

Olivia flopped back down. "I suppose you are going to write that I have a short attention span."

"I already have."

Silence, then: "Really?"

"I believe I said you bored easily."

"Well," her friend replied, with only the barest moment of reflection, "that much is true."

Miranda looked back down at the writing desk. Her candle was shedding flickers of light on the blotter, and she suddenly felt tired. Tired, but unfortunately, not sleepy.

Weary, perhaps. Restless.

"I'm exhausted," Olivia declared, sliding off the bed. Her maid had left her nightclothes atop the covers, and Miranda respectfully turned her head while Olivia changed into them.

"How long do you think Turner will remain here in the country?" Miranda asked, trying not to bite her tongue. She hated that she was still so desperate for a glimpse of him, but it had been this way for years. Even when he'd married, and she'd sat in the pews at his wedding, and watching him meant watching him watch his bride with all the love and devotion that burned in her own heart—

She'd still watched. She still loved him. She always would. He was the man who'd made her believe in herself. He had no idea what he'd done to her—what he'd done *for* her—and he probably never would. But Miranda still ached for him. And she probably always would.

Olivia crawled into bed. "Will you be up long?" she asked, her voice thick with the beginnings of slumber.

"Not long," Miranda assured her. Olivia could not fall asleep while a candle burned so close. Miranda could not understand it, as the fire in the grate did not seem to bother her, but she had seen Olivia toss and turn with her own eyes, and so, when she realized that her mind was still racing and "not long" had been a bit of a lie, she leaned forward and blew out the candle.

"I'll take this elsewhere," she said, tucking her journal under her arm.

"Thankthsh," Olivia mumbled, and by the time Miranda pulled on a wrapper and reached the corridor, she was asleep.

Miranda tucked her journal under her chin and wedged it against her breastbone to free her hands so that she could tie the sash around her waist. She was a frequent overnight guest at Haverbreaks, but still, it wouldn't do to be wandering the halls of someone else's home in nothing but her nightgown.

It was a dark night, with nothing but the moonlight filtering through the windows to guide her, but Miranda could have made her way from Olivia's room to the library with her eyes closed. Olivia always fell asleep before she did—too many thoughts rumbling about in her head, Olivia pronounced—and so Miranda frequently took her diary to another room to record her ponderings. She supposed she could have asked for a bedchamber of her own, but Olivia's mother did not believe in needless extravagance, and she saw no reason to heat two rooms when one would suffice.

Miranda did not mind. In fact, she was grateful for the company. Her own home was far too quiet these days. Her beloved mother had passed away nearly a year earlier, and Miranda had been left alone with her father. In his grief, he had closeted himself away with his precious manuscripts, leaving his daughter to fend for herself. Miranda had turned to the Bevelstokes for love and friendship, and they welcomed her with open arms. Olivia even wore black for three weeks in honor of Lady Cheever.

"If one of my first cousins died, I'd be forced to do the same," Olivia had said at the funeral. "And I certainly loved your mama better than any of my cousins."

"Olivia!" Miranda was touched, but nonetheless, she thought she ought to be shocked.

Olivia rolled her eyes. "Have you met my cousins?"

And she'd laughed. At her own mother's funeral, Miranda had laughed. It was, she'd later realized, the most precious gift her friend could have offered.

"I love you, Livvy," she said.

Olivia took her hand. "I know you do," she said softly. "And I, you." Then she squared her shoulders and assumed her usual stance. "I should be quite incorrigible without you, you know. My mother often says you are the only reason I have not committed some irredeemable offense."

It was probably for that reason, Miranda reflected, that Lady Rudland had offered to sponsor her for a season in London. Upon receiving the invitation, her father had sighed with relief and quickly forwarded the necessary funds. Sir Rupert Cheever was not an exceptionally wealthy man, but he had enough to cover a season in London for his only daughter. What he did not possess was the necessary patience—or, to be frank, the interest—to take her himself.

Their debut was delayed for a year. Miranda could not go while in mourning for her mother, and Lady Rudland had decided to allow Olivia to wait, as well. Twenty would

do as well as nineteen, she'd announced. And it was true;
no one was worried about Olivia making a grand match.
With her stunning looks, vivacious personality and, as
Olivia wryly pointed out, her hefty dowry, she was sure to
be a success.

But Leticia's death, in addition to being tragic, had
been particularly ill-timed; now there was another period
of mourning to be observed. Olivia could get away with
just six weeks, however, as Leticia had not been a sister
in blood.

They would be only a little bit late in their arrival for the
season. It couldn't be helped.

Secretly, Miranda was glad. The thought of a London
ball positively terrified her. It wasn't that she was shy, precisely, because she didn't think she was. It was just that
she did not enjoy large crowds, and the thought of so many
people staring at her in judgment was just awful.

Can't be helped, she thought as she made her way down
the stairs. And at any rate, it would be far worse to be stuck
out in Ambleside, without Olivia for company.

Miranda paused at the bottom of the stairs, deciding
where to go. The west sitting room had the better desk, but
the library tended to be warmer, and it was a bit of a chilly
night. On the other hand—

Hmmm . . . what was that?

She leaned to the side, peering down the hall. Someone had a fire burning in Lord Rudland's study. Miranda
couldn't imagine that anyone was still up and about—the
Bevelstokes always retired early.

She moved quietly along the runner carpet until she reached the open door.

"Oh!"

Turner looked up from his father's chair. "Miss Miranda," he drawled, not adjusting one muscle of his lazy sprawl. "*Quelle* surprise."

Turner wasn't certain why he *wasn't* surprised to see Miss Miranda Cheever standing in the doorway of his father's study. When he'd heard footsteps in the hall, he'd somehow known it had to be she. True, his family tended to sleep like the dead, and it was almost inconceivable that one of them might be up and about, wandering the halls in search of a snack or something to read.

But it had been more than the process of elimination that had led him to Miranda as the obvious choice. She was a watcher, that one, always there, always observing the scene with those owlish eyes of hers. He couldn't remember when he'd first met her—probably before the chit had been out of leading strings. She was a fixture, really, somehow always *there*, even at times like these, when it ought to have been only family.

"I'll go," she said.

"No, don't," he replied, because . . . because *why*?

Because he felt like making mischief?

Because he'd had too much to drink?

Because he didn't want to be alone?

"Stay," he said, waving his arm expansively. Surely there had to be somewhere else to sit in here. "Have a drink."

Her eyes widened.

"Didn't think they could get any bigger," he muttered.

"I can't drink," she said.

"Can't you?"

"I *shouldn't*," she corrected, and he thought he saw her brows draw together. Good, he'd irritated her. It was good to know he could still provoke a woman, even one as unschooled as she.

"You're here," he said with a shrug. "You might as well have a brandy."

For a moment she held still, and he could swear he could hear her brain whirring. Finally, she set her little book on a table near the door and stepped forward. "Just one," she said.

He smiled. "Because you know your limit?"

Her eyes met his. "Because I *don't* know my limit."

"Such wisdom in one so young," he murmured.

"I'm nineteen," she said, not defiantly, just as statement of fact.

He lifted a brow. "As I said . . ."

"When you were nineteen . . ."

He smiled caustically, noticing that she did not finish the statement. "When I was nineteen," he repeated for her, handing her a liberal portion of brandy, "I was a fool." He looked at the glass he'd poured for himself, equal in volume to Miranda's. He downed it in one long, satisfying gulp.

The glass landed on the table with a clunk, and Turner leaned back, letting his head rest in his palms, his elbows bent out to the sides. "As are all nineteen-year-olds, I should add," he finished.

He eyed her. She hadn't touched her drink. She hadn't

even yet sat down. "Present company quite possibly excluded," he amended.

"I thought brandy was meant to go in a snifter," she said.

He watched as she moved carefully to a seat. It wasn't next to him, but it wasn't quite across from him, either. Her eyes never left his, and he couldn't help but wonder what she thought he might do. Pounce?

"Brandy," he announced, as if speaking to an audience that numbered more than one, "is best served in whatever one has handy. In this case—" He picked up his tumbler and regarded it, watching firelight dance along the facets. He didn't bother to finish his sentence. It didn't seem necessary, and besides, he was busy pouring himself another drink.

"Cheers." And down it went.

He looked over at her. She was still just sitting there, watching him. He couldn't tell if she disapproved; her expression was far too inscrutable for that. But he wished that she would say something. Anything would do, really, even more nonsense about stemware would be enough to nudge his mind off the fact that it was still half eleven, and he had thirty more minutes to go before he could declare this wretched day over.

"So tell me, Miss Miranda, how did you enjoy the service?" he asked, daring her with his eyes to say something beyond the usual platitudes.

Surprise registered on her face—the first emotion of the night he was clearly able to discern. "You mean the funeral?"

"Only service of the day," he said, with considerable jauntiness.

"It was, er, interesting."

"Oh, come now, Miss Cheever, you can do better than that."

She caught her lower lip between her teeth. Leticia used to do that, he recalled. Back when she still pretended to be an innocent. It had stopped when his ring had been safely on her finger.

He poured another drink.

"Don't you think—"

"*No*," he said forcefully. There wasn't enough brandy in the world for a night like this.

And then she reached forward, picked up her glass, and took a sip. "I thought you were splendid."

God *damn* it. He coughed and spluttered, as if he were the innocent, taking his first taste of brandy. "I beg your pardon?"

She smiled placidly. "It might help to take smaller sips."

He glared at her.

"It's rare that someone speaks honestly of the dead," she said. "I'm not certain that that was the most appropriate venue, but . . . well . . . she wasn't a terribly nice person, was she?"

She looked so serene, so innocent, but her eyes . . . they were sharp.

"Why, Miss Cheever," he murmured, "I do believe you've a bit of a vindictive streak."

She shrugged and took another sip of her drink—a small

one, he noted. "Not at all," she said, although he was quite certain he did not believe her, "but I am a good observer."

He chuckled. "Indeed."

She stiffened. "I beg your pardon."

He'd ruffled her. He didn't know why he found this so satisfying, but he couldn't help but be pleased. And it had been so long since he'd been pleased about anything. He leaned forward, just to see if he could make her squirm. "I've been watching you."

She paled. Even in the firelight he could see it.

"Do you know what I've seen?" he murmured.

Her lips parted, and she shook her head.

"*You* have been watching me."

She stood, the suddenness of the movement nearly knocking her chair over. "I should go," she said. "This is highly irregular, and it's late, and—"

"Oh, come now, Miss Cheever," he said, rising to his feet. "Don't fret. You watch everyone. Do you think I hadn't noticed?"

He reached out and took her arm. She froze. But she didn't turn around.

His fingers tightened. Just a touch. Just enough to keep her from leaving, because he didn't want her to leave. He didn't want to be alone. He had twenty more minutes, and he wanted her to be angry, just as he was angry, just as he'd been angry for years.

"Tell me, Miss Cheever," he whispered, touching two fingers to the underside of her chin. "Have you ever been kissed?"

Chapter 2

It would not have been an overstatement to say that Miranda had been dreaming of this moment for years. And in her dreams, she always seemed to know what to say. But reality, it seemed, was far less articulate, and she couldn't do anything but stare at him, breathless—*literally*, she thought, quite literally without breath.

Funny, she'd always thought it was a metaphor. *Breathless. Breathless.*

"I thought not," he was saying, and she could barely hear him over the frantic racing of her thoughts. She should run, but she was frozen, and she shouldn't do this, but she wanted to, at least she *thought* she wanted to— she'd certainly thought about wanting to since she was ten and didn't particularly even know what it was she'd been wanting and—

And his lips touched hers. "Lovely," he murmured, raining delicate, seductive kisses along her cheek until he reached the line of her jaw.

It felt like heaven. It felt like nothing she knew. There was a quickening within her, a strange tension, coiling and stretching, and she wasn't sure what she was meant to do, so she stood there, accepting his kisses as he moved across her face, along her cheekbone, back to her lips.

"Open your mouth," he ordered, and she did, because this was Turner, and she wanted this. Hadn't she always wanted this?

His tongue dipped inside, and she felt herself being pulled more tightly against him. His fingers were demanding, and then his mouth was demanding, and then she realized that this was wrong. This wasn't the moment she'd been dreaming of for years. He didn't want her. She didn't know why he was kissing her, but he didn't want her. And he certainly did not love her. There was no kindness in this kiss.

"Kiss me back, damn it," he growled, and he pressed his lips against hers with renewed insistence. It was hard, and it was angry, and for the first time that night, Miranda began to feel afraid.

"No," she tried to say, but her voice was lost against his mouth. His hand had somehow found her bottom, and was squeezing, pressing her up against him in the most intimate of places. And she didn't understand how she could want this and not want this, how he could make her tingle and make her scared, how she could love him and hate him at the very same time, in equal measures.

"No," she said again, wedging her hands between them, palms against his chest. "No!"

And then he stepped away, utterly abrupt, without even the slightest hint of a desire to linger.

"Miranda Cheever," he murmured, except it was really more of a drawl, "who knew?"

She slapped him.

His eyes narrowed, but he said nothing.

"Why did you do that?" she demanded, her voice steady even as the rest of her shook.

"Kiss you?" He shrugged. "Why not?"

"No," she shot back, horrified by the note of pain she heard in her voice. She wanted to be furious. She *was* furious, but she wanted to sound it. She wanted him to *know*. "You may not take the easy way out. You lost that privilege."

He chuckled, damn him, and said, "You're quite entertaining as a dominatrix."

"Stop it," she cried. He kept talking about things she did not understand, and she hated him for it. "Why did you kiss me? You don't love me."

Her fingernails bit into her palms. *Stupid, stupid girl.* Why did she say that?

But he only smiled. "I forget that you are only nineteen and thus do not realize that love is never a prerequisite for a kiss."

"I don't think you even like me."

"Nonsense. Of course I do." He blinked, as if he were trying to remember how well, exactly, he knew her. "Well, I certainly don't dislike you."

"I'm not Leticia," she whispered.

In a split second, his hand had wrapped around her upper arm, squeezing nearly to the point of pain. "Don't you *ever* mention her name again. Do you hear me?"

Miranda stared in shock at the raw fury emanating from his eyes. "I'm sorry," she said hastily. "Please let me go."

But he didn't. He loosened his grip, but only slightly, and it was almost as if he were staring through her. At a ghost. At Leticia's ghost.

"Turner, please," Miranda whispered. "You're hurting me."

Something cleared in his expression, and he stepped back. "I'm sorry," he said. He looked to the side—at the window? At the clock? "My apologies," he said curtly. "For assaulting you. For everything."

Miranda swallowed. She should leave. She should slap him again and *then* leave, but she was a wretch, and she couldn't help herself when she said, "I'm sorry she made you so unhappy."

His eyes flew to hers. "Gossip travels all the way to the schoolroom, does it?"

"No!" she said quickly. "It's just that . . . I could tell."

"Oh?"

She chewed on her lip, wondering what she should say. There *had* been gossip in the schoolroom. But more than that, she'd seen it for herself. He'd been so in love at his wedding. His eyes had shone with it, and when he looked at Leticia, Miranda could practically see the world falling away. It was as if they were in their own little world, just the two of them, and she was watching from the outside.

And the next time she saw him . . . it had been different.

"Miranda," he prodded.

She looked up and gently said, "Anyone who knew you

before your marriage could tell that you were unhappy."

"And how is that?" He stared down at her, and there was something so urgent in his eyes that Miranda could only tell him the truth.

"You used to laugh," she said softly. "You used to laugh, and your eyes twinkled."

"And now?"

"Now you're just cold and hard."

He closed his eyes, and for a moment Miranda thought he was in pain. But in the end he gave her a piercing stare, and one corner of his mouth tilted up in a wry mockery of a smile. "So I am." He crossed his arms and leaned insolently against a bookcase. "Pray tell me, Miss Cheever, when did you grow so perceptive?"

Miranda swallowed, fighting the disappointment that rose in her throat. His demons had won again. For a moment—when his eyes had been closed—it had almost seemed as if he heard her. Not her words, but the meaning behind them. "I've always been so," she said. "You used to comment on it when I was little."

"Those big brown eyes," he said with a heartless chuckle. "Following me everywhere. Do you think I didn't know you fancied me?"

Tears pricked Miranda's eyes. How could he be so cruel to say it? "You were very kind to me as a child," she said softly.

"I daresay I was. But that was a long time ago."

"No one realizes that more than I."

He said nothing, and she said nothing. And then finally—

"*Go.*"

His voice was hoarse and pained and full of heart-break.

She went.

And in her diary that night, she wrote nothing.

The following morning, Miranda woke with one clear objective. She wanted to go home. She didn't care if she missed breakfast, she didn't care if the heavens opened and she had to slog through the driving rain. She just didn't want to be *here*, with him, in the same building, on the same property.

It was all too sad. He was gone. The Turner she'd known, the Turner she'd adored—he was gone. She'd sensed it, of course. She'd sensed it on his visits home. The first time it had been his eyes. The next his mouth, and the white lines of anger etched at the corners.

She'd sensed it, but until now she had not truly allowed herself to *know* it.

"You're awake."

It was Olivia, fully dressed and looking charming, even in her mourning black.

"Unfortunately," Miranda muttered.

"What was that?"

Miranda opened her mouth, then remembered that Olivia wasn't going to wait for an answer, so why expend the energy?

"Well, hurry up," Olivia said. "Get dressed, and I'll have my maid do the finishing touches. She's positively magical with hair."

Miranda wondered when Olivia would notice that she had not moved a muscle.

"Get *up*, Miranda."

Miranda nearly jumped a foot. "Good heavens, Olivia. Has no one told you it's rude to bellow in another human being's ear?"

Olivia's face loomed over hers, a little too close. "You don't look quite human this morning, to tell the truth."

Miranda rolled over. "I don't feel human."

"You'll feel better after breakfast."

"I'm not hungry."

"But you can't miss breakfast."

Miranda clenched her teeth. Such chirpiness ought to be illegal before noon.

"Miranda."

Miranda shoved a pillow over her head. "If you say my name one more time, I will have to kill you."

"But we have work to do."

Miranda paused. What the devil was Livvy talking about? "Work?" she echoed.

"Yes, work." Olivia wrenched the pillow away and tossed it on the floor. "I've had the most wonderful idea. It came to me in a dream."

"You're joking."

"Very well, I'm joking, but it did come to me this morning as I was lying in bed." Olivia smiled—a rather feline sort of smile, actually, the sort that meant she'd either had a flash of brilliance or was going to destroy the world as they knew it. And then she waited—it was about the only time she ever waited—and so Miranda rewarded her with "Very well, what is it?"

"You."

"Me."

"And Winston."

For a moment, Miranda couldn't speak. Then—"You're mad."

Olivia shrugged and sat back. "Or very, very clever. Think of it, Miranda. It's perfect."

Miranda couldn't imagine thinking of anything involving gentlemen just at the moment, much less one with the Bevelstoke surname, even if it wasn't Turner.

"You know him well, and you're of an age," Olivia said, ticking the items off on her fingers.

Miranda shook her head and escaped off the other side of the bed.

But Olivia was nimble, and she was by her side within seconds. "You don't really want a season," she continued. "You've said so on numerous occasions. And you hate making conversation with people you don't know."

Miranda attempted to dodge her by scooting to the wardrobe.

"Since you *know* Winston—as I have already pointed out—that eliminates the need to make conversation with strangers, and besides"—Olivia's smiling face came into view—"it means we shall be *sisters*."

Miranda went still, her fingers clutching the day dress she'd taken from the wardrobe. "That would be lovely, Olivia," she said, because really, what else could she say?

"Oh, I'm *thrilled* you agree!" Olivia exclaimed, and she threw her arms around her. "It shall be wonderful. Splendid. Beyond splendid. It shall be perfection."

Miranda stood still, wondering how on earth she had just managed to get herself into such a tangle.

Olivia pulled back, still beaming. "Winston will have no idea what has hit him."

"Is the purpose of this to make a match or simply to somehow best your brother?"

"Well, both, of course," Olivia freely admitted. She released Miranda and plopped herself down in a nearby chair. "Does it matter?"

Miranda opened her mouth, but Olivia was quicker. "Of course not," she said. "All that matters is the commonality of the goal, Miranda. Truly, I'm surprised we have not given this serious thought before."

As her back was to Olivia, Miranda allowed herself a wince. Of course she had not given it serious thought. She had been too busy dreaming of Turner.

"And I saw Winston looking at you last night."

"There were only five people in the room, Olivia. He couldn't very well *not* look at me."

"It was all in the *how*," Olivia persisted. "It was as if he'd never seen you before."

Miranda started pulling on her clothes. "I'm quite certain you're mistaken."

"I'm not. Here, turn around, I'll do your buttons. I'm never wrong about things like these."

Miranda stood patiently as Olivia did up her frock. And then it occurred to her—

"When have you had the opportunity to be right? We're buried in the country. It's not as if we're witness to anyone falling in love."

"Of course we are. There was Billy Evans and—"

"They *had* to get married, Olivia. You know that."

Olivia finished the last button, moved her hands to Miranda's shoulders, and twisted her until they were facing. Her expression was arch, even for Olivia. "Yes, but *why* did they have to get married? Because they were in love."

"I don't recall your predicting the match."

"Nonsense. Of course I did. You were in Scotland. And I couldn't tell you in a letter—it makes it all seem so utterly sordid to put it into writing."

Miranda wasn't sure why that should be the case— an unplanned pregnancy was an unplanned pregnancy was an unplanned pregnancy. Putting it down in writing wasn't going to change anything. But regardless, Olivia did have a point. Miranda went to Scotland for six weeks every year to visit her maternal grandparents, and Billy Evans did get married while she was gone. Trust Olivia to come up with the one argument she couldn't refute.

"Shall we go to breakfast?" Miranda asked wearily. There was no way she was going to get out of making an appearance, and besides, Turner had been somewhat disguised the night before. If there was any justice in the world, he'd be plastered to his bed with a throbbing head all morning.

"Not until Maria does your hair," Olivia decided. "We must not leave anything to chance. It is your *job* to be beautiful now. Oh, don't stare at me like that. You're far prettier than you think you are."

"Olivia."

"No, no, bad choice of words. You're not pretty. *I'm* pretty. Pretty and dull. You have something more."

"A long face."

"Not really. Not as much as when you were small, at least." Olivia tilted her head to the side. And said nothing.

Nothing. Olivia.

"What is it?" Miranda asked suspiciously.

"I think you've grown into yourself."

It was what Turner had said, all those years ago. *Someday you're going to grow into yourself, and you will be as beautiful as you already are smart.* Miranda hated that she remembered it. And she really hated that it made her want to cry.

Olivia, seeing the emotion in her eyes, misted up as well. "Oh, Miranda," she said, embracing her tightly. "I love you, too. We shall be the best of sisters. I cannot wait."

By the time Miranda arrived at breakfast (a full thirty minutes later; she vowed she had never spent so long dressing her hair, and then she vowed she never would again), her stomach was roaring.

"Good morning, family," Olivia said cheerily as she took a plate from the sideboard. "Where is Turner?"

Miranda sent up a silent prayer of thanks for his absence.

"Still in bed, I imagine," Lady Rudland replied. "The

poor man. He's had a shock. It's been a dreadful week."

No one said anything. None of them had liked Leticia.

Olivia picked up the silence. "Right," she said. "Well, I hope he does not grow too hungry. He did not dine with us last night, either."

"Olivia, his wife just died," Winston said. "Of a broken neck, no less. Pray give him a spot of leniency."

"It is because I love him that I am concerned for his welfare," Olivia said, with the testiness she reserved only for her twin brother. "The man is not eating."

"I had a tray sent up to his room," their mother said, putting an end to the squabble. "Good morning, Miranda."

Miranda started. She'd been busy watching Olivia and Winston. "Good morning, Lady Rudland," she said quickly. "I trust you slept well."

"As well as can be expected." The countess sighed and took a sip of her tea. "These are trying times. But I must thank you again for spending the night. I know it was a solace to Olivia."

"Of course," Miranda murmured. "I was happy to be of help." She followed Olivia to the sideboard and fixed herself a plate for breakfast. When she returned to the table, she found that Olivia had left her a seat next to Winston.

She sat and looked up at the Bevelstokes. They were all smiling at her, Lord and Lady Rudland quite benignly, Olivia with a hint of shrewdness, and Winston. . .

"Good morning, Miranda," he said warmly. And his eyes . . . They held. . .

Interest?

Good heavens, could Olivia have been right? There *was*

something different in the way he was looking at her.

"Very well, thank you," Miranda said, completely unsettled. Winston was practically her brother, wasn't he? He couldn't possibly think of her like— And she couldn't, either. But if he could, then could she? And—

"Do you intend to remain at Haverbreaks through the morning?" he asked. "I thought we might go for a ride. Perhaps after breakfast?"

Dear God. Olivia was right.

Miranda felt her lips part with surprise. "I, er, I hadn't decided."

Olivia kicked her under the table.

"Oh!"

"Has the mackerel gone off?" Lady Rudland inquired.

Miranda shook her head. "Sorry," she said, clearing her throat. "Ehrm, it was just a bone, I think."

"It's why I never eat fish for breakfast," Olivia announced.

"What say you, Miranda?" Winston persisted. He smiled—a lazy, boyish masterpiece that was certain to break a thousand hearts. "Shall we go for a ride?"

Miranda carefully edged her legs farther from Olivia and said, "I didn't bring a habit, I'm afraid." It was the truth, and it was really too bad, because she was beginning to think that an outing with Winston might be just the thing to banish Turner from her mind.

"You can borrow one of mine," Olivia said, smiling sweetly over her toast. "It will be only a little too big."

"It's settled, then," Winston said. "It shall be splendid to catch up. It has been an age since we have had the chance."

Miranda found herself smiling. Winston was so easy to be with, even now, when she was befuddled by his intentions. "It's been several years, I think. I always manage to be in Scotland when you're home from school."

"But not today," he announced happily. He picked up his tea, smiling at her over the cup, and Miranda was struck by how very much he looked like Turner when he was younger. Winston was twenty now, just a year older than Turner had been when she'd fallen in love with him.

When they'd first met, she corrected. She hadn't fallen in love with him. She'd merely thought she had. She knew better now.

11 APRIL 1819

> *Splendid ride with Winston today. He is much like his brother—if his brother were kind and considerate and still in possession of a sense of humor.*

Turner had not slept well, but this did not surprise him; he rarely slept well anymore. And indeed, come morning, he was still irritable and still angry—mostly with himself.

What the hell had he been thinking? Kissing Miranda Cheever. The girl was practically his little sister. He'd been angry, and maybe just a little bit drunk, but that was no excuse for such poor behavior. Leticia had killed many things within him, but by God, he was still a gentleman. Otherwise, what had he left?

He hadn't even desired her. Not really. He knew desire,

knew that gut-wrenching need to possess and claim, and what he'd felt for Miranda. . .

Well, he didn't know what it was, but it hadn't been that.

It was those big brown eyes of hers. They saw everything. They unnerved him. Always had. Even as a child, she had seemed uncannily wise. As he'd stood there in his father's study, he'd felt exposed, transparent. She was just a chit, barely out of the schoolroom, and yet she saw through him. The intrusion had been infuriating, and so he lashed out in the only way that had seemed appropriate at the time.

Except nothing could have been less appropriate.

And now he was going to have to apologize. God, but the thought of it was intolerable. It would be so much easier to pretend it had never happened and ignore her for the rest of his life, but that clearly wasn't going to wash, not if he intended to maintain ties with his sister. And besides that, he hoped he had some shred of gentlemanly decency left within him.

Leticia had killed most of what was good and innocent within him, but surely there had to be something left. And when a gentleman wronged a lady, a gentleman apologized.

By the time Turner went down to breakfast, his family had departed, which suited him fine. He ate quickly and gulped down his coffee, taking it black as a penance and not even flinching when it rolled hot and bitter down his throat.

"Will there be anything else?"

Turner looked up at the footman, hovering at his side. "No," he said. "Not at this time."

The footman stepped back, but he did not exit the room, and Turner decided at that moment that it was time to depart Haverbreaks. There were too many people here. Hell, his mother had probably given instructions to all the servants to keep a close eye on him.

Still scowling, he shoved back in his chair and strode out into the hall. He'd alert his valet that they would be departing posthaste. They could be gone in an hour. All that remained was to find Miranda and get this bloody business over and done with so he could go back to skulking about in his own home and—

Laughter.

He looked up. Winston and Miranda had just entered, rosy-cheeked and practically blooming with fresh air and sunshine.

Turner quirked a brow and stopped, waiting to see how long it took them to notice his presence.

"And *that*," Miranda was saying, clearly coming to the close of a story, "was when I knew Olivia could not be trusted with the chocolate."

Winston laughed, his eyes surveying her warmly. "You've changed, Miranda."

She blushed prettily. "Not so very much. Mostly I have just grown up."

"That you have."

Turner thought he might gag.

"Did you think you could go away to school and find me just the way you left me?"

Winston grinned. "Something like that. But I must say I'm pleased with the way you've turned out." He touched her hair, which had been coiled into a neat chignon. "I daresay I won't be yanking on this anymore."

She blushed again, and, really, this simply could not be tolerated.

"Good morning," Turner said loudly, not bothering to move from his spot across the hall.

"I believe it is now afternoon," Winston replied.

"For the uninitiated, perhaps," Turner said with a mocking half smile.

"In London morning lasts until two?" Miranda asked coolly.

"Only if the evening prior was disappointing in its results."

"Turner," Winston said reproachfully.

Turner shrugged. "I need to speak with Miss Cheever," he said, not bothering to look at his brother. Miranda's lips parted—with surprise, he supposed, and perhaps a bit of anger as well.

"I should think that is up to Miranda," Winston said.

Turner kept his eyes on Miranda. "Inform me when you are ready to return home. I will escort you."

Winston's mouth opened in dismay. "See here," he said stiffly. "She is a lady, and you would do well to offer her the courtesy of asking permission."

Turner turned to his brother and paused, staring until the younger man squirmed. He looked back to Miranda and said it again. "I will escort you home."

"I've—"

He cut her off with a pointed look, and she acquiesced with a nod. "Of course, my lord," she said, the corners of her mouth uncharacteristically tight. She turned to Winston. "He wanted to discuss an illuminated manuscript with my father. I'd quite forgotten."

Clever Miranda. Turner almost smiled.

"Turner?" Winston said doubtfully. "An illuminated manuscript?"

"It's a new passion of mine," Turner said blandly.

Winston looked from him to Miranda and back, then finally gave in with a stiff nod. "Very well," he said. "It has been a pleasure, Miranda."

"Indeed," she said, and from her tone, Turner knew that she did not lie.

Turner did not relinquish his position between the two young lovers, and Winston shot him an irritated glance before facing Miranda and saying, "Will I see you again before I return to Oxford?"

"I hope so. I have no firm plans for the next few days, and—"

Turner yawned.

Miranda cleared her throat. "I am sure we can make arrangements. Perhaps you and Olivia can come by for tea."

"I would enjoy that very much."

Turner managed to extend his bored mien to his fingernails, which he inspected with a significant lack of interest.

"Or if Olivia cannot visit," Miranda continued, her voice impressively steely, "perhaps you can come by yourself."

Winston's eyes grew warm with interest. "I would be delighted," he murmured, leaning over her hand.

"Are you ready?" Turner barked.

Miranda moved not a muscle as she ground out, "No."

"Well, hurry it along, then, I haven't all day."

Winston turned to him in disbelief. "What is wrong with you?"

It was a good question. Fifteen minutes earlier, his only aim was to escape his parents' house with all possible haste, and now he'd all but insisted that he take the time to escort Miranda home.

Very well, he *had* insisted, but he had his reasons.

"I am quite well," Turner returned. "Best I've been in years. Since 1816, to be precise."

Winston shifted his weight uncomfortably from foot to foot, and Miranda turned away. 1816 was, they all knew, the year of Turner's marriage.

"June," he added, just to be perverse.

"I beg your pardon?" Winston said stiffly.

"June. June of 1816." And then he beamed at both of them, a patently false, self-congratulatory sort of smile. He turned to Miranda. "I will await you in the front hall. Don't be late."

Chapter 3

Don't be late?

Don't be late??!

For what, Miranda fumed for about the sixteenth time as she yanked on her clothing. They hadn't set a time. He hadn't even asked to escort her home. He'd ordered her, and then, after he'd instructed her to tell him when she was ready to leave, he'd not bothered to wait for an answer.

Was he so eager to have her gone?

Miranda didn't know whether to laugh or cry.

"Are you leaving already?"

It was Olivia, slipping in from the corridor.

"I need to return home," Miranda said, choosing that moment to pull her dress over her head. She didn't particularly wish Olivia to see her face. "Your habit is on the bed," she added, the words muffled by the muslin.

"But why? Your father won't miss you."

Kind of her to point it out, Miranda thought uncharitably, even though she'd voiced the same opinion to Olivia on countless occasions.

"Miranda," Olivia persisted.

Miranda turned her back so that Olivia could do up her buttons. "I don't wish to overstay my welcome."

"What? Don't be silly. My mother would have you live with us if it were possible. You will, in fact, once we go to London."

"We're not in London."

"What has that to do with anything?"

Nothing. Miranda clenched her teeth.

"Did you have a row with Winston?"

"Of course not." Because, really, who could have a row with Winston? Aside from Olivia.

"Then what is the matter?"

"It is nothing." Miranda forced herself into a calmer disposition and reached for her gloves. "Your brother wishes to ask my father about an illuminated manuscript."

"Winston?" Olivia asked doubtfully.

"Turner."

"Turner?"

Good heavens, was she *ever* without questions?

"Yes," Miranda answered, "and he plans to leave soon, so he needs to escort me now."

The last bit was entirely fabricated, but Miranda thought it rather inspired, under the circumstances. Besides, maybe now he'd have to go back to his home in Northumberland, and the world could go back to its usual position, tilting contentedly on its axis, spinning 'round the sun.

Olivia leaned against the doorframe, situating herself

in such a way that Miranda could not ignore her. "Then why are you in such a beastly mood? You've always liked Turner, haven't you?"

Miranda almost laughed.

And then she almost cried.

How dare he order her about like some recalcitrant trollop.

How dare he make her so miserable here, at Haver-breaks, which had been more of a home to her these past few years than it had to him.

She turned away. She couldn't let Olivia see her face.

How dare he kiss her and not mean it.

"Miranda?" Olivia said softly. "Are you all right?"

"I'm perfectly well," Miranda choked out, brushing quickly by her as she flew toward the door.

"You don't sound—"

"I'm sad about Leticia," Miranda snapped. And she was. Anyone who had made Turner that miserable surely deserved to be mourned.

But Olivia, being Olivia, would not be swayed, and as Miranda hurried down the stairs to the front hall, she was right at her heels.

"Leticia!" she exclaimed. "You must be joking."

Miranda skidded 'round the landing, holding tight to the banister to keep herself from flying.

"Leticia was a nasty old witch," Olivia continued. "She made Turner dreadfully unhappy."

Precisely.

"Miranda! Miranda! Oh, Turner. Good day."

"Olivia," he said politely, giving her a tiny nod.

"Miranda says she is mourning Leticia. Is that not insupportable?"

"Olivia!" Miranda gasped. Turner might have detested his dead wife—enough to say so at her funeral, even—but there were certain things that were quite beyond the bounds of decency.

Turner just looked at Miranda, one of his brows rising into a mockingly quizzical expression.

"Oh, stuff. He hated her, and we all knew it."

"Candid as always, dear sister," Turner murmured.

"You've always said you don't enjoy hypocrisy," she returned.

"True enough." He looked to Miranda. "Shall we?"

"You're taking her home?" Olivia asked, even though Miranda had just told her that he was.

"I need to speak with her father."

"Can't Winston take her?"

"Olivia!" Miranda wasn't sure what embarrassed her more—that Olivia was matchmaking or that she was doing it in front of Turner.

"Winston doesn't need to speak with her father," Turner said smoothly.

"Well, can't he come along?"

"Not in my curricle."

Olivia's eyes grew round with longing. "You're taking your curricle?" It was newly built, high, fast, and sleek, and Olivia had been dying to take the reins.

Turner grinned, and for a moment he almost looked like himself again—the man Miranda had known and loved, all those years ago. "Maybe I'll even let her drive," he said, clearly for no other reason than to torture his sister.

It worked, too. Olivia made a strange, gurgling sound, as if she were choking on her own envy.

"Ta, dear sis!" Turner said with a smirk. He slipped his arm through Miranda's and drew her toward the door. "I shall see you later . . . or perhaps you'll see me. As I drive by."

Miranda bit back a laugh as they headed down the steps to the drive. "You're terrible," she said.

He shrugged. "She deserves it."

"No," Miranda said, feeling that she ought to stand up for her dearest friend, even if she had enjoyed the scene to an unseemly degree.

"No?"

"Very well, yes, but you're still terrible."

"Oh, absolutely," he agreed, and as Miranda let him help her up into the curricle, she wondered how this had all come about, that she was sitting beside him and she was actually smiling and thinking that maybe she didn't hate him, and maybe he could be redeemed.

They drove in silence for the first few minutes. The curricle was very smart, and Miranda could not help but feel terribly stylish as they sped along, high above the road.

"You made quite a conquest this afternoon," Turner finally said.

Miranda stiffened.

"Winston seems quite taken with you."

Still, she said nothing. There was nothing she could say, nothing that would leave her with dignity intact. She could deny it, and sound like a coquette, or she could agree and sound boastful. Or taunting. Or, God forbid, as if she wished to make him jealous.

"I suppose I ought to give you my blessing."

Miranda turned to face him in shock, but Turner kept his eyes on the road as he added, "It would certainly be an advantageous match for you, and he could undoubtedly do no better. You may be lacking in the funds a younger son so earnestly needs, but you make up for it in sense. And sensibility, for that matter."

"Oh. I—I—" Miranda blinked. She hadn't the faintest idea what to say. It was a compliment, and not even a back-handed one at that, but still, it fell a bit flat. She didn't want him to rave about all her stellar qualities if the only reason was to pair her with his brother.

And she didn't want to be *sensible*. For once she wanted to be beautiful, or exotic, or captivating.

Good heavens. *Sensible*. It was a miserable designation.

Miranda realized he was waiting for her to finish her halting reply, so she muttered, "Thank you."

"I do not wish for my brother to make the same mistakes that I did."

She looked to him at that. His face was pinched, his eyes pointed determinedly at the road, as if a single glance in her direction might send the world crashing down around them. "Mistakes?" she echoed softly.

"Mistake," he said, his voice clipped. "Singular."

"Leticia." There. She'd said it.

The curricle slowed, then stopped. And finally, he looked at her. "Indeed."

"What did she do to you?" she asked softly. It was too

personal, and highly inappropriate, but she could not stop herself, not when his eyes were focused so intently on hers.

But it was the wrong thing to say. Clearly, because his jaw tensed, and he turned away as he said, "Nothing that is fit for a lady's ears."

"Turner—"

He whirled back to face her, his eyes flaring. "Do you know how she died?"

Miranda was shaking her head even as she said, "Her neck. She fell."

"From a horse," he bit off. "She was thrown from a horse—"

"I know."

"—riding to meet her lover."

That, she hadn't known.

"She was also with child."

Good God. "Oh, Turner, I'm so s—"

He cut her off. "*Don't* say it. I'm not."

Her hand covered her open mouth.

"It wasn't mine."

She swallowed. What could she say? There was nothing to say.

"The first wasn't mine, either," he added. His nostrils flared, and his eyes narrowed, and there was a twist to his lips—almost as if he were daring her. Silently daring her to ask.

"T—" She tried to say his name, because she thought she ought to speak, but the truth was, she was blessedly thankful when he cut her off.

"She was carrying when we married. It's why we married, if you must know." He laughed caustically at that. "*If you must know*," he said again. "That's rich, considering *I* didn't know."

The pain in his voice cut through her, but not nearly as much as the self-loathing. She had wondered how he had come to this, and now she knew . . . and she knew she could never hate him.

"I'm sorry," she said, because she was, and because anything more would have been too much.

"It wasn't your—" He cut himself off, cleared his throat. And then, after several seconds, he said, "Thank you."

He picked up the reins again, but before he could set them in motion, she asked, "What will you do now?"

He smiled at that. Well, not really, but the corner of his mouth moved a little. "What will I do?" he echoed.

"Will you go to Northumberland? To London?" *Will you remarry?*

"What will I do," he mused. "Whatever I please, I imagine."

Miranda cleared her throat. "I know that your mother was hoping that you would make yourself present in London during Olivia's season."

"Olivia doesn't need my help."

"No." She swallowed. Painfully. That was her pride sliding down her throat. "But I do."

He turned and assessed her with raised brows. "You? I thought you had my little brother wrapped up neatly with a bow."

"No," she said quickly. "I mean, I don't know. He's rather young, don't you think?"

"Older than you."

"By three months," she shot back. "He's still at university. He's not going to wish to marry soon."

His head tilted, and his gaze grew penetrating. "And you do?" he murmured.

Miranda fought the urge to leap over the side of the curricle. Surely there were some conversations a lady shouldn't have to endure.

Surely this had to be one of them.

"I would like to marry someday, yes," she said haltingly, hating that her cheeks were growing warm.

He stared at her. And he stared at her. And then he stared at her some more.

Or maybe it was barely a glance. She really couldn't tell any longer, but she was beyond relieved when he finally broke the silence—however long it had lasted—and said, "Very well. I shall consider it. I owe you that, at least."

Good Lord, her head was spinning. "Owe me what?"

"An apology, to begin with. What happened last night . . . It was unforgivable. It's why I insisted upon escorting you home." He cleared his throat, and for the barest of moments looked away. "I owe you an apology, and I thought you'd rather I did it in private."

She stared straight ahead.

"A public apology would require that we tell my family just what exactly I was apologizing for," he continued. "I didn't think you'd want them to know."

"You mean *you* don't want them to know."

He sighed and raked his hand through his hair. "No, I

don't. I can't say I'm proud of my behavior, and I would rather my family didn't know. But I was also thinking of you."

"Apology accepted," she said softly.

Turner let out a long, weary sigh. "I don't know why I did it," he continued. "It wasn't even desire. I don't know what it was. But it wasn't your fault."

She gave him a look. It wasn't difficult to decipher.

"Ah, bloody—" He let out an irritated breath and looked away. *Brilliant job, Turner. Kiss a girl and then tell her you didn't do it out of desire.* "I'm sorry, Miranda. That came out the wrong way. I'm being an ass. I can't seem to help myself these days."

"Perhaps you ought to write a book," she said bitterly. "One hundred and one ways to insult a young lady. I daresay you're up to at least fifty by now."

He took a deep breath. He wasn't used to apologizing. "It's not that you aren't attractive."

Miranda's expression turned to disbelief. Not at his words, he realized—at the mere fact that he was saying them, that she was being forced to sit there and listen as he embarrassed them both. He should stop, he knew, but the hurt in her eyes had awakened a painful little corner of his heart that he'd kept shuttered for years, and he had this strange compulsion to make things right.

Miranda was nineteen. Her experience with men consisted of Winston and himself. Both of whom had heretofore been brotherly figures. The poor girl must be confused as hell. Winston had suddenly decided that she was Venus, Queen Elizabeth, and the Virgin Mary all rolled into one, and Turner had all but forced himself on her. Not exactly an average day in the life of a young country miss.

And yet here she was. Her back straight. Her chin high. And she didn't hate him. She should, but she didn't.

"No," he said, actually taking her hand in his. "You must listen to me. You *are* attractive. Quite." He let his eyes settle on her face and took his first really good look at her in years. She wasn't classically pretty, but there was something about those big brown eyes that was rather engaging. Her skin was flawless and quite elegantly pale, providing a luminescent contrast to her dark hair, which was, Turner suddenly noticed, rather thick, with just the slightest tendency to curl. It looked soft, too. He had touched it the night before. Why didn't he remember what it felt like? Surely he would have noticed its texture.

"Turner," Miranda said.

He was staring at her. Why was he staring at her?

His gaze moved down to her lips as she said his name. A sensual little mouth, she had. Full lips, very kissable.

"Turner?"

"Quite," he said softly, as if just coming to an unbelievable realization.

"Quite what?"

"Quite attractive." He shook his head slightly, pulling himself out of the spell she had somehow cast over him. "You're quite attractive."

She let out a sigh. "Turner, please don't lie to spare my feelings. It shows a lack of respect for my intellect, and that is more insulting than anything you can say about my appearance."

He drew back and quirked a smile. "I'm not lying." He sounded surprised.

Miranda caught her lower lip nervously between her teeth. "Oh." She sounded just as surprised as he had. "Well, thank you, then. I think."

"I'm not usually so clumsy with compliments that they cannot be identified."

"I am sure you are not," she said tartly.

"Now why do I suddenly feel like you're accusing me of something?"

Her eyes widened. Had her tone been that cold? "I don't know what you're talking about," she said quickly.

For a moment it looked as if he might question her further, but then he must have decided against it, because he picked up the reins and offered her a bland smile as he said, "Shall we?"

They rode on for several minutes, Miranda stealing glances at Turner when she could. His expression was unreadable, placid even, and it was more than a bit irritating, when her own thoughts were in such a turmoil. He'd said he hadn't desired her, but then why had he kissed her? What had been the point? And then it just slipped out— "Why *did* you kiss me?"

For a moment it looked as if Turner were choking, although on what, Miranda could not imagine. The horses slowed a bit, sensing a lack of attention from their driver, and Turner looked at her with obvious shock.

Miranda saw his distress and decided that he couldn't find any kind way to answer her question. "Forget that I asked," she said quickly. "It doesn't matter."

But she didn't regret having asked. What had she to lose? He wasn't going to mock her and he wasn't going to spread tales. She had only the embarrassment of this one moment, and that could never compare with the embarrassment of the night before, so—

"It was me," he said quite suddenly. "Just me. And you were unfortunate enough to be standing next to me."

Miranda saw the bleakness in his blue eyes and placed her hand on his sleeve. "It's all right to be angry with her."

He did not pretend not to know what she was talking about. "She's dead, Miranda."

"That doesn't mean she wasn't an exceptionally awful person when she was alive."

He looked at her strangely and then burst out laughing. "Oh, Miranda, sometimes you say the damnedest things."

She smiled. "Now *that* I will definitely take as a compliment."

"Remind me never to put you up for the position of Sunday school teacher."

"I have never quite mastered Christian virtue, I'm afraid."

"Oh, really?" He looked amused.

"I still hold a grudge against poor little Fiona Bennet."

"And she is . . . ?"

"That dreadful girl who called me ugly at Olivia and Winston's eleventh birthday party."

"Dear God, how many years ago was that? Remind me not to cross you."

She quirked a brow. "See that you don't."

"You, my dear girl, are decidedly lacking as pertains to charitable nature."

She shrugged, marveling at how he'd managed to make her feel so carefree and happy in such a short time. "Don't tell your mother. She thinks me a saint."

"Compared to Olivia, I'm sure you are."

Miranda wagged her finger at him. "Nothing bad about Olivia, if you please. I'm quite devoted to her."

"Faithful as a hound you are, if you'll excuse my less than attractive simile."

"I adore hounds."

And it was then that they arrived at Miranda's home.

I adore hounds. That would be her final comment. Wonderful. For the rest of his life, he would associate her with dogs.

Turner helped her down and then glanced up at the sky, which had begun to darken. "I hope you don't mind if I do not walk you in," he murmured.

"Of course not," Miranda said. She was a practical girl. It was silly for him to get wet when she was perfectly able to let herself into her own home.

"Good luck," he said, hopping back up into his curricle.

"With what?"

"London, life." He shrugged. "Whatever you wish."

She smiled ruefully. If he only knew.

19 MAY 1819

> *We arrived in London today. I swear I have never seen the like of it. It is big and noisy and crowded and actually rather smelly.*
>
> *Lady Rudland says we are late. Many people are already in town, and the season began*

over a month ago. But there was nothing to be done—Livvy would have looked dreadfully ill-bred to be out and about when she is meant to be mourning Leticia. As it is, we cheated a bit and came early, although only for fittings and preparations. We may not attend events until the mourning is complete.

Thank heavens only six weeks were required. Poor Turner must do a year.

I have quite forgiven him, I'm afraid. I know I should not, but I cannot bring myself to despise him. Surely I must hold some kind of record for the longest stint of unrequited love.

I am pathetic.

I am a hound.

I am a pathetic hound.

And I waste paper quite dreadfully.

Chapter 4

Turner had planned to spend the spring and summer in Northumberland, where he could decline to mourn his wife with some degree of privacy, but his mother had employed an astonishing number of tactics—the most lethal being guilt, of course—to force his hand and compel him to come down to London in support of Olivia.

He had not given in when she had pointed out that he was a leader in society and thus his presence at Olivia's ball would ensure attendance by all the best young gentlemen.

He had not given in when she had said that he shouldn't molder away in the country, and it would do him good to be out and about among friends.

He had, however, given in when she had appeared on his doorstep and said, without even the benefit of a salutation, "She's your *sister*."

And so here he was, at Rudland House in London, surrounded by five hundred of, if not the country's finest, at least its most pompous.

Still, Olivia was going to have to find a husband from among this lot, Miranda, too, and Turner was bloody well not going to allow either one of them to make a match as disastrous as his own had been. London was teeming with male equivalents to Leticia, most of whom began their names with Lord This or Sir That. And Turner quite doubted that his mother would be privy to the more salacious of the gossip that ran through their circles.

Still, it didn't mean that he would be required to make too many appearances. He was here, at their debut ball, and he'd squire them about now and then, perhaps if there was something at the theater he actually cared to see, and beyond that, he'd monitor their progress from behind the scenes. By the end of summer, he'd be done with all this nonsense, and he could go back to—

Well, he could go back to whatever it was he'd been thinking about planning to do. Study crop rotation, perhaps. Take up archery. Visit the local public house. He rather liked their ale. And no one ever asked questions about the recently departed Lady Turner.

"Darling, you're here!" His mother suddenly filled his vision, lovely in her purple gown.

"I told you I would make it in time," he replied, finishing off the glass of champagne he'd been holding in his hand. "Weren't you alerted to my arrival?"

"No," she replied, somewhat distractedly. "I have been running about like a madwoman with all the last-moment details. I'm sure the servants did not wish to bother me."

"Or they could not find you," Turner remarked, idly scanning the crowd. It was a mad crush—a success by any measure. He did not see either of the guests of honor, but then again, he'd been quite content to remain in the shadows for the twenty minutes or so he'd been present.

"I have secured permission for both girls to waltz," Lady Rudland said, "so please do your duty by both of them."

"A direct order," he murmured.

"Especially Miranda," she added, apparently not having heard his comment.

"What do you mean, especially Miranda?"

His mother turned to him with no-nonsense eyes. "Miranda is a remarkable girl, and I love her dearly, but we both know that she is not the sort that society normally favors."

Turner gave her a sharp look. "We both also know that society is rarely an excellent judge of character. Leticia, if you recall, was a grand success."

"And so is Olivia, if this evening is any indication," his mother shot back tartly. "Society is capricious and rewards the bad as often as the good. But it never rewards the quiet."

It was at that moment that Turner caught sight of Miranda, standing near Olivia by the door to the hall.

Near Olivia, but worlds apart.

It wasn't that Miranda was being ignored, because she surely was not. She was smiling at a young gentleman who appeared to be asking her to dance. But she had nothing like the crowd surrounding Olivia, who, Turner had to admit, shone like a radiant jewel placed in its proper setting. Olivia's eyes sparkled, and when she laughed, music seemed to fill the air.

There was something captivating about his sister. Even Turner had to admit it.

But Miranda was different. She watched. She smiled, but it was almost as if she had a secret, as if she were jotting notes in her mind about the people she met.

"Go dance with her," his mother urged.

"Miranda?" he asked, surprised. He would have thought she'd wish him to bestow his first dance with Olivia.

Lady Rudland nodded. "It will be a huge coup for her. You have not danced since . . . since I cannot even recall. Long before Leticia died."

Turner felt his jaw tighten, and he would have said something, except his mother suddenly gasped, which was not half as surprising as what followed, which, he was quite certain, was the first incidence of blasphemy ever to cross her lips.

"Mother?" he queried.

"Where is your armband?" she whispered urgently.

"My armband," he said, with some irony.

"For Leticia," she added, as if he did not know that.

"I believe I told you that I have chosen not to mourn her."

"But this is London," she hissed. "And your sister's debut."

He shrugged. "My coat is black."

"Your coats are always black."

"Perhaps I am in perpetual mourning then," he said mildly, "for innocence lost."

"You will create a scandal," she fairly hissed.

"No," he said pointedly, "Leticia created scandals. I am simply refusing to mourn my scandalous wife."

"Do you wish to ruin your sister?"

"My actions will not reflect half so badly upon her as my dear departed's would have done."

"That is neither here nor there, Turner. The fact of the matter is your wife *died*, and—"

"I *saw* the body," he retorted, effectively halting her arguments.

Lady Rudland drew back. "There is no need to be vulgar about it."

Turner's head began to pound. "I apologize for that, then."

"I wish you would reconsider."

"I would prefer that I did not cause you distress," he said with a bit of a sigh, "but I will not change my mind. You may have me here in London without an armband, or you may have me in Northumberland . . . also without an armband," he finished after a pause. "It is your decision."

His mother's jaw clenched, and she did not say anything, so he simply shrugged and said, "I shall find Miranda, then."

And he did.

Miranda had been in town for two weeks, and while she was not sure she could term herself a success, she did not think she qualified as a failure, either. She was right where she'd expected herself to be—somewhere in the middle, with a dance card that was always half full and a journal that was overflowing with observations of the inane, insane, and occasionally in pain. (That would be Lord Chisselworth, who tripped on a step at the Mottram ball and sprained his ankle. Of the inane and insane, there were too many to count.)

All in all, she thought herself rather accomplished for one with her particular set of God-given talents and attributes. In her diary, she wrote—

> *Am meant to be honing my social skills, but as Olivia pointed out, idle chatter has never been my forte. But I have perfected my gentle, vacant smile, and it seems to be doing the trick. Had three requests for my company at supper!*

It helped, of course, that her position as Olivia's closest friend was well known. Olivia had taken the *ton* by storm—as they all had known she would—and Miranda benefited by association. There were the gentlemen who reached Olivia's side too late to secure a dance, and there were those who were simply too terrified to speak with her. (At such times, Miranda always seemed like a more comfortable choice.)

But even with all the overflow attention, Miranda was still standing alone when she heard an achingly familiar voice—

"Never say I have caught you without company, Miss Cheever."

Turner.

She could not help but smile. He was devastatingly handsome in his dark evening clothes, and the candlelight flickered gold against his hair. "You came," she said simply.

"Didn't you think I would?"

Lady Rudland had said he was planning on it, but Miranda hadn't been so sure. He had made it abundantly clear that he wanted no part of society that year. Or possibly any year. It was hard to say just yet.

"I understand she had to blackmail you into attendance," she said, as they assumed side-by-side positions, both gazing idly out at the crowd.

He feigned affront. "Blackmail? What an ugly word. And incorrect in this instance."

"Oh?"

He leaned toward her ever so slightly. "It was guilt."

"Guilt?" Her lips twitched, and she turned to him with mischievous eyes. "What did you do?"

"It's what I didn't do. Or rather, what I wasn't doing." He gave a careless shrug. "I'm told that you and Olivia will be successes if I offer my support."

"I expect Olivia would be a success if she were penniless *and* born on the wrong side of the blanket."

"I have no worries for you, either," Turner said, smiling down at her in a somewhat annoyingly benevolent manner. Then he scowled. "And what would my mother blackmail me with, pray tell?"

Miranda smiled to herself. She liked it when he was disconcerted. He always seemed so in control of himself to her, whereas her heart always managed to thump in triplicate whenever she saw him. Luckily the years had made her comfortable with him. If she hadn't known him for so long, she doubted she would be able to manage a conversation in his presence. Besides, he would surely suspect something if she were tongue-tied each time they met.

"Oh, I don't know," she pretended to ponder. "Stories of when you were small and such."

"Hush your mouth. I was a perfect angel."

She raised her brows dubiously. "You must think I'm very gullible."

"No, just too polite to contradict me."

Miranda rolled her eyes and turned back to the crowd. Olivia was holding court across the room, surrounded by her usual bevy of gentlemen.

"Livvy's a natural at this, isn't she?" she said.

Turner nodded his assent. "Where are all of *your* admirers, Miss Cheever? I find it difficult to believe you haven't any."

She blushed at his compliment. "One or two, I suppose. I tend to blend into the woodwork when Olivia is near."

He shot her a disbelieving look. "Let me see your dance card."

Reluctantly, she handed it over to him. He gave it a quick examination, then returned it. "I was right," he said. "It is very nearly filled."

"Most of them found their way to me only because I was standing next to Olivia."

"Don't be silly. And it's nothing to get upset about."

"Oh, but I'm not," she replied, surprised that he should think so. "Why? Do I look upset?"

He drew back and surveyed her. "No. No, you don't. How odd."

"Odd?"

"I have never known a lady who did not wish for a gaggle of eligible young men surrounding her at a ball."

Miranda bristled at the condescension in his voice and was not quite able to keep the insolence out of *hers*, as she said, "Well, now you do."

But he just chuckled. "And how, dear girl, are you going to find a husband with that attitude? Oh, don't look at me as if I am being patronizing—"

Which only made her teeth grind harder.

"—you yourself told me that you wish to find a husband this season."

He was right, drat the man. Which left her with no option other than to say, "Don't call me 'dear girl,' if you please."

He grinned. "Why, Miss Cheever, do I detect a bit of temper in you?"

"I've always had a temper," she bit off.

"Apparently so." He was still smiling as he said it, which was all the more irritating.

"I thought you were meant to be moody and brooding," she grumbled.

He gave her a lopsided shrug. "You seem to bring out the best in me."

Miranda gave him a pointed look. Had he forgotten the night of Leticia's funeral? "The best?" she nearly drawled. "Really?"

He had the grace to look sheepish, at least. "Or occasionally the worst. But tonight, only the best." At her lifted brows, he added, "I am here to do my duty by you."

Duty. Such a solid, boring word.

"Hand me back your dance card, if you will."

She held it out. It was a festive little thing, with curli-
cues and a small pencil ribbon-tied to the corner. Turner's
eyes grazed over it, and then narrowed. "Why have you
left all of your waltzes free, Miranda? My mother told me
quite specifically that she had secured permission for both
you and Olivia to waltz."

"Oh, it's not that." She clenched her teeth for a split second, trying to control the flush that she knew was going to
start creeping up her neck any second now. "It's just that,
well, if you must know—"

"Out with it, Miss Cheever."

"Why do you always call me Miss Cheever when you're
mocking me?"

"Nonsense. I also call you Miss Cheever when I'm
scolding you."

Oh, well, *that* was an improvement.

"Miranda?"

"It is nothing," she muttered.

But he would not let it go. "It is quite obviously *some*-
thing, Miranda. You—"

"Oh, very well, if you must know, I was hoping *you*
would waltz with me."

He drew back, his eyes betraying his surprise.

"Or Winston," she said quickly, because there was
safety—or at least fewer chances of embarrassment—in
numbers.

"We are interchangeable, then?" Turner murmured.

"No, of course not. But I am not skilled at the waltz, and
I would feel more comfortable if my first time in public is
with someone I know," she hastily improvised.

"Someone who wouldn't take mortal offense if you trod on his toes?"

"Something like that," she mumbled. How had she got herself into this bind? He would either know she was in love with him or think her a silly twit scared to dance in public.

But Turner, bless his heart, was already saying, "I would be honored to dance a waltz with you." He took the little pencil and signed his name to her dance card. "There. You are now promised to me for the first waltz."

"Thank you. I shall look forward to it."

"Good. So do I. Shall I put myself down for another? I can't think of anyone else here with whom I'd rather to be forced into conversation for the four or so minutes of the waltz."

"I had no idea I was such a chore," Miranda said, grimacing.

"Oh, you're not," he assured her. "But everyone else is. Here you are, I'm putting myself down for the last waltz, too. You'll have to fend for yourself for the rest of them. It wouldn't do to dance with you more than twice."

Heavens no, Miranda thought acerbically. Someone might think he hadn't been browbeaten into dancing with her. But she knew what was expected of her, so she smiled tightly and said, "No, of course not."

"Very well, then," Turner said, with the tone of finality men liked to use when they were ready to end a conversation, regardless of whether anyone else was. "I see young Hardy over there is coming this way to claim the next dance. I'm going to get something to drink. I shall see you at the first waltz."

And then he left her standing in the corner, murmuring his greetings to Mr. Hardy as he departed. Miranda bobbed a dutiful curtsy at her dance partner and then took his gloved hand and followed him onto the dance floor for a quadrille. She was not surprised when, after commenting on her gown and the weather, he asked after Olivia.

Miranda answered his questions as politely as she was able, trying not to encourage him overmuch. Judging from the crowd around her friend, Mr. Hardy's chances were slim indeed.

The dance was over with merciful speed, and Miranda quickly made her way over to Olivia.

"Oh, Miranda, dear," she exclaimed. "Where have you been? I've been telling everyone about you."

"You have not," Miranda said, raising her brows disbelievingly.

"Indeed I have. Haven't I?" Olivia poked a gentleman in the side, and he immediately nodded. "Would I lie to you?"

Miranda bit back a smile. "If it suited your purposes."

"Oh, stop. You're terrible. And where *have* you been?"

"I needed a breath of fresh air, so I escaped to a corner and had a glass of lemonade. Turner kept me company."

"Oh, has he arrived, then? I shall have to save a dance for him."

Miranda was doubtful. "I don't think you have any left to save."

"That cannot be so." Olivia looked down at her dance card. "Oh, dear. I shall have to cross one of these off."

"Olivia, you can't do that."

"Why ever not? Listen, Miranda, I must tell you—" She broke off suddenly, remembering the presence of her many admirers. She turned, smiling radiantly at them all.

Miranda would not have been surprised if they had dropped to the floor, one by one, like proverbial flies.

"Would any of you gentlemen mind fetching some lemonade?" Olivia asked sweetly. "I'm utterly parched."

There was a rush of assurances, followed by a flurry of movement, and Miranda could only stare in awe as she watched them scuttle off in a pack. "They're like sheep," she whispered.

"Well, yes," Olivia agreed, "except for the ones who are more like goats."

Miranda had about two seconds to attempt to decipher *that* before Olivia added, "Brilliant of me, wasn't it, to be rid of all of them at once. I tell you, I'm getting quite good at all this."

Miranda nodded, not bothering to speak. Really, there was no use in forming a proper comeback, because when Olivia was telling a story—

"What I was going to say," Olivia continued, unknowingly confirming Miranda's hypothesis, "is that really, most of them are dreadful bores."

Miranda could not resist giving her friend a little jab. "One would certainly never be able to tell that from watching you in action."

"Oh, I'm not saying I'm not enjoying myself." Olivia

gave her a vaguely sardonic look. "I mean, really, I'm not going to cut off my nose to spite my mother."

"To spite your mother," Miranda repeated, trying to recall the origin of the original proverb. "Somewhere someone is surely rolling in his grave."

Olivia cocked her head. "Shakespeare, do you think?"

"No." Blast, now she wasn't going to be able to stop thinking about it. "It wasn't Shakespeare."

"Machiavelli?"

Miranda mentally ran down her list of famous writers. "I don't think so."

"Turner?"

"Who?"

"My *brother*."

Miranda's head snapped up. "Turner?"

Olivia leaned a bit to the side, stretching her neck as she peered past Miranda. "He looks quite purposeful."

Miranda looked down at her dance card. "It must be time for our waltz."

Olivia tilted her head to the side in a ponderous sort of motion. "He looks handsome as well, doesn't he?"

Miranda blinked and tried not to sigh. Turner did look handsome. Almost unbearably so. And now that he was a widower, surely every unmarried lady—and all their mamas—would be after him like a shot.

"Do you think he'll marry again?" Olivia murmured.

"I—I don't know." Miranda swallowed. "I would think he'd have to, wouldn't you?"

"Well, there is always Winston to provide an heir. And if you—euf!"

Miranda's elbow. In her ribs.

Turner arrived at their sides and bowed smartly.

"Lovely to see you, brother," Olivia said with a wide smile. "I'd almost given up on your attendance."

"Nonsense. Mother would have had me filleted." His eyes narrowed (almost imperceptibly, but then again, Miranda tended to notice everything about him), and he asked, "Why'd Miranda jab you in the ribs?"

"I didn't!" Miranda protested. And then, when his stare turned quite dubious, she mumbled, "It was more of a tap."

"Jab, tap, it has all the hallmarks of a conversation that's a damned sight more entertaining than any of the rest in this ballroom."

"Turner!" Olivia protested.

Turner dismissed her with a flick of his head and turned to Miranda. "Do you think she objects to my language or my judgment of the attendees of your ball as idiots?"

"I think it was your language," Miranda said mildly. "She said most of them were idiots, too."

"That is not at all what I said," Olivia put in. "I said they were bores."

"Sheep," Miranda confirmed.

"Goats," Olivia added with a shrug.

Turner began to look alarmed. "Good God, do the two of you speak your own language?"

"No, we are being perfectly clear," Olivia said, "but tell me, do you know who first said, 'Do not cut off your nose to spite your face'?"

"I'm not certain I see the connection," Turner murmured.

"It's not Shakespeare," Miranda said.

Olivia shook her head. "Who else would it be?"

"Well," Miranda said, "any one of thousands of notable writers of the English language."

"Was this why you, er, tapped her in the ribs?" Turner inquired.

"Yes," Miranda replied, seizing the opportunity. Unfortunately, Olivia beat her by one half second with "No."

Turner looked from one to the other with an amused expression.

"It was about Winston," Olivia said impatiently.

"Ah, Winston." Turner looked about. "He's here, is he not?" Then he plucked Miranda's dance card from her fingers. "Why has he not claimed a dance or three? Aren't the two of you planning to make a match of it?"

Miranda gritted her teeth together and declined to answer. Which was a perfectly reasonable choice, as she knew that Olivia would not allow the opportunity to pass her by.

"Of course there is nothing official," she was saying, "but *everyone* agrees that it would be a splendid match."

"Everyone?" Turner asked softly, looking at Miranda.

"Who wouldn't?" Olivia replied with an impatient face.

The orchestra picked up their instruments, and the first strains of a waltz floated through the air.

"I believe this is my dance," Turner said, and Miranda realized that his eyes had not left hers.

She trembled.

"Shall we?" he murmured, and he held out his arm.

She nodded, needing a moment to regain her voice. He did things to her, she realized. Strange, shivery things that left her breathless. He need only to look at her—not in his usual, conversational way, but to really look at her, to let his eyes settle on hers, deeply blue and insightful, and she felt naked, her soul bared. And the worst of it all was—he had no idea. There she was, with her every emotion exposed, and Turner most probably saw nothing but the dull brown of her eyes.

She was his little sister's little friend, and in all likelihood, that was all she ever would be.

"You are leaving me here all alone, then?" Olivia said, not petulantly, but with a little sigh nonetheless.

"Have no fear," Miranda assured her, "you shan't be alone for long. I think I see your flock returning with lemonade."

Olivia made a face. "Have you ever noticed, Turner, that Miranda has quite the driest sense of humor?"

Miranda tilted her head to the side and suppressed a smile. "Why do I suspect that your tone was not precisely complimentary?"

Olivia gave her a dismissive little wave. "Off with you. Have a nice dance with Turner."

Turner took Miranda's elbow and led her out onto the dance floor. "You do have a rather odd sense of humor, you know," he murmured.

"Do I?"

"Yes, but it's what I like best about you, so please don't change."

She tried not to feel absurdly pleased. "I shall contrive not to, my lord."

He winced as he put his arms around her for the waltz.

"'My lord,' is it now? Since when have you grown so proper?"

"It's all this time in London. Your mother has been beating etiquette into me." She smiled sweetly. "Nigel."

He scowled. "I believe I prefer 'my lord.'"

"I prefer Turner."

His hand tightened at her waist. "Good. Keep it that way."

Miranda let out a little sigh as they lapsed into silence. As waltzes went, this one was fairly sedate. There were no breathless whirls, nothing that would leave her dizzy and spinning. And it gave her every opportunity to savor the moment, to relish the feel of her hand in his. She breathed in the scent of him, felt the heat from his body, and simply enjoyed.

It all felt so perfect . . . so perfectly right. It was almost impossible to imagine that he did not feel it, too.

But he didn't. She did not delude herself that she could wish his desire into being. When she looked up at him, he was glancing out at someone in the crowd, his gaze just a little bit clouded, as if he were working through a problem in his mind. It was not the look of a man in love. And neither was what followed, when he finally peered down at her and said, "You're not bad at the waltz, Miranda. In fact, you're really quite accomplished. I don't see why you were so nervous about it."

His expression was kind. Brotherly.

It was heartbreaking.

"I haven't had much practice recently," she improvised, since he seemed to be waiting for an answer.

"Even with Winston?"

"Winston?" she echoed.

His eyes grew amused. "My younger brother, if you re-call."

"Right," she said. "No. I mean, no, I haven't danced with Winston in years."

"Really?"

She looked up at him quickly. There was something odd in his voice, almost—but not quite—a faint note of pleasure. Not jealousy, unfortunately—she didn't think he would care one way or another if she danced with his brother. But she had the strangest sensation that he was congratulating himself, as if he had predicted her answer correctly and was pleased by his astuteness.

Good heavens, she was thinking far too much. She was *over*thinking—Olivia was forever accusing her of it, and for once, Miranda had to concede that she was right.

"I don't often see Winston," Miranda said, hoping that a conversation would stop her from obsessing about completely unanswerable questions—such as the true meaning of the word *really*.

"Oh?" Turner prompted, adding a touch of pressure to the small of her back as they turned to the right.

"He's usually at university. Even now he's not quite done with his term."

"I expect you shall see a great deal more of him over the summer."

"I expect so." She cleared her throat. "Er, how long do you plan to stay?"

"In London?"

She nodded.

He paused, and they did a lovely little whirl to the left before he finally said, "I'm not certain. Not long, I think."

"I see."

"I'm supposed to be in mourning, anyway. Mother was aghast that I left off the armband."

"I'm not," she declared.

He smiled down at her, and this time it wasn't brotherly. It wasn't full of passion and desire, but at least it was something new. It was sly and conspiring and it made her feel a part of a team. "Why, Miss Cheever," he murmured mischievously, "do I detect a hint of the rebel in you?"

Her chin rose a full inch. "I have never understood the necessity of donning black for someone with whom one is not acquainted, and I certainly don't see the logic in mourning a person one finds detestable."

For a moment his face remained blank, and then he grinned. "Who were you forced to mourn?"

Her lips slid into a smile. "A cousin."

He leaned in a hair closer. "Has anyone ever told you it's unseemly to smile when discussing the death of a relation?"

"I'd never even met the man."

"Still . . ."

Miranda let out a ladylike snort. She knew that he was goading her, but she was having far too much fun to stop. "He lived his entire life in the Caribbean," she added. It wasn't strictly true, but it was mostly true.

"Bloodthirsty little wench, you are," he murmured.

She shrugged. Coming from Turner, it seemed a compliment.

"I do believe you shall be a welcome member of the family," he said. "Provided you can tolerate my younger brother for lengthy periods of time."

Miranda tried for a sincere smile. Marrying Winston was not her preferred method of becoming a member of the Bevelstoke family. And despite Olivia's urgings and machinations, Miranda did not think a match was forthcoming.

There were many excellent reasons to consider marrying Winston, but there was one compelling reason not to, and he was standing right in front of her.

If Miranda was going to marry someone she did not love, it was *not* going to be the brother of the man she did.

Or thought she did. She kept trying to convince herself that she didn't, that it had all been a schoolgirl crush, and that she would outgrow it—that she already *had* outgrown it, and just didn't realize it yet.

She was in the *habit* of thinking herself in love with him. That's all it was.

But then he would do something utterly loathsome, like smile, and all her hard work flew out the window, and she had to start anew.

One day it would stick. One day she would wake up and realize it had been two days of sensible Turnerless thought, and then it would be magically three and then four and—

"Miranda?"

She looked up. He was watching her with an expression of amusement, and it would have been patronizing except his eyes were crinkling at the corners . . . and for a moment he looked unburdened, and young, and maybe even content.

And she was still in love with him. At least for the rest of the evening, there would be no convincing herself otherwise. Come morning, she'd start again, but for tonight, she wasn't going to bother to try.

The music ended, and Turner let go of her hand, stepping back to execute an elegant bow. Miranda curtsied in turn, and then took his arm as he led her to the perimeter of the room.

"Where do you suppose we might find Olivia?" he murmured, craning his neck. "I suppose I'll have to boot one of the gentlemen off her card and dance with her."

"Goodness, don't make it sound such a chore," Miranda returned. "We're not so very dreadful."

He turned and looked at her with a touch of surprise. "I didn't say anything about *you*. Don't mind dancing with you in the least."

As compliments went, it was lukewarm at best, but Miranda still found a way to hold it next to her heart.

And *that*, she thought miserably, had to be proof that she'd sunk quite as low as she could go. Unrequited love, she was discovering, was much worse when one actually *saw* the object of one's desire. She'd spent nearly ten years daydreaming about Turner, waiting patiently for whatever news the Bevelstokes happened to drop at afternoon tea, and then trying to hide her bliss and joy (not to mention her terror at being found out) when he happened to visit once or twice per year.

She'd thought that nothing could be more pathetic, but as it happened, she was wrong. This was definitely worse. Before, she'd been a nonentity. Now she was a comfortable old shoe.

Gad.

She stole a glance at him. He wasn't looking at her. He wasn't *not* looking at her, and he certainly wasn't avoiding looking at her. He simply wasn't looking at her.

She perturbed him not at all.

"There's Olivia," she said, sighing. Her friend was surrounded, as usual, by a ridiculously large assortment of gentlemen.

Turner regarded his sister with narrowed eyes. "It doesn't look as if any of them are misbehaving, does it? It's been a long day, and I'd rather not have to play the ferocious older brother tonight."

Miranda rose onto her toes for a closer look. "I think you're safe."

"Good." And then he realized that his head was tilted to the side, and he was watching his sister with a strangely detached eye. "Hmmm."

"Hmmm?"

He turned back to Miranda, who was still at his side, watching him with those ever curious brown eyes.

"Turner?" he heard her say, and he replied with another "Hmmm?"

"You look a bit queer."

No *Are you quite all right?* or *Are you unwell?* Just *You look a bit queer.*

It made him smile. It made him think how much he actually liked this girl, and how much he'd wronged her the day of Leticia's funeral. And it made him want to do something nice for her. He looked at his sister one last time, and then said, as he slowly turned back around, "If I were a young buck, which mind you I'm not . . ."

"Turner, you're not even thirty."

Her expression turned impatient—in a somewhat governessy way that he found oddly entertaining, and he gave her a lazy, one-shouldered shrug as he answered, "Yes, well, I feel older. Ancient these days, to tell the truth." Then he realized that she was staring at him expectantly, so he cleared his throat and said, "I was merely trying to say that if *I* were nosing around the crop of new debutantes, I don't believe Olivia would catch my eye."

Miranda's brows rose. "Well, she *is* your sister. Aside from the illegalities—"

Oh, for the love of— "I was *attempting* to compliment you," he interrupted.

"Oh." She cleared her throat. Blushed a little, although it was difficult to be sure in the dim light. "Well, in that case, please do go right ahead."

"Olivia is quite beautiful," he continued. "Even I, her older brother, can see that. But there is something lacking behind her eyes."

Which elicited an immediate gasp. "Turner, that is a terrible thing to say. You know as well as I do that Olivia is very intelligent. Far more so than most of the men who are swarming around her."

He watched her indulgently. She was such a loyal little thing. He had no doubt she'd take a bullet for Olivia if the need ever arose. It was a good thing she was here. Aside

from whatever calming tendencies she had on his sister—
and he rather suspected the entire Bevelstoke family owed
her an enormous debt of gratitude for that—Miranda was,
he was fairly certain, the only thing that was going to make
his time in London bearable. God knew he hadn't wanted
to come. The last thing he needed just then were women
angling for position, attempting to fill Leticia's miserable
little shoes. But with Miranda about, at least he was assured of some decent conversation.

"Of course Olivia is intelligent," he said in a placating
voice. "Allow me to restate myself. I personally would not
find her intriguing."

She pursed her lips, and the governess was back. "Well,
that's your prerogative, I suppose."

He smiled and leaned in, just a hint. "I think I'd be far
more likely to make my way to *your* side."

"Don't be silly," she mumbled.

"I'm not," he assured her. "But then again, I am older
than most of those fools with my sister. Perhaps my tastes
have mellowed. But the point is moot, I suppose, because
I'm not a young buck, and I'm not nosing around this
year's crop of debutantes."

"And you're not looking for a wife." It was a statement,
not a question.

"*God*, no," he blurted out. "What on earth would I do
with a wife?"

2 JUNE 1819

> *Lady Rudland announced at breakfast that
> last night's ball was a smashing success. I could*

not help but smile over her choice of words—I do not think anyone refused her invitation, and I vow the room was as crowded as any I have ever experienced. I certainly felt smashed up against all sorts of perfect strangers. I do believe I must be a country girl at heart because I am not so certain that I wish to ever again be quite so intimate with my fellow man.

I said so at breakfast, and Turner spit his coffee. Lady Rudland sent him a murderous glare, but I cannot imagine she is that enamored of her table linens.

Turner intends to remain in town for only a week or two, he is staying with us at Rudland House, which is lovely and terrible, all at once.

Lady Rudland reported that some crotchety old dowager (her words, not mine, and she would not reveal her identity in any case) said that I was acting Too Familiar with Turner and that people might get the Wrong Idea.

She said that she told the c.o.d. (cod! how apt!) that Turner and I are practically brother and sister, and that it is only natural that I would rely upon him at my debut ball, and that there are no Wrong Ideas to be had.

I am wondering if there is ever a Right Idea in London.

Chapter 5

A week or so later, the sun was shining so brightly that Miranda and Olivia, missing their frequent sojourns in the country, decided to spend the morning exploring London. At Olivia's insistence, they began in the shopping district.

"I certainly don't need another dress," Miranda said as they strolled down the street, their maids a respectful distance behind them.

"Neither do I, but it's always great fun to look, and besides, we might find a trinket or such to buy with our pin money. Your birthday will be here before we know it. You should purchase yourself a treat."

"Perhaps."

They wandered through dress shops, milliners, jewelers, and sweet shops before Miranda found what she hadn't even known she'd been looking for.

"Look at that, Olivia," she breathed. "Isn't it magnificent?"

"Isn't what magnificent?" Olivia replied, peering into the elegantly dressed window of the bookshop.

"That." Miranda pointed her finger toward an exquisitely bound copy of *Le Morte d'Arthur* by Sir Thomas Malory. It looked rich and lovely, and Miranda wanted nothing more than to lean right through the window and inhale the air that wafted around it.

For the first time in her life, she saw something that she simply had to have. Forget economy. Forget practicality. She sighed—a deep, soulful, needy breath, and said, "I think I finally understand what you mean about shoes."

"Shoes?" Olivia echoed, looking down at her feet. "Shoes?"

Miranda didn't bother to explain further. She was too busy tilting her head so that she could peer at the gold leaf that edged the pages.

"And we've read that already," Olivia continued. "I believe it was two years ago—when Miss Lacey was hired on as our governess. Don't you recall? She was all aghast that we hadn't got to it yet."

"It's not about reading it," Miranda said, pressing even closer to the glass. "Is it not the most beautiful thing you've ever seen?"

Olivia regarded her friend with a doubtful expression. "Er . . . no."

Miranda shook her head slightly and looked up at Olivia. "I suppose that's what makes something art. What can send one person into raptures may fail to move another even the tiniest bit."

"Miranda, that's a *book*."

"That book," Miranda decided firmly, "is a piece of art."

"It looks rather old."

"I know." Miranda sighed happily.

"Are you going to buy it?"

"If I have enough money."

"I would think you must. You haven't spent your pin money in years. You always put it in that porcelain vase Turner sent you for your birthday five years ago."

"Six."

Olivia blinked. "Six what?"

"It was six years ago."

"Five years ago, six years ago—what is the difference?" Olivia burst out, looking rather exasperated by Miranda's exactitude. "The point is, you have quite a bit of money tucked away, and if you truly want that book, you should buy it to celebrate your twentieth birthday. You never buy anything for yourself."

Miranda turned back to the temptation in the window. The book had been set on a pedestal and opened to a page in the middle. A brightly colored illustration depicted Arthur and Guinevere. "It's going to be expensive," she said ruefully.

Olivia gave her a little shove and said, "You'll never know if you don't go in and ask."

"You're right. I'll do it!" Miranda flashed her a smile that hovered somewhere between excitement and nervousness and headed into the store. The cozy bookshop was decorated in rich, masculine tones, with overstuffed leather chairs strategically placed for those who might want to sit and leaf through a volume.

"I don't see the proprietor," Olivia whispered in Miranda's ear.

"Right there." Miranda gestured with her head toward a thin, balding man about the age of their parents. "See, he's helping that man find a book. I'll just wait until he is available. I don't wish to be a bother."

The two ladies waited patiently for a few minutes while the bookseller was busy. Every so often, he shot them a scowling glance, which quite perplexed Miranda, as both she and Olivia were finely dressed and obviously able to afford most of his merchandise. Finally, he finished up his task and bustled toward them.

"I was wondering, sir—" Miranda began.

"This is a *gentlemen's* bookshop," he said in a hostile voice.

"Oh." Miranda drew back, rather put off by his attitude. But she desperately wanted the Malory book, so she swallowed her pride, smiled sweetly, and continued. "I apologize. I did not realize. But I was hoping I—"

"I said this is a gentlemen's shop." His beady little eyes narrowed. "Kindly depart."

Kindly? She stared at him, her lips parting with astonishment. *Kindly?* With *that* sort of tone?

"Let's go, Miranda," Olivia said, taking hold of her sleeve. "We should go."

Miranda clenched her teeth and did not budge. "I would like to purchase a book."

"I'm sure you would," the bookseller said snidely. "And the ladies' bookshop is only a quarter of a mile away."

"The ladies' bookshop doesn't have what I want."

He smirked. "Then I'm sure you shouldn't be reading it."

"I don't believe it is your place to make that judgment, sir," Miranda said coldly.

"Miranda," Olivia whispered, wide-eyed.

"Just one moment," she replied, never taking her eyes off the repulsive little man. "Sir, I can assure you that I possess ample funds. And if you would only allow me to inspect *Le-Morte d'Arthur*, I might be persuaded to part with them."

He crossed his arms. "I don't sell books to women."

And really, that was too much. "I *beg* your pardon."

"Leave," he spat, "or I will have you forcibly removed."

"That would be a mistake, sir," Miranda countered sharply. "Do you know who we are?" It was not her habit to pull rank, but she was not averse to doing so if the occasion warranted.

The bookseller was unimpressed. "I am certain I do not care."

"Miranda," Olivia pleaded, looking acutely uncomfortable.

"I am Miss Miranda Cheever, daughter of Sir Rupert Cheever, and this," Miranda said with a flourish, "is Lady Olivia Bevelstoke, daughter of the Earl of Rudland. I suggest you reconsider your policy."

He met her haughty glare with one of his own. "I don't care if you're bloody Princess Charlotte. Get out of my shop."

Miranda narrowed her eyes before she moved to leave.

It was bad enough that he'd insulted her. But to impugn the memory of the princess—it was beyond the pale. "You have not heard the end of this, sir."

"Out!"

She took Olivia's arm and left the premises in a huff, giving the door a good slam just to be contrary. "Can you believe him?" she said once they were safely outside. "That was appalling. It was criminal. It was—"

"A *gentlemen's* bookshop," Olivia cut in, looking at her as if she'd suddenly sprouted a spare head.

"And?"

Olivia stiffened at her nearly belligerent tone. "There are gentlemen's bookshops, and there are ladies' bookshops. It's the way of things."

Miranda's fists curled into tight little balls. "It's a bloody stupid way, if you ask me."

"Miranda!" Olivia audibly gasped. "What did you just say?"

Miranda had the grace to blush at her foul language. "Do you see how upset he made me? Have you ever known me to curse aloud before?"

"No, and I'm not sure I want to know how much cursing you're doing in your mind."

"It's asinine," Miranda fumed. "Absolutely asinine. *He* had something I wanted to buy, and *I* had the money to pay for it. It should have been a simple matter."

Olivia glanced down the road. "Why don't we just go to the ladies' bookshop?"

"There is nothing I would rather do under normal circumstances. I certainly would prefer not to patronize that dreadful man's store. But I doubt they will have the same copy of *Le Morte d'Arthur*, Livvy. I'm certain it's a singular item. And *worse*—" Miranda's voice rose as the injustice of it all sank in more firmly. "And worse—"

"It gets worse?"

Miranda shot her an irritated look but nonetheless replied, "Yes. It does. The worst of it is, even if there were two copies, which I'm quite certain there are not, the ladies' bookshop probably would not carry one, anyway, because no one would think that a lady would wish for such a book!"

"They wouldn't?"

"No. It's probably full of Byron and Mrs. Radcliffe novels."

"I like Byron and Mrs. Radcliffe novels," Olivia said, sounding vaguely affronted.

"So do I," Miranda assured her, "but I enjoy other literature as well. And I *certainly* do not think it is the place of that man"—she jabbed an angry finger toward the bookshop window—"to decide what I may or may not read."

Olivia stared at her for a moment, then politely asked, "Are you quite done?"

Miranda smoothed her skirts and sniffed. "Quite."

Olivia's back was to the bookshop, and she sent a rueful glance over her shoulder before placing a comforting hand on Miranda's arm. "We'll get Father to buy it for you. Or Turner."

"That's not the point. I cannot believe you're not as upset about this as I am."

Olivia sighed. "When did you become such a crusader, Miranda? I thought I was meant to be the unrestrained one of the duo."

Miranda's jaw began to ache from clenching. "I suppose," she nearly growled, "that I have never had anything to get this upset about before."

Olivia's head drew back, just a touch. "Remind me to take pains not to upset you in the future."

"I'm going to get that book."

"Fine, we'll just—"

"And *he* is going to know that I've got it." Miranda gave the bookshop one last belligerent stare and then strode off in the direction of home.

"Of course I'll buy the book for you, Miranda," Turner said congenially. He'd been enjoying a rather leisurely afternoon, reading the newspaper and pondering life as an unattached gentleman, when his sister had burst into the room, announcing that Miranda desperately needed a favor.

It all been rather entertaining, actually, especially the death stare Miranda had bestowed upon Olivia at her use of the word *desperate*.

"I don't want you to buy it *for* me," Miranda ground out. "I want you to buy it *with* me."

Turner sat back in his comfortable chair. "Is there a difference?"

"A *world* of difference."

"A world," Olivia confirmed, but she was grinning, and he rather suspected she didn't see the distinction, either.

Miranda threw her another glare, and Olivia actually backed up and exclaimed. "What? I'm supporting you!"

"Don't you think it's *wrong*," Miranda continued ferociously, returning to both her diatribe and his face, "that I cannot shop in a certain store simply because I am a woman?"

He smiled lazily at her. "Miranda, there are certain places where women cannot go."

"I am not asking to enter one of your precious clubs. I merely wish to purchase a book. There isn't anything remotely unsuitable about it. It is an antique, for heaven's sake."

"Miranda, if that gentleman owns that shop, he can decide who he does and doesn't want sell to."

She crossed her arms. "Well, perhaps he shouldn't be allowed to. Perhaps there ought to be a law that says that booksellers cannot bar women from their stores."

He raised an ironic brow at her. "You haven't been reading that tract by Mary Wollstonecraft, have you?"

"Mary who?" Miranda asked in a distracted voice.

"Good."

"Don't change the subject, please, Turner. Do you or do you not agree that I should be allowed to buy that book?"

He sighed, quite exhausted by her unexpected stubbornness. And over a *book*. "Miranda, why should you be allowed in a gentlemen's bookshop? You can't even vote."

Her sputter of outrage was colossal. "And that's another thing—"

Turner quickly realized that he had made a tactical error. "Forget I mentioned suffrage. Please. I'll go with you to buy the book."

"You will?" Her eyes lit up and glowed soft and brown. "Thank you."

"Shall we go on Friday? I don't believe I'm engaged for the afternoon."

"Oh, I want to go, too," Olivia piped in.

"Absolutely not," Turner said firmly. "One of you is all I can manage. My nerves, you know."

"Your nerves?"

He gave her A Look. "You try them."

"Turner!" Olivia exclaimed. She turned to Miranda. "Miranda!"

But Miranda was still focused on Turner. "Could we go now?" she asked him, giving every impression of not having heard a word of their squabble. "I don't want that bookseller to forget about me."

"Judging from Olivia's rendition of your adventure," Turner said wryly, "I doubt that is likely to happen."

"But could we please go today? Please. *Please*."

"You do realize you're begging."

"I don't care," she said promptly.

He pondered this. "It occurs to me that I could use this situation to my advantage."

Miranda gave him a blank look. "What would be the point of that?"

"Oh, I don't know. One never knows when one might want to call in a favor."

"Since I have nothing you could possibly want, I advise

you to forget your nefarious plans and simply take me to
the bookshop."

"Very well. Let's be off."

He thought she might jump with glee. Good Lord.

"It's not far," she was saying. "We can walk there."

"Are you certain I cannot come with you?" Olivia asked,
following them into the hall.

"Stay," Turner ordered benignly as he watched Miranda charge the door. "Someone will need to call the watch
when we don't return in one piece."

Ten minutes later, Miranda was standing in front of the
bookshop from which she'd been ejected earlier that day.

"Gad, Miranda," she heard Turner murmur beside her.
"You look a bit a frightening."

"Good," she replied succinctly, and she stepped forward.

Turner placed a restraining hand on her arm. "Allow me
to enter before you," he suggested, an amused glint in his
eye. "The mere sight of you may send the poor man into
an apoplectic fit."

Miranda scowled at him but let him pass. There was no
way the bookseller would best her this time. She'd come
armed with a titled gentleman and a healthy dose of rage.
The book was all but hers.

A bell jingled as Turner entered the shop. Miranda followed right behind him, practically stepping on his heels.

"May I assist you, sir?" the bookseller asked, all fawn-
ing politeness.

"Yes, I'm interested in . . ." His words trailed off as he
looked around the store.

"That book," Miranda said firmly, pointing toward the display in the window.

"Yes, that's the one." Turner offered the bookseller a bland smile.

"You!" the bookseller spluttered, his face turning pink with ire. "Out! Get out of my shop!" He grabbed Miranda's arm and tried to drag her to the door.

"Stop! Stop, I say!" Miranda, not one to let herself be abused by a man she considered to be an idiot, grabbed her reticule and thwacked him on the head.

Turner groaned.

"Simmons!" the bookseller yelled out, summoning his assistant. "Fetch a constable. This young lady is deranged."

"I'm not deranged, you overgrown goat!"

Turner pondered his options. Really, there could be no good outcome.

"I'm a paying customer," Miranda continued hotly. "And I want to buy *Le Morte d'Arthur*!"

"I'll die before it reaches your hands, you ill-mannered trollop!"

Trollop? That was really too much for Miranda, a young lady whose sensibilities were usually more modest than one might have guessed from her current behavior. "You vile, vile man," she hissed. She raised her reticule again.

Trollop? Turner sighed. It was an insult he really couldn't overlook. Still, he couldn't let Miranda attack the poor man. He grabbed the reticule from her hand. She glared daggers at him for his interference. He narrowed his eyes and gave her a warning look.

He cleared his throat and turned to the bookseller. "Sir, I must insist that you apologize to the lady."

The bookseller crossed his arms defiantly.

Turner glanced at Miranda. Her arms were crossed in much the same manner. He looked back at the older man and said, a little more forcefully, "You will apologize to the lady."

"She is a menace," the bookseller said viciously.

"Why, you—" Miranda would have launched herself at him if Turner had not pulled her back with a quick grab to the back of her dress. The older man balled his fist and assumed a predatory stance that was quite at odds with his bookish appearance.

"You be quiet," Turner hissed at her, feeling the beginnings of fury uncurl in his chest.

The bookseller shot her a triumphant look.

"Oh, that was a mistake," Turner said. Good God, did the man have no common sense? Miranda jolted forward, which meant that Turner had to hold on to her dress even more firmly, which meant that the bookseller assumed even more of a smirk, which meant that the whole bloody farce was going to spiral into a full-blown hurricane if Turner did not settle the matter then and there.

He gave the bookseller his iciest, most aristocratic stare. "Apologize to the lady, or I will make you very sorry, indeed."

But the bookseller was clearly a raving idiot, because he did not accept the offer Turner had, in his estimation, so generously offered. Instead, he jutted his jaw belligerently and announced, "I have nothing for which to apologize. That woman came into my store . . ."

"Ah, hell," Turner muttered. There was no avoiding it now.

" . . . disturbed my customers, insulted me . . ."

Turner balled his hand into a fist and swung, clipping the bookseller neatly next to his nose.

"Oh my good Lord," Miranda breathed. "I think you broke his nose."

Turner shot her a scathing glance before looking down at the bookseller on the floor. "I don't think so. He isn't bleeding enough."

"Pity," Miranda muttered.

Turner grabbed her arm and hauled her up close to him. The bloodthirsty little wench was going to get herself killed. "Not another word until we get out of here."

Miranda's eyes widened, but she wisely shut her mouth and allowed him to pull her out of the store. As they passed by the window, however, she caught sight of *Le Morte d'Arthur* and burst out, "My book!"

That was *it*. Turner slammed to a halt. "I don't want to hear another word about your damned book, do you hear me?"

Her mouth fell open.

"Do you understand what just happened? I struck a man."

"But wouldn't you agree he needed striking?"

"Not half as much as you need throttling!"

She drew back, clearly affronted.

"Contrary to whatever it is that you think of me," he bit off, "I don't go about my days pondering when and where I might next be reduced to violence."

"But—"

"But *nothing*, Miranda. You insulted the man—"

"He insulted me!"

"I was handling the matter," he said between clenched teeth. "That's why you brought me here, to handle everything. Isn't that so?"

Miranda scowled and moved her chin in a sharp, reluctant nod.

"What the devil was the matter with you? What if that man had had less restraint? What if—"

"You thought he showed restraint?" she asked, dumbfounded.

"At least as much as you did!" He grabbed her shoulders and almost began to shake. "Good God, Miranda, you do realize that there are many men who would not blink an eye before striking a woman? Or worse," he added meaningfully.

He waited for her answer, but she was just staring at him, her eyes huge and unblinking. And he had the most unsettling feeling that she saw something that he did not.

Something in *him*.

And then she said, "I'm sorry, Turner."

"For what?" he asked less than graciously. "For making a scene in the middle of a quiet bookstore? For not keeping your mouth shut when you should have? For—"

"For upsetting you," she said quietly. "I'm sorry. It was not well done of me."

Her soft words cut cleanly through his anger, and he sighed. "Just don't do anything like that again, will you?"

"I promise."

"Good." He realized that he was still clutching her shoulders and loosened his grip. Then he realized that her shoulders felt quite nice. Surprised, he let go altogether.

She tilted her head to the side as a worried expression crossed her face. "At least I think I promise. I shall certainly *try* not to do anything to upset you like that."

Turner had a sudden vision of Miranda trying not to upset him. The vision upset him. "What has happened to you? We depend upon you to be levelheaded. Lord knows you've steered Olivia out of trouble more than once."

Her lips pressed together, and then she said, "Don't confuse levelheaded with meek, Turner. They're not the same thing at all. And I am certainly not meek."

She wasn't being defiant, he realized. She was simply stating fact—one that he suspected his family had overlooked for years. "Have no fear," he said wearily, "if ever I entertained the notion that you were meek, you have certainly disabused me of it this afternoon."

But God help him, she wasn't done. "If I see something that is so obviously *wrong*," she said earnestly, "I can hardly sit by and do nothing."

She was going to kill him. He was sure of it. "Just try to stay away from obvious mischief. Could you do that for me?"

"But I didn't think this was particularly mischievous. And I did—"

He held up his hand. "No more. Not another word on

the topic. It'll take ten years off my life just talking about it." He took her arm and steered her toward home.

Dear God, what was wrong with him? His pulse was still racing, and she hadn't even been in any danger. Not really. He doubted the bookseller could have got a good punch in. And furthermore, why the devil was he so worried about Miranda? Of course he cared about her. She was like a little sister to him. But then he tried to imagine Olivia in her place. All he could feel was mild amusement.

Something was very wrong if Miranda could make him this furious.

Chapter 6

"Winston will be here soon." Olivia sailed into the rose salon on that statement, bestowing upon Miranda her sunniest of smiles.

Miranda looked up from her book—a dog-eared and decidedly unglamorous copy of *Le Morte d'Arthur* she'd borrowed from Lord Rudland's library. "Really?" she murmured, even though she knew very well that Winston was expected that afternoon.

"Really?" Olivia mimicked. "Is that all you can say? Pardon, but I was under the impression you were in love with the boy, oh, excuse me—he's a man now, isn't he?"

Miranda returned to her reading. "I told you I'm not in love with him."

"Well, you should be," Olivia retorted. "And you would be, if you would deign to spend some time with him."

Miranda's eyes, which had been resolutely moving over the words on the page, slammed to a halt. She looked up. "I beg your pardon. Isn't he in Oxford?"

"Well, yes," Olivia said, waving off the comment as if the sixty miles' distance was of no consequence, "but he was here last week, and you barely spent any time with him."

"That's not true," Miranda replied. "We rode in Hyde Park, went to Gunter's for ices, and even took a boat out into the Serpentine that one day it was actually warm."

Olivia plopped down in a nearby chair, crossing her arms. "It's not enough."

"You've gone mad," Miranda said. She gave her head a little shake and turned back to her book.

"I *know* that you will love him. You need only to spend enough time in his company."

Miranda pressed her lips together and kept her eyes firmly on her book. This was not a conversation that could go anywhere sensible.

"He will be here for only two days," Olivia mused. "We're going to need to work quickly."

Miranda flipped a page and said, "You do what you wish, Olivia, but I will not be party to your schemes." Then she looked up in alarm. "No, I've changed my mind. Don't do what you wish. If I leave matters up to you, I'll find myself drugged and on my way to Gretna Green before I know it."

"An intriguing thought."

"Livvy, no matchmaking. I want you to promise me."

Olivia's expression turned arch. "I won't make a promise I might not keep."

"*Olivia.*"

"Oh, very well. But you cannot stop Winston if *he* has

matchmaking in mind. And judging from his recent behavior, he very well might."

"Just so long as *you* don't interfere."

Olivia sniffed and tried to look affronted. "I am hurt that you would even think I would do such a thing."

"Oh, *please*." Miranda turned back to her book, but it was nearly impossible to focus on the plot when in her mind she was counting down . . . *twenty, nineteen, eighteen. . .*

Surely Olivia would not be able to remain silent for more than twenty seconds.

Seventeen . . . sixteen. . .

"Winston will make a lovely husband, don't you think?"

Four seconds. That was remarkable, even for Olivia.

"He's young, of course, but so are we."

Miranda studiously ignored her.

"Turner probably would have made a fine husband, as well, if Leticia hadn't gone and ruined him."

Miranda's head snapped up. "Don't you think that's an unkind remark?"

Olivia gave a little smile. "I knew you were listening to me."

"It's nearly impossible not to," Miranda muttered.

"I was merely saying that—" Olivia's chin rose, and her gaze moved to the doorway behind Miranda. "And here he is now. What a coincidence."

"Winston," Miranda said cheerfully, twisting in her seat so that she could peer over the edge of the sofa. Except it wasn't Winston.

"Sorry to disappoint," Turner said, one corner of his mouth twisting into a lazy and extremely slight smile.

"Sorry," Miranda mumbled, feeling rather unexpectedly foolish. "We were speaking of him."

"We were speaking of you, too," Olivia said. "More recently, in fact, which is why I remarked upon your entrance."

"Diabolical things, I hope."

"Oh, indeed," Olivia said.

Miranda managed a close-lipped smile as he took a seat across from her.

Olivia leaned forward and rested her chin coquettishly in her hand. "I was just telling Miranda that I thought you would make someone a terrible husband."

He looked amused as he sat back. "True enough."

"But I was *about* to say that with the proper training," Olivia continued, "you could be rehabilitated."

Turner stood. "I'm leaving."

"No, don't go!" Olivia called out with a laugh. "I am teasing, of course. You're quite beyond redemption. But Winston . . . Now, Winston is like a lump of clay."

"I shan't tell him you said that," Miranda murmured.

"Don't say you don't agree," Olivia said provocatively. "He hasn't had time to turn dreadful, the way most men do."

Turner watched his sister with undisguised amazement. "How is it possible that I am sitting here listening to you lecture on the management of men?"

Olivia opened her mouth to reply—something clever and cunning, to be sure—but just then the butler appeared in the doorway and saved them all. "Your mother requires your company, Lady Olivia."

"I shall be back," Olivia warned as she exited the room. "I am most eager to complete this conversation." And then, with a devilish smile and a wag of her fingers, she departed.

Turner stifled a groan—his sister was going to be the death of someone, just hopefully not him—and looked to Miranda. She was curled up on the sofa, her feet tucked under her, a large, dusty tome in her lap.

"Heavy reading?" he murmured.

She held up the book.

"Oh," he said, his lips twitching.

"Don't laugh," she warned.

"I wouldn't dream of it."

"Don't lie, either," she said, her mouth assuming that governess expression she seemed to do so well.

He leaned back with a chuckle. "Now *that* I cannot promise."

For a moment she just sat there, looking equal parts stern and serious, and then her face changed. Nothing dramatic, nothing to raise alarm, but enough so that it was clear that she'd been debating something in her mind. And that she'd reached a decision.

"What *do* you think of Winston?" she asked.

"My brother," he stated.

She held out her hand and flicked her wrist, as if to say— *Who else?*

"Well," he said, stalling because, really, what did she expect him to say? "He's my brother."

Her eyes glanced upward sarcastically. "Positively re-
velatory of you."

"What exactly is it you are asking me?"

"I want to know what you think of him," she insisted.

His heart slammed in his chest for no reason he could
identify. "Are you asking me," he inquired carefully, "if I
believe that Winston would make a good husband?"

She gave him that owlish stare of hers, and then she
blinked, and—it was the strangest thing—it was almost as
if she were clearing her head before she said, in quite the
most conversational tone, "It does seem that everyone is
trying to make a match of us."

"Everyone?"

"Well, Olivia."

"Hardly the person I'd turn to for romantic advice."

"So you don't think I should set my cap for Winston,"
she said, leaning forward.

Turner blinked. He knew Miranda, and he'd known her
for years, which was why he was quite certain that she had
not adjusted her position with the intention of showcas-
ing her surprisingly lovely bosom. But rather distractingly,
that had been the end result.

"Turner?" she murmured.

"He's too young," he blurted out.

"For me?"

"For anyone. Good God, he's barely twenty-one."

"Actually, he's still twenty."

"Exactly," he said uncomfortably, wishing very much
there was some way to adjust his cravat without looking
like a fool. It was starting to feel rather warm, and it was

getting difficult to keep his attention focused on something other than Miranda without being obvious about it.

She sat back. Thank God.

And she said nothing.

Until finally he could not help himself. "Do you intend to pursue him, then?"

"Winston?" She appeared to be pondering it. "I don't know."

He snorted. "If you don't know, then clearly you should not."

She turned and looked him directly in the eye. "Is that what you think? That love should be obvious and clear?"

"Who said anything about love?" His voice was slightly unkind, which he regretted, but surely she understood that this was an untenable conversation.

"Hmmm."

He had the unpleasant sensation that she'd judged him, and he'd come up lacking. A conclusion that was reinforced when she returned her attention to the book in her lap.

And he sat there, like an idiot, really, just watching her read her book, trying to devise some sort of cunning remark.

She looked up, her face irritatingly placid. "Do you have plans for the afternoon?"

"None," he bit off, even though he had had every intention of taking his gelding out for a trot.

"Oh. Winston is expected soon."

"I'm aware."

"It's why we were talking about him," she explained, as if that mattered. "He is coming for my birthday."

"Yes, of course."

She leaned forward again, God help him. "You did remember?" she asked. "We are to have a family supper tomorrow evening."

"Of course I remembered," he muttered, even though he had not.

"Hmmm," she murmured, "thank you for your thoughts, anyway."

"My thoughts," he echoed. What the devil was she talking about now?

"About Winston. There is much to consider, and I did wish for your opinion."

"Well. Now you have it."

"Yes." She smiled. "I'm glad. It is because I have such great respect for you."

Somehow she was managing to make him feel like he was some kind of ancient relic. "You have great respect for me?" The words slipped distastefully off his tongue.

"Well, yes. Did you think I wouldn't?"

"Frankly, Miranda, most of the time I have no idea what you think," he snapped.

"I think about *you*."

His eyes flew to hers.

"And Winston, of course. And Olivia. As if one could live in the same house with her and not think about her." She snapped her book shut and stood. "I imagine I should go seek her out. She and your mother are at odds over some frocks Olivia wishes to order, and I promised to aid the cause."

He stood and escorted her to the door. "Olivia's or my mother's?"

"Why, your mother's, of course," Miranda said with a laugh. "I'm young, but I'm no fool."

And with that, she departed.

10 JUNE 1819

> *Odd conversation with Turner this after-noon. It was not my intention to try to make him jealous, although I suppose it could have been interpreted that way, if anyone knew of my feelings for him, which of course they do not.*
>
> *It was my intention, however, to inspire cer-tain notions of guilt as pertains to* Le Morte d'Arthur. *In this, I do not believe I succeeded.*

Later that afternoon, Turner returned from a ride in Hyde Park with his friend Lord Westholme, only to find Olivia loitering in the main hall.

"Shush," she said.

It was enough to pique anyone's interest, and so Turner immediately went to her side. "Why are we being quiet?" he asked, refusing to whisper.

She shot him an angry glare. "I'm eavesdropping."

Turner could not imagine upon whom, as she was edged up against the stairwell that led down to the kitchens. But then he heard it—a lilt of laughter.

"Is that Miranda?" he asked.

Olivia nodded. "Winston just arrived, and they have gone downstairs."

"Why?"

Olivia peered around the corner, then snapped back to face Turner. "Winston was hungry."

Turner yanked off his gloves. "And he needs Miranda to feed him?"

"No, he's gone down for some of Mrs. Cook's butter biscuits. I was going to join them, as I hate being left alone, but now that you're here, I believe I'll let you keep me company instead."

Turner glanced past her down the hall, even though he couldn't possibly see his brother and Miranda. "I'm rather hungry myself," he murmured thoughtfully.

"Abstain," Olivia ordered. "They need time."

"To eat?"

Her eyes actually rolled up. "To fall in love."

There was something rather galling about receiving such a disdainful look from one's younger sister, but Turner decided that he would take, if not the high road, then at least something middle-ish, and so he gave her a somewhat arch look and returned with a pithy "And they intend to do this over biscuits and tea in a single afternoon?"

"It's a start," Olivia retorted. "I don't see you doing anything to further the match."

That, Turner thought with unexpected forcefulness, was because any fool could see that it would be a dreadful misalliance. He loved Winston dearly, and held him in as high an esteem as anyone could hold a twenty-year-old boy, but he was *clearly* the wrong man for Miranda. It was true that he had only come to know her well these past few weeks, but even he could see that she was wise beyond her years. She needed someone who was more mature, older, better able to appreciate her finer points. Someone who could keep a firm hand on her when her temper made one of its rare appearances.

Winston, he supposed, could be that man . . . in ten years.

Turner looked to his sister and said, rather firmly, "I need food."

"Turner, don't!" But Olivia couldn't stop him. By the time she even tried he was halfway down the hall.

The Bevelstokes had always run a relatively informal house, at least when they were not entertaining guests, and so none of the servants had been particularly surprised when Winston had poked his head into the kitchen, melted Mrs. Cook with his sweetest, most puppy-dog expression, and then plopped down at a table with Miranda to wait while she whipped up some of her famous butter biscuits. They had just been laid on the table, still steaming and smelling like heaven, when Miranda heard a loud thump behind her.

She turned, blinking, to see Turner standing at the base of the stairs, looking rakish, sheepish, and utterly adorable, all at once. She sighed. She couldn't help it.

"Took the stairs two at a time," he explained, although she wasn't quite certain of the significance of it.

"Turner," Winston grunted, too busy eating his third biscuit to greet him more eloquently.

"Olivia said you two were down here," Turner said. "Good timing on my part. I'm famished."

"We've a plate of biscuits if you want some," Miranda said, motioning to a dish on the table.

Turner shrugged his shoulders and sat down next to her. "Mrs. Cook's?"

Winston nodded.

Turner took three, then turned to Mrs. Cook with the same puppyish expression Winston had adopted earlier. "Oh, very well," she huffed, clearly adoring the attention, "I'll make more."

Just then Olivia appeared in the doorway, her lips pursed as she glared at her elder brother. "Turner," she said in an irritated voice. "I told you I wanted to show you the new, er, book I got."

Miranda stifled a groan. She'd *told* Olivia to stop trying to force a match.

"Turner," Olivia ground out.

Miranda decided that if Olivia ever asked her about it, she'd say that she just could not help herself when she looked up, smiled sweetly, and asked, "And what book would that be?"

Olivia glared long pointy swords at her. "You know the one."

"Would it be the one about the Ottoman Empire, the one about fur trappers in Canada, or the one about the philosophy of Adam Smith?"

"The Smith fellow," Olivia bit out.

"Really?" Winston asked, turning to his twin with renewed interest. "I had no idea you enjoyed that sort of thing. We've been reading *Wealth of Nations* this year. It's quite an interesting mixture of philosophy and economics."

Olivia smiled tightly. "I'm certain it is. I'll be sure to give you my opinion once I finish reading it."

"How far along are you?" Turner asked.

"Just a few pages."

Or at least that was what Miranda thought she heard. It was difficult to tell over the grinding of Olivia's teeth.

"D'you want a biscuit, Olivia?" Turner asked, and then he flashed *Miranda* a grin, as if to say, *We're in this together.*

He looked boyish. He looked young. He looked . . . happy.

And Miranda melted.

Olivia crossed the room to sit next to Winston, but on the way she leaned down and hissed in Miranda's ear, "I was trying to help you."

Miranda, however, was still recovering from Turner's smile. Her stomach felt as if it had just dropped to her feet, her head was dizzy, and her heart felt like it was thumping out an entire symphony. Either she was in love or she had contracted influenza. She stole a peek at Turner's chiseled profile and sighed.

All signs pointed to love.

"Miranda. Miranda!"

She looked up at Olivia, who was impatiently calling her name.

"Winston wants to know my opinion on *Wealth of Nations*

when I finish reading it. I told him you would be reading it along with me. I'm sure we can purchase another copy."

"What? Oh, yes, of course, I love to read." It was only when she saw Olivia's smirk that Miranda realized just what she'd agreed to.

"Now, Miranda," Winston said, leaning across the table and patting her hand with his. "You must tell me how you have been enjoying the season."

"Those biscuits are delicious," Turner declared loudly, reaching for one. "Excuse me, Winston, could you move your arm?"

Winston retrieved his hand, and Turner took a biscuit and popped it into his mouth. He smiled broadly. "Wonderful as always, Mrs. Cook!"

"I'll have another plate for you in just a few minutes," she assured him, beaming at the praise.

Miranda waited through the exchange and then said to Winston, "It has been quite lovely. I only wish you were here more often to enjoy it with us."

Winston turned to her with a lazy smile that ought to have made her heart skip. "As do I," he said, "but I'll be down for part of the summer."

"You won't have much time for the ladies, I'm afraid," Turner put in helpfully. "If I recall, my summer holidays were spent carousing with my friends. Great fun. You won't wish to miss it."

Miranda looked at him oddly. He sounded almost *too* jolly.

"I'm sure it was," Winston replied. "But I'd like to attend some of the *ton* events, too."

"Good idea," Olivia said. "You'll want to acquire some town polish."

Winston turned to her. "I have sufficient polish, thank you very much."

"Of course you do, but there is nothing like actual experience to, er, polish a man."

Winston flushed. "I have experience, Olivia."

Miranda's eyes widened.

Turner stood in one smooth movement. "I do believe this conversation is rapidly deteriorating to a level that is not fit for gentle ears."

Winston looked as if he might like to say something more, but luckily for the cause of familial peace, Olivia clapped her hands together with a cheerful "Well said!"

But Miranda should have known better than to trust her—at least when matchmaking was on the table. And sure enough, she soon found herself on the receiving end of Olivia's most devious smile.

"Miranda," she said, rather too prettily.

"Er, yes?"

"Didn't you tell me that you wanted to take Winston to that glove shop we noticed last week? They've the most amazingly well-made gloves," Olivia continued, directing this to Winston. "For both men and women. We thought you might need a pair. Weren't sure what sort of quality was available up at Oxford, you know."

It was quite the most obvious speech, and Miranda was sure Olivia knew it. She stole a glance at Turner, who was watching the proceedings with an air of amusement. Or maybe it was disgust. Sometimes it was difficult to discern.

"What do you say, dear brother?" Olivia said in her most charming voice. "Shall we go?"

"I can't think of anything I would enjoy more."

Miranda opened her mouth to say something, then saw the futility and shut it. She was going to kill Olivia. She was going to sneak into her bedroom and skin the meddling girl alive. But for now, her only choice was to agree. She did not wish to do anything that might lead Winston to believe she had romantic feelings for him, but it would be the height of insensitivity to attempt to wiggle out of the outing right in front of him.

And so, when she realized that three pairs of eyes were focused expectantly on her, there was nothing to do but say, "We could go today. It would be lovely."

"I'll join you," Turner announced, rising rather decisively to his feet.

Miranda turned to him with surprise, as did both Olivia and Winston. He had never shown interest in accompanying them on any of their outings back in Ambleside, and in truth, why should he have done? He was nine years their senior.

"I need a pair of gloves," he said simply, his lip curling slightly as if to say— *Why else would I come along?*

"Of course," Winston said, still blinking at the unexpected attention from his older brother.

"Good of you to suggest it," Turner said briskly. "Thank you, Olivia."

She did not look as if she were very welcome.

"It will be lovely to have you along," Miranda said,

perhaps a touch more enthusiastically than she'd intended. "You don't mind, do you, Winston?"

"No, of course not." But he looked as if he did. At least a little bit.

"Are you almost done with your milk and biscuits, Winston?" Turner asked. "We ought to be on our way. It looks like it might cloud over in the afternoon."

Winston perversely reached for another biscuit, the largest one on the table. "We can take a closed carriage."

"I'm going to fetch my coat," Miranda said, standing up. "The two of you can decide on carriages and such. Shall we meet in the rose salon? In twenty minutes?"

"I'll escort you upstairs," Winston said quickly. "I need to retrieve something from my traveling case."

The pair left the kitchen, and Olivia immediately turned on Turner with an expression that was positively feline. "What is *wrong* with you?"

He regarded her blandly. "I beg your pardon?"

"I have been working with every breath in my body to make a match of those two, and you are ruining it all."

"Do try not to be such a thespian," he said with a brief shake of his head. "I am merely purchasing gloves. It won't stop a wedding, if indeed one is imminent."

Olivia scowled. "If I didn't know better, I'd think you were jealous."

For a moment, Turner could do nothing but stare. And then he found his sense—and his voice—and bit off, "Well, you do know better. So I will thank you not to make unfounded accusations."

Jealous of Miranda. Good Lord, what would she think of next?

Olivia crossed her arms. "Well, you were certainly acting strangely."

Turner had, in his lifetime, treated his younger sister in a number of ways. Generally speaking, he employed benign neglect. Occasionally, he adopted a more avuncular role, surprising her with gifts and flattery when it was convenient for him to do so. But the gap in their ages had ensured that he had never treated her as an equal, never spoken to her without first considering her a child.

But now, with her accusing him of this, of wanting *Miranda*, of all things, he lashed out without measuring his words, without scaling them down in size and sentiment. And his voice was hard, biting, and sharp as he said, "If you would look beyond your own desire to have Miranda constantly at your beck and call, you would see that she and Winston are extremely ill-suited."

Olivia gasped at the unexpected attack, but she recovered quickly. "Beck and call?" she repeated furiously. "Now who is making unfounded accusations? You know as well as anyone that I adore Miranda and want nothing more than her happiness. Furthermore, she lacks beauty and a dowry, and—"

"Oh, for the love of—" Turner clamped his mouth shut before he cursed in front of his sister. "You sell her short," he snapped. Why did people persist in seeing Miranda as the gangly girl she'd once been? She might not fit the society's current standards of beauty, as did Olivia, but she had something far deeper and more interesting. One could look at her and know that there was something behind the eyes. And when she smiled, it wasn't practiced, it wasn't mocking—oh, very well, sometimes it was mocking, but he could excuse that, as she possessed the exact same sense of humor as he did. And truly, trapped in London for the season as they were, they were bound to come across any number of things worth mocking.

"Winston would be an excellent match for her," Olivia continued hotly. "And she for—" She stopped, gasped, and clamped her hand over her mouth.

"Oh, what now?" Turner said irritably.

"This isn't about Miranda, is it? It is about Winston. You don't think *she* is good enough for him."

"No," he retorted, instantly and in a strange, almost indignant voice. "No," he said again, this time measuring the word more carefully. "Nothing could be further from the truth. They are too young to marry. Winston especially."

Olivia immediately took umbrage. "That is not true, we are—"

"He is too young," he cut in coldly, "and you need look no further than this room to see why a man should not wed too young."

She did not understand right away. Turner saw the exact moment that she did, saw the comprehension, and then the pity.

And he *hated* the pity.

"I'm sorry," Olivia blurted out—the two words guaranteed to set him even more on edge. And then she said it again. "I'm sorry."

And ran off.

Miranda had been waiting in the rose salon for several minutes when a maid arrived in the doorway and said, "Beg pardon, miss, but Lady Olivia has asked me to tell you that she will not be down."

Miranda set down the figurine she'd been examining and looked to the maid with surprise. "Is she unwell?"

The maid looked hesitant, and Miranda did not wish to put her in a difficult position when she could simply seek out Olivia herself, so she said, "Never you mind. I shall ask her myself."

The maid bobbed a curtsy, and Miranda turned to the table next to her to make sure she'd put the figurine back in its proper position, then, giving it one more backward glance—she knew Lady Rudland liked her curios to be displayed just so—she stepped toward the door.

And crashed into a large, male body.

Turner. She knew it even before he spoke. It could have been Winston, or it could have been a footman, or it could have even been—heaven help her, the embarrassment—Lord Rudland, but it wasn't. It was Turner. She knew his scent. She knew the sound of his breath.

She knew the way the air felt when she was near him.

And that was when she knew, for sure and forever, that it was love.

It was love, and it was the love of a woman for a man. The young girl who'd thought him a white knight was gone. She was a woman now. She knew his flaws and she saw his shortcomings, and still she loved him.

She loved him, and she wanted to heal him, and she wanted—

She didn't know what she wanted. She wanted it all. She wanted everything. She—

"Miranda?"

His hands were still at her arms. She looked up, even though she knew it would be almost unbearable to face the blue of his eyes. She knew what she would not see there.

And she didn't. There was no love, no revelation. But he looked strange, different.

And she felt hot.

"I'm sorry," she stammered, pulling away. "I should be more careful."

But he didn't release her. Not right away. He was looking at her, at her mouth, and Miranda thought for one lovely, blessed second that maybe he wanted to kiss her. Her breath caught, and her lips parted, and—

And then it was over.

He stepped away. "My apologies," he said, with almost no inflection whatsoever. "I should be more careful, as well."

"I was going to find Olivia," she said, mostly because she had no idea what else to say. "She sent word that she will not be coming down."

His expression changed—just enough and with just enough cynicism that she knew he knew what was wrong. "Leave be," he said. "She'll be fine."

"But—"

"For once," he said sharply, "let Olivia deal with her own problems."

Miranda's lips parted with surprise at his tone. But she was saved from having to respond by the arrival of Winston.

"Ready to leave?" he asked jovially, completely unaware of the tensions in the room. "Where's Olivia?"

"She's not coming," Miranda and Turner said in unison.

Winston looked from one to the other, slightly nonplussed by their joint reply. "Why?" he asked.

"She's not feeling well," Miranda lied.

"That's too bad," Winston said, not sounding particularly unhappy. He held out his arm to Miranda. "Shall we?"

Miranda looked to Turner. "Are you still coming?"

"No." And it didn't take him even two seconds to reply.

11 JUNE 1819

My birthday today—lovely and strange.

The Bevelstokes held a family supper in my honor. It was so very sweet and kind, especially as my own father has likely forgot that today is anything other than the day that a certain Greek scholar did a certain special mathematical computation or some such other Very Important Thing.

From Lord and Lady Rudland: a beautiful pair of aquamarine earrings. I know I should not accept something so dear, but I could not make a fuss at the supper table, and I did say, "I can't . . ." (if with something of a lack of conviction) and was roundly shushed.

From Winston: a set of lovely lace handkerchiefs.

From Olivia: a box of stationery, engraved with my name. She enclosed a little note marked, "For Your Eyes Only," which said, "I hope you shan't be able to use this for long!" Which of course means she hopes my name shall soon be Bevelstoke.

I did not comment.

And from Turner, a bottle of scent. Violets. I immediately thought of the violet ribbon he pinned to my hair when I was ten, but of course he would not have remembered such a thing. I said nothing about it; it would have been far too embarrassing to be revealed as so maudlin. But I thought it a lovely and sweet gift.

I cannot seem to sleep. Ten minutes have passed since I wrote the previous sentence, and although I yawn quite frequently, my eyelids do not seem the least bit heavy. I think I shall go down to the kitchens to see if I might get a glass of warm milk.

Or perhaps I will not go to the kitchens. It is not likely that anyone will be down there to assist me, and while I am perfectly able to heat some milk, the chef will probably have palpita-

tions when he sees that someone has used one of his pots without his knowledge. And more importantly, I am twenty years old now. I can have a glass of sherry to help me sleep if I want.

　I think that is what I will do.

Chapter 7

Turner had been through one candle and three glasses of brandy, and now he was sitting in the dark in his father's study, staring out the window, listening to the leaves of a nearby tree rustle in the wind and slap up against the glass.

Dull, perhaps, but just now he was embracing dull. Dull was precisely what he wanted after a day such as this.

First there had been Olivia, accusing him of wanting Miranda. Then there had been Miranda, and he had—

Dear Lord, he had wanted her.

He knew the exact moment he had realized it. It wasn't when she had bumped into him. It wasn't when his hands had gone 'round her upper arms to steady her. She'd felt nice, yes, but he hadn't noticed. Not like that.

The moment . . . the moment that could quite possibly ruin him had occurred a split second later, when she looked up.

It was her eyes. It had always been her eyes. He had just been too stupid to realize it.

And as they stood there, for what felt like an eternity, he felt himself changing. He felt his body coiling and his breath ceasing altogether, and then his fingers tightened, and her eyes—they widened even more.

And he wanted her. Like nothing he could have imagined, like nothing that was proper and good, he wanted her.

He had never been so disgusted with himself.

He didn't love her. He *couldn't* love her. He was quite certain he could not love anyone, not after the destruction Leticia had wrought on his heart. It was lust, pure and simple, and it was lust for what was quite possibly the least suitable woman in all England.

He poured himself another drink. They said that what didn't kill a man made him stronger, but this. . .

This was going to kill him.

And then, as he sat there, pondering his own weaknesses, he saw her.

It was a test. It could only be a test. Someone somewhere was determined to test his mettle as a gentleman, and he was going to fail. He would try, he would hold back as long as he could, but deep down, in a little corner of his soul that he didn't particularly like to examine, he knew. He would fail.

She moved like a ghost, almost glowing in some billowy white gown. It was plain cotton, he was sure, prim and proper and perfectly virginal.

It made him desperate for her.

He clutched the sides of his chair and held on for all he was worth.

* * *

Miranda felt a little uneasy at entering Lord Rudland's study, but she had not found what she was looking for in the rose salon, and she knew that he kept a decanter on a shelf by the door. She could be in and out in under a minute; surely mere seconds would not count as an invasion of privacy.

"Now where are those glasses?" she murmured, setting her candle down on the table. "Here we are." She found the bottle of sherry and poured herself a small amount.

"I hope you are not making this a habit," a voice drawled out.

The glass slipped through her fingers and landed on the floor with a loud smash.

"Tsk, tsk, tsk."

She followed his voice until she saw him, seated in a wingback chair, his hands perched awkwardly on the arms. The light was dim, but even so, she could see the expression on his face, sardonic and dry. "Turner?" she whispered foolishly, as if maybe, possibly, it could be someone else.

"The very one."

"But what are you—why are you here?" She took a step forward. "Ouch!" A shard of glass pierced the skin on the ball of her foot.

"You little fool. Coming down here with bare feet." He rose from his chair and strode across the room.

"I wasn't planning on breaking a glass," Miranda replied in a defensive tone, leaning down and plucking the splinter out.

"It doesn't matter. You'll catch the death of a cold wandering around like that." He scooped her up in his arms and carried her away from the broken glass.

It crossed Miranda's mind just then that she was as close to heaven as she had ever been in her short life. His body was warm, and she could feel the heat of him pouring through her nightgown. Her skin tingled from his nearness, and her breath started coming in strange little pants.

It was the scent of him. That must be it. She had never been this near to him before, never been close enough to smell his uniquely male essence. He smelled like warm wood and brandy, and a little of something else, something she couldn't quite pinpoint. Something that was simply Turner. Clutching his neck, she allowed her head to drop closer to his chest just so she could take another deep breath of him.

And then, just when she was convinced that life was as perfect as it could possibly be, he dumped her unceremoniously on the sofa.

"What was that for?" she asked, scrambling to sit up straight.

"What are you doing here?"

"What are *you* doing here?"

He sat down across from her on a low table. "I asked you first."

"We sound like a pair of children, she said, tucking her legs beneath her. But she answered him, nonetheless. It seemed silly to argue over such a thing. "I couldn't sleep. I thought a glass of sherry might do the trick."

"Because you've reached the ripe old age of twenty," he said mockingly.

But she would not take his bait. She just tilted her head in gracious acknowledgment that said— *Exactly*.

He chuckled at that. "Then, by all means, allow me to assist in your downfall." He stood and walked to a nearby cabinet. "But if you are going to drink, then by God, do it properly. Brandy is what you need, preferably the sort smuggled from France."

Miranda watched as he plucked two snifters from a shelf and set them down on the table. His hands were steady and—could hands be beautiful?—as he poured two liberal doses. "My mother occasionally gave me brandy when I was small. When I got caught in the rain," she explained. "Just a sip to warm me up."

He turned and looked at her, his eyes piercing even in the dark. "Are you cold now?"

"No. Why?"

"You're shivering."

Miranda looked down at her traitorous arms. She *was* shivering, but it wasn't the cold that had caused it. She hugged her arms to her body, hoping he would not pursue the subject further.

He walked back across the room and handed her the brandy, his body infused with lean, masculine grace. "Don't drink it all at once."

She shot him an extremely irritated expression at his condescending tone before taking a sip. "Why *are* you here?" she asked.

He sat down across from her and lazily propped one

ankle on the opposite knee. "I had to discuss some estate matters with my father, so he invited me to share a drink with him after our meal. I never left."

"And you've been sitting here in the dark all by yourself?"

"I like the dark."

"No one likes the dark."

He laughed aloud, and she felt terribly green and young.

"Ah, Miranda," he said, still chuckling. "Thank you for that."

She narrowed her eyes. "How much have you had to drink?"

"An impertinent question."

"Aha, so you have had too much."

He leaned forward. "Do I look drunk to you?"

She drew back involuntarily, unprepared for the unwavering intensity of his gaze. "No," she said slowly. "But you're far more experienced than I am, and I would imagine that you know how to handle your liquor. You probably could drink eight times as much as I do and not show it at all."

Turner laughed harshly. "All true, every bit of it. And you, dear girl, should learn to stay away from men who are 'far more experienced' than you."

Miranda took another sip of her drink, just barely resisting the urge to toss it back in one gulp. But it would burn, and she would choke, and then he would laugh.

And she would want to die of the embarrassment.

He'd been in a foul mood all evening. Cutting and

mocking when they were alone, and silent and surly when they were not. She cursed her traitorous heart for loving him so; it would have been far easier to adore Winston, whose smile was sunny and open, who had doted upon her the entire evening.

But no, she wanted him. Turner, whose quicksilver moods meant that he was laughing and joking with her one moment, and treating her like an antidote the next.

Love was for idiots. Fools. And she was the biggest fool of them all.

"What are you thinking about?" he demanded.

She said, "Your brother." Just to be perverse. It was a little bit true, anyway.

"Ah," he said, adding more brandy to his glass. "Winston. Nice fellow."

"Yes," she said. Almost defiantly.

"Jolly."

"Lovely."

"Young."

She shrugged. "So am I. Perhaps we are well matched."

He said nothing. She finished her drink.

"Don't you agree?" she asked.

Still, he did not speak.

"About Winston," she pushed. "He's your brother. You want him to be happy, don't you? Do you think I'd be good for him? Do you think I'd make him happy?"

"Why are you asking me this?" he asked, his voice low and almost disembodied in the night.

She shrugged, then slipped her finger into her glass to

dab up the last drops. After licking her skin, she looked up.

"At your service," he murmured, and splashed two more fingers of brandy into the snifter.

Miranda nodded her thanks and then answered his question. "I want to know," she said simply, "and I don't know who else to ask. Olivia is so eager to see me married off to Winston, she'd say whatever she thought would bring me to the altar quickest."

She waited, counting the seconds until he spoke. One, two, three . . . and then he took a ragged breath.

It was almost like a surrender.

"I don't know, Miranda." He sounded tired, weary. "I don't see why you wouldn't make him happy. You'd make anyone happy."

Even you? Miranda ached to say the words, but instead she asked, "Do you think he'd make me happy?"

It took him longer to answer this question. And then finally, in slow, measured tones: "I'm not sure."

"Why not? What's wrong with him?"

"Nothing is wrong with him. I'm just not certain he'd make you happy."

"But why?" She was being impertinent, she knew, but if she could just get Turner to tell her why Winston wouldn't make her happy, maybe he'd realize why *he* would.

"I don't know, Miranda." He raked his hand through his hair until the gold strands stood at an awkward angle. "Must we have this conversation?"

"Yes," she said intently. "Yes."

"Very well." He leaned forward, his eyes narrowing as if to prepare her for unpleasant news. "You lack the current societal standards of beauty, you're too sarcastic by half, and you don't particularly like to make polite conversation. Frankly, Miranda, I really cannot see you wanting a typical society marriage."

She swallowed. "And?"

He looked away from her for a long minute before finally turning back. "And most men will not appreciate you. If your husband tries to mold you into something you're not, you will be spectacularly unhappy."

There was something electric in the air, and Miranda was quite unable to take her eyes off him. "And do you think there is anyone out there who will appreciate me?" she whispered.

The question hung heavily in the air, mesmerizing them both until Turner finally answered, "Yes."

But his eyes fell to his glass, and then he drained the last of the brandy, and his sigh was that of a man satisfied by drink, not one pondering love and romance.

She looked away. The moment—if there had been one, if it hadn't been just a figment of her imagination—was gone, and the silence that remained was not one of comfort. It was awkward and ungainly, and *she* felt awkward and ungainly, and so, eager to fill the space between them, she blurted the first completely unimportant thing she could think of.

"Do you plan to attend the Worthington ball next week?"

He turned, one of his brows lifting in query over her unexpected question. "I might."

"I wish you would. You're always so kind to dance with

me twice. Otherwise I should be sadly lacking in partners."
She was babbling, but she wasn't sure she cared. In any
case, she couldn't seem to stop herself. "If Winston could
attend, I wouldn't need you, but I understand he has to
return to Oxford in the morning."

Turner flashed her a strange look. It wasn't quite a smile,
and it wasn't quite mocking, and it wasn't even quite ironic. Miranda hated that he was so inscrutable; it gave her
absolutely no indication how to proceed. But she plowed
on, anyway. At this point, what had she to lose?

"Will you go?" she asked. "I would so appreciate it."

He regarded her for a moment, then said, "I will be
there."

"Thank you. I'm quite grateful."

"I'm delighted to be of use," he said dryly.

She nodded, her movements spurred more by nervous
energy than anything else. "You need only dance with me
once, if that is all you can manage. But if you might do it
at the outset, I would appreciate it. Other men do seem to
follow your lead."

"Strange as it may seem," he murmured.

"It's not so strange," she said, offering him a one-
shouldered shrug. She was beginning to feel the effects
of the liquor. She was not yet impaired, but she felt rather
warm, perhaps a little daring. "You're quite handsome."

He seemed not to know how to reply. Miranda congrat-
ulated herself. It was so rarely that she managed to discon-
cert him.

The feeling was heady, and so she took another gulp of

her brandy, careful this time to let it slide down her throat more smoothly, and said, "You're rather like Winston."

"I beg your pardon."

His voice was sharp, and she probably should have taken it as a warning, but she could not seem to step out of the ditch she was rapidly digging 'round herself. "Well, you both have blue eyes and blond hair, although I suppose his is a bit lighter. And you stand in a similar manner, although—"

"That's enough, Miranda."

"Oh, but—"

"I said, that's *enough*."

She silenced at his caustic tone, then muttered, "There is no need to take offense."

"You've had too much to drink."

"Don't be silly. I'm not the least bit drunk. I'm sure you've drunk ten times as much as I have."

He regarded her with a deceptively lazy stare. "That's not quite true, but as you said earlier, I have a great deal more experience than you do."

"I did say that, didn't I? I think I was right. I don't think you're the least bit drunk."

He inclined his head and said softly, "Not drunk. Just a trifle reckless."

"Reckless, are you?" she murmured, testing the word on her tongue. "What an interesting description. I think I am reckless, too."

"You certainly must be, or you would have gone right back upstairs when you saw me."

"And I wouldn't have compared you to Winston."

His eyes glinted steely blue. "You certainly would not have done that."

"You don't *mind*, do you?"

There was a long, dead silence, and for a moment Miranda thought she'd gone too far. How could she have been so foolish, so conceited to think that he might want her? Why on earth would he care if she compared him to his younger brother? She was nothing more than a child to him, the homely little girl he'd befriended because he'd felt sorry for her. She should never have dreamed that he might one day come to care for her.

"Forgive me," she muttered, jerking to her feet. "I overstep." And then, because it was still there, she drained the rest of her brandy and rushed toward the door.

"Aaaah!"

"What the devil?" Turner shot to his feet.

"I forgot about the glass," she whimpered. "The broken glass."

"Oh, Christ, Miranda, don't cry." He walked swiftly across the room and for the second time that evening scooped her into his arms.

"I'm so stupid. So bloody stupid," she said with a sniffle. The tears were more for her lost dignity than for pain, and for that reason they were harder to stop.

"Don't curse. I've never heard you curse before. I'll have to wash your mouth out with soap," he teased, carrying her back to the sofa.

His gentle tone affected her more than stern words ever could, and she took a few great gulps of air, trying to control the sobs that were hovering somewhere at the back of her throat.

He set her gently back down on the sofa. "Let me see that foot now, all right?"

She shook her head. "I can take care of it."

"Don't be silly. You're shaking like a leaf." He walked over to the liquor cabinet and picked up the candle she'd left there earlier.

She watched him as he crossed back to her and set the candle down on an end table. "Here now, we've got a bit of light. Let me see your foot."

Reluctantly, she let him pick up her foot and place it in his lap. "I'm so stupid."

"Will you stop saying that? You're the least stupid female I know."

"Thank you. I— Ouch!"

"Sit still and stop twisting around."

"I want to see what you're doing."

"Well, unless you're a contortionist, you can't, so you'll have to trust me."

"Are you almost done?"

"Almost." He pinched his finger around another shard of glass and pulled.

She stiffened in pain.

"I've only one or two left."

"What if you don't get them all out?"

"I will."

"What if you don't?"

"Good God, woman, have I ever told you that you're persistent?"

She almost smiled. "Yes."

And he almost smiled back. "If I miss one, it'll probably just work its way out in a few days. Splinters usually do."

"Wouldn't it be nice if life were as simple as a splinter?" she said sadly.

He looked up. "Working its way out in a few days?"

She nodded.

He held her gaze for another moment, and then turned back to his work, plucking one last shard of glass from her skin. "There you are. You'll be as good as new in no time."

But he made no move to take her foot off his lap.

"I'm sorry I was so clumsy."

"Don't be. It was an accident."

Was it her imagination or was he whispering? And his eyes looked so tender. Miranda twisted herself around so that she was sitting up next to him. "Turner?"

"Don't say anything," he said hoarsely.

"But I—"

"Please!"

Miranda didn't understand the urgency in his voice, didn't recognize the desire lacing his words. She only knew that he was close, and she could feel him, and she could smell him . . . and she wanted to taste him. "Turner, I—"

"No more," he said raggedly, and he pulled her up next to him, her breasts flattening against his firmly muscled chest. His eyes were gleaming fiercely, and she suddenly realized—suddenly *knew*—that nothing was going to stop the slow descent of his lips onto hers.

And then he was kissing her, his lips hot and hungry against her mouth. His desire was fierce, raw, and consuming. He wanted her. She could not believe it, could barely even summon the presence of mind to *think* it, but she knew it.

He wanted her.

It made her bold. It made her womanly. It brought forth some kind of secret knowledge that had been buried within her, since before she was born perhaps, and she kissed him back, her lips moving with artless wonder, her tongue darting out to taste the hot salt of his skin.

Turner's hands pressed into her back, imprisoning her against him, and then they could no longer remain upright, and they sank into the cushions, Turner covering Miranda's body with his own.

He was wild. He was mad. That could be the only explanation, but he could not seem to get enough of her. His hands roamed everywhere, testing, touching, squeezing, and all he could think—when he could think at all—was that he wanted her. He wanted her in every possible way. He wanted to devour her. He wanted to worship her.

He wanted to lose himself within her.

He whispered her name, moaned it against her skin. And when she whispered his in return, he felt his hands move to the tiny buttons at the neck of her nightgown. Each fastening seemed to melt away beneath his fingertips until she was undone, and all that was left was for him to slide the fabric along her skin. He could feel the swell of her breasts beneath the gown, but he wanted more. He wanted the heat of her, the smell, the taste.

His lips moved down her throat, following the elegant curve to her collarbone, right where the edge of her nightgown met her skin. He nudged it down, tasting one new inch of her, exploring the soft, salty sweetness, and shuddering with pleasure when the flat planes of her chest gave way to the gentle swell of her breast.

Dear God, he wanted her.

He cupped her through her clothing, pressing her up, raising her closer to his mouth. She groaned, and it was all he could do to hold himself back, to force his desire to move slowly. His mouth moved closer, edging toward the ultimate prize, even as his hand slipped under the hemline of her nightgown, sliding up the silky skin of her calf.

Then his hand reached her thigh, and she very nearly screamed.

"Shhh," he crooned, silencing her with a kiss. "You'll wake up the neighbors. You'll wake up my . . ."

Parents.

It was like a bucket of cold water being dumped over him.

"Oh, my *God*."

"What, Turner?" Her breath was coming in ragged gasps.

"Oh, my God. *Miranda*." He said her name with all the shock that was flooding his mind. It was as if he'd been asleep, in a dream, and he'd been woken and—

"Turner, I—"

"Quiet," he whispered harshly, and he rolled himself off

her with such force that he landed on the carpet beside her. "Oh, dear God," he said. And then again, because it bore repeating.

"Oh. Dear. God."

"Turner?"

"Get up. You have to get up."

"But—"

He looked down at her, which was a big mistake. Her nightgown was still gathered near her hips, and her legs— good God, who would have thought they'd be quite so lovely and long—and he just wanted to—

No.

He shuddered with the force of his own refusal.

"Now, Miranda," he ground out.

"But I don—"

He yanked her to her feet. He didn't particularly wish to take her hand; frankly, he did not trust himself to touch her, however unromantic the grasp. But he had to get her moving. He had to get her out of there.

"Go," he ordered. "For love of God, if you have any sense, *go.*"

But she was just standing there, staring at him in shock, and her hair was mussed, and her lips were swollen, and he wanted her.

Dear Lord, he still wanted her.

"This will not happen again," he said, his voice tight.

She said nothing. He watched her face warily. Please, *please* don't let her cry.

He held himself ferociously still. If he moved, he might

touch her. He wouldn't be able to help himself. "You'd better go upstairs," he said in a low voice.

She nodded jerkily and fled the room.

Turner stared at the doorway. Holy bloody hell. What was he going to do?

12 JUNE 1819

I am without words. Utterly.

Chapter 8

Turner woke up the next morning with a blistering head-
ache that had nothing to do with alcohol.

He *wished* it had been the brandy. Brandy would have
been a hell of a lot simpler than this.

Miranda.

What the hell had he been thinking?

Nothing. He obviously hadn't been thinking at all. At
least not with his head.

He had kissed Miranda. Hell, he had practically mauled
her. And it was difficult to imagine that there might exist
anywhere in Britain a young woman *less* suitable for his
attentions than Miss Miranda Cheever.

He was going to roast somewhere for this.

If he were a better man, he supposed, he would marry
her. A young woman could lose her reputation for far less
than this. *But no one had seen*, a little voice inside him
insisted. No one knew but the two of them. And Miranda
wouldn't say anything. She wasn't the sort.

And he wasn't a better man. Leticia had seen to that. She had killed whatever was good and kind inside him. But he still had his sense. And there was no way he was going to let himself anywhere near Miranda again. One mistake might be understandable.

Two would be his undoing.

And three. . .

Good God, he shouldn't even be *thinking* about three.

He needed distance, that was it. Distance. If he stayed away from Miranda, he couldn't be tempted, and she'd eventually forget about their illicit encounter and find herself some nice jolly fellow to wed. The image of her in another man's arms was unexpectedly distasteful, but Turner decided that was because it was early in the morning, and he was tired, and he'd kissed her only six or so hours earlier, and—

And there could be a hundred different reasons, none of them important enough to examine further.

In the meantime, he'd have to avoid her. Maybe he should leave town. Get away. He could go to the country. He hadn't really meant to remain in London very long, anyway.

He opened his eyes and groaned. Had he no self-control? Miranda was an inexperienced chit of twenty. She wasn't like Leticia, wise to all of her womanly skills, and willing to use them to her advantage.

Miranda would be tempting, but resistible. Turner was man enough to keep his head around her. All the same, he probably ought not to be living in the same house. And while he was making changes, perhaps it was time to in-spect the women of the *ton* this year. There were many discreet young widows. He'd been far too long without female company.

If anything could help him forget one woman, it was another.

"Turner is moving out."

"What?" Miranda had been arranging flowers in a porce-lain vase. It was only through agile hands and tremendous good luck that the precious antique did not go crashing to the ground.

"He's already gone," Olivia said with a shrug. "His va-let is packing his things right now."

Miranda set the vase back on the table with achingly careful fingers. Slow, steady, breathe in, breathe out. And then finally, when she was certain she could speak without shaking, she asked, "Is he leaving town?"

"No, I don't believe so," Olivia said, settling down on the chaise with a yawn. "He'd not meant to remain in town this long, so he is taking an apartment."

He was taking an apartment? Miranda fought against the horrible, hollow feeling that was sinking in her chest. He was taking an apartment. Just to get away from her.

It would have been humiliating if it weren't so sad. Or maybe it was both.

"It's probably for the best," Olivia continued, oblivi-ous to her friend's distress. "I know he says he will never marry again—"

"He said that?" Miranda froze. How was it possible she did not know this? She knew he'd said he wasn't looking for a wife, but surely he had not meant forever.

"Oh, yes," Olivia replied. "He said so the other day. He was quite adamant. I thought Mother would have a fit over it. As it was, she very nearly swooned."

"Your mother?" Miranda was having difficulty imagining it.

"Well, no, but if her nerves were less constitutional, surely she would have done."

Most of the time Miranda enjoyed her friend's meandering manner, but just now she wanted to *throttle* her.

"Anyway," Olivia said, sighing as she settled into a reclining position, "he said he will not marry, but I am quite certain he will reconsider. He must simply get past the grief." She paused, glancing over at Miranda with a wry expression. "Or the lack thereof."

Miranda smiled tightly. So tightly, in fact, that she was fairly certain it ought to be termed something else altogether.

"But despite what he says," Olivia continued, settling back down and closing her eyes, "he certainly will never find a bride whilst living here. Goodness, how could anyone court in the company of a mother, father, and two younger sisters?"

"Two?"

"Well, one, of course, but you might as well count as a second. He certainly cannot behave in any manner he might *like* to behave while you are in his presence."

Miranda did not know if she ought to laugh or cry.

"And even if he does not choose a bride anytime soon," Olivia added, "he ought to take a mistress. Surely that will help him forget Leticia."

Miranda did not see how she could possibly comment.

"And certainly he cannot do that while he is living *here*." Olivia opened her eyes and propped herself up on her elbows. "So really, it is all for the best. Wouldn't you agree?"

Miranda nodded. Because she had to. Because she felt too stunned to cry.

19 JUNE 1819

> *He has been gone a week now, and I am quite beyond myself.*
>
> *If he had just left—that, I could have forgiven. But he has not come back!*
>
> *He has not called upon me. He has not sent a letter. And although I hear whispers and gossip that he is out and about and being seen in society, he is certainly never seen by me. If I am in attendance at an event, then he is not. Once I thought I saw him from across a room, but I cannot be certain, as it was only his back as he made his departure.*
>
> *I don't know what I may do about all of this. I cannot call upon him. It would be the height of impropriety. Lady Rudland has forbidden even Olivia from visiting him; he is at The Albany, and it is strictly gentlemen. No families or widows.*

* * *

"What do you plan to wear to the Worthington ball to-night?" Olivia asked, splashing three sugars into her tea.

"Is that tonight?" Miranda's fingers tightened around her teacup. Turner had promised her he'd attend the Worthington ball and dance with her. Surely he wouldn't renege on a promise.

He would be there. And if he wasn't. . .

She would simply have to make sure he was.

"I'm wearing my green silk," Olivia said. "Unless you want to wear your green dress. You do look lovely in green."

"Do you think so?" Miranda straightened. Suddenly it was imperative that she look her absolute best.

"Mmm-hmm. But it wouldn't do for both of us to wear the same color, so you'll have to decide soon."

"What do you recommend?" Miranda wasn't hopeless when it came to fashion, but she would never have as good an eye as Olivia.

Olivia tilted her head to the side as she examined her friend. "With your coloring, I do wish you could wear something more vivid, but Mama says we are still too new. But maybe . . ." She jumped up, snatched a pale sage green pillow from a nearby chair, and held it up under Miranda's chin. "Hmmm."

"Are you planning to redecorate me?"

"Hold this," Olivia ordered, and she backed up several steps, letting out a ladylike "Euf!" when her foot caught on a table leg. "Yes, yes," she murmured, catching her balance with the arm of the sofa. "It's perfect."

Miranda looked down. And then up. "I'm to wear a pillow?"

"No, you will wear my green silk. It is precisely the same color. We shall have Annie take it in today."

"But what will you wear?"

"Oh, anything," Olivia said with a wave of her hand. "Something pink. The gentlemen always seem to go mad for pink. Makes me look like a confection, I'm told."

"You don't mind being a confection?" Because Miranda would hate it.

"I don't mind them thinking it," Olivia corrected. "It gives me the upper hand. There is often benefit in being underestimated. But you . . ." She shook her head. "You need something more subtle. Sophisticated."

Miranda picked up her tea for one last sip, then stood, smoothing out the soft muslin of her day frock. "I should go try it on now," she said. "To give Annie time to make the alterations."

And besides that, she had some correspondence to attend to.

Turner was discovering, as he tied his cravat with nimble fingers, that his talent for the invective was broader and deeper than he'd realized. He'd found a hundred things to malign since he'd received that blasted note from Miranda earlier that afternoon. But most of all, he was cursing himself, and whatever sodding sense of honor he still possessed.

Attending the Worthington ball was the height of folly— quite the most asinine thing he could possibly do. But he couldn't bloody well break a promise to the chit, even if it was for her own good.

Holy hell. This was not what he needed right now.

He looked back down at the note. He had promised to dance with her if she lacked partners, had he? Well, that shouldn't be a problem. He'd simply make sure she had more partners than she knew what to do with. She'd be the bloody belle of the ball.

He supposed that as long as he had to attend this deuced party, he ought to go ahead and examine the young widows. With any luck, Miranda would see exactly where he planned to devote his attentions, and she'd realize that she ought to look elsewhere.

He winced. He didn't like the thought of upsetting her. Hell, he liked the chit. He always had.

He gave his head a shake. He wasn't going to upset her. Not much, anyway. And besides, he would make it up to her.

Belle of the ball, he reminded himself as he stepped into his carriage and steeled himself for what was certain to be a most trying evening.

Belle. Of. The. Ball.

Olivia spotted Turner the moment he entered. "Oh, look," she said, nudging Miranda with her elbow. "My brother is here."

"He is?" Miranda replied breathlessly.

"Mmm-hmm." Olivia straightened, her brows coming together. "I haven't seen him for ages, now that I think on it. Have you?"

Miranda shook her head absently as she craned her neck, trying to spot Turner.

"He's over there speaking with Duncan Abbott," Olivia informed her. "I wonder what they're talking about. Mr. Abbott is quite political."

"Is he?"

"Oh, yes. I should love to have a discussion with him, but he probably wouldn't care to discuss politics with a woman. Annoying, that."

Miranda was about to nod her agreement when Olivia furrowed her brow again and said in an irritated voice, "Now he's talking to Lord Westholme."

"Olivia, the man is allowed to speak with whomever he likes," Miranda said, but inside, she, too, was growing irritated that Turner was not making his way over to them.

"I know, but he ought to come and greet us first. We're family."

"Well, you are, at least."

"Don't be silly. You're family, too, Miranda." Olivia's mouth opened in an outraged little O. "Will you look at that? He's gone in quite the opposite direction."

"Who is that man he's talking to? I don't recognize him."

"The Duke of Ashbourne. Devilishly handsome fellow, don't you think? I think he's been abroad. Having a holiday with his wife. They're quite devoted to one another, I understand."

Miranda thought it a positive sign to hear that at least one *ton* marriage was happy. Still, Turner certainly wasn't about to ask for *her* hand if he couldn't be bothered to walk across a ballroom to say hello. She frowned.

"Excuse me, Lady Olivia. I believe this is my dance."

Olivia and Miranda looked up. A handsome young man whose name neither could recall was standing before them.

"Of course," Olivia said quickly. "How silly of me to have forgotten."

"I believe I will get a glass of lemonade," Miranda said with a smile. She knew that Olivia always felt awkward when she went off for a dance and left Miranda alone.

"Are you certain?"

"Go. Go."

Olivia floated out onto the dance floor, and Miranda started to make her way to a footman who was pouring lemonade. As usual, she had been claimed for only about half of the dances. And where was Turner, she might ask, after he had promised to dance with her if she lacked partners?

Horrid, horrid man.

Somehow, it felt good to malign him in her mind, even if she didn't quite believe it.

Miranda had made it about halfway to the lemonade when she felt a firm masculine hand on her elbow. Turner? She whirled around, but was disappointed to find a gentleman she did not know but whose face looked vaguely familiar.

"Miss Cheever?"

Miranda nodded.

"May I have the pleasure of this dance?"

"Why yes, of course, but I do not believe we have been introduced."

"Oh, forgive me, please. I am Westholme."

Lord Westholme? Wasn't he the gentleman Turner had been talking to just a few moments earlier? Miranda smiled at him, but her mind was frowning. She had never been a great believer in coincidences.

Lord Westholme proved to be an excellent dancer, and the pair whirled effortlessly around the floor. When the music drew to a close, he bowed elegantly and escorted her to the perimeter of the room.

"Thank you for a lovely dance, Lord Westholme," Miranda said graciously.

"It is I who should thank you, Miss Cheever. I hope that we may repeat this pleasure soon."

Miranda noticed that Lord Westholme had managed to deposit her as far away from the lemonade as possible. It had been a white lie when she told Olivia she was thirsty, but now she was really quite parched. With a sigh, she realized that she would have to wiggle her way back through the crowd. She had not taken two steps toward the refreshments when another elegant, eminently eligible young man stepped in front of her. She recognized this one immediately. It was Mr. Abbott, the politically minded gentlemen with whom Turner had also been conversing.

Within seconds, Miranda was back on the dance floor and growing very irritated, indeed.

Not that she could fault her partners. If Turner had found it necessary to bribe men into dancing with her, at least he'd chosen handsome, well-mannered ones. Nevertheless, when Mr. Abbott led her from the dance floor, and she saw the Duke of Ashbourne making his way toward her, Miranda beat a hasty retreat.

Did he think she had no pride? Did he think she would appreciate his cajoling his friends into asking her to dance? It was humiliating. And even worse was the implication that he was getting those men to dance with her because he couldn't be bothered to do so himself. Tears pricked her eyes, and Miranda, terrified that she would spill them in the ballroom in full view of the *ton*, darted out into a deserted corridor.

She leaned back against a wall and took great big gulps of air. His rejection didn't just sting. It stabbed. It shot bullets. And its aim was accurate to a degree.

This was not like all those years when he had viewed her as a child. Then at least she could be consoled by telling herself that he did not know what he was missing. But now he did. Now he knew exactly what he was missing, and he didn't care a bit.

Miranda could not remain in the hallway all night, but she was not ready to return to the party, so she made her way out to the garden. It was a small patch of green, but well proportioned and tastefully laid out. Miranda sat down on a stone bench in the corner of the garden that faced back toward the house. Large glass doors opened onto the ballroom, and for several minutes she watched the lords and ladies twirling to the music. She sniffled and pulled off one of her gloves so she could wipe her nose with her hand. "My kingdom for a handkerchief," she said with a sigh.

Maybe she could feign illness and go home.

She tested out a little cough. Maybe she really *was* ill. Really, there was no sense in her staying the rest of the ball. The aim was to be pretty and sociable and engaging, wasn't it? There was no way she was going to manage any of *that* this evening.

And then she saw a flash of gold.

Gold-touched hair, to be more precise.

It was Turner. *Of course*. How could it not be he, when she was sitting off by herself, pathetic and alone? He was walking through the French doors that led to the garden.

And there was a woman on his arm.

A strange lump rolled about in her throat, and Miranda did not know whether to laugh or cry. Would she be spared no humiliation? Breath catching in her throat, she scooted down to the edge of the bench where she would be more hidden by shadows.

Who *was* that? She'd seen her before. Lady Something-or-other. A widow, she'd heard, and very, very wealthy and independent. She didn't look like a widow. Truth be told, she didn't look much older than Miranda.

Murmuring an insincere apology to no one in particular, Miranda strained her ears to hear their conversation. But the wind was carrying their words in the opposite direction, so she heard only the barest of snatches. Finally, after what sounded like "I'm not certain," from the lady's lips, Turner leaned down and kissed her.

Miranda's heart shattered.

The lady murmured something she could not hear and returned to the ballroom. Turner remained in the garden, his hands on his hips, staring enigmatically up at the moon.

Go away, Miranda wanted to scream. *Go!* She was trapped there until he left, and all she wanted was to go home and curl up in her bed. And possibly never get out. But that did not appear to be an option just then, so she scooted farther along the bench, trying to cloak herself with even more shadows.

Turner's head moved sharply in her direction. Blast! He'd heard her. He squinted his eyes and took a couple of steps in her direction. Then he shut his eyes and slowly shook his head.

"Damn it, Miranda," he said with a sigh. "Please tell me that isn't you."

And here the evening had been going so well. He had managed to avoid Miranda completely, he had finally got himself introduced to the lovely Widow Bidwell—only twenty-five years young—and the champagne wasn't even that bad, either.

But no, the gods were clearly not inclined to grant him any favors. There she was. Miranda. Sitting on a bench, watching him. Presumably watching him kiss the widow.

Good Lord.

"Damn it, Miranda," he said with a sigh. "Please tell me that isn't you."

"It isn't me."

She was trying to sound proud, but her voice held a hollow edge that pierced him. He closed his eyes for a moment because, damn it, she wasn't supposed to *be* there. He wasn't supposed to have these sorts of complications in his life. Why couldn't anything ever be simple and easy?

"Why are you here?" he asked.

She shrugged a little. "I wanted some fresh air."

He took a few more steps toward her until he was as deeply embedded in the shadows as she was. "Were you spying on me?"

"You must have a very high opinion of yourself."

"Were you?" he demanded.

"No, of course not," she retorted, her chin drawing back with anger. "I don't stoop to spying. You ought to inspect your gardens more carefully the next time you plan a tryst."

He crossed his arms. "I find it difficult to believe that your being out here has nothing to do with my presence."

"Do tell, then," she bit off, "if I had followed you here, how could I have got all the way back to this bench without your noticing me?"

He ignored the question, mostly because she was right. He raked a hand through his hair, and then grabbed a hunk and squeezed, the tugging sensation at his scalp somehow helping him to rein in his temper.

"You're going to yank it out," Miranda said in an aggravatingly even voice.

He took a deep breath. He flexed his fingers. And his voice was almost steady when he demanded, "What is this about, Miranda?"

"What is it about?" she echoed, rising to her feet. "What is it about? How dare you! It's about your ignoring me for a week and treating me like something that needs to be swept under a rug. It's about your thinking I have so little pride that I'd appreciate your bribing your friends to ask me to dance. It's about your rudeness and your selfishness and your inability to—"

He placed his hand over her mouth. "For God's sake, keep your voice down. What happened last week was wrong, Miranda. And you're a fool to call in your promises and force me to attend tonight."

"But you did it," she whispered. "You came."

"I came," he spat out, "because I am looking for a mistress. *Not* a wife."

She lurched backward. And she stared at him. She stared until he thought her eyes would burn holes in him. And then finally, in a voice so low it hurt, she said, "I don't like you right now, Turner."

That was convenient. He didn't much like himself just then, either.

Miranda's chin lifted, but she was trembling as she said, "If you'll excuse me. I have a ball to attend. Thanks to you, I have a goodly number of dance partners, and I wouldn't want to offend any of them."

He watched as she stalked off. And then he watched the door. And then he left.

20 JUNE 1819

I saw that widow again tonight after I went back into the ballroom. I asked Olivia who she was, and she said her name is Katherine Bidwell. She is the Countess of Pembleton. She married Lord Pembleton when he was nearly sixty and promptly produced a son. Lord Pembleton passed soon after, and now she is in complete power of his fortune until the boy is of age. Smart woman. To have such inde-

pendence. She probably won't want to marry again, which I'm sure suits Turner perfectly.

I had to dance with him once. Lady Rudland insisted upon it. And then, as if the evening could not get any worse, she pulled me aside to comment on my sudden popularity. The Duke of Ashbourne danced with me! (Exclamation point hers.) He is married, of course, and very happily, but still, he does not waste his time with little misses just out of the schoolroom. Lady R. was just thrilled and so very proud of me. I thought I might cry.

I am home now, however, and I resolve to invent some sort of illness so that I do not have to go out for a few days. A week, if I can manage it.

Do you know what disturbs me the most? Lady Pembleton is not even considered beautiful. Oh, she is not unpleasing to look at, but she is no diamond of the first water. Her hair is plain brown, and so are her eyes.

Just like mine.

Chapter 9

Miranda spent the next week pretending to read Greek tragedies. It was impossible to keep her mind focused on a book long enough to actually read one, but as long as she had to stare at the words on the page every now and then, she figured she might as well choose something that suited her mood.

A comedy would have made her cry. And a love story, God forbid, would have made her want to perish on the spot.

Olivia, who'd never been known for her lack of interest in other people's business, had been relentless in her quest to discover the reason for Miranda's morose mood. In fact, the only times she wasn't interrogating Miranda were when she was trying to brighten her mood. She was in the midst of one of these cheering-up sessions, regaling Miranda with the tales of a certain countess who'd thrown her husband out of the house until he agreed to let her buy four miniature poodles as pets, when Lady Rudland rapped on the door.

"Oh, good," she said, poking her head into the room. "You're both here. Olivia, don't sit like that. It's very un-ladylike."

Olivia dutifully adjusted her position before asking, "What is it, Mama?"

"I wanted to inform you that we have been invited to Lady Chester's home for a country visit next week."

"Who is Lady Chester?" Miranda inquired, setting her now dog-eared volume of Aeschylus down in her lap.

"A cousin of ours," Olivia replied. "Third or fourth, I can't remember."

"Second," Lady Rudland corrected. "And I accepted the invitation on our behalf. It would be rude not to attend, as she's such a close relation."

"Is Turner going?" Olivia asked.

Miranda wanted to thank her friend a thousand times over for asking the question she didn't dare voice.

"He had better. He has wormed his way out of his familial obligations for far too long," Lady Rudland said with uncharacteristic steeliness. "If he doesn't, he'll have to answer to me."

"Heavens," Olivia deadpanned. "What a terrifying thought."

"I don't know what is wrong with the boy," Lady Rudland said with a shake of her head. "It is almost as if he is avoiding us."

No, Miranda thought with a sad smile, *only me*.

* * *

Turner tapped his foot impatiently as he waited for his family to come down. For about the fifteenth time that morning, he found himself wishing that he were more like the rest of the men of the *ton*, most of whom either ignored their mothers or treated them like pieces of fluff. But somehow his mother had managed to get him to agree to this blasted week-long house party, at which, of course, Miranda would also be in attendance.

He was an idiot. That fact was growing clearer to him by the day.

An idiot who had apparently offended fate, because as soon as his mother arrived in the front hall she said, "You're going to have to ride with Miranda."

Apparently the gods had a sick sense of humor.

He cleared his throat. "Do you think that's wise, Mother?"

She gave him an impatient look. "You're not going to seduce the girl, are you?"

Holy bloody hell. "Of course not. It's just that she has her reputation to consider. What will people say when we arrive in the same carriage? Everyone will know we've spent several hours alone."

"Everyone thinks of the two of you as brother and sister. And we shall meet up a mile from Chester Park and switch everyone about so that you may arrive with your father. There won't be any problem. Besides, your father and I need to have a word alone with Olivia."

"What did she do now?"

"Apparently she called Georgiana Elster a silly widgeon."

"Georgiana Elster *is* a silly widgeon."

"To her face, Turner! She said it to her face."

"Lack of judgment on her part but nothing that requires a two-hour scolding, I think."

"That's not all."

Turner sighed. His mother's mind was made up. Two hours alone with Miranda. What had he done to deserve this torture?

"She called Sir Robert Kent an overgrown stoat."

"To his face, I suppose."

Lady Rudland nodded.

"What *is* a stoat?"

"I haven't the slightest idea, but I can't imagine it's complimentary."

"A stoat is a weasel, I think," Miranda said as she entered the hall in a creamy blue traveling dress. She smiled at them both, annoyingly composed.

"Good morning, Miranda," Lady Rudland said briskly. "You're to ride with Turner."

"I am?" She nearly choked on her words and had to cover for it with a few coughs. Turner took a rather juvenile satisfaction in that.

"Yes. Lord Rudland and I need to have a word with Olivia. She has been saying rather inappropriate things in public."

A groan was heard on the stairs. Three heads swiveled around to watch Olivia as she descended. "Is that really necessary, Mama? I didn't mean any harm. I would never have called Lady Finchcoombe a miserable harridan if I thought it might get back to her."

The blood drained from Lady Rudland's face. "You called Lady Finchcoombe a miserable *what*?"

"You didn't know about that?" Olivia asked weakly.

"Turner, Miranda, I suggest you leave now. We will see you in a few hours."

They walked in silence to the waiting carriage, and Turner held out his hand to assist Miranda as she climbed up. Her gloved fingers felt electric in his own, but she must not have felt the same, because she sounded singularly un-affected as she muttered, "I hope my presence is not too much a trial for you, my lord."

Turner's reply was a cross between a grunt and a sigh.

"I didn't arrange this, you know."

He sat down across from her. "I know."

"I had no idea we'd—" She looked up. "You know?"

"I know. Mother was quite determined to get Olivia alone."

"Oh. Thank you for believing me, then."

He let out a pent-up breath, staring out the window for a moment as the carriage lurched into motion. "Miranda, I don't think you're some sort of habitual liar."

"No, of course not," she said quickly. "But you did look rather furious when you helped me into the carriage."

"I was furious at fate, Miranda, not you."

"What an improvement," she said coldly. "Well, if you'll excuse me. I brought along a book." She twisted around so that as much of her back was facing him as possible and began to read.

Turner waited about thirty seconds before asking, "What's that you're reading?"

Miranda froze, then moved slowly, as if completing the most odious of chores. She held up the book.

"Aeschylus. How depressing."

"It fits my mood."

"Oh dear, was that a barb?"

"Don't be condescending, Turner. Under the circumstances, it's hardly appropriate."

He raised his brows. "And what, precisely, might that mean?"

"It means that after all that has, er, *occurred* between us, your superior attitude is no longer justified."

"My, but that was a long sentence."

Miranda let her glare be her reply. This time, when she picked up the book again, it covered her face entirely.

Turner chuckled and leaned back, surprised by how much he was enjoying himself. The quiet ones were always the most interesting. Miranda might not ever choose to place herself at the center of attention, but she could hold her own in a conversation with wit and style. Baiting her was great fun. And he didn't feel the least bit guilty for it. For all her disgruntled behavior, he had no doubt that she enjoyed the verbal sparring every bit as much as he did.

This trip might not be quite so hellish. He just had to make sure he kept her engaged in this sort of amusing conversation and didn't stare too long at her mouth.

He really liked her mouth.

But he wasn't going to think about that. He was going to resume their conversation and try to enjoy himself the way he had before they had become embroiled in this mess. He rather missed his old friendship with Miranda, and he supposed that as long as they were trapped together in this carriage for two hours, he might as well see what he could do to patch things up.

"What are you reading?" he asked.

She looked up irritably. "Aeschylus. Didn't you already ask me that?"

"I meant *which* Aeschylus," he improvised.

To his great amusement, she had to look down at the book before replying, "*The Eumenides.*"

He winced.

"You don't like it?"

"All those furious women? I think not. Give me a nice adventure story any day."

"I like furious women."

"You feel a great empathy? Oh dear, no, don't grind your teeth, Miranda, you'd not enjoy a visit to the dentist, I promise you."

Her expression was such that he could do nothing but laugh. "Oh, don't be so sensitive, Miranda."

Still glaring at him, she muttered, "So sorry, my lord," and then somehow managed to drop an obsequious curtsy right there in the middle of the carriage.

Turner's chuckles exploded into rollicking laughter. "Oh, Miranda," he said, wiping his eyes. "You are a gem."

When he finally recovered, she was staring at him like he was a lunatic. He thought briefly about holding up his hands like claws and letting out some sort of strange, animalistic sound, just to confirm her suspicions. But in the end he just sat back and grinned.

She shook her head. "I don't understand you."

He didn't respond, not wishing to let the conversation slip back into serious waters. She picked up her book again, and this time he busied himself by timing how many minutes passed before she turned a page. When the score was five and zero, he quirked a smile. "Difficult reading?"

Miranda slowly lowered the book and leveled a deadly gaze in his direction. "Excuse me?"

"A lot of big words?"

She just stared at him.

"You haven't turned a page since you started."

She let out a vocal growl and with great determination flipped a page over.

"Is that English or Greek?"

"I beg your pardon?"

"If it's the Greek, it might explain your speed."

Her lips parted.

"Or lack thereof," he said with a shrug.

"I can read Greek," she bit off.

"Yes, and it's a noteworthy achievement."

She looked down at her hands. They were gripping the book so tightly, her knuckles were turning white. "Thank you," she ground out.

But he wasn't done. "Uncommon for a female, wouldn't you say?"

This time, she decided to ignore him.

"Olivia can't read in the Greek," he said conversationally.

"Olivia doesn't have a father who does nothing *but* read in the Greek," she said without looking up. She tried to concentrate on the words at the top of the new page, but they didn't make much sense, as she hadn't finished reading the previous one. She hadn't even started.

She tapped a gloved finger against the book as she pretended to read. She didn't suppose there was any way she could flip back to the previous page without his noticing. It didn't matter much anyway, for she doubted she'd manage to get any reading done while he was staring at her in that heavy-lidded way of his. It was deadly, she decided. It made her hot and shivery, and it did this simultaneously *and* while she was thoroughly irritated with the man.

She was fairly certain he had no interest in seducing her, but he was doing a rather good job of it, regardless.

"A peculiar talent, that."

Miranda sucked in her lips and looked up at him. "Yes?"

"Reading without moving your eyes."

She counted to three before responding. "Some of us don't have to mouth out the words when we read, Turner."

"Touché, Miranda. I knew there was still some spark left in you."

Her nails bit into the cushioned seat. *One, two, three. Keep counting. Four, five, six.* At this rate she was going to have to go to fifty if she wanted to control her temper.

Turner saw her moving her head slightly along some unknown rhythm and grew curious. "What are you doing?"

Eighteen, nineteen— "What?"

"What are you doing?"

Twenty. "You're growing extremely annoying, Turner."

"I'm persistent." He grinned. "I thought you of all people

would appreciate the trait. Now, what were you doing? Your head was bobbing along in a most curious fashion."

"If you must know," she said cuttingly, "I was counting in my head so that I might control my temper."

He regarded her for a moment, then said, "One shudders to think what you might have said to me if you hadn't stopped to count first."

"I'm losing my patience."

"No!" he said with mock disbelief.

She picked the book up again, trying to dismiss him.

"Stop torturing that poor book, Miranda. We both know you aren't reading it."

"Will you just leave me alone!" she finally exploded.

"What number are you up to?"

"What?"

"What number? You said you were counting so as not to offend my tender sensibilities."

"I don't know. Twenty. Thirty. I don't know. I stopped counting about four insults ago."

"You made it all the way up to thirty? You've been lying to me, Miranda. I don't think you've lost your patience with me at all."

"Yes . . . I . . . have," she ground out.

"I don't think so."

"Aaaargh!" She threw the book at him. It clipped him neatly on the side of his head.

"Ouch!"

"Don't be a baby."

"Don't be a tyrant."

"Stop goading me!"

"I wasn't goading you."

"Oh, *please*, Turner."

"Oh, all right," he said petulantly, rubbing the side of his head. "I was goading you. But I wouldn't have done it if you weren't ignoring me."

"Excuse me, but I rather thought you wanted me to ignore you."

"Where the devil did you get that idea?"

Miranda's mouth fell open. "Are you mad? You have avoided me like the plague for at least the last fortnight. You've even avoided your mother just to avoid me."

"Now that's not true."

"Tell that to your mother."

He winced. "Miranda, I would like for us to be friends."

She shook her head. Were there any crueler words in the English language? "It's not possible."

"Why not?"

"You can't have it both ways," Miranda continued, using every ounce of her energy to keep her voice from shaking. "You can't kiss me and then say you wish to be friends. You can't humiliate me the way you did at the Worthingtons' and then claim that you like me."

"We must forget what happened," he said softly. "We must put it behind us, if not for the sake of our friendship, then for my family."

"Can you do that?" Miranda demanded. "Can you truly forget? Because I cannot."

"Of course you can," he said, a little too easily.

"I lack your sophistication, Turner," she said, and then added bitterly, "Or perhaps I lack your shallowness."

"I'm not shallow, Miranda," he shot back. "I'm sensible. Lord knows, one of us has to be."

She wished she had something to say. She wished she had some scathing retort that would cut him off at the knees, render him speechless, leaving him quivering in a gelatinous, messy heap of pathetic rot.

But instead she just had herself, and the horrible, angry tears burning behind her eyes. And she wasn't even certain she could manage a proper glare, so she looked away, counting the buildings as they passed by her window and wishing that she were anywhere else.

Any*one* else.

And that was the worst, because in all her life, even with a best friend who was prettier, richer, and better-connected than she was, Miranda had never wished to be anyone other than who she was.

Turner had, in his life, done things of which he was not proud. He had drunk too much and vomited on a priceless rug. He had gambled with money he did not have. He had once even ridden his horse too hard and with too little care and left the horse lame for a week.

But never had he felt quite so low as he did when he looked at Miranda's profile, aimed so determinedly toward the window.

So determinedly *away* from him.

He did not speak for a long while. They passed out of London, through the outskirts where the buildings grew fewer and farther between, and then finally into open, rolling fields.

She didn't look at him once. He knew. He was watching.

And so finally, since he could not tolerate another hour of this silence, nor could he bring himself to ponder what, exactly, this silence meant, he spoke.

"I do not mean to insult, Miranda," he said quietly, "but I know when something is a bad idea. And dallying with you is an *extremely* bad idea."

She didn't turn, but he heard her say, "Why?"

He stared at her in disbelief. "What are you thinking, Miranda? Don't you give a damn for your reputation? If word gets out about us, you'll be ruined."

"Or you'll have to marry me," she said in a low, mocking voice.

"Which I have no intention of doing. You know that." He swore under his breath. Dear God, that had come out wrong. "I don't want to marry anyone," he explained. "You know *that*, as well."

"What I *know*," she shot back, her eyes flashing with unconcealed fury, "is that—" And then she stopped, clamping her mouth shut and crossing her arms.

"What?" he demanded.

She turned back to the window. "You wouldn't understand." And then: "Nor would you listen."

Her contemptuous tone was like nails under his skin. "Oh, please. Petulance does not suit you."

She whirled around. "And how should I act? Tell me, what am I supposed to feel?"

His lip curled. "Grateful?"

"Grateful?"

He sat back, his entire body a study of insolence. "I could have seduced you, you know. Easily. But I didn't."

She gasped and drew back, and when she spoke, her voice was low and lethal. "You're hateful, Turner."

"I'm just telling you the truth. And do you know why I didn't do more? Why I didn't peel your nightgown from your body and lay you down and take you right there on the sofa?"

Her eyes widened and her breath grew audible, and he knew he was being crude and crass and, yes, hateful, but he could not stop himself, could not stop the bluntness, because, damn it, she had to understand. She had to understand who he really was, and what he was capable of, and what he was not.

And this—*this*. Her. He had managed to do the honorable thing for her, and she wasn't even grateful?

"I'll tell you," he practically hissed. "I stopped out of *respect* for you. And I'll tell you something—" He stopped, swore, and she looked at him in question, daringly, provokingly, as if to say— *You don't even know what you mean to say.*

But that was the problem. He did know, and he had been about to tell her how much he had wanted her. How if they had been anywhere but his parents' home, he was not certain he would have stopped.

He was not certain he could have stopped.

But she did not need to know that. She should not know it. That sort of power over him, he did not need.

"Can you believe it," he muttered, more to himself than to her. "I did not want to ruin your future."

"Leave my future to me," she replied angrily. "I know what I'm doing."

He snorted disdainfully. "You're twenty years old. You think you know everything."

She glared at him.

"When I was twenty, I thought I knew everything." he said with a shrug.

Her eyes turned sad. "So did I," she said softly.

Turner tried to ignore the unpleasant knot of guilt twisting about in his belly. He wasn't even sure *why* he felt guilty, and in fact the whole thing was ridiculous. He shouldn't be made to feel guilty for *not* taking her innocence, and all he could think to say was, "You'll thank me for this someday."

She looked at him in disbelief. "You sound like your mother."

"You're getting surly."

"Can you blame me? You're treating me like a child, when you know very well I'm a woman."

The knot of guilt grew tentacles.

"I can make my own decisions," she said defiantly.

"Obviously not." He leaned forward, a dangerous glint in his eyes. "Or you wouldn't have let me push down your dress last week and kiss your breasts."

She blushed with the deep crimson of shame, and her voice shook with accusation as she said, "Don't try to say that this is my fault."

He closed his eyes and raked both hands through his hair, aware that he had just said something very, very stupid. "Of course it's not your fault, Miranda. Please forget I said that."

"Just like you want me to forget you kissed me." Her voice was devoid of emotion.

"Yes." He looked over at her and saw a kind of deadness in her eyes, something he had never before seen on her face. "Oh, God, Miranda, don't look like that."

"Don't do this, do do that," she burst out. "Forget this, don't forget that. Make up your mind, Turner. I don't know what you want. And I don't think you do, either."

"I'm nine years older than you," he said in an awful voice. "*Don't* talk down to me."

"So sorry, Your Highness."

"Don't do this, Miranda."

And her face, which had been so closed and bitter, suddenly exploded with emotion. "Stop telling me what to do! Did it ever occur to you that I *wanted* you to kiss me? That I wanted you to want me? And you do, you know. I'm not so naive that you can convince me you don't."

Turner could only stare at her, whispering, "You don't know what you're saying."

"Yes, I do!" Her eyes flashed, and her hands curled into shaking fists, and he had a terrible, awful premonition that this was it, this was the moment. Everything depended on this moment, and he knew, without even a thought to what she would say, and what he would say in return, that it would not end well.

"I know exactly what I'm saying," she said. "I want you."

His body tightened, and his heart thundered in his chest. But he could not allow this to continue. "Miranda, you only think you want me," he said quickly. "You have never kissed anyone else, and—"

"Don't patronize me." Her eyes locked with his, and they were hot with desire. "I know what I want, and I want you."

He took a ragged breath. He deserved to be sainted for what he was about to say. "No, you don't. It's an infatuation."

"Damn you!" she exploded. "Are you blind? Are you deaf, dumb, and blind? It's not an infatuation, you idiot! I love you!"

Oh, my God.

"I've always loved you! Since I first met you nine years ago. I've loved you all along, every minute."

"Oh, my God."

"And don't try to tell me that it's a childhood crush because it's not. It may have been at one point, but it's not any longer."

He said nothing. He just sat there like an imbecile and stared at her.

"I just—I know my own heart, and I love you, Turner. And if you have even the tiniest shred of decency, you'll say something, because I've said *everything* I possibly can, and I can't bear the silence, and—oh, for heaven's sake! Will you at least blink?"

He couldn't even manage that.

Chapter 10

Two days later, Turner still seemed to be in something of a daze.

Miranda hadn't tried to speak with him, hadn't even approached him, but every now and then, she would catch him looking at her with an unfathomable expression. She knew that she had unsettled him because he didn't even have the presence of mind to look away when their eyes met. He'd just stare at her for a few moments longer, then blink and turn away.

Miranda kept hoping that just one time he'd nod.

Still, for most of the weekend they managed to never be in the same place at the same time. If Turner went riding, Miranda explored the orangery. If Miranda took a walk in the gardens, Turner played cards.

Very civilized. Very adult.

And, Miranda thought more than once, very heart-breaking.

They did not see each other even at meals. Lady Chester

prided herself on her matchmaking abilities, and because it was unfathomable that Turner and Miranda might become romantically involved, she did not seat them near each other. Turner was always surrounded by a gaggle of pretty young things, and Miranda more often than not was relegated to keeping company with graying widowers. She supposed Lady Chester did not hold much stock in her ability to snare an eligible husband. Olivia, by contrast, was always seated with three extremely handsome and wealthy men, one to her left, one to her right, and one across the table.

Miranda learned quite a bit about home remedies for gout.

Lady Chester had, however, left the pairings for one of her planned events to chance, and that was her annual treasure hunt. The guests were to search in teams of two. And since the aim of all the guests was to get married or embark upon an affair (depending, of course, on one's current marital status), each team would be made up of one male and one female. Lady Chester had written out her guests' names on slips of paper and then put all the ladies in one bag and the gentlemen in the other.

She was presently dipping her hand into one of these bags. Miranda felt sick to her stomach.

"Sir Anthony Waldove and . . ." Lady Chester thrust her hand into the other bag. "Lady Rudland."

Miranda exhaled, not realizing until then that she had been holding her breath. She would do anything to be paired up with Turner—and anything to avoid it.

"Poor Mama," Olivia whispered in her ear. "Sir Anthony

Waldove is really quite dim. She will have to do all the work."

Miranda put her finger to her lips. "I can't hear."

"Mr. William Fitzhugh and . . . Miss Charlotte Gladdish."

"With whom do you wish to be paired?" Olivia asked.

Miranda shrugged. If she was not assigned to Turner, it didn't really matter.

"Lord Turner and . . ."

Miranda's heart stopped beating.

". . . Lady Olivia Bevelstoke. Isn't that sweet? We have been doing this for five years, and this is our first brother-sister team."

Miranda began to breathe again, not certain if she was disappointed or relieved.

Olivia, however, had no doubt of her own feelings. "*Quel disaster*," she muttered, in her typically broken French. "All these gentlemen, and I'm stuck with my brother. When is the next time I will be allowed to wander off alone with a gentleman? It's a waste, I tell you, a waste."

"It could be worse," Miranda said pragmatically. "Not all the gentlemen here are, er, gentlemen. At least you know that Turner won't attempt to ravish you."

"It's a small consolation, I assure you."

"Livvy—"

"Shush, they just called out Lord Westholme."

"And for the ladies . . ." Lady Chester trilled. "Miss Miranda Cheever!"

Olivia nudged her. "Lucky you."

Miranda just shrugged.

"Oh, don't act like such a jade," Olivia admonished her. "Don't you think he's divine? I'd give my left foot to switch places with you. Say, why *don't* we switch places? There aren't any rules against it. And you like Turner, after all."

Only too much, Miranda thought gloomily.

"Well? Will you do it? Unless you have your eye on Lord Westholme as well?"

"No," Miranda replied, trying not to sound dismayed. "No, of course not."

"Then let's do it," Olivia said excitedly.

Miranda didn't know if she ought to jump at the chance or run to her room and hide in the wardrobe. Either way, she didn't have much of an excuse to refuse Olivia's request. Livvy would certainly want to know why she didn't want to be alone with Turner. And then what would she say? *I just told your brother that I love him, and I'm afraid that he hates me? I can't be alone with Turner because I'm afraid he might ravish me? I can't be alone with him because I'm afraid I might ravish him?*

Just thought of it made Miranda want to laugh.

Or cry.

But Olivia was staring at her expectantly, in that Olivia-ish way she'd perfected at, oh, the age of three, and Miranda realized that it didn't really matter what she said or did, she was going to end up partnered with Turner.

It wasn't that Olivia was spoiled, although she was, perhaps, a little bit. It was just that any attempts on Miranda's part to dodge the issue would be met by an interrogation so precise and so persistent that she would surely end up revealing everything.

At which point she would have to flee the country. Or at least find a bed to crawl under. For a week.

So she sighed. And she nodded. And she thought about bright sides and silver linings and deduced that neither was in evidence.

Olivia grabbed her hand and squeezed. "Oh, Miranda, thank you!"

"I hope Turner doesn't mind," Miranda said cautiously.

"Oh, he won't mind. He'll probably get down on his knees and thank his lucky stars he doesn't have to spend the entire afternoon with me. He thinks I'm a brat."

"He does not."

"He does. He often tells me I ought to be more like you."

Miranda turned in surprise. "Does he really?"

"Mmm-hmm." But Olivia's attention was back on Lady Chester, who was completing the task of matching off the ladies and gentlemen. When she was done, the men rose to seek out their partners.

"Miranda and I have exchanged places!" Olivia exclaimed when Turner reached her side. "You don't mind, do you?"

He said, "Of course not," but Miranda wouldn't have bet even a farthing that he was telling the truth. After all, what else could he say?

Lord Westholme arrived soon after, and although he was polite enough to try to hide it, he appeared delighted by the switch.

Turner said nothing.

Olivia shot Miranda a perplexed frown, which Miranda ignored.

"Here is your first clue!" Lady Chester called out. "Would the gentlemen please come forward to collect their envelopes?"

Turner and Lord Westholme walked to the center of the room and returned a few seconds later with crisp white envelopes.

"Let's open ours outside," Olivia said to Lord Westholme, flashing a mischievous smile at Turner and Miranda. "I wouldn't want anyone to overhear us while we discuss our strategy."

The other competitors apparently had the same idea, because a moment later, Turner and Miranda found themselves very much alone.

He took a deep breath and planted his hands on his hips.

"I didn't ask to switch," Miranda said quickly. "Olivia wanted me to."

He raised a brow.

"I didn't!" she protested. "Livvy is interested in Lord Westholme, and she thinks you think she's a brat."

"She *is* a brat."

Miranda was not particularly inclined to disagree at that moment, but she nonetheless said, "She could hardly have known what she was doing when she paired us together."

"You could have refused the switch," he said pointedly.

"Oh? And on what grounds?" Miranda demanded testily. He didn't have to be *quite* so upset that they had ended up as partners. "How would you suggest I explain to her that we ought not spend the afternoon together?"

Turner didn't answer because, she presumed, he had no

answer. He merely turned on his heel and stalked out of the room.

Miranda watched him for a moment, and then, when it became apparent that he had no intention of waiting for her, she let out a little huff and scurried along after him. "Turner, will you slow down!"

He stopped short, the exaggerated motions of his body clearly displaying his impatience with her.

When she reached his side, his face held a bored, annoyed expression. "Yes?" he drawled.

She did her best to maintain her temper. "Could we at least try to be civil to one another?"

"I'm not angry with you, Miranda."

"Well, you certainly do a good imitation of it."

"I'm frustrated," he said, in a way that she was fairly certain was meant to shock her. And then he grumbled, "In more ways than you could possibly imagine."

Miranda could imagine and often did, and she blushed. "Open the envelope, will you?" she muttered.

He handed it to her, and she tore it open. "'Find your next clue 'neath a miniature sun,'" she read.

She glanced over at him. He wasn't even looking at her. He wasn't particularly *not* looking at her, he was just staring off and up into nothingness, looking as if he'd rather be somewhere else.

"The orangery," she declared, almost at the point at which she did not care if he was going to participate or not. "I've always thought that oranges were like tiny pieces of the sun."

He nodded brusquely and gestured with his arm for

her to lead. But there was something rather impolite and condescending about his movements, and she felt an overwhelming urge to grind her teeth together and growl as she stalked forward.

Without a word, she marched out of the house toward the orangery. He really couldn't wait to get this deuced treasure hunt over with, could he? Well, she'd be only too happy to oblige him. She was rather clever; these clues shouldn't be too difficult to decipher. They could be back in their respective rooms in an hour.

Sure enough, they found a pile of envelopes underneath an orange tree. Wordlessly, Turner reached down for one and then handed it to her.

With equal silence, Miranda tore the envelope open. She read the clue and then handed it to Turner.

THE ROMANS COULD HELP YOU FIND
THE NEXT CLUE.

If he was irritated by her silent treatment, he did not show it. He merely folded up the slip of paper and looked at her with an expression of bored expectation.

"It's underneath an arch," she said in a matter-of-fact tone. "The Romans were the first to use them in architecture. There are several in the garden."

Sure enough, ten minutes later they had retrieved another envelope.

"Do you know how many clues we must get through before we're done?" Turner asked.

It was his first sentence since they'd begun, and it concerned when he might be rid of her. Miranda gritted her teeth at the insult, shook her head, and opened the envelope. She had to remain poised. If she let him make even one chink in her facade, she'd fall completely to pieces. Schooling her features into impassivity, she unfolded the slip of paper and read, " 'You'll need to hunt for the next clue.' "

"Something to do with hunting, I imagine," Turner said.

She lifted her brows. "You've decided to participate?"

"Don't be petty, Miranda."

She let out an irritated exhale and decided to ignore him. "There is a small hunting lodge to the east. It will take us approximately fifteen minutes to walk there."

"And how did you discover this lodge?"

"I've been walking quite a bit."

"Whenever I'm in the house, I imagine."

Miranda saw no reason to deny his statement.

Turner squinted toward the horizon. "Do you think Lady Chester would send us so far from the main house?"

"I've been right up to now," Miranda retorted.

"So you have," he said with a bored shrug. "Lead on."

They had trudged through the woods for about ten minutes when Turner cast a dubious eye at the darkening sky. "Looks like rain," he said laconically.

Miranda looked up. He was right. "What do you want to do?"

"Right this minute?"

"No, next week. Of course right this minute, you dolt."

"A dolt?" He smiled, his white teeth nearly blinding her. "You wound me."

Miranda's eyes narrowed. "Why are you suddenly being so nice to me?"

"Was I?" he murmured, and she was mortified.

"Oh, Miranda," he continued with a patronizing sigh, "maybe I like to be nice to you."

"Maybe you don't."

"Maybe I do," he said pointedly. "And maybe you sometimes just make it difficult."

"Maybe," she said with equal arrogance, "it's going to rain, and we ought to get going."

A clap of thunder drowned out her last word. "Maybe you're right," Turner replied, grimacing at the sky. "Are we closer to the lodge or the house?"

"The lodge."

"Then let's hurry. I have no wish to get caught in an electrical storm in the middle of the woods."

Miranda could not disagree with him, despite her concerns for propriety, so she started walking faster toward the hunting lodge. But they had hardly gone ten yards when the first raindrops fell. Another ten yards and it was a torrential downpour.

Turner grabbed her hand and began to run, pulling her along the path. Miranda stumbled along behind him, wondering if it was any use to run, as they were already soaked to the skin.

A few minutes later they found themselves in front of the two-room hunting lodge. Turner took hold of the doorknob and turned it, but the door did not budge. "Bloody hell," he muttered.

"Is it locked?" Miranda asked through clattering teeth.

He nodded curtly.

"What are we going to do?"

He answered her by slamming his shoulder into the door.

Miranda bit her lip. That had to hurt. She tried a window. Locked.

Turner shoved the door again.

Miranda slipped around to the side of the house and tried another window. With a little effort it slid up. At the same moment, she heard Turner come tumbling through the doorway. She briefly considered crawling through the window anyway, but then decided to do the magnanimous thing and lowered it. He had gone to a great deal of trouble to break down the door. The least she could do was let him believe himself her knight in shining armor.

"Miranda!"

She came running back around front. "I'm right here." She hurried into the house and shut the door behind her.

"What the devil were you doing out there?"

"Being a far kinder person than you could imagine," she muttered, now wishing she'd gone through the window.

"Eh?"

"Just looking around," she said. "Did you damage the door?"

"Not very much. The deadbolt is broken, though."

She winced. "Did you hurt your shoulder?"

"It's fine." He peeled off his sodden coat and hung it on a peg on the wall. "Take off your . . ." He motioned to her light pelisse. ". . . whatever it is you call that."

Miranda hugged her arms to herself and shook her head.

He gave her an impatient look. "It's a bit late for missish modesty."

"Someone could come in at any moment."

"I doubt it," he said. "I imagine they're all safe and warm in Lord Chester's study, gazing upon all of the heads he's got mounted on the wall."

Miranda tried to ignore the lump that had just sprouted in her throat. She'd forgotten what an avid hunter Lord Chester was. She quickly scanned the room. Turner was correct. Not a white envelope in sight. No one was likely to stumble across them anytime soon, and from the looks of it outside, the rain had no intention of letting up.

"Please tell me you're not one of those ladies who chooses modesty over health."

"No, of course not." Miranda shrugged off her pelisse and hung it on the peg next to his. "Do you know how to build a fire?" she asked.

"Provided we've dry wood."

"Oh, but there must be some here. It's a hunting lodge, after all." She looked up at Turner with hopeful eyes. "Don't most men like to be warm while they hunt?"

"*After* they hunt," he corrected absently as he looked around for wood. "And most men, Lord Chester included, I imagine, are sufficiently lazy that the short trip back to the main house is far more preferable than putting in the effort to build a fire here."

"Oh." Miranda stood still for a moment, watching him as he moved about the room. Then she said, "I'm going to go into the other room to see if there are any dry clothes we can use."

"Good idea." Turner watched her back as she disappeared from sight. The rain had plastered her shirt to her body, and he could see the warm, pink tones of her skin through the wet material. His loins, which had been unbelievably cold from the soaking, grew hot and heavy with remarkable speed. He cursed and then stubbed his toe as he lifted the lid off a wooden chest to look for wood.

Dear God, what had he done to deserve this? If he had been handed a pen and paper and ordered to compose the perfect torture, he would never have come up with this. And he had a very active imagination.

"I found some wood in here!"

Turner followed the sound of Miranda's voice into the next room.

"It's over there." She pointed to a pile of logs near a fireplace. "I reckon Lord Chester prefers to use this fireplace when he's here."

Turner eyed the large bed with its soft quilts and fluffy pillows. He had a fairly good idea why Lord Chester preferred this room, and it did not involve the somewhat portly Lady Chester. He immediately put a log in the fireplace.

"Don't you think we ought to use the one in the other room?" Miranda asked. She, too, had seen the large bed.

"This one has obviously seen more use. It is dangerous to use a dirty chimney. It could be clogged."

Miranda nodded slowly, and he could tell that she was trying very hard not to look uncomfortable. She continued to look for dry clothing while Turner attended to the fire, but all she found were some scratchy-looking old blankets. Turner watched as she draped one over her shoulders.

"Cashmere?" he drawled.

Her eyes widened. She hadn't, he realized, been aware that he had been looking at her. He smiled, or really, it was more of a baring of his teeth. Maybe she was uncomfortable, but damn it, so was he. Did she think this was easy for him? She'd said she loved him, for God's sake. Why the *devil* had she gone and done that? Did she know nothing about men? Could it be possible that she didn't understand that that was the one thing guaranteed to terrify him?

He didn't want to be entrusted with her heart. He didn't want the responsibility. He'd been married. He'd had his own heart crushed, stomped upon, and tossed in a flaming rubbish heap. The last thing he wanted was custody of someone else's, especially Miranda's.

"Use the quilt on the bed," he said with a shrug. It had to be more comfortable than what she'd found.

But she shook her head. "I don't want to muss it. I don't want anyone to know we were here."

"Mmm, yes," he said unkindly, "I'd have to marry you then, wouldn't I?"

She looked so stricken that he muttered an apology. Good Lord, he was turning into someone he didn't particularly like. He didn't want to hurt her. He just wanted to—

Hell, he didn't know what he wanted. He couldn't even think more than ten minutes into the future, just then, couldn't focus on anything beyond keeping his hands to himself.

He busied himself with the fire, letting out a satisfied

grunt when a tiny orange flame finally curled around a log. "Easy now," he murmured, carefully setting a smaller stick near the flame. "There we are, there we are . . . and—*yes*!"

"Turner?"

"Got the fire burning," he mumbled, feeling a trifle foolish for his excitement. He stood and turned. She was still clutching the threadbare blanket around her shoulders.

"A fine lot of good that'll do you once it's soaked from your shirt," he commented.

"I don't have much choice, do I?"

"That's up to you, I suppose. As for me, I'm drying off." His fingers went to the buttons on his shirt.

"Maybe I should go to the other room," she whispered.

Turner noted that she didn't move an inch. He shrugged, and then he shrugged his shirt off entirely.

"I should go," she whispered again.

"Then go," he said. But his lips curved.

She opened her mouth as if to say something, then closed it. "I—" She broke off, a look of horror crossing her features.

"You what?"

"I should go." And this time she did, leaving the room with alacrity.

Turner shook his head as she left. Women. Did anyone understand them? First she said she loved him. Then she said she wanted to seduce him. Then she avoided him for two days. Now she looked terrified.

He shook his head again, this time faster, his hair spraying water across the room. Wrapping one of the blankets around his shoulders, he stood in front of the fire and dried himself off. His legs felt damned uncomfortable, though. He shot a sidelong look at the door. Miranda had shut it behind her when she left, and given her present state of maidenly embarrassment, he doubted she'd enter without knocking.

He peeled off his breeches with great haste. The fire began to warm him almost immediately. He glanced again at the door. Just to be on the safe side, he lowered the blanket and tucked it around his waist. It looked a bit like a kilt, actually.

He thought again about the expression on her face just before she'd run from the room. Maidenly embarrassment and something else. Was it fascination? Desire?

And what had she been about to say? It hadn't been "I should go," which was what she *did* say.

If he had stepped up to her, taken her face in his hands, and whispered, "Tell me," what would she have said?

3 JULY 1819

> *I almost told him again. And I think he knew it. I think he knew what I was going to say.*

Chapter 11

Turner was so busy thinking about how much he'd like to touch Miranda—anywhere and everywhere—that he completely forgot that she must be freezing her backside off in the other room. It was only when he realized that he was finally toasty warm that it occurred to him that she was not.

Cursing himself up and down and ten times for an idiot, he stood up and strode to the door that she had shut between them. He yanked it open and then uttered another stream of curses when he saw her huddled on the floor, shaking with near violence.

"You little fool," he said. "Are you trying to kill yourself?"

She looked up, her eyes widening at the sight of him. Turner suddenly remembered he was barely dressed.

"Bugger it," he muttered to himself, then shook his head in exasperation and hauled her to her feet.

Miranda snapped out of her daze and began to struggle. "What are you doing?"

"Shaking some sense into you."

"I'm perfectly fine," she said, though her shivers proved her a liar.

"The devil you are. I'm freezing just talking to you. Come by the fire."

She looked longingly at the orange flames crackling in the next room. "Only if you stay here."

"Fine," he said. Anything to get her warm. With a slightly less than gentle prod, he pointed her in the right direction.

Miranda stopped near the fire and held her hands out. A low moan of contentment escaped her lips, traveling across the room and punching Turner right in the gut.

He stepped forward, mesmerized by the pale, almost translucent skin of the back of her neck.

Miranda sighed again, then turned around to warm her back. She jumped away an inch, startled by the sight of him standing so close. "You said you'd leave," she accused.

"I lied." He shrugged. "I haven't the least bit of faith that you'll dry yourself off properly."

"I'm not a child."

He glanced down at her breasts. Her day dress was white, and plastered to her skin as it was, he could just make out the dark blush of her nipples. "Clearly, you are not."

Her arms flew to her chest.

"Turn around if you don't want me looking at you."

She did, but not before her mouth fell open at his audacity.

Turner stared at her back for a long moment. It was nearly as lovely as the front of her had been. The skin on her neck was somehow beautiful, and a few tendrils of her hair had escaped her coiffure and were curling from the damp. She smelled like wet roses, and it took all his strength not to reach out and slide his hand down the length of her arm.

No, not her arm, her hip. Or maybe her leg. Or maybe—

He took a ragged breath.

"Is something wrong?" She didn't turn around, but her voice sounded nervous.

"Not at all. Are you warming up?"

"Oh, yes." But even as she said that, she shivered.

Before Turner could give himself the chance to talk himself out of it, he reached out and unfastened her skirt.

A strangled yelp emerged from her mouth.

"You'll never get warm with this thing clinging to you like an icicle." He started to pull the fabric down.

"I don't think . . . I know . . . This really . . ."

"Yes?"

"This is a very bad idea."

"Probably." The skirt fell to the floor in a sodden heap, leaving her clad in her thin chemise, which clung like a second skin.

"Oh, my God." She tried to cover herself, but she obviously didn't know where to start. She crossed her arms, then moved one hand down to cover where her legs met. Then she must have realized that she wasn't even facing him, so she reached around and put her hands on her backside.

Turner half expected her to squeeze.

"Would you please just go away?" she said in a mortified whisper.

He meant to. Dear God, he knew he ought to obey her
request. But his legs steadfastly refused to move, and
he couldn't take his eyes off the sight of her exquisitely
rounded backside covered by her slender hands.

Hands that were still shaking from the cold.

He cursed again, remembering just why he had yanked
off her skirt to begin with. "Get closer to the fire," he ordered.

"Any closer and I'll be in it!" she snapped. "Just go
away."

He took a step back. He liked her better when she was
spitting fire.

"Away!"

He walked to the door and shut it. Miranda remained utterly still for a moment, then finally let the blanket around
her shoulders fall to the floor as she knelt before the fire.

Turner's heart thumped loudly in his chest—so loud, in
fact, he was surprised it didn't alert her to his presence.

She sighed and stretched.

He grew even harder—a feat he didn't think possible.

She lifted her heavy tresses off her neck and rolled her
head around languorously.

Turner groaned.

Miranda's head spun around. "You knave!" she spat
out, forgetting to cover herself.

"Knave?" He had to raise a brow at the old-fashioned
word.

"Knave, rake, devil, whatever you want to call it."

"Guilty as charged, I'm afraid."

"If you were a gentleman, you'd leave."

"But you love me," he said, not sure why he was reminding her of it.

"You are horrid to bring that up," she whispered.

"Why?"

Miranda looked at him sharply, shocked that he'd asked. "Why do I love you? I don't know. You certainly don't deserve it."

"No," he agreed.

"It doesn't matter, anyway. I don't think I love you anymore," she said quickly. Anything to preserve her battered pride. "You were right. It was a schoolgirl infatuation."

"No, it wasn't. And you don't fall out of love with someone so quickly."

Miranda's eyes widened. What was he saying? Did he want her love? "Turner, what do you want?"

"You." The word was the barest of whispers, as if he could hardly bring himself to say it.

"No, you don't," she said, more out of nervousness than anything else. "You said so."

He took a step forward. He'd go to hell for this, but first he would have heaven. "I want you," he said. And he did. He wanted her with more power, more heat and intensity than he could even comprehend. It went beyond desire.

It went beyond need.

It wasn't explainable, and it sure as hell wasn't rational, but it was there, and it could not be denied.

Slowly, he closed the distance between them. Miranda stood frozen by the fire, her lips parted, her breath growing shallow. "What are you going to do?" she whispered.

"That should be obvious by now." And in one fluid movement, he leaned down and scooped her up.

Miranda didn't move, didn't struggle against him. The warmth of his body was intoxicating. It poured into her, melting her bones, making her feel deliciously wanton. "Oh, Turner," she sighed.

"Oh, yes." His lips trailed along the line of her jaw as he laid her gently and reverently on the bed.

In that last moment before he covered her body with his own, Miranda could only stare up at him, thinking that she'd loved him forever, that her every dream, her every waking thought, had been leading to this moment. He hadn't yet uttered the words that would make her heart soar, but just now that didn't seem to matter. His blue eyes blazed so brightly, with such intensity that she thought he must love her a little. And that seemed to be enough.

Enough to make this possible.

Enough to make this right.

Enough to make this perfect.

Miranda sank into the mattress as his weight settled atop her. She reached out to touch his thick hair. "It's so soft," she murmured. "What a waste."

Turner raised his head and looked down at her with amusement. "A waste?"

"On a man," she said with a shy smile. "Like long eyelashes. Women would kill for them."

"They would, would they?" He grinned down at her. "And how do my eyelashes rate?"

"Very, very highly."

"And would you kill for long eyelashes?"

"I would kill for *yours*."

"Really? Don't you think they'd be a bit fair with your dark hair?"

She swatted him playfully. "I want them fluttering against my face, not attached to my eyelids, silly."

"Did you just call me silly?"

She grinned at him. "I did."

"Does this feel silly?" He stroked his hand up her bare leg.

She shook her head, her breath leaving her body in mere seconds.

"Does this?" His hand closed over her breast.

She moaned incoherently.

"Does it?"

"No," she managed to get out.

"How does it feel?"

"Good."

"Is that all?"

"Wonderful."

"And?"

Miranda took a ragged breath, trying not to concentrate on his forefinger, which was tracing lazy circles through the thin silk covering her puckered nipple. And she said the only word that seemed to describe it. "Sparkling."

He smiled with surprise. "Sparkling?"

It was all she could do just to nod. The heat of him touched her everywhere, and he was so solid and heavy and male. Miranda felt as if she were slipping over the edge of a precipice. She was falling, falling, but she didn't want to be saved. She just wanted to take him along with her.

He was nibbling on her ear, and then his mouth was at the hollow of her shoulder, his teeth tugging at the thin strap of her chemise. "How do you feel?" he asked huskily.

"Hot." The one word seemed to describe every inch of her body.

"Mmm, good. I like you that way." His hand stole under the silken fabric and cupped her bare breast.

"Oh, dear God! Oh, Turner!" She arched her back beneath him, inadvertently giving him a bigger handful.

"God or me?" he said teasingly.

Miranda's breath was coming in short gasps. "I . . . don't . . . know."

Turner slid his other hand under the hem of her chemise and pushed it up until he felt her softly curved hip. "Under the circumstances," he murmured into her neck, "I think it's me."

She smiled weakly. "Please, no religion." She did not need to be reminded that her actions went against every tenet she'd been taught in church, school, home, and everywhere else.

"On one condition."

She opened her eyes wide in question.

"You must take off this blasted thing."

"I can't." She choked on the words.

"It's lovely and soft, and I'll buy you a hundred of them, but if you don't get rid of it now, it'll be shreds." As if to demonstrate his urgency, he ground his hips closer to her, reminding her of the intensity of his arousal.

"I just can't. I don't know why." She gulped. "But you can."

One corner of his mouth lifted in a knowing grin. "Not an answer I was expecting, but certainly one I endorse." He knelt above her and pushed the chemise higher and higher until it passed her breasts and slid over her head.

Miranda felt the chill air blow over her bare skin, but strangely, she no longer felt any need to cover herself. It seemed perfectly natural that this man should be able to see and touch every last inch of her. His eyes raked possessively over her glowing skin, and she thrilled at the fierceness of his expression. She wanted to belong to him in every way a woman could belong to a man. She wanted to lose herself in his heat and strength.

And she wanted him to surrender to her with equal totality.

She reached up and laid her hand against his chest, allowing her fingertips to brush over his flat brown nipple. He flinched in reaction.

"Did I hurt you?" she whispered anxiously.

He shook his head. "Again," he rasped.

Imitating his earlier caresses, she caught the very tip of his nipple between her thumb and forefinger. It hardened under her touch, causing her to smile with delight. Like a child discovering a new toy, she reached out to play with the other. Turner, realizing that he was rapidly losing control under her curious fingers, clapped his hand over hers, holding it immobile. He stared down at her for a full minute, his blue eyes fierce. His gaze was so intense that

Miranda had to fight the urge to look away. But she forced herself to keep her eyes level with his. She wanted him to know that she wasn't afraid, that she wasn't ashamed, and most importantly, that she'd meant it when she said she loved him.

"Touch me," she whispered.

But he seemed frozen in place, his hand still holding hers to his chest. He looked odd, torn, almost . . . afraid.

"I don't want to hurt you," he rasped.

And she wasn't sure how she had come to reassure him, but she murmured, "You won't."

"I—"

"Please," she begged. She needed him. She needed him *now*.

Her impassioned plea broke through his reserve, and with a groan he pulled her up against him for a hard kiss before lowering her back to the bed. This time he came along with her, the hard length of his body pressing her breasts flat. His hands were everywhere, and he was moaning her name, and each touch, each sound seemed to stoke the flame within her.

She needed to feel him. Every inch.

She yanked at his makeshift kilt, wanting to get rid of the last barrier between them. She felt the friction of it sliding away, and then there was nothing there . . . except Turner.

She gasped at his arousal. "Oh, my God."

And that made him chuckle. "No, just me." He buried his face in the hollow of her neck. "Told you that already."

"But you're so . . ."

"Big?" He smiled against her. "That's your fault, sweet-ling."

"Oh, no." She squirmed beneath him. "I couldn't have done that."

He pressed himself more firmly against her. "Shhh."

"But I want to . . ."

"You will." He silenced her with a hot kiss, not even sure what he'd just promised her. Once he had her moaning again, he dragged his mouth away from hers, forging a searing path down to her navel. His tongue traced a circle around it and then dipped scandalously inside. His hands were at her thighs, easing them open, spreading her for his invasion.

He wanted to kiss her. He wanted to devour her, but he did not think she was ready for such an intimacy, so instead, he pushed one of his hands up. . .

And slipped one finger inside.

"Turner!" she cried, and he could not help but smile with satisfaction. He flicked his thumb over the soft, pink folds, reveling in the way she was writhing beneath him. He had to hold her hips firmly down with his free hand just to keep her from rolling off the bed.

"Open for me," he groaned, dragging his mouth back up to hers.

He heard her let out a little cry of pleasure, and her legs seemed almost to melt, sliding farther apart until the tip of his arousal was pressing against her, probing her softness. Turner moved his lips to her ear and whispered, "I'm go-ing to make love to you now."

Breathless, she nodded.

"I'm going to make you mine."

"Oh, yes, *please*."

He moved slowly forward, patient against her tight innocence. It was killing him, but he was going to restrain himself. He wanted more than anything to plunge into her with hard, furious strokes, but that would have to wait for another time. Not her first.

"Turner?" she whispered, and he realized he'd held still for several seconds. Gritting his teeth, he slowly withdrew until only the very tip of him remained inside her.

Miranda clutched at his shoulders. "Oh, no, Turner. Don't go!"

"Shhh. Don't worry. I'm still here." He moved back in.

"Don't leave me," she whispered.

"I won't." He reached her maidenhead and groaned at its resistance. "This is going to hurt, Miranda."

"I don't care." Her fingers bit into his skin.

"You may later." He pressed a little farther, trying to go as gently as possible.

She arched beneath him, moaning his name. Her arms were wrapped around him, and her fingers pressed spasmodically into his back. "*Please*, Turner," she begged. "Oh, please. Please, please."

Unable to control himself any longer, Turner plunged forward to the hilt, shuddering at the exquisite feeling of her squeezing around him. But Miranda stiffened beneath him, and he heard her wince.

"I'm sorry," he said quickly, trying to keep still and ignore the painful demands of his body. "I'm sorry. I'm so sorry. Does it hurt?"

She squeezed her eyes shut and shook her head.

He kissed away the tiny tears forming in the corners of her eyes. "Don't lie."

"Just a little," she admitted in a whisper. "It was more surprise than anything else."

"I'll make it better," he said fervently. "I promise I will." Propping himself up on this forearms to keep her free of his weight, he began again to move—slow, sure strokes, each bringing a jolt of pure desire with its sweet friction.

And all the while, his jaw was clenched in concentration, every muscle in his body tight and coiled with the strain of keeping himself in check. *In and out, in and out,* he chanted to himself. If he moved off rhythm for even just a second, he'd lose control completely. He had to keep this good for her. He wasn't worried for himself—he knew he would reach heaven before the night was through.

But for Miranda . . . All he knew was that he felt an intense responsibility to make sure that she found bliss as well. He'd never been with a virgin before, so he wasn't certain how likely this would be, but by God, he was going to try. He was afraid that even speaking would set him off, but he managed to say, "How do you feel?"

Miranda opened her eyes and blinked. "Good." She sounded surprised. "It doesn't hurt anymore."

"At all?"

She shook her head. "I feel splendid. And . . . hungry." She ran her fingers hesitantly along the length of his back.

Turner shuddered at her feather-light touch and felt his control slipping.

"How do *you* feel?" she whispered. "Are you hungry, too?"

He grunted something she couldn't understand and began to move faster. Miranda felt a quickening in her abdomen, then an unbearable tightness. Her fingers and toes began to tingle, and then just when she was certain that her body would shatter into a thousand tiny pieces, something inside her snapped, and her hips jerked up off the mattress with such force that she actually lifted him.

"Oh, Turner!" she yelled. "Help me!"

He pumped forward relentlessly. "I will," he groaned. "I swear it." And then he cried out, and his face looked almost pained, and then finally, he breathed, and he sank against her.

They lay entwined for several minutes, damp with exertion. Miranda loved his weight on top of her, loved this feeling of languid contentment. She idly stroked his hair with her hand, wishing the world around them would just go away. How long could they stay here, cocooned in the small hunting lodge, before they would be missed?

"How do you feel?" she asked softly.

His lips curled into a boyish smile. "How do you think I feel?"

"Good, I hope."

He rolled off her, propped himself up on one elbow, and caught her under her chin with two fingers. "Good, I *know*," he said, deliberately emphasizing the final word.

Miranda smiled. One couldn't hope for better than that.

"How do you feel?" he said quietly, concern marking his brow. "Are you sore?"

"I don't think so." She shifted her weight as if to test her body. "I might be later."

"You will."

Miranda frowned. Had he so much experience deflowering virgins, then? He'd said Leticia had already been with child when they'd married. And then she pushed the thought from her mind. She did not want to be thinking of Leticia. Not now. Turner's dead wife had no place in bed with them.

And she found herself dreaming of babies. Little blond ones, with bright blue eyes, smiling up at her with delight. A miniature Turner, that's what she wanted. She supposed a babe might take after her and be saddled with her less remarkable coloring, but in her mind, it was all Turner, right down to the dimples.

When she finally opened her eyes, she saw him gazing down at her, and he touched her mouth, right where the corner had been curling up. "What has you in such a reverie?" he murmured, his voice thick with satisfaction.

Miranda avoided his gaze, embarrassed by the direction of her thoughts. "Nothing important," she murmured. "Is it still raining?"

"I don't know," he replied, and he rose to peek out the window.

Miranda pulled the sheets over her nude body, wishing that she hadn't inquired about the weather. If the rain had let up, they would have to return to the main house. They had surely been missed by now. They could claim that they had sought shelter in the rain, but that excuse would ring hollow if they did not return just as soon as the weather cleared.

He pushed the curtains back into place and turned to face her, and Miranda caught her breath at the sheer male beauty of him. She had seen drawings of statues in her father's many books, and he even possessed a miniature of the David statue in Florence. But nothing compared to the living, breathing man standing before her, and she dropped her gaze to the floor, fearing that the mere sight of him would seduce her anew.

"It's still raining," he said evenly. "But it's getting lighter. We should clean up our, er, mess, so that we'll be ready to go just as soon as it clears."

Miranda nodded. "Could you hand me my clothing?"

He raised a brow. "Modest now?"

She nodded. Perhaps it was silly, after her wanton behavior, but she was not so sophisticated that she could rise from a bed nude with someone else in the room. She jerked her head toward her skirt, which was still lying on the floor in a heap. "Could you please?"

He picked it up and handed it to her. It was still wet in places since she hadn't bothered to lay it out flat, but as it had been rather close to the fire, it wasn't too dreadful. She quickly dressed and put the bed aright, pulling the sheets neat and tight, the way she saw the maids doing it at home. It was harder work than she'd expected, what with the bed pushed up against the wall.

By the time they and the lodge were presentable, the

rain had thinned down to a vague drizzle. "I don't suppose our clothing will get much wetter than it already is," Miranda said as she poked her hand out the window to test the rain.

He nodded, and they made their way back to the main house. He did not speak, and Miranda couldn't bring herself to break the silence, either. What happened now? Did he have to marry her? He *should*, of course, and if he was the gentleman she'd always thought him to be, he would, but no one knew that she had been compromised. And he knew her too well to worry that she would tell someone in order to trap him into marriage.

Fifteen minutes later, they stood just before the steps leading up to the front door of Chester House. Turner paused and looked at Miranda, his eyes serious and intent. "Will you be all right?" he asked gently.

She blinked several times. Why was he asking her this now?

"We won't be able to speak once we go inside," he explained.

She nodded, trying to ignore the sinking feeling in her belly. Something was not quite right.

He cleared his throat and stretched his neck as if his cravat were too tight. He cleared his throat again, and then for a third time. "You will notify me if a situation should arise for which we must act quickly."

Miranda nodded again, trying to discern whether that had been a statement or a question. A little of both, she decided. And she wasn't sure why it mattered.

Turner took a deep breath. "I will need a bit of time to think."

"About what?" she asked, before she had the chance to think the better of it. Shouldn't it all be simple now? What was there left to debate?

"Myself, mostly," he said, his voice a little hoarse, and maybe a little detached. "But I will see you shortly, and I will make everything right. You do not need to worry."

And then, because she was sick of waiting, and she was sick of being so bloody *convenient*, she blurted out, "Are you going to marry me?"

Because by God, it was as if the man were speaking through fog.

He looked taken aback by her shrill query, but nonetheless, he said brusquely, "Of course."

And while Miranda waited for the jubilation she knew she ought to feel, he added, "But I see no reason to rush unless we are presented with a compelling reason."

She nodded and swallowed. A baby. He wanted to marry her only if there was a baby. He would still do it regardless, but he'd take his sweet time.

"If we marry right away," he said, "it will be obvious that we *had* to."

"That *you* had to," Miranda muttered.

He leaned in. "Hmmm?"

"Nothing." Because it would be humiliating to say it again. Because it was humiliating that she'd said it once already.

"We should go in," he said.

She nodded. She was getting very good at nodding.

Ever the gentleman, Turner inclined his head and took her arm. Then he led her into the drawing room and acted as if he hadn't a care in the world.

3 JULY 1819

And after it happened, he did not speak to me once.

Chapter 12

When Turner returned home the next day, he retreated into his study with a glass of brandy and a muddled mind. Lady Chester's house party wasn't due to conclude for a few more days, but he had made up some story about pressing matters with his solicitors in the city and left early. He was fairly certain that he could behave as if nothing had happened, but of Miranda he was not so sure. She was an innocent—or at least she had been—and unused to such playacting. And for the sake of her reputation, all must appear scrupulously normal.

He did regret that he had been unable to explain to her the reasons for his early departure. He did not think that she would be affronted; he had, after all, told her that he needed time to think. He had also told her that they would marry; surely she would not doubt his intentions for his having taken a few days to ruminate upon his unexpected situation.

The enormity of his actions was not lost on him. He had

seduced a young, unmarried lady. One he actually liked and respected. One his family adored.

For a man who had not wished to remarry, he had clearly not been thinking with his head.

Groaning, he sank down into a chair and remembered the rules he and his friends had set down years ago when they'd left Oxford for the pleasures of London and the *ton*. There were only two. No married ladies, unless it was extremely obvious that her husband did not mind. And above all, no virgins. Never, never, never seduce a virgin.

Never.

He took another swig of his drink. Good Lord. If he'd needed a woman, there were dozens who would have been more suitable. The lovely young widowed countess had been coming along quite nicely. Katherine would have been the perfect mistress, and there would have been no need to marry her.

Marriage.

He'd done it once, with a romantic heart and stars in his eyes, and he'd been crushed. It was laughable, really. The laws of England gave absolute authority in a marriage to the husband, but he had never felt less in control of his life than when he'd been married.

Leticia had ground his heart into dust and left him an angry, soulless man. He was glad that she'd died. *Glad.* What sort of man did that make him? When the butler had found him in his study, and haltingly informed him that there had been an accident, and his wife was dead, Turner had not even felt relief. Relief would have at least been an innocent emotion. No, Turner's first thought had been—

Thank God.

And no matter how despicable Leticia might have been, no matter how many times he wished he had never married her, should he not have felt something more charitable at her passing? Or at the very least, something that was not entirely *un*charitable?

And now . . . and now . . . Well, the truth was, he did not wish to marry. It was what he had decided when they'd brought Leticia's broken body into the house, and it was what he'd confirmed when he'd stood over her grave. He'd had a wife. He did not want another one. At least not anytime soon.

But despite Leticia's best attempts, she had apparently not killed everything right and good in him, because here he was, planning his marriage to Miranda.

He knew she was a good woman, and he knew she would never betray him, but dear Lord she could be headstrong. Turner thought of her in the bookshop, assaulting the proprietor with her reticule. Now she would be his *wife*. It would be up to him to keep her out of trouble.

He swore and took another drink. He did not want that kind of responsibility. It was too much. He just wanted a rest. Was that too much to ask? A rest from having to think about anyone other than himself. A rest from having to care, from having to protect his heart from another beating.

Was it so very selfish? Probably. But after Leticia, he deserved a bit of selfishness. Surely, he must.

But on the other hand, marriage could bring a few welcome benefits. His skin began to tingle just thinking of Miranda. In bed. Underneath him. And then when he started to imagine what the future might bring. . .

Miranda. Back in bed. And then back in bed. And back in bed. And back—

Who would've thought? *Miranda*.

Marriage. To Miranda.

And, he reasoned, draining the last of his drink, he did like her better than almost anyone else. She was certainly more interesting and more fun to talk to than any of the other ladies of the *ton*. If one had to have a wife, it might as well be Miranda. She was a damned sight better than anyone else out there.

It occurred to him that he was not approaching this with a terribly romantic outlook. He was going to need more time to think. Perhaps he should go to bed and hope that his mind was clearer in the morning. With a sigh, he placed his glass back down on the table and stood up, then thought better of it and picked his glass back up. Another brandy might be just thing.

The next morning, Turner's head was throbbing, and his mind certainly was not any more disposed to deal with the matter at hand than it had been the night before. Of course, he still planned to marry Miranda—a gentleman did not compromise a wellborn lady without paying the consequences.

But he hated this feeling of being rushed. It didn't matter that this mess was entirely of his own making; he needed to feel that he had sorted everything out to his own satisfaction.

This was why, when he went down for breakfast, the letter from his friend Lord Harry Winthrop was such a welcome diversion. Harry was contemplating buying some property in Kent. Would Turner like to come down and take a look at it and offer his opinion?

Turner was out the door in under an hour. It was only for a few days. He would take care of Miranda when he got back.

Miranda didn't mind terribly that Turner had left the house party early. She would have done the same had she been able. Besides, she could think more clearly with him gone, and although there wasn't really much to debate—she had behaved in a manner contrary to every tenet of her upbringing, and if she did not marry Turner, she would be forever disgraced—it was a bit of a relief to feel at least slightly in control of her emotions.

When they returned to London a few days later, Miranda fully expected Turner to show his face immediately. She didn't particularly want to trap him into marriage, but a gentleman was a gentleman and a lady was a lady, and when the two of them were put together, a wedding usually followed. He knew that. He'd said he would marry her.

And surely he would *want* to do it. She had been so deeply moved by their intimacy—he must have felt something, too. It could not have been one-sided, at least not completely.

She managed a casual tone when she asked Lady Rudland where he was, but his mother replied that she hadn't the slightest idea except that he had left town. Miranda's chest grew tight, and she murmured, "Oh," or "I see," or something like that before dashing up the stairs to her room, where she wept as quietly as she could.

But soon her optimistic side broke through, and she decided that perhaps he had been called away from town on emergency estate business. It was a long way up to Northumberland. He would certainly be gone at least a week.

A week came and went, and frustration built up next to the despair in Miranda's heart. She could not inquire as to his whereabouts—no one in the Bevelstoke family realized that the two were close—Miranda had always been considered Olivia's friend, not Turner's—and if she asked repeatedly where he was, it would look suspicious. And it went without saying that Miranda could have no logical reason to go to Turner's lodgings and inquire herself. That would ruin her reputation completely. At least now her disgrace was still a private matter.

When another week passed, however, she decided that she couldn't bear to remain in London any longer. She fabricated an illness for her father and told the Bevelstokes that she had to return to Cumberland immediately to care for him. They were all terribly concerned, and Miranda felt somewhat guilty when Lady Rudland insisted that she travel back in their coach with two outriders and a maid.

But it had to be done. She could not remain in London any longer. It hurt too much.

A few days later, she was home. Her father was perplexed. He didn't know very much about young women, but he'd been assured that they all wanted seasons in London. But he didn't mind; Miranda was certainly never a bother. Half the time he didn't even realize she was there. So he patted her on the hand and returned to his precious manuscripts.

As for Miranda, she almost convinced herself that she was happy to be back at home. She'd missed the green fields and clean air of the Lakes, the sedate pace of the village, the early-to-bed and early-to-rise attitude. Well, perhaps not that—with no commitments and nothing to do, she slept in until noon and stayed up late every night, scribbling furiously in her journal.

A letter arrived from Olivia only two days after Miranda did. Miranda smiled as she opened it—trust Olivia to be so impatient that she would send up a missive right away. Miranda's eyes flew over the letter for Turner's name before reading it, but there was no mention of him. Not quite sure if she was disappointed or relieved, she turned back to the beginning and began to read. London was dull without her, Olivia wrote. She hadn't realized how much she had enjoyed Miranda's wry observations of society until they were gone. When was she coming home? Was her father improved? If not, was he at least improv*ing*? (Thrice underlined, in typical Olivia fashion.) Miranda read those sentences with a pang in her conscience. Her father was downstairs in his study poring over his manuscripts without even the teeniest of sniffles.

With a sigh, Miranda shoved her conscience over to the side and folded Olivia's letter, placing it in her desk drawer. A lie wasn't always a sin, she decided. Surely she was justified in whatever she had to do to get away from

London, where all she could do was sit and wait and hope that Turner would stop by.

Of course, all she did in the country was sit and think about him. One evening she forced herself to count how many times his name appeared in her journal entry, and to her supreme disgust, the total was thirty-seven.

Clearly, this trip to the country was not clearing her mind.

Then, after a week and a half, Olivia arrived on a surprise visit.

"Livvy, what are you doing here?" Miranda asked as she rushed into the parlor where her friend was waiting. "Is someone hurt? Is something wrong?"

"Not at all," Olivia returned breezily. "I've just come up to retrieve you. You are desperately needed in London."

Miranda's heart began to thump erratically. "By whom?"

"By me!" Olivia linked arms with her and led her into the sitting room. "Good heavens, I am an utter disaster without you."

"Your mother let you leave town in the middle of the season? I don't believe it."

"She practically shoved me out the door. I've been beastly since you left."

Miranda laughed despite herself. "Surely it hasn't been that bad."

"I do not jest. Mama always told me that you were a good influence, but I don't think she realized just how much until you left." Olivia flashed a guilty smile. "I can't seem to curb my tongue."

"You never could." Miranda smiled and led the way to a sofa. "Would you like some tea?"

Olivia nodded. "I don't understand why I get into so much trouble. Most of what I say isn't half as bad as what *you* say. You've the wickedest tongue in London."

Miranda pulled the bell cord for a maid. "I do not."

"Oh, yes, you do. You are the worst. And I know you know it. *And* you never get into trouble for any of it. It's terribly unfair."

"Yes, well, perhaps I don't say things quite as *loudly* as you do," Miranda replied, biting back a smile.

"You're right," Olivia sighed. "I know you're right, but it's still vastly annoying. You really do have a wicked sense of humor."

"Oh, come now, I'm not that bad."

Olivia let out a short laugh. "Oh, yes you are. Turner always says so, too, so I know it's not just me."

Miranda gulped down the quickly forming lump in her throat at the mention of his name. "Is he back in town, then?" she asked, oh-so-casually.

"No. I haven't seen him in ages. He's off in Kent somewhere with his friends."

Kent? One couldn't travel much farther from Cumberland and still remain in Britain, Miranda thought gloomily. "He's been gone quite some time."

"Yes, he has, hasn't he? But then again, he's off with Lord Harry Winthrop, and Harry has always been more than a little wild, if you know what I mean."

Miranda feared that she did.

"I'm sure they've just got carried away with wine,

women, and the sort," Olivia continued. "There won't be any proper ladies in attendance, I'm sure."

The lump in Miranda's throat quickly reappeared. The thought of Turner with another woman was violently painful, especially now that she knew just how close a man and woman could be. She had made up all sorts of reasons for his absence—her days were *filled* with rationalizations and excuses on his behalf. It was, she thought bitterly, her only pastime.

But she had never thought that he was off with another woman. He knew how painful it was to be betrayed. How could he do the same to her?

He didn't want her. The truth stung and it slapped and it dug its nasty little nails right into her heart.

He didn't want her, and she still wanted him so badly, and it *hurt*. It was physical. She could feel it, squeezing and pinching, and thank heavens Olivia was examining her father's prized Grecian vase, because she did not think she could keep her agony off her face.

With some sort of grunted comment that wasn't meant to be understood, Miranda stood and quickly crossed to the window, pretending to look out over the horizon. "Well, he must be having a good time," she managed to get out.

"Turner?" she heard from behind her. "He must, or he wouldn't be staying so long. Mama is in a despair, or she would be, if she weren't so busy despairing over me. Now, do you mind if I stay here with you? Haverbreaks is so big and drafty when no one is home."

"Of course I don't mind." Miranda remained at the window for a few moments longer, until she thought that she could look at Olivia without bursting into tears. She had been so emotional lately. "It will be quite a treat for me. It's a bit lonely with only Father to keep me company."

"Oh, yes. How is he? Improving, I hope."

"Father?" Miranda was grateful for the interruption provided by the maid who answered her earlier summons. She ordered some tea before turning back to Olivia. "Ehm, he is much improved."

"I shall have to stop in and wish him well. Mama asked me to send her regards as well."

"Oh, no, you shouldn't do that," Miranda said quickly. "He doesn't like to be reminded of his illness. He's very proud, you know."

Olivia, who had never been one to mince words, said, "How very odd."

"Yes, well, it's a *masculine* complaint," Miranda improvised. She had heard so much about feminine complaints; surely the men had to have some sort of ailment that was exclusively theirs. And if they didn't, she could not imagine that Olivia would know otherwise.

But Miranda hadn't counted on her friend's insatiable curiosity. "Oh, really?" she breathed, leaning forward. "What exactly is a *masculine* complaint?"

"I shouldn't talk about it," Miranda said hastily, offering her father a silent apology. "It would embarrass him greatly."

"But—"

"And your mother would be most upset with me. It's really not fit for tender ears."

"Tender ears?" Olivia snorted. "As if your ears were any less tender than mine."

Her ears might not be, but the rest of her certainly was, Miranda thought wryly. "No more on the subject," she said firmly. "I shall leave it up to your magnificent imagination."

Olivia grumbled a bit at that but finally sighed and asked, "When are you coming home?"

"I am home," Miranda reminded her.

"Yes, yes, of course. This is your *official* home, I know, but I assure you, the entire Bevelstoke family misses you very much, so when are you returning to London?"

Miranda caught her lower lip between her teeth. The *entire* Bevelstoke family obviously did not miss her, or a certain member would not have remained so long in Kent. But still, returning to London was the only way she could fight for her happiness, and sitting up here in Cumberland, crying into her journal and gazing morosely out the window, made her feel like a spineless twit.

"If I'm a twit," she muttered to herself, "at least I shall be a vertebrate twit."

"What did you say?"

"I said I *will* go back to London," Miranda said with great determination. "Father is well enough to get along without me."

"Splendid. When shall we leave?"

"Oh, in two or three days' time, I think." Miranda was not so brave that she didn't want to put off the inevitable by a few days. "I need to pack my things, and you are surely tired from traveling across the country."

"I am a bit. Perhaps we ought to stay a week. Assuming you are not weary of the country life already. I would not mind a short break from the congestion of London."

"Oh, no, that's just fine," Miranda assured her. Turner could wait. He certainly wasn't going to marry someone else in the meantime, and she could use the time to bolster her courage.

"Perfect. Then shall we go riding this afternoon? I'm dying for a good gallop."

"That sounds lovely." The tea arrived, and Miranda busied herself with pouring the steaming liquid. "I think a week is just perfect."

A week later, Miranda was convinced beyond anything that she could not return to London. Ever. Her monthly, which was so regular that it truly was monthly, had not arrived. She should have bled a few days before Olivia came. She had managed to stave off her worry for the first few days by telling herself that it was only because she was overset. Then, in the excitement of Olivia's arrival, she had forgotten about it. But now she was well over a week late. And emptying her stomach every single morning. Miranda had led a sheltered life, but she was a country girl, and she knew what that meant.

Dear God, a baby. What was she to do? She had to tell Turner; there was no getting around that. As much as she did not wish to use an innocent life to force a marriage that was obviously not fated to occur, how could she deny her child his birthright? But the thought of traveling to London was pure agony. And she was sick of chasing him and waiting for him and hoping and praying that maybe one day he'd come to love her. For once, he could bloody well come to her.

And he would, wouldn't he? He was a gentleman. He might not love her, but surely she had not misjudged him so completely. He would not shirk his duty.

Miranda smiled weakly to herself. So it had come to this. She was a duty. She would have him—after so many years of dreaming, she would actually be Lady Turner, but she would be nothing but a duty. She placed her hand on her belly. This should be a moment of joy, but instead all she wanted to do was cry.

A knock sounded on her bedroom door. Miranda looked up with a startled expression and didn't say anything.

"Miranda!" Olivia's voice was insistent. "Open the door. I can hear you crying."

Miranda took a deep breath and walked over to the door. It would not be easy to keep this a secret from Olivia, but she had to try. Olivia was intensely loyal, and she would never betray Miranda's trust, but still, Turner was her brother. There was no telling what Olivia would do. Miranda wouldn't put it past her to put a pistol to his back and march him north herself.

Miranda took a quick look in the mirror before heading to the door. Her tears she could wipe away, but she would have to blame her red-rimmed eyes on the summer garden. She took a few deep breaths, and then pasted on the brightest smile she was able and answered the door.

She did not fool Olivia for a minute.

"Good heavens, Miranda," she said, rushing to put her arms around her. "Whatever has happened to you?"

"I'm well," Miranda assured her. "My eyes always itch this time of year."

Olivia stood back, regarded her for a moment, then kicked the door shut. "But you are so pale."

Miranda's stomach began to churn, and she swallowed convulsively. "I think I've caught some sort of . . ." She waved her hand in the air, hoping that would finish her sentence for her. "Perhaps I should sit down."

"It couldn't have been something you ate," Olivia said, helping her to her bed. "You hardly touched your food yesterday, and in any case, I had everything you did and more." She nudged Miranda forward on the bed while she fluffed the pillows. "And I feel as fine as ever."

"Probably a head cold," Miranda mumbled. "You should probably return to London without me. I wouldn't wish for you to fall sick as well."

"Nonsense. I can't leave you alone like this."

"I'm not alone. My father is here."

Olivia gave her a look. "You know I would never wish to disparage your father, but I hardly think he knows what to do with an invalid. Half the time, I'm not even sure he remembers we are here."

Miranda closed her eyes and sank into the pillows. Olivia was right, of course. She adored her father, but truly, when it came to matters that involved actually interacting with another human being, he was fairly well hopeless.

Olivia perched on the edge of the bed, the mattress

sighing with her weight. Miranda tried to ignore her, tried to pretend that she didn't know, even with her eyes closed, that Olivia was staring at her, just waiting for her to acknowledge her presence.

"Please tell me what is wrong, Miranda," Olivia said softly. "Is it your father?"

Miranda shook her head, but just at that moment Olivia shifted her weight. The mattress rocked beneath them, rather like the movement of a boat, and although Miranda had never been seasick a day in her life, her stomach began to churn, and it suddenly became imperative—

Miranda leaped from the bed, knocking Olivia to the floor. She reached the chamber pot just in time.

"Good gracious," Olivia said, keeping a respectful— and self-preservational—distance. "How long have you been like this?"

Miranda declined to answer. But her stomach heaved in reply.

Olivia took a step back. "Er, is there anything I can do?"

Miranda shook her head, thankful her hair was neatly pulled back.

Olivia watched for another few moments, then went over to the basin and wet a cloth. "Here you are," she said, holding it forward, her arm entirely outstretched.

Miranda took it gratefully. "Thank you," she whispered, wiping her face.

"I don't think this is a head cold," Olivia said.

Miranda shook her head.

"I'm quite certain the fish last night was perfectly good, and I can't imagine—"

Miranda did not have to see Olivia's face to interpret her gasp. She knew. She might not yet quite believe it, but she knew.

"Miranda?"

Miranda remained frozen in place, hanging pathetically over the chamber pot.

"Are you—did you—?"

Miranda swallowed convulsively. And she nodded.

"Oh, my. Oh, my. Oh oh oh oh oh . . ."

It was perhaps the first time in her life that Miranda had heard Olivia at a complete loss for words. Miranda finished wiping her mouth, and then, her stomach finally at a somewhat even keel, moved away from the chamber pot and sat up a little straighter.

Olivia was still staring at her as if she'd seen an apparition. "How?" she finally asked.

"The usual way," Miranda retorted. "I assure you, there is no cause to alert the Church."

"I'm sorry. I'm sorry. I'm sorry," Olivia said hurriedly. "I didn't mean to upset you. It's just that . . . well . . . you must know . . . well . . . this is just such a *surprise*."

"It surprised me, too," Miranda replied in a somewhat flat voice.

"It couldn't have been that much of a surprise," Olivia said without thinking. "I mean, if you had done . . . if you had been . . ." She let her words trail off, realizing that her foot was lodged firmly in her mouth.

"It was still a surprise, Olivia."

Olivia was silent for a few moments as she absorbed this shock. "Miranda, I have to ask . . ."

"Don't!" Miranda warned her. "Please don't ask me who."

"Was it Winston?"

"No!" she replied forcefully. And then muttered, "Good heavens."

"Then who?"

"I can't tell you," Miranda said, her voice breaking. "It was . . . it was someone totally unsuitable. I . . . I don't know what I was thinking, but please don't ask me again. I don't want to talk about it."

"That's fine," Olivia said, clearly realizing that it would be unwise to push her any further. "I won't ask you again, I promise. But what are we going to do?"

Miranda could not help but feel a little warmed by her use of the word *we*.

"I say, Miranda, are you certain you're expecting?" Olivia asked suddenly, her eyes brightening with hope. "You could just be late. I'm late all the time."

Miranda threw an obvious glance at the chamber pot. And then she shook her head and said, "I'm never late. Never."

"You'll have to go somewhere," Olivia said. "The scandal will be amazing."

Miranda nodded. She planned to post a letter to Turner, but she could not tell that to Olivia.

"The best thing to do would be to get you out of the country. The continent, perhaps. How is your French?"

"Dismal."

Olivia sighed wearily. "You never were very good with languages."

"Nor were you," Miranda said testily.

Olivia declined to dignify that with a response, instead suggesting, "Why don't you go to Scotland?"

"To my grandparents?"

"Yes. Don't tell me they would turn you out because of your condition. You're always talking about how kind they are."

Scotland. Yes, that was the perfect solution. She would notify Turner, and he could join her there. They would be able to marry without posting banns, and then all would be, if not well, at least settled.

"I shall accompany you," Olivia said decisively. "I will stay as long as I can."

"But what will your mother say?"

"Oh, I'll tell her that someone's gone ill. It worked before, didn't it?" Olivia leveled a shrewd look at Miranda, one that clearly said that she knew that she had made up the story about her father.

"That's an awful lot of ill people."

Olivia shrugged. "It's an epidemic. All the more reason for her to remain in London. But what will you tell your father?"

"Oh, anything," Miranda replied dismissively. "He doesn't pay very much attention to what I do."

"Well, for once that is an advantage. We'll leave today."

"Today?" Miranda echoed weakly.

"We're already packed, after all, and there is no time to wait."

Miranda looked down at her still-flat stomach. "No, I don't suppose there is."

13 AUGUST 1819

Olivia and I arrived in Edinburgh today. Grandmama and Grandpapa were rather surprised to see me. They were even more surprised when I told them the reason for my visit. They were very silent and very grave, but not for one moment did they let me think that they were disappointed in or ashamed of me. I shall always love them for that.

Livvy sent off a note to her parents saying that she had accompanied me up to Scotland. Every morning she asks me if my monthly has arrived. As I anticipated, it has not. I find myself looking down at my belly constantly. I don't know what I expect to see. Surely one does not bulge out overnight, and certainly not this early.

I must tell Turner. I know I must, but I cannot seem to escape Olivia, and I cannot write the letter in her presence. Much as I adore her, I will have to shoo her away. I certainly cannot have her here when Turner arrives, which he will surely do once he receives my missive, assuming, of course, I am ever able to send it.

Oh, heavens, there she is now.

Chapter 13

Turner wasn't exactly certain why he had remained so long in Kent. The two-day jaunt quickly extended itself when Lord Harry decided that he did indeed wish to purchase the property, and furthermore, he wanted to have some friends over for a raucous house party immediately. There wasn't any way for Turner to extricate himself politely, and to be honest, he didn't really want to leave, not when that meant returning to London and facing up to his responsibilities.

Not that he was plotting a way to weasel out of marrying Miranda. Quite the opposite, in fact. Once he had resigned himself to the idea of remarrying, it no longer seemed like such a dreadful fate.

But still, he was hesitant to return. If he hadn't rushed out of town on the flimsiest of excuses, he could have cleared up the matter right away. But the longer he waited, the more he wanted to keep on waiting. How on earth would he explain his absence?

So the two-day trip slipped into a week-long house party that in turn slid into a three-week-long free-for-all with hunting, races, and plenty of loose women who'd been given free rein of the house. Turner was careful not to partake of the last. He might be shirking his responsibility to Miranda, but the least he could do was remain faithful.

Then Winston found his way down to Kent and proceeded to join the party with abandon so reckless that Turner felt compelled to stay and offer some fraternal guidance. This required another two weeks of his time, which he gave gladly, for it assuaged some of the guilt he'd been feeling. He couldn't abandon his brother, could he? If he didn't watch out for Winston, the poor boy would probably end up with a raging case of the French pox.

But finally he realized that he could not put off the inevitable any longer, and he returned to London, feeling rather like an ass. Miranda was probably fuming. He'd be lucky if she'd have him. And so, with not a little trepidation, he marched up the steps to his parents' home and let himself into the front hall.

The butler materialized immediately. "Huntley," Turner said in greeting. "Is Miss Cheever in? Or my sister?"

"No, my lord."

"Hmmm. When are they expected back?"

"I do not know, my lord."

"This afternoon? Suppertime?"

"Not for several weeks, I imagine."

"Several weeks!" Turner had not anticipated this. "Where the devil are they?"

Huntley stiffened at Turner's use of the invective. "Scotland, my lord."

"Scotland?" Bloody hell. What the devil were they doing up there? Miranda had relations in Edinburgh, but if there had been plans to visit them, he had not been made aware.

Wait a moment, Miranda wasn't promised to some Scottish gentleman who was connected to her grandparents, was she? *Someone* would surely have told him if that were the case. Miranda, for one. And the Lord knew Olivia couldn't keep a secret.

Turner strode to the bottom of the stairs and began to yell. "Mother! Mother!" He turned back to Huntley. "I assume my mother has not also hightailed it off to Scotland?"

"No, she is in residence here, my lord."

"Mother!"

Lady Rudland came hurrying down. "Turner, what on earth is the matter? And where have you been? Taking yourself off to Kent without even telling us."

"Why are Olivia and Miranda in Scotland?"

Lady Rudland raised her eyebrows at his interest. "Illness in the family. Miranda's family, that is."

Turner declined to point out that that much was obvious, as the Bevelstokes didn't have any family in Scotland. "And Olivia went with her?"

"Well, they are very close, you know."

"When are they expected back?"

"I can't say about Miranda, but I have already written to Olivia, insisting that she return. She is expected in just a few days."

"Good," Turner muttered.

"I'm sure she'll be pleased by your brotherly devotion."

Turner's eyes narrowed. Was that a note of sarcasm in his mother's voice? He couldn't be certain. "I'll see you soon, Mother."

"I'm sure you will. Oh, and Turner?"

"Yes?"

"Why don't you see about spending a bit more time with your valet? You're looking quite ragged."

Turner was growling when he let himself out.

Two days later, Turner was informed that his sister had returned to London. Turner rushed out to find her immediately. If there was one thing he hated, it was waiting. And if there was one thing he hated even more, it was feeling guilty.

And he felt bloody guilty for having made Miranda wait for what was now more than six weeks.

Olivia was in her bedroom when he arrived. Rather than wait for her in the sitting room, Turner headed up the stairs and knocked on her door.

"Turner!" Olivia exclaimed. "My goodness! What are you doing up here?"

"Really, Olivia, I used to live here. Remember?"

"Yes, yes, of course." She smiled and sat back down. "To what do I owe this pleasure?"

Turner opened his mouth and then shut it, not at all certain what he wanted to ask her. He couldn't very well just come out and say, "I seduced your best friend and now I need to make things right, so would it be appropriate for me to seek her out at her grandparents' home while one of them is ill?"

He opened his mouth again.

"Yes, Turner?"

He shut it, feeling the fool.

"Did you want to ask me something?"

"How was Scotland?" he blurted out.

"Lovely. Have you ever been?"

"No. And Miranda?"

Olivia hesitated before replying, "She is well. She sends her regards."

Somehow, Turner doubted that. He took a breath. He had to proceed cautiously. "She is in good spirits?"

"Ehrm, yes. Yes, she is."

"She wasn't upset about missing out on the rest of the season?"

"No, of course not. She never enjoyed it very much to begin with. You know that."

"Right." He turned around and faced the window, his hand beating an impatient tattoo against one of his legs. "Is she coming back soon?"

"Not for several months, I imagine."

"Then her grandmother is quite ill?"

"Quite."

"I shall have to send my condolences."

"It hasn't come to that yet." Olivia said quickly. "The

doctor says it will take some time, ehrm, at least half a year, maybe a little more, but he thinks she will recover."

"I see. And just what is this malady?"

"A female complaint," Olivia said, her voice perhaps a little too pert.

Turner raised a brow. A female complaint in a grand-mother. How very intriguing. And suspicious. He turned back around. "I hope this isn't catching. I shouldn't like to see Miranda fall ill."

"Oh, no. The, er, malady present in that household is definitely not communicable." When Turner did not re-move his heavy stare from her face, she added, "Just look at me. I was there for over a fortnight, and I am healthy as a horse."

"So you are. But I must say, I'm worried about Miranda."

"Oh, but you shouldn't be," Olivia insisted. "She's just fine, really she is."

Turner narrowed his eyes. His sister's cheeks had gone a little pink. "You're not telling me something."

"I . . . I don't know what you're talking about," she stammered. "And why are you asking me so many ques-tions about Miranda?"

"She's a good friend of mine as well," he replied silkily. "And I suggest you try telling me the truth."

Olivia scooted across the bed as he strode toward her. "I don't know what you're talking about."

"Is she involved with a man?" he demanded. "Is she? Is that why you've concocted this over-obvious story about some sick relative?"

"It's not a story," she protested.

"Tell me the truth!"

Her mouth clamped shut.

"Olivia," he said dangerously.

"Turner!" Her voice grew shrill. "I don't like that look in your eye. I'm going to call for Mother."

"Mother's half my size. She won't be able to stop me from strangling you, brat."

Her eyes bugged out. "Turner, you've gone mad."

"Who is he?"

"I don't know!" she burst out. "I don't know."

"So there *is* someone."

"Yes! No! Not anymore!"

"What the devil is going on?" Jealousy, pure and raging hot, raced through him.

"Nothing!"

"Tell me what has happened to Miranda." He circled around the bed until he had Olivia cornered. A very primitive sense of fear coursed through him. Fear that he might lose Miranda and fear she was in some way hurt. What if something had happened to her? He had never dreamed that Miranda's welfare could cause this throat-choking worry within him, but there you had it, and Christ, this was awful. He had never wanted to care about her this much.

Olivia's head darted back and forth as she looked for a means to escape. "She's fine, Turner. I swear it."

His large hands descended on her shoulders. "Olivia," he said in a very low voice, his blue eyes gleaming with fury and fear. "I'm going to say this but once. When we were children, I never once struck you, despite, I might add, ample reason." He paused, leaning in menacingly. "But I am not averse to starting right now."

Her lower lip began to quiver.

"If you do not tell me right this instant what kind of trouble Miranda has gotten herself into, you will be very sorry indeed."

A hundred different emotions crossed Olivia's face, most of them somehow related to panic or fear. "Turner," she beseeched him, "she is my dearest friend. I cannot betray her trust."

"What is wrong with her?" he ground out.

"Turner . . ."

"Tell me!"

"No, I can't, I . . ." Olivia went white. "*Oh, my God.*"

"What?"

"Oh, my God," she breathed. "It's you."

A look Turner had never seen before, on his sister, or indeed anyone, came over her face, and then—

"How could you!" she screamed, pummeling his upper body with her meager fists. "How could you? You're a beast! Do you hear me? A beast! And it was positively wretched of you to leave her like that."

Turner stood stock-still throughout her tirade, trying to make sense of her words and her rage. "Olivia," he said slowly. "What are you talking about?"

"Miranda is pregnant," she hissed. "Pregnant."

"Oh, my God." Turner's hands fell away from her arms and he sank down onto the bed in shock.

"I assume you're the father," she said coldly. "That is

disgusting. For God's sake, Turner. You're practically her brother."

His nostrils flared. "Hardly."

"You're older than she is, and more experienced. You shouldn't have taken advantage of her."

"I am not going to explain my actions to you," he bit out coldly.

Olivia snorted.

"Why didn't she tell me?"

"You were off in Kent, if you recall. Drinking and whoring and—"

"I wasn't whoring," he snapped. "I haven't been with another woman since Miranda."

"Pardon me if I find that hard to believe, big brother. You are despicable. Get out of my room."

"Pregnant." He repeated the word as if saying it again would make it easier to believe. "Miranda. A baby. My God."

"It's a little late for prayer," Olivia said icily. "Your behavior has been worse than reprehensible."

"I didn't know she was pregnant."

"Does it matter?"

Turner didn't answer. He couldn't answer, not when he knew that he was so obviously in the wrong. He let his head fall into his hands, his mind still reeling in shock. Dear God, when he thought about how selfish he had been . . . He had put off confronting Miranda simply because he was too lazy. He had figured she'd be here waiting for him when he returned. Because . . . because . . .

Because that's what she did. Hadn't she been waiting for him for years? Hadn't she said . . .

He was an ass. There could be no other explanation or excuse. He'd just assumed . . . and then he'd taken advantage . . . and . . .

Never in his wildest dreams had he imagined that she was off some three hundred miles to the north, coping with an unexpected pregnancy that would soon become an illegitimate child.

He'd told her to notify him if this happened. Why hadn't she written? Why hadn't she said something?

He looked down at his hands. They looked strange, and foreign, and when he flexed his fingers, his muscles were tight and awkward.

"Turner?"

He could hear his sister whispering his name, but somehow he couldn't respond. He could feel his throat moving, but he couldn't speak, couldn't even breathe. All he could manage was to sit there like a fool, thinking of Miranda.

Alone.

She was alone, and probably terrified. She was alone, when she should have been married and comfortably ensconced in his Northumberland home with fresh air and wholesome food and where he could keep an eye out on her.

A baby.

Funny how he had always assumed he'd let Winston carry on the family name, because now he wanted more than anything to touch Miranda's swollen belly, to hold this child in his arms. He hoped it would be a girl. He hoped she would have brown eyes. He could get his heir later on. With Miranda in his bed, he wasn't worried about conceiving again.

"What are you going to do about it?" Olivia demanded.

Turner slowly lifted his head. His sister was standing militantly before him, hands on hips. "What do you think I'm going to do about it?" he countered.

"I don't know, Turner," and for once Olivia's voice lacked an edge. Turner realized that this wasn't a retort. It wasn't a dare. Olivia honestly was not convinced that he intended to do the right thing and marry Miranda.

Turner had never felt like less of a man.

With a deep, shuddering breath, he stood and cleared his throat. "Olivia, would you be so kind as to provide me with Miranda's address in Scotland?"

"Gladly." She marched over to her desk and whipped out a piece of paper onto which she hastily scrawled a few lines. "Here you are."

Turner took the scrap of paper, folded it, and put it into his pocket. "Thank you."

Olivia very pointedly did not reply.

"I shan't be seeing you for some time, I think."

"At least seven months, I should hope," she retorted.

Turner raced across England up to Edinburgh, completing the journey in an amazing four and a half days. He was tired and dusty when he reached the Scottish capital, but that didn't seem to matter. Every day that Miranda was left alone was another day that she could—hell, he didn't know what she could do, but he didn't want to find out.

He checked the address one last time before heading up the steps. Miranda's grandparents lived in a fairly new home in a fashionable section of Edinburgh. They were gentry, he'd once heard, and had some property farther north. He sighed in relief that they were spending the summer down near the border. He wouldn't have relished having to continue his trip up into the Highlands. He was exhausted as it was.

He gave the door a firm knock. A butler answered it and greeted him with as snooty an English accent as one could find in the residence of a duke.

"I am here to see Miss Cheever," Turner said in clipped tones.

The butler looked disdainfully at Turner's rumpled clothing. "She is not in."

"Is that so?" Turner's tone implied that he did not believe him. He wouldn't be surprised if she had given his description to the entire household and instructed them to bar his entrance.

"You will have to return at a later time. I should be happy, however, to convey a message if—"

"I'll wait." Turner pushed right past him into a small salon off the main hall.

"Now see here, sir!" the butler protested.

Turner whipped out one of his cards and handed it to him. The butler looked at his name, looked at him, and then looked at his name again. He obviously didn't expect a viscount to look so disheveled. Turner smiled wryly. There were times a title could be damned convenient.

"If you would like to wait, my lord," the butler said in a

more subdued tone, "I shall have a maid bring in some tea."

"Please do."

As the butler slipped out the door, Turner began to wander through the room, slowly examining his surroundings. Miranda's grandparents had obvious good taste. The furnishings were understated and of a classic style, one that would never seem gauche or hopelessly out of date. As he idly examined a landscape painting, he pondered, as he had done a thousand times since leaving London, what he was going to say to Miranda. The butler hadn't called the guard as soon as he knew his name. That was a good sign, he supposed.

Tea arrived a few minutes later, and when Miranda didn't show up soon thereafter, Turner decided that the butler had not been lying about her whereabouts. No matter. He would wait as long as it took. He'd get his way in the end—of that he had no doubt.

Miranda was a sensible girl. She knew that the world was a cold and unfriendly place to illegitimate children. And their mothers. No matter how angry she was with him— and she would be, of that he had no doubt—she would not wish to consign her child to such a difficult life.

It was his child, too. It deserved the protection of his name. As did Miranda. He really didn't like the thought of her remaining much longer on her own, even if her grandparents had agreed to take her in during this awkward time.

Turner sat with his tea for half an hour, plowing through at least six of the scones that had been brought with them. It had been a long trip from London, and he had not stopped often for food. He was marveling at how much better these tasted than anything he'd ever had in England when he heard the front door open.

"MacDownes!"

Miranda's voice. Turner stood up, a half-eaten scone still dangling from his fingers. Footsteps sounded in the hall, presumably belonging to the butler.

"Could you relieve me of some of these bundles? I know I should have just had them sent home, but I was too impatient."

Turner heard the sound of packages changing hands, followed by the butler's voice. "Miss Cheever, I must inform you that you have a visitor waiting for you in the salon."

"A visitor? Me? How odd. It must be one of the Macleans. I have always been friendly with them while in Scotland, and they must have heard I was in town."

"I do not believe he is of Scottish origin, miss."

"Really, then who . . ."

Turner almost smiled as her voice trailed off in shock. He could just see her mouth dropping open.

"He was most insistent, miss," MacDownes continued. "I have his card right here."

There was a long silence until Miranda finally said, "Please tell him that I am not available." Her voice quavered on the last word, and then she dashed up the stairs.

Turner strode out into the hall just in time to crash into MacDownes, who was probably relishing the idea of tossing him out.

"She doesn't want to see you, my lord," the butler intoned, not without the barest hint of a smile.

Turner pushed past him. "She damned well will."

"I don't think so, my lord." MacDownes caught hold of his coat.

"Look, my man," Turner said, trying to sound icily congenial, if such a thing was possible. "I am not averse to hitting you."

"And I am not averse to hitting you."

Turner surveyed the older man with disdain. "Get out of my way."

The butler crossed his arms and stood his ground.

Turner scowled at him and yanked his coat free, striding to the bottom of the stairs. "Miranda!" he yelled out. "Get down here right now! Right now! We have things to dis—"

Thwack!

Good God, the butler had punched him in the jaw. Stunned, Turner stroked his tender flesh. "Are you mad?"

"Not at all, my lord. I take great pride in my work."

The butler had assumed a fighting position with the ease and grace of a professional. Leave it to Miranda to hire a pugilist as a butler.

"Look," Turner said in a conciliatory tone. "I need to speak with her immediately. It's of the utmost importance. The lady's honor is at stake."

Thwack! Turner reeled from a second blow.

"That, my lord, is for implying that Miss Cheever is anything less than honorable."

Turner narrowed his eyes menacingly but decided that he wouldn't have a chance against Miranda's mad butler, not when he'd already been on the receiving end of two disorienting blows. "Tell Miss Cheever," he said scathingly, "that I will be back, and she bloody well had better receive me." He strode furiously out of the house and down the front steps.

Utterly enraged that the chit would completely refuse to see him, he turned back to look at the house. She was standing at an open upstairs window, her fingers nervously covering her mouth. Turner scowled at her and then realized that he was still holding his half-eaten scone.

He lobbed it hard through the window, where it caught her square on the chest.

There was some satisfaction in that.

24 AUGUST 1819

> *Oh, dear.*
>
> *I never sent the letter, of course. I spent an entire day composing it, and then just when I had it ready to post, it became unnecessary.*
>
> *I did not know whether to weep or rejoice.*
>
> *And now Turner is here. He must have beat the truth—or rather, what used to be the truth—out of Olivia. She would never have betrayed me otherwise. Poor Livvy. He can be terrifying when he is furious.*
>
> *Which, apparently, he still is. He threw a scone at me. A scone! It is difficult to fathom.*

Chapter 14

Two hours later, Turner made another appearance. This time, Miranda was waiting for him.

She wrenched the front door open before he could even knock. He didn't so much as stumble, however, just stood there with his perfect posture, his arm halfway up, his hand fisted and ready to connect with the door.

"Oh, for goodness' sake," she said in an irritated tone. "Come in."

Turner raised his brows. "Were you watching for me?"

"Of course."

And because she knew she could not put this off any longer, she marched to the sitting room without a backward glance.

He'd follow.

"What do you want?" she demanded.

"A most pleasant greeting, Miranda," he said smoothly, looking clean and crisp and handsome and utterly at ease and—oh! she wanted to kill him. "Who has been teaching you manners?" he continued. "Attila the Hun?"

She gritted her teeth and repeated the question. "What do you want?"

"Why, to marry you, of course."

It was, of course, the one thing she'd been waiting for since the first moment she'd laid eyes upon him. And never in her life had she been so proud of herself as when she said, "No, thank you."

"No . . . thank you?"

"No, thank you," she repeated pertly. "If that is all, I will show you out."

But he caught her wrist as she made as if to leave the room. "Not so fast."

She could do this. She knew she could. She had her pride, and she no longer had any compelling reason to marry him. And she shouldn't. No matter how much her heart ached, she could not give in. He did not love her. He did not even hold her in high enough regard to contact her even once in the month and a half since they had come together at the hunter's lodge.

He might have been a gentleman, but he was not much of one.

"Miranda," he said silkily, and she knew he was trying to seduce her, if not into his bed, then into acquiescence.

She took a deep breath. "You came here, you did the right thing, and I refused. You have nothing more to feel guilty about, so you can return to England with a clear conscience. Good-bye, Turner."

"I don't think so, Miranda," he said, tightening his grip on her. "We have much to discuss, you and I."

"Ehrm, not much, really. Thank you for your concern, though." Her arm tingled where he held her, and she knew that if she was to hold on to her resolve, she had to be rid of him as soon as possible.

Turner kicked the door shut. "I disagree."

"Turner, don't!" Miranda tugged her arm and tried to get back to the door to reopen it, but he blocked her way. "This is my grandparents' house. I'll not have them shamed by any improper behavior."

"I should think you'd be more concerned by their possibly hearing what I have to say to you."

She took one look at his implacable expression and shut her mouth. "Very well. Say whatever it is you came here to say."

His finger began to draw lazy circles in her palm. "I've been thinking about you, Miranda."

"Have you? That's very flattering."

He ignored her snide tone and moved closer. "Have you been thinking about me?"

Oh, dear Lord. If he only knew. "On occasion."

"Only on occasion?"

"Quite rarely."

He pulled her toward him, his hand sliding sinuously along her arm. "How rarely?" he murmured.

"Almost never." But her voice was growing softer, and far less sure.

"Really?" He raised one of his brows in an incredulous

expression. "I think all this Scottish food has been addling your brain. Have you been eating haggis?"

"Haggis?" she asked breathlessly. She could feel her chest growing light, as if the air itself had become something intoxicating, as if she might grow drunk, just breathing in his presence.

"Mmm-hmm. Hideous food, I think."

"It's—it's not bad." What was he talking about? And why was he looking at her that way? His eyes looked like sapphires. No, like a moonlit sky. Oh, dear. Was that her resolve flying out the window?

Turner smiled indulgently. "Your memory is quite diminished, darling. I think you need some reminding." His lips descended gently on hers, spreading fire quickly throughout her body. She sagged against him, sighing his name.

He pulled her more tightly against him, the force of his arousal pressing against her. "Can you feel what you do to me?" he whispered. "Can you?"

Miranda nodded shakily, barely aware that she was standing in the middle of her grandparents' salon.

"Only you can do that to me, Miranda," he murmured huskily. "Only you."

That remark struck a discordant chord within her, and she stiffened in his arms. Hadn't he just spent more than a month in Kent with his friend Lord Harry Whatever-his-name-was? And hadn't Olivia blithely informed her that the festivities would have included wine, whiskey, and women? Loose women. Lots of them.

"What's wrong, darling?"

His words were whispered against her skin, and a part of her wanted to melt right back against him. But she would not be seduced. Not this time. Before she could change her mind, she planted her palms against his chest and pushed. "Don't try to do this to me," she warned.

"Do what?" His face was the picture of innocence.

If Miranda had had a vase in her hands, she would have thrown it at him. Or better yet, a half-eaten scone. "Seduce me into bending to your will."

"Why not?"

"Why not?" she repeated incredulously. "Why not? Because I . . . Because you . . ."

"Because why?" He was grinning now.

"Because—oh!" Her fists balled up at her sides, and she actually stamped her foot. Which made her even more furious. To be reduced to this—it was humiliating.

"Now, now, Miranda."

"Don't 'now, now' me, you overbearing, patronizing—"

"You're angry with me, I gather."

She narrowed her eyes. "You always were clever, Turner."

He ignored her sarcasm. "Well, here you have it—I'm sorry. I never intended to remain so long in Kent. I don't know why I did it, but I did, and I'm sorry. It was meant to be a two-day trip."

"A two-day trip that lasted nearly two months?" she scoffed. "Pardon me if I have difficulty believing you."

"I wasn't in Kent the entire time. When I returned to London, my mother said you were tending to a sick relative. It wasn't until Olivia returned that I learned otherwise."

"I don't care how long you were . . . wherever you were!" she yelled, crossing her arms tightly across her chest. "You shouldn't have abandoned me like that. I can understand that you needed time to think, because I know you never wanted to marry me, but good heavens, Turner, did you need seven weeks? You cannot treat a woman like that! It's rude and unconscionable and . . . and downright ungentlemanly!"

Was that the worst thing she could think to call him? Turner resisted the urge to smile. This wasn't going to be nearly as bad as he thought. "You're right," he said quietly.

"And furthermore—what?" She blinked.

"You're right."

"I am?"

"Don't you want to be?"

She opened her mouth, shut it, and then said, "Stop trying to confuse me."

"I'm not. I'm agreeing with you, in case you hadn't noticed." He offered her his most engaging smile. "Is my apology accepted?"

Miranda sighed. It ought to be illegal for a man to have this much charm. "Yes, fine. It's accepted. But what," she asked suspiciously, "were you doing in Kent?"

"Mostly getting drunk."

"Is that all?"

"A bit of hunting."

"And?"

"And I did my best to keep Winston out of trouble when he found his way down there from Oxford. That chore kept me an extra fortnight, I'll have you know."

"And?"

"Are you trying to ask me if there were women there?"

Her eyes slid away from his face. "Perhaps."

"There were."

She tried to swallow the enormous lump that suddenly popped up in her throat as she stepped aside to clear his path to the door. "I think you should leave," she said quietly.

He gripped her upper arms and forced her to look at him. "I never touched any of them, Miranda. Not one."

The intensity of his voice was enough to make her want to cry. "Why not?" she whispered.

"I knew I was going to marry you. I know how it feels to be cuckolded." He cleared his throat. "I would not do that to you."

"Why not?" The words were barely a whisper.

"Because I have a care for your feelings. And I hold you in the highest regard."

She pulled away from him and walked over to the window. It was early evening, but the days were long during the Scottish summertime. The sun was high in the sky, and people were still walking to and fro, completing their daily errands as if they didn't have a care in the world. Miranda wanted to be one of those people, wanted to walk down the street away from her problems and never return.

Turner wanted to marry her. He had remained faithful to her. She should be dancing with joy. But she could not shake the feeling that he was doing this out of duty, not out of any love or affection for her. Except for desire, of course. It was abundantly clear that he desired her.

A tear trickled down her face. It wasn't enough. It might be, if she didn't love him so well. But this . . . It was too uneven. It would sicken her slowly, until she was nothing but a sad, lonely shell.

"Turner, I . . . I appreciate your coming all the way up here to see me. I know it was a long trip. And it was truly . . ." She searched for the right word. " . . . honorable of you to stay away from all those women in Kent. I'm sure they were very pretty."

"Not half as pretty as you," he whispered.

She swallowed convulsively. This was getting harder by the second. She clutched at the windowsill. "I cannot marry you."

Dead silence. Miranda didn't turn around. She could not see him, but she could feel the rage emanating from his body. *Please, please just leave the room*, she silently pleaded. *Don't come over here. And please—oh, please, don't touch me*.

Her prayers went unanswered, and his hands descended brutally on her shoulders, spinning her around to face him. "What did you say?"

"I said I cannot marry you," she replied tremulously. She let her gaze fall to the floor. His blue eyes were burning holes into her.

"Look at me, damn it! What are you thinking? You have to marry me."

She shook her head.

"You little fool."

Miranda didn't know what to say to that so she said nothing.

"Have you forgotten this?" He yanked her hard against him and plundered her lips with his. "Have you?"

"No."

"Then have you forgotten that you told me you loved me?" he demanded.

Miranda wanted to die on the spot. "No."

"That should count for something," he said, shaking her until some of her hair broke free of its pins. "Doesn't it?"

"And have you ever said you loved me?" she shot back.

He stared at her mutely.

"Do you love me?" Her cheeks were flaming with anger and embarrassment. "Do you?"

Turner swallowed, suddenly feeling as if he were choking. The walls seemed close, and he could not say anything, could not utter the words she wanted to hear.

"I see," she said in a low voice.

A muscle worked spasmodically in his throat. Why couldn't he say it? He wasn't sure if he loved her, but he wasn't sure that he didn't. And he sure as hell didn't want to hurt her, so why didn't he just say those three words that would make her happy?

He had told Leticia he loved her.

"Miranda," he said haltingly. "I—"

"Don't say it if you don't mean it!" she burst out, her voice catching on the words.

Turner spun on his heel and walked across the room to where he had noticed a decanter of brandy. There was a bottle of whiskey on the shelf beneath it, and without asking her permission, he poured himself a glass. It went down in one fiery gulp, but it didn't make him feel any better. "Miranda," he said, wishing his voice were just a little steadier. "I'm not perfect."

"You were supposed to be!" she cried. "Do you know how wonderful you were to me when I was little? And you didn't even try. You were just . . . just *you*. And you made me feel like I wasn't such an awkward little thing. And then you changed, but I thought I could change you back. And I tried, oh, how I tried, but it wasn't enough. *I* wasn't enough."

"Miranda, it isn't you . . ."

"Don't make excuses for me! I can't be what you need, and I hate you for that! Do you hear me? I hate you!" Overcome, she turned away and hugged her arms to herself, trying to control the tremors that shook her body.

"You don't hate me." His voice was soft and oddly soothing.

"No," she said, choking back a sob. "I don't. But I hate Leticia. If she weren't already dead, I'd kill her myself."

One corner of his mouth tilted upward in a wry smile.

"I'd do it slowly and painfully."

"You really do have a vicious streak, puss," he said, offering her a cajoling smile.

She tried to smile, but her lips just wouldn't obey.

There was a long pause before Turner spoke again. "I will try to make you happy, but I can't be everything you want."

"I know," she said sadly. "I thought you could, but I was wrong."

"But we could still have a good marriage, Miranda. Better than most."

"Better than most" might mean only that they spoke to each other at least once a day. Yes, they might have a good marriage. Good, but empty. She didn't think she could bear living with him without his love. She shook her head.

"Damn it, Miranda! You have to marry me!" When she didn't acknowledge his outburst, he yelled, "For the love of God, woman, you're carrying my child!"

And there it was. She'd known that had to be the reason he'd traveled so far, and with such single-minded purpose. And as much as she appreciated his sense of honor— belated though it might have been—there was no getting around the fact that the baby was gone. She had bled, and then her appetite had returned, and her chamber pot had gone back to its regular manner of use.

Her mother had told her about this, had said that she had gone through exactly the same thing twice before Miranda and three times after. It had been, perhaps, an indelicate subject for a young woman not even out of the school- room, but Lady Cheever had known that she was dying, and she had wished to pass along to her daughter as much womanly knowledge as she could. She had told Miranda not to mourn if the same should happen to her, that she had always felt that those lost babes were never meant to be.

Miranda wet her lips and swallowed. And then, in a low, solemn voice, she said, "I'm not carrying your child. I was, but I'm not any longer."

Turner said nothing. And then: "I don't believe you."

Miranda stood stunned. "I beg your pardon."

He shrugged. "I don't believe you. Olivia told me you were pregnant."

"I *was*, when Olivia was here."

"How do I know you're not simply trying to be rid of me?"

"Because I'm not an *idiot*," she snapped. "Do you think I'd refuse to wed you if I were carrying your child?"

He seemed to consider that for a moment, and then he crossed his arms. "Well, you're still compromised, and you're still marrying me."

"No," she said derisively, "I'm not."

"Oh, you will," he said, his eyes glittering ruthlessly. "You just don't know it yet."

She backed away from him. "I don't see how you're going to force me."

He took a step forward. "I don't see how you're going to stop me."

"I'll yell for MacDownes."

"I don't think you will."

"I will. I swear it." She opened her mouth and then looked sideways at him to see if he caught her warning.

"Go ahead," he said, shrugging casually. "He won't catch me off guard this time."

"Mac—"

He clamped his hand on her mouth with stunning speed. "You little fool. Aside from the fact that I have no wish for your aging pugilistic butler to interrupt my privacy, did you stop to consider that his barging in here will only hasten our marriage? You wouldn't want to get caught in a compromising position, would you?"

Miranda grumbled something against his hand and then punched him in the hip until he removed it. But she did not call out for MacDownes again. Much as she was loath to admit it, he had a point. "Why didn't you just let me yell, then?" she taunted. "Hmmm? Isn't marriage what you want?"

"Yes, but I thought you might prefer to enter into it with a little dignity."

Miranda had no ready response, so she crossed her arms.

"Now I want you to listen to me," he said in a low voice, taking her chin in his hand and forcing her to look at him. "And listen carefully, because I'm only going to say this once. You are going to marry me before the week is out. Since you have conveniently run off to Scotland, we don't need a special license. You're just lucky I don't haul you off to a church right this instant. Get yourself a dress and get yourself some flowers, because, sweetheart, you're getting yourself a new name."

She shot him a scathing glare, unable to think of any words to sufficiently express her fury.

"And don't even think about running off again," he said lazily. "For your information, I have rented rooms just two doors down and have arranged for surveillance on this house twenty-four hours a day. You won't make it to the end of the street."

"My God," she breathed. "You've gone mad."

He laughed at that. "Consider that statement if you will. If I brought ten people in here and explained that I had taken your virginity, asked you to marry me, and you refused, who do you think they would think is mad?"

She was fuming so badly, she thought she might explode.

"Not me!" he said brightly. "Now buck up, puss, and look on the bright side. We shall make more babies and have a splendid time doing so, I promise never to beat you or forbid you to do anything that is not utterly foolish, and you'll finally be sisters with Olivia. What more could you want?"

Love. But she couldn't voice the word.

"All in all, Miranda, you could be in a far worse position."

She still didn't say anything.

"Many women would be thrilled to change places with you."

She wondered if there was any way to wipe the smug expression off his face without doing him permanent harm.

He leaned forward suggestively. "And I can promise you I shall be very, very attentive to your needs."

She clasped her hands behind her back because they were starting to shake with frustration and rage.

"You'll thank me for this someday."

And that was *it*. "Aaaaargh!" she yelled incoherently, launching herself onto him.

"What on earth?" Turner twisted around, trying to get her and her pummeling fists off him.

"Don't you ever—ever say, 'You'll thank me for this someday' again! Do you hear me! Ever!"

"Stop, woman! Good God, you've gone mad!" He raised his arms to shield his face. The position was rather cowardly for his taste, but the alternative was to have her accidentally jab him in the eye. There wasn't much else to do, as he couldn't exactly defend himself. He had never hit a woman, and he wasn't about to start now.

"And don't ever use that patronizing tone with me again," she demanded, poking him furiously in the chest.

"Calm down, dear. I promise I'll never use that patronizing tone with you again."

"You're using it now," she ground out.

"Not in the least."

"Yes, you were."

"No, I wasn't."

"Yes, you were."

Good Lord, this was growing tedious. "Miranda, we're acting like children."

She seemed to grow taller, and her eyes took on a wild look that should have struck fear in his heart. And as she gave her head a little shake, she spat, "I don't care."

"Well, maybe if you start acting like an adult, I'll stop speaking to you in my so-called patronizing tone."

Her eyes narrowed, and she growled from the back of her throat. "Do you know something, Turner? Sometimes you act like a complete ass." With that, she balled her hand into a fist, pulled back her arm, and let fly.

"Holy bloody hell!" His hand shot up to his eye, and he touched his burning skin in disbelief. "Who the hell taught you to throw a punch?"

She smiled smugly. "MacDownes."

24 AUGUST 1819—LATER IN THE EVENING

MacDownes informed Grandmother and Grandfather of my visitor today, and they quickly guessed who he is to me. Grandfather blustered for about ten minutes about how could that son of a something I cannot possibly write show his face, until Grandmother finally calmed him down and asked me why he had come.

I cannot lie to them. I never have been able to. I told them the truth—that he had come to marry me. They reacted with great joy and even greater relief until I told them that I refused. Grandfather launched into another tirade, only this time the object was me, and my lack of common sense. Or at least I think that was what he said. He is from the Highlands, and although he speaks the King's English with a perfect accent, his brogue breaks through when he gets upset.

He was, to understate, particularly upset.

So now I find myself with all three of them aligned against me. I fear I might be fighting a losing battle.

Chapter 15

Given the opposition against her, it was remarkable that Miranda held out as long as she did, which was three days.

Her grandmother launched the attack, using the sweet and sensible approach. "Now, dear," she had said, "I understand that Lord Turner was perhaps a bit tardy in his attentions, but he did come up to scratch, and well, you *did* . . ."

"You don't need to say it," Miranda had replied, blushing furiously.

"Well, you did."

"I *know*." Heaven above, she knew. She could rarely think of anything else.

"But really, sweetling, what is wrong with the viscount? He seems a rather nice fellow, and he has assured us that he will be able to provide for you and look after you properly."

Miranda gritted her teeth. Turner had stopped by the

evening before to introduce himself to her grandparents. Trust him to make her grandmother fall in love with him in under an hour. That man ought to be kept away from women of all ages.

"And he's quite handsome, I think," her grandmother continued. "Don't you think so? Of course you think so. After all, his is not the kind of face that some think is handsome and some don't. His is the kind that *everyone* finds handsome. Don't you agree?"

Miranda did agree, but she wasn't about to say so.

"Of course, handsome is as handsome does, and so many well-formed people have ill-formed minds."

Miranda wasn't even going to touch that one.

"But he appears to have all his wits about him, and he's quite affable, too. All in all, Miranda, you could do much worse." When her granddaughter did not reply, she said with uncharacteristic severity, "And I don't think you'll be able to do better."

It stung, but it was true. Still, Miranda said, "I could remain unmarried."

Since her grandmother did not view that as a viable option, she did not dignify it with a response. "I'm not talking about his title," she said sharply. "Or his fortune. He would be a good catch if he hadn't a farthing."

Miranda found a way to respond that involved a non-committal throat sound, a bit of a head shake, a bit of a head twist, and a shrug. And that, she hoped, would be that.

But it wasn't. The end wasn't nearly in sight. Turner took up the next round by trying to appeal to her romantic nature.

Large bouquets of flowers arrived every two or so hours, every one with a note reading, "Marry me, Miranda."

Miranda did her best to ignore them, which wasn't easy, because they soon filled every corner of the house. He made great inroads with her grandmother, however, who was redoubled in her resolve to see her Miranda married to the charming and generous viscount.

Her grandfather tried next, his approach considerably more aggressive. "For the love of God, lassie," he roared. "Have you lost your mind?"

Since Miranda was no longer quite so certain she knew the answer to that question, she did not reply.

Turner went next, this time making a tactical mistake. He sent a note reading, "I forgive you for hitting me." Miranda was initially enraged. It was that condescending tone which had caused her to punch him in the first place. Then she recognized it for what it was—a gentle warning. He was not going to put up with her stubbornness for much longer.

On the second day of the siege, she decided she needed some fresh air—really, the scent of all those flowers was positively cloying—so Miranda picked up her bonnet and headed out to the nearby Queen Street Garden.

Turner began to follow her immediately. He had not been jesting when he had told her that he was keeping her house under surveillance. He had not bothered to mention, however, that he wasn't hiring professionals to keep watch. His poor beleaguered valet had that honor, and after eight straight hours of staring out the window, he was much relieved when the lady in question finally departed, and he could abandon his post.

Turner smiled as he watched Miranda make her way to the park with quick, efficient steps, then frowned when he realized that she had not taken a maid along with her. Edinburgh was not as dangerous as London, but surely a gentle lady did not venture out by herself. This sort of behavior would need to stop once they were married.

And they *would* get married. End of discussion.

He was, however, going to have to approach this matter with a certain measure of finesse. In retrospect, the note expressing his forgiveness was probably a mistake. Hell, he'd known it would irk her even as he wrote it, but he couldn't seem to help himself. Not when, every time he looked in the mirror, he was greeted by his blackened eye.

Miranda entered the park and strode along for several minutes until she found an unoccupied bench. She brushed away some dust, sat down, and pulled a book out of the bag she'd been carrying with her.

Turner smiled from his vantage point fifty yards or so away. He liked watching her. It surprised him how content he felt just standing there under a tree, watching her read a book. Her fingers arched so delicately as she turned each page. He had a sudden vision of her sitting behind the desk in the sitting room attached to his bedroom at his home in Northumberland. She was writing a letter, probably to Olivia, and smiling as she recounted the day's events.

Turner suddenly realized that this marriage wasn't just

the right thing, it was also a good thing, and he was going to be quite happy with her.

Whistling to himself, he ambled over to where she was sitting and plopped down next to her. "Hello, puss."

She looked up and sighed, rolling her eyes at the same time. "Oh, it's *you*."

"I certainly hope no one else uses endearments."

She grimaced as she caught sight of his face. "I'm sorry about your eye."

"Oh, I've already forgiven you for that, if you recall."

She stiffened. "I recall."

"Yes," he murmured. "I rather thought you would."

She waited for a moment, most probably for him to leave. Then she turned pointedly back to her book and announced, "I'm trying to read."

"I see that. Very good of you, you know. I like a female who broadens her mind." He plucked the volume from her fingers and turned it over to read the title. "*Pride and Prejudice*. Are you enjoying it?"

"I *was*."

He ignored her barb as he flipped to the first page, holding her place with his index finger. "'It is a truth universally acknowledged,'" he read aloud, "'that a single man in possession of a good fortune must be in want of a wife.'"

Miranda tried to grab her book back, but he moved it out of her reach.

"Hmmm," he mused. "An interesting thought. *I* certainly am in want of a wife."

"Go to London," she retorted. "You'll find lots of women there."

"And I am in possession of a good fortune." He leaned forward and grinned at her. "Just in case you didn't realize."

"I cannot tell you how relieved I am in the knowledge that you will never starve."

He chuckled. "Oh, Miranda, why don't you just give up? You can't win this one."

"I don't imagine there are many priests who will marry a couple without the woman's consent."

"You'll consent," he said in a pleasant tone.

"Oh?"

"You love me, remember?"

Miranda's mouth tightened. "That was a very long time ago."

"What, two, three months? Not so long. It'll come back to you."

"Not the way you're acting."

"Such a pointy tongue," he said with a sly smile. And then he leaned in. "If you must know, it's one of the things I like best about you."

She had to flex her fingers to keep herself from wrapping them around his neck. "I believe I've had my fill of fresh air," she announced, holding her book tightly to her chest as she stood. "I'm going home."

He stood immediately. "Then I shall accompany you, Lady Turner."

She whirled around. "*What* did you just call me?"

"Just testing the name," he murmured. "It fits quite well, I think. You might as well accustom yourself to it as soon as possible."

Miranda shook her head and resumed her walk home. She tried to keep a few steps ahead of him, but his legs were far longer, and he had no trouble remaining even with her. "You know, Miranda," he said affably, "if you could give me one good reason why we should not be married, I would leave you alone."

"I don't like you."

"That's a lie, so it doesn't count."

She thought for a few more moments, still walking as quickly as she could. "I don't need your money."

"Of course you don't. Olivia told me last year that your mother left you a small bequest. Enough to live on. But it's a bit shortsighted to refuse to marry someone because you don't wish to have *more* money, wouldn't you think?"

She ground her teeth together and kept walking. They reached the steps leading up to her grandparents' house, and Miranda marched up. But before she could enter, Turner's hand settled upon her wrist with just enough pressure to assure her that he had lost his levity.

And yet he was still smiling when he said, "You see? Not a single reason."

She should have been nervous.

"Perhaps not," she said icily, "but nor is there a reason *to* do it."

"Your reputation is not a reason?" he asked softly.

Her eyes met his warily. "But my reputation is not in danger."

"Is it not?"

She sucked in her breath. "You wouldn't."

He shrugged, a tiny movement of his shoulder that sent

a shiver down her spine. "I am not ordinarily described as ruthless, but do not underestimate me, Miranda. I *shall* marry you."

"Why do you even *want* to?" she cried. He didn't have to do it. No one was forcing him. Miranda had practically offered him an escape route on a silver platter.

"I am a gentleman," he bit off. "I take care of my transgressions."

"I am a transgression?" she whispered. Because the air had been knocked from her lungs. A whisper was all she could do.

He stood across from her, looking as uncomfortable as she had ever seen him. "I should not have seduced you. I should have known better. And I should not have abandoned you for so many weeks following. For that I have no excuse, save my own shortcomings. But I will not allow my honor to be tossed aside. And you will marry me."

"Do you want me, or do you want your honor?" Miranda whispered.

He looked at her as if she had missed an important lesson. And then he said, "They are the same thing."

28 AUGUST 1819

I married him.

The wedding was small. Tiny, really, the only guests Miranda's grandparents, the vicar's wife, and—at Miranda's insistence—MacDownes.

At Turner's insistence, they departed for his home in Northumberland directly following the ceremony, which, also at his insistence, had been held at a shockingly early hour so that they might get a good start back to Rosedale, the Restoration-era manse that the new couple would call home.

After Miranda said her good-byes, he helped her up into the carriage, his hands lingering at her waist before he gave her a boost. An odd, unfamiliar emotion washed over him, and Turner was slightly bemused to realize that it was contentment.

Marriage to Leticia had been about many things, but never peace. Turner had entered into the union on a giddy rush of desire and excitement that had turned quickly to disillusionment and crushing sense of loss. And when that was through, all that had been left was anger.

He rather liked the idea of being married to Miranda. She could be trusted. She would never betray him, with her body or with her words. And although he did not feel the obsession he had done with Leticia, he desired her—*Miranda*—with an intensity that he still could not quite believe. Every time he saw her, smelled her, heard her voice . . . He wanted her. He wanted to lay his hand on her arm, to feel the heat from her body. He wanted to brush up close, to breathe her in as they crossed paths.

Every time he closed his eyes, he was back at the hunting lodge, covering her body with his, powered by something deep within him, something primitive and possessive, and just a little bit wild.

She was his. And she would be again.

He entered the carriage after her and sat down on the same side, although not directly next to her. He wanted nothing more than to settle at her side and pull her into his lap, but he sensed that she needed a bit of time.

They would be many hours in the carriage this day. He could afford to take his time.

He watched her for several minutes as the carriage rolled away from Edinburgh. She was tightly clutching the folds of her mint green wedding gown. Her knuckles were turning white, a testament to her frayed nerves. Twice, Turner reached out to touch her, then pulled back, unsure if his overture would be welcome. After a few more minutes, however, he said softly, "If you wish to cry, I shan't judge you."

She didn't turn around. "I'm fine."

"Are you?"

She swallowed. "Of course. I just got married, didn't I? Isn't that what every woman wants?"

"Is it what you want?"

"It's a little late to worry about that now, don't you think?"

He smiled wryly. "I'm not so dreadful, Miranda."

She let out a nervous laugh. "Of course not. You're what I've always wanted. That's what you've been telling me for days, have you not? I've loved you forever."

He found himself wishing that her words did not hold such a mocking tone. "Come over here," he said, taking hold of her arm and hauling her over to his side of the carriage.

"I like it here . . . wait . . . Oh!" She was firmly pressed against his side, his arm an iron band around her.

"This is much better, don't you think?"

"I can't see out the window now," she said sourly.

"Nothing there you haven't seen before." He pushed aside the curtain and peeked outside. "Let's see, trees, grass, a cottage or two. All fairly ordinary stuff." He took her hand in his and idly stroked her fingers. "Do you like the ring?" he asked. "It's rather plain, I know, but simple gold bands are a custom in my family."

Miranda's breathing grew quicker as her hands were warmed by his caress. "It's lovely. I—I shouldn't like anything ostentatious."

"I didn't think you would. You're a rather elegant little creature."

She blushed, nervously twisting her ring 'round and 'round on her finger. "Oh, but it's Olivia who picks out all my fashions."

"Nonetheless, I'm sure you wouldn't let her choose anything loud or garish."

Miranda stole a glance at him. He was smiling at her rather gently, almost benignly, but his fingers were doing wicked things to her wrist, sending flutters and sparks to her very core. And then he lifted her hand to his mouth, pressing a devastatingly soft kiss on the inside of her wrist. "I've something else for you," he murmured.

She didn't dare look at him again. Not if she wanted to maintain even a shred of her composure.

"Turn around," he ordered gently. He placed two fingers below her chin and tilted her face toward his. Fishing into his pocket, he pulled out a velvet-covered jeweler's box. "In all the rush this week, I forgot to give you a proper engagement ring."

"Oh, but that's not necessary," she said quickly, not really meaning it.

"Shut up, puss," he said with a grin. "And accept your gift gracefully."

"Yes, sir," she murmured, easing the lid off the box. Inside sparkled a brilliant diamond, oval-cut and framed by two small sapphires. "It's lovely, Turner," she whispered. "It matches your eyes."

"That wasn't my intention, I assure you," he said in a husky voice. He took the ring out of the box and slid it on her slender finger. "Does it fit?"

"Perfectly."

"Are you certain?"

"I'm positive, Turner. I . . . thank you. It was very thoughtful." Before she could talk herself out of it, she leaned up and gave him a quick kiss on the cheek.

He captured her face in his hands. "I'm not going to be such a terrible husband, you'll see." His face drew closer until his lips brushed hers in a gentle kiss. She leaned in toward him, seduced by his warmth and the soft murmurings of his mouth. "So soft," he whispered, pulling the pins from her hair so that he could run his hands through it. "So soft, and so sweet. I never dreamed . . ."

Miranda arched her neck to allow his lips greater access. "Never dreamed what?"

His lips moved lightly across her skin. "That you'd be like this. That I'd want you like this. That it *could* be like this."

"I always knew. I always knew." The words slipped out before she could judge the wisdom of speaking them, and then she decided she didn't care. Not when he was kissing her like this, not when his breath was coming in ragged gasps to match her own.

"Such a clever one, you are," he murmured. "I should have listened to you long ago." He began to ease her dress from her shoulders, then pressed his lips against the top of her breast, and the fire of it proved to be too much for Miranda. She arched her back against him, and when his fingers went to the buttons of her dress, she offered no resistance. In seconds, her gown slid down, and his mouth found the tip of her breast.

Miranda moaned at the shock and the pleasure. "Oh, Turner, I . . ." She sighed. "More . . ."

"A command I am only too happy to obey." His lips moved to her other breast, where they repeated the same torture.

He kissed and he suckled, and all the while, his hands wandered. Up her leg, around her waist—it was as if he was trying to mark her, to brand her forever as his own.

She felt wanton. She felt womanly. And she felt a need that burned from some strange, fiery place, deep within her. "I want you," she breathed, her fingers sinking into his hair. "I want . . ."

His fingers wandered higher, to her most tender flesh.

"I want *that*."

He chuckled against her neck. "At your service, Lady Turner."

She didn't even have time to be surprised by her new name. He was doing something—dear God, she didn't even know *what*—and it was all she could do not to scream.

And then he pulled away—not his fingers; she would

have killed him if he'd tried—but his head, just far enough to gaze down on her with a delicious smile. "I know something else you'll like," he taunted.

Miranda's lips parted with breathless surprise as he sank to his knees on the floor of the carriage. "Turner?" she whispered, because surely he could do nothing from down there. Surely he wouldn't. . .

She gasped as his head disappeared under her skirts.

Then she gasped again when she felt him, hot and demanding, kissing a trail along her thigh.

And then there could be no more doubt as to his intention. His fingers, which had been doing such a fine job arousing her, shifted position. He was spreading her open, she realized wildly, separating her, preparing her for . . .

His lips.

After that there was very little rational thought. Whatever she'd thought she'd felt the first time—and the first time had been very good, indeed—it was nothing compared to this. His mouth was wicked, and she was bewitched. And when she shattered, it was with every ounce of her body, every last drop of her soul.

Dear heavens, she thought, trying desperately to find her breath. *How could anyone survive such a thing?*

Turner's smiling face suddenly appeared before hers. "Your first wedding gift," he said.

"I . . . I . . ."

"'Thank you' will suffice," he said, cheeky as ever.

"Thank you," she sighed.

He kissed her gently on the mouth. "You are very, very welcome."

Miranda watched him as he adjusted her dress, covering her carefully and finishing with a platonic pat on the arm. His passion seemed to have completely cooled, whereas she still felt as if a flame were licking at her from the inside out. "Don't you . . . er, you didn't . . ."

A wry smile touched his features. "There isn't much I want more, but unless you want your wedding night in a moving carriage, I'll find a way to abstain."

"That wasn't a wedding night?" she asked doubtfully.

He shook his head. "Just a little treat for you."

"Oh." Miranda was trying to remember why she had protested the marriage so fiercely. A lifetime of little treats sounded rather lovely.

Her body spent, she felt a languor descending over her, and she settled sleepily into his side. "We'll do this again?" she mumbled, burrowing into his warmth.

"Oh, yes," he murmured, smiling to himself as he watched her drift off. "I promise."

Chapter 16

Rosedale was, by aristocratic standards, of modest proportions. The warm and elegant home had been in the Bevelstoke family for several generations, and it was customary for the eldest son to use it as his country home before he ascended to the earldom and the much grander Haverbreaks. Turner loved Rosedale, loved its plain stone walls and crenellated roofs. And most of all, he loved the wild landscape, domesticated only by the hundreds of roses that had been planted with wild abandon around the house.

They arrived fairly late at night, having stopped for a leisurely lunch near the border. Miranda had long since fallen asleep—she'd warned him that the motion of a carriage always made her drowsy—but Turner did not mind. He liked the quiet of the night, with only the sounds of the horses and the carriage and the wind in the air. He liked the moonlight, drifting in through the windows. And he liked glancing down at his new wife, who was not at all elegant in her sleep—her mouth was open, and truth be told, she snored just a bit. But he liked that. He didn't know why he liked it, but he did.

And he liked knowing it.

He hopped down from the carriage, placed one finger on his lips when one of the outriders approached to help, then reached back in and scooped Miranda into his arms. She had never been to Rosedale, even though it was not so far from the Lakes. He hoped she would grow to love it as he did. He thought she would. He knew her well, he was beginning to realize. He wasn't sure when it had happened, but he could look at something and think, *Miranda would like that*.

Turner had stopped here on his way up to Scotland, and the servants had been instructed to have the house ready. It was, although he had not sent word of their exact arrival, and so the staff had not been assembled for an introduction to the new viscountess. Turner was glad for that; he wouldn't have wanted to wake Miranda up.

When he made his way inside his bedchamber, he noticed thankfully that a fire was burning in the hearth. It might have been August, but the Northumberland nights held a distinctive chill. As he set Miranda softly down on the bed, a pair of footmen brought in their meager luggage. Turner whispered to the butler that his new wife could meet the staff in the morning, or perhaps later in the day, and then shut the door.

Miranda, who had gone from snoring to restless mumbling, shifted position and hugged a pillow to her chest. Turner returned to her side and shushed softly in her ear. She seemed to recognize his voice in her sleep; she let out a contented sigh and immediately rolled over.

"No sleep just yet," he murmured. "Let's get you out of these clothes." She was lying on her side, so he went to work on the buttons marching down her back. "Can you sit up for just a moment? So I can remove your dress?"

Like a sleepy child, she allowed herself to be pulled into a sitting position. "Where are we?" she yawned, not quite awake.

"Rosedale. Your new home." He wiggled her skirts up past her hips so that he could pull them over her head.

"Oh. It's nice." She flopped back down on the bed.

He smiled indulgently and nudged her back up. "Just another few seconds." With one deft motion, he pulled her dress over her head, leaving her clad in her chemise.

"Good," Miranda murmured, trying to crawl under the covers.

"Not so fast." He caught hold of her ankle. "We don't sleep with clothing here." The chemise joined her gown on the floor. Miranda, barely realizing that she was nude, finally made it under the bedclothes, sighed in utter contentment, and promptly fell asleep.

Turner chuckled and shook his head as he watched his wife. Had he noticed before that her eyelashes were so long? Perhaps it was just the candlelight. He, too, was tired, so he stripped off his clothing in quick, efficient movements and crawled into bed. She was lying on her side, curled up like a child, so he snaked an arm around her and pulled her to the center of the bed, where he could cuddle up against her warmth. Her skin was unbearably soft, and he idly stroked his hand against her midriff. Something he touched must have tickled her, for she let out a soft squeal and rolled over.

"Everything is going to be just fine," he whispered. They had affection and they had attraction, and that was more than most couples. He leaned forward to kiss her sleepy mouth, tracing its outline lightly with his tongue.

Her eyelids fluttered open.

"You must be Sleeping Beauty," he murmured. "Awakened by a kiss."

"Where are we?" she asked, her voice groggy.

"At Rosedale. You asked me that already."

"Did I? I don't remember."

Quite unable to help himself, he leaned forward and kissed her again. "Ah, Miranda, you're very sweet."

She let out a small sigh of contentment at his kiss, but it was obvious that she was having trouble keeping her eyelids open. "Turner?"

"Yes, puss?"

"I'm sorry."

"Sorry about what?"

"I'm sorry. I just can't . . . that is, I'm so tired." She yawned. "Can't do my duty."

He smiled wryly as he pulled her into his arms. "Shhh," he whispered, leaning down to kiss her temple. "Don't think of it as a duty. It's far too splendid for that. And I'm not such a cad as to force myself on a woman who is exhausted. We have plenty of time. Don't worry."

But she was already asleep.

He brushed his lips against her hair. "We have an entire lifetime."

* * *

Miranda woke first the next morning, letting out a great big yawn as she opened her eyes. Daylight was peeking in around the curtains, but it definitely wasn't the sun that was causing her bed to be so cozy and warm. Turner's arm had been thrown over her waist at some point during the night, and she was curled up against him. Lord, but the man radiated heat.

She scooted around to allow herself a better view of him while he slept. His face always held a boyish appeal, but in slumber the effect was exaggerated. He looked a perfect angel, without a trace of the cynicism that sometimes clouded his eyes.

"We have Leticia to thank for that," Miranda murmured softly, touching his cheek.

He stirred, mumbling something in his sleep.

"Not yet, my love," she whispered, feeling brave enough to use endearments when she knew he could not hear her. "I like to watch you sleep."

Turner slept, and she listened to him breathe.

It was heaven.

Eventually he stirred, his body stretching its way awake before his eyelids lifted. And then there he was, watching her with sleepy eyes, smiling.

"Morning," he said groggily.

"Good morning."

He yawned. "Have you been awake long?"

"Just a little while."

"Are you hungry? I could have some breakfast sent up."

She shook her head.

He yawned again and then smiled at her. "You're very pink in the morning."

"Pink?" She couldn't help but be intrigued.

"Mmm-hmm. Your skin . . . it glows."

"It does not."

"It does. Trust me."

"My mother always told me to be suspicious of men who said, 'Trust me.'"

"Yes, well, your mother never knew me very well," he said offhandedly. He touched her lips with his index finger. "These are pink, too."

"Are they?" she asked in a breathy voice.

"Mmm-hmm. Very pink. But not, I think, as pink as some other parts of you."

Miranda turned positively scarlet.

"These, for example," he murmured, grazing his palms over her nipples. His hand stole back up and tenderly cupped her cheek. "You were very tired last night."

"Yes, I was."

"Much too tired to attend to some important business."

She swallowed nervously, trying not to let out a little moan as his hand trailed softly up her back.

"I think it's time we consummated this marriage," he murmured, his lips warm and wicked at her ear. And then he pulled her against him, and she realized just how soon he wanted to take care of the matter.

Miranda gave him a smile full of humor-tinged reproof. "We took care of that quite some time ago. A trifle prematurely, if you recall."

"Doesn't count," he said blithely, waving off her comment. "We weren't married."

"If it didn't *count*, we wouldn't *be* married."

Turner acknowledged her point with a rakish smile. "Ah, well, I suppose you're right. But everything worked out in the end. You can hardly be upset with me for being so tremendously virile."

Miranda might have been fairly innocent, but she knew enough to roll her eyes at that. She could not remark, however, as his hand had moved to her breast, and he was doing something to the tip that she could swear she felt between her legs.

She felt herself sliding, slipping off the pillow and onto her back, and she felt herself sliding on the inside, too, as his every touch seemed to melt another inch of her body. He kissed her breasts, her stomach, her legs. There seemed to be no part of her that did not interest him. Miranda didn't know what to do. She lay on her back beneath his exploring hands and mouth, squirming and moaning whenever the sensations began to overwhelm her.

"Do you like that?" Turner murmured as he inspected the back of her knee with his lips.

"I like everything," she gasped.

He moved back up to her mouth and dropped a quick kiss onto it. "I cannot tell you how much it pleases me to hear you say that."

"This can't be proper."

He grinned. "No less so than what I did to you in the carriage."

She flushed at the memory, then bit her lip to keep from asking him to do it again.

But he read her mind, or at least her face, and he let out a purr of pleasure as he kissed his way down the length of her body to her womanhood. His lips touched first the inside of one thigh, then the other.

"Oh, yes," she sighed, beyond embarrassment now. She didn't care if it made her a brazen hussy. She just wanted the pleasure.

"So sweet," he murmured, and he placed one of his hands on her soft tuft of hair and opened her even more. His hot breath touched her skin, and her legs tensed, even though she knew she wanted this. "No, no, no," he said, amusement in his voice as he gently pried her apart. And then he leaned down and kissed that most sensitive nub of flesh.

Miranda, quite unable to say anything coherent, squealed from the sheer sensation of his kisses. Was it pleasure or pain? She wasn't certain. Her hands, which had been balled into fists at her sides, flew down to Turner's head and planted themselves in his hair. When her hips began to writhe beneath him, he made a move as if to get up, but her hands held his head firmly in place. He finally eased his way from her grasp and moved back up her body until his lips were on level with hers. "I thought you weren't going to let me up for air," he murmured.

Miranda didn't think it possible in her position, but she blushed.

He nibbled on her ear. "Did you like that?"

She nodded, unable to voice the words.

"There are many, many things for you to learn."

"Could I . . . ?" Oh, how to ask it?

He smiled indulgently at her. "Could you what?"

She swallowed down her embarrassment. "Could I touch *you*?"

In response, he took her hand and guided it down his body. When they reached his manhood, her hand jerked back reflexively. It was much hotter than she'd expected, and much, much harder. Turner patiently moved her hand back to him, and this time she made a few tentative strokes, marveling at how soft the skin was. "It's so different," she marveled. "So very odd."

He chuckled, partly because that was the only way he could contain the desire that was racing through him. "It's never seemed odd to me."

"I want to see it."

"Oh, God, Miranda." This, between clenched teeth.

"No, I do." She pushed down the covers until he was bared to her eyes. "Oh, my goodness," she breathed. That had fit into her? She could barely believe it. Still immensely curious, she wrapped her hand around him and gently squeezed.

Turner nearly came off the bed.

She let go of him immediately. "Did I hurt you?"

"No," he rasped. "Do it again."

Miranda's lips curved into a feminine smile of satisfaction as she repeated her caresses. "Can I kiss you?"

"You'd better not," he said hoarsely.

"Oh. I thought maybe since you had kissed me . . ."

Turner let out a primitive growl and flipped her over

onto her back and settled himself between her thighs. "Later. You can do it later." Unable to control his passion any longer, his mouth descended onto hers with stunning force, claiming her as his own. He nudged her thigh with his knee, forcing her to open wider.

Miranda instinctively tilted her hips to allow him easier entry. He slid into her effortlessly, and she marveled that her body could stretch to fit him. He began stroking slowly back and forth, back and forth, moving inside her with a slow but steady rhythm. "Oh, Miranda," he moaned. "Oh, my God."

"I know. I know." Her head lolled from side to side. The weight of him was pinning her down, and yet she could not keep still.

"You're mine," he growled, stepping up the pace. "Mine."

She moaned in response.

He held still, his eyes strange and penetrating as he said, "Say it."

"I'm yours," she whispered.

"Every inch of you. Every luscious inch of you. From here"—he cupped her breast—"to here"—he slid his finger along the curve of her cheek—"to here." He pulled out until only the very tip of him remained within her and then pumped back in to the hilt.

"Oh, God yes, Turner. Anything you want."

"I want *you*."

"I'm yours. I swear it."

"No one else, Miranda. Promise me." He again pulled himself almost out.

She felt utterly bereft without him inside her and almost cried out. "I promise," she gasped. "Please . . . just come back to me."

He slid back in, causing her to both sigh with relief and pant with desire. "There will be no other men. Do you hear me?"

Miranda knew that his urgent words stemmed from Leticia's betrayal, but she was too caught up in the passion of the moment to even think of scolding him for comparing her to his late wife. "None, I swear! I've never wanted anyone else."

"And you never will," he said firmly, as if he could make it true simply by saying it.

"Never! Please, Turner, please . . . I need you. I need . . ."

"I know what you need." His lips closed around one of her nipples as he sped up his movements inside her. She felt pressure building in her body. Spasms of pleasure were shooting through her belly, down her arms, and up her legs. And then suddenly she knew she could not possibly bear another moment without expiring on the spot, and her entire body convulsed, clenching around his manhood like a silken glove. She screamed his name, grasping at his arms as her shoulders came off the bed in the force of her climax.

The sheer sensuality of her release pushed Turner over the edge, and he cried out hoarsely as he plunged forward one last time, driving himself in to the hilt. His pleasure was intense, and he could not believe the speed with which he poured himself into her. He collapsed on top of her, utterly spent. Never had it been this good, never. Not even the last time with Miranda. It was as if every movement, every touch was intensified now that he knew she was his and his alone. He was startled by his possessiveness, stunned by the way he had made her swear her fidelity to him, and disgusted by the fact that he had manipulated her passion to suit his childish needs.

Was she angry? Did she hate him for it? He lifted his head up and looked down into her face. Her eyes were closed, and her lips were curved into a half smile. She looked every inch the satisfied woman, and he quickly decided that if she wasn't offended by his actions or questions, he wasn't going to argue with her.

"You look pink, puss," he murmured, stroking her cheek.

"Still?" she asked lazily, not even opening her eyes.

"Even more so."

Turner smiled, propping himself up on his elbows to take some of his weight off her. He ran his finger along the curve of her cheek, starting at the corner of her mouth and then winding up at the tender skin near her eye. He nudged her lashes. "Open up."

She lifted her lids. "Good morning."

"Indeed." He grinned boyishly.

She squirmed beneath his intense stare. "Aren't you growing uncomfortable?"

"I like it up here."

"But your arms—"

"Are strong enough to hold me up for quite a while longer. Besides, I enjoy looking at you."

Shyly, she averted her gaze.

"No, no, no. No escape. Look back here." He touched her chin and nudged it until she was facing him again. "You're very beautiful, you know."

"I am not," she said in a voice that said she *knew* he was lying.

"Will you stop quibbling with me over this point? I'm older than you and have seen a lot of women."

"Seen?" she asked dubiously.

"That, my dear wife, is another topic altogether, and one that does not require discussion. I merely wanted to point out that I am probably a bit more of a connoisseur than you are, and you should take my word on the matter. If I say you're beautiful, then you're beautiful."

"Really, Turner, you're very sweet—"

He leaned down until his nose rested on hers. "You're starting to irritate me, wife."

"Good heavens, I wouldn't want to do that."

"I should think not."

Her lips curved into a mischief-tinged smile. "You're very handsome."

"Thank you," he said magnanimously. "Now, did you see how nicely I accepted your compliment?"

"You rather ruined the effect by pointing out your good manners."

He shook his head. "Such a mouth on you. I'm going to have to do something about that."

"Kiss it?" she said hopefully.

"Mmm, not a problem." His tongue darted out and traced the outline of her lips. "Very nice. Very tasty."

"I'm not a fruit tart, you know," she retorted.

"There's that mouth again," he said, sighing.

"I imagine you'll have to keep kissing me."

He sighed as if that were a great chore. "Oh, all right." This time, he poked into her mouth and ran his tongue along the smooth surface of her teeth. When he lifted his head again and looked back down at her face, she was glowing. It seemed the only word to describe the radiance that emanated from her skin. "My Lord, Miranda," he said hoarsely. "You really are beautiful."

He lowered himself down, rolled onto his side, and gathered her into his arms. "I've never seen anyone look quite as you do right this minute," he murmured, pulling her more tightly against him. "Let's just lie here like this for a spell."

He drifted off to sleep, thinking that this was an excellent way to start off a marriage.

6 NOVEMBER 1819

Today marked the tenth week of my marriage—and the third since when I should last have bled. I should not be surprised that I have conceived again so quickly—Turner is a most attentive husband.

I do not complain.

12 JANUARY 1820

As I stepped into the bath this evening, I could swear I saw a slight swell to my belly. I believe in it now. I believe it is here to stay.

30 APRIL 1820

Oh, I am large. And nearly three months re-main. Turner seems to adore my roundness. He is convinced it shall be a girl. He whispers, "I love you," to my belly.

But just to my belly. Not to me. To be fair, I have not said the words, either, but I am sure he knows that I do. After all, I did tell him before our marriage, and he once said that a person does not fall out of love so easily.

I know he cares for me. Why can he not love me? Or if he does, why can he not say it?

Chapter 17

The months passed, and the newlyweds settled into a comfortable and affectionate routine. Turner, who had lived through a hellish existence with Leticia, was constantly surprised at how pleasant marriage could be when one undertook it with the right person. Miranda was a complete delight to him. He loved to watch her read a book, brush her hair, give instructions to the housekeeper—he loved to watch her do anything. And he found himself constantly looking for excuses to touch her. He would point out an invisible speck of dust on her dress and then brush it aside. A lock of her hair had fallen astray, he would murmur as he pushed it back into place.

And she never seemed to mind. Sometimes, if she was busy with something, she would swat his hand away, but more often she merely smiled, and sometimes she'd move her head—just a touch, just enough to rest her cheek in his hand.

But sometimes, when she did not realize he was watching her, he caught her looking at him with such longing. She always looked away, so quickly that he often could not even be sure that the moment had occurred. But he knew that it had, because when he closed his own eyes at night, he saw hers, with that flash of sadness that clawed at his gut.

He knew what she wanted. It should have been easy. Three simple words. And really, shouldn't he just say them? Even if he didn't mean them, wouldn't it be worth it just to see her happy?

Sometimes he tried to say it, tried to make his mouth form the words, but he always seemed to get this choking feeling, as if his very breath were being squeezed from his throat.

And the irony was—he thought he might love her. He knew that he would be utterly bereft if something were to happen to her. But then again, he'd thought he loved Leticia, and look where that had got him. He loved everything *about* Miranda, from the way her nose turned up slightly at the end to her dry wit which she never spared on him. But was that the same as loving the person?

And if he did, how would he know? This time, he wanted to be sure. He wanted some sort of scientific proof. He had loved on faith once before, believing that his giddy mix of desire and obsession had to be love. Because what else could it have been?

But now he was older. Wiser, too, which was a good thing, and far more cynical, which was not.

Most of the time he was able to push these worries from

his head. He was a man, and frankly, that's what men did.
Women could discuss and ruminate (and most likely discuss again, following) all they wanted. He preferred to
ponder a matter once, maybe twice, and be done with it.

Which was why it was particularly galling that he
seemed unable to let this particular problem go. His life
was lovely. Happy. Delightful. He shouldn't be wasting
valuable thought and energy pondering the state of his own
heart. He ought to be able to enjoy his many blessings and
not have to *think* about it.

He was doing precisely this—concentrating on why he
did not wish to be thinking about all this—when he heard
a knock on his study door.

"Come in!"

Miranda's head peeked into the doorway. "Am I bothering you?"

"No, of course not. Come in."

She pushed the door the rest of the way open and entered the room. Turner had to stifle a smile at the sight of
her. Lately her belly seemed to precede the rest of her into
a room by a good five seconds. She saw his grin and looked
down at herself ruefully. "I'm enormous, aren't I?"

"That you are."

She sighed. "You might have lied to spare my feelings
and told me that I'm not so very big. Women in my condition are very emotional, you know." She walked over to a
chair near his desk and put her arms on the armrests to ease
herself down into it.

Turner jumped to his feet immediately to help her into
the chair. "I believe I like you big."

She snorted. "You just like seeing tangible proof of your own virility."

He smiled at that. "Has she kicked today?"

"No, and I'm not so sure he's a she."

"Of course he's a she. It's perfectly obvious."

"I suppose you're planning to open a practice in psychic midwifery?"

His brows rose. "Watch your mouth, wife."

Miranda rolled her eyes and held out a piece of paper. "I received a letter from your mother today. I thought you might like to read it."

He took the letter from her hands, idly pacing the room as he read the missive. He had put off telling his family about his marriage for as long as possible, but after two months, Miranda had convinced him that he couldn't possibly avoid it any longer. As expected, they were shocked (with the exception of Olivia, who'd had some inkling as to what was going on), and had rushed immediately to Rosedale to inspect the situation. His mother had been heard to murmur, "I never dreamed . . ." a few hundred times, and Winston's nose had been put a little out of joint, but all in all, Miranda made a smooth transition from Cheever to Bevelstoke. After all, she had practically been a part of the family before.

"Winston has got into a bit of trouble at Oxford," Turner murmured, his eyes quickly moving across his mother's words.

"Yes, well, that is to be expected, I imagine."

He looked up at her with an amused expression. "What does that mean?"

"Don't think I never heard about *your* exploits at university."

He grinned. "I'm much more mature now."

"I should hope so."

He walked over to her and dropped a kiss first on her nose and then on her belly.

"I wish I could have gone to Oxford," she said longingly. "I should have loved to listen to all of those lectures."

"Not all of them. Trust me, some were dismal."

"I still think I would have liked it."

He shrugged. "Perhaps. You're certainly a deuced sight more intelligent than most of the men I knew there."

"After having spent nearly a season in London, I have to say that it is not terribly difficult to be more intelligent than most of the men of the *ton*."

"Present company excluded, I hope."

She nodded graciously. "Of course."

He shook his head as he moved back to his desk. This was what he loved most about being married to her—these quirky little conversations that filled their days. He sat back down and picked up a document he'd been perusing before she came in. "It looks as if I will need to go to London."

"Now? Is anyone even there?"

"Very few," he admitted. Parliament was not in session, and most of the *ton* had vacated town for their country homes. "But a good friend of mine is there, and he needs my support for a business venture."

"Would you like me to go with you?"

"There is nothing I would like better, but I will not have you traveling at such a time."

"I feel perfectly healthy."

"And I believe you, but it seems ill-advised to take unnecessary chances. And it must be said—you've become rather . . ." He cleared his throat. "Unwieldy."

Miranda grimaced. "I wonder what you could possibly have said that might have made me feel less attractive."

His lips twitched, and he leaned forward and kissed her cheek. "I won't be gone long. No more than a fortnight, I should think."

"A fortnight?" she said forlornly.

"I'll have at least four days' travel each way. With all the rain recently, the roads will certainly be dreadful."

"I shall miss you."

He paused for a moment before answering, "I shall miss you, too."

At first she did not speak. And then she sighed, a tiny, wistful sound that squeezed around his heart. But then her demeanor changed and she looked a bit more brisk. "I suppose there is plenty to keep me busy," she said with a sigh. "I should like to redecorate the west parlor. The upholstery is dreadfully faded. Perhaps I will invite Olivia for a visit. She is so good at these things."

Turner smiled warmly at her. It gave him great joy that she was coming to love his home as much as he did. "I trust your judgment. You don't need Olivia."

"I should enjoy her company while you're gone, though."

"Then by all means, invite her." He glanced at the clock. "I say, are you hungry? It's well past noon."

She rubbed her stomach absently. "Not too hungry, I think. But I could have a bite or two."

"More than two," he said firmly. "More than three. You're not just eating for yourself now, you know."

Miranda looked ruefully down at her swollen belly. "Believe me, I know."

He stood up and strode over to the door. "I'll run down to the kitchen and get something."

"You could just ring for it."

"No, no, it will be much faster this way."

"But I'm not—" It was too late. He'd already run out the door and couldn't hear her. She smiled to herself as she sat and curved her legs underneath her. No one could doubt Turner's concern for her and the baby's welfare. It was there in the way he fluffed the pillows for her before she crawled into bed, the way he made sure that she ate good, wholesome food, and especially in the way he insisted on putting his ear to her stomach every night to hear the baby moving about.

"I think she kicked!" he would exclaim excitedly.

"It was probably a burp," Miranda had teased him once.

Turner completely missed her humor and raised his head, concern clouding his eyes. "Can they burp in there? Is it normal?"

She let out a soft, indulgent laugh. "I don't know."

"Perhaps I ought to ask the physician."

She took his hand and pulled him up until he was lying by her side. "I'm sure everything is just fine."

"But—"

"If you send for the physician, he is going to think you're insane."

"But—"

"Let's just go to sleep. That's it, hold me. Tighter." She sighed and snuggled up next to him. "There. I can sleep now."

Back in the study, Miranda smiled as she remembered the interchange. A hundred times a day he did similar things, showing her how much he loved her. Didn't he? How could he look at her so tenderly and not love her? Why was she so unsure of his feelings?

Because he never voiced them aloud, she retorted silently. Oh, he complimented her and frequently made comments about how *glad* he was that he had married her.

It was the most pinpointedly cruel sort of torture, and he had no idea he was committing it. He thought he was being kind and attentive, and he *was*.

But every time he looked at her, and he smiled in that warm and secret way of his, and she thought—for one breathless second she thought he would lean forward and whisper—

I love you.

—and then every time, when it didn't happen, and he just brushed his lips by her cheek, or tousled her hair, or asked her if she'd enjoyed her bloody pudding, for heaven's sake—

She felt something inside crumpling. A little squeeze, making just a little crease, but all those folds on her heart were adding up, and every day, it seemed a little harder to pretend that her life was precisely how she wished it.

She tried to be patient. The last thing she wanted from him was falsehood. *I love you* was devastating when there wasn't any feeling behind it.

But she didn't want to think about this. Not right now, not when he was being so sweet and attentive, and she should have been utterly and completely happy.

And she was. Truly. Almost. It was only one tiny little piece of her that kept pushing it way to the fore, and it was getting annoying, really, because she didn't want to waste all her thought and energy thinking about something over which she had no control.

She just wanted to live in the moment, to enjoy her many blessings without having to *think* about it.

Turner made a timely entrance, striding back into the room and dropping a gentle kiss on the top of her head. "Mrs. Hingham says she'll send up a plate of food in a few minutes."

"I told you you shouldn't have bothered to go down," Miranda scolded. "I knew that nothing would be ready."

"If I hadn't gone down myself," he said in a matter-of-fact tone, "I would have had to wait for a maid to come and see what I wanted, then I would have had to wait for her to go down to the kitchens, then I would have had to wait while Mrs. Hingham prepared our food, then—"

Miranda held her hand up. "Enough! I see your point."

"It will arrive more quickly this way." He leaned forward with a devilish grin. "I'm not a patient person."

Neither was she, Miranda thought ruefully.

But her husband, oblivious to her stormy thoughts,

merely smiled as he gazed out the window. A light dusting of snow covered the trees.

A footman and a maid slipped into the room, bringing food and setting it up on Turner's desk.

"Aren't you worried about your papers?" Miranda asked.

"They'll be fine." He shoved them all into a pile.

"But won't they get mixed up?"

He shrugged. "I'm hungry. That's more important. *You're* more important."

The maid let out a little sigh at his romantic words. Miranda smiled tightly. The household staff probably thought he professed his love to her whenever they were out of earshot.

"Now then," Turner said briskly. "Here is some beef and vegetable stew, puss. I want you to eat every bite."

Miranda looked dubiously at the tureen he'd set in front of her. It would take a small army of pregnant women to finish it all. "You're joking," she said.

"Not at all." He dipped the spoon into the stew and held it up in front of her mouth.

"Really, Turner, I can't—"

He darted the spoon into her mouth.

She choked in surprise for a second, then chewed and swallowed. "I can feed myself."

"But this is much more fun."

"For you, perha—"

In went the spoon again.

Miranda swallowed. "This is ridiculous."

"Not at all."

"Is this some way to teach me not to talk so much?"

"No, although I missed a great opportunity with that last sentence."

"Turner, you're incorr—"

Got her again. "Incorrigible?"

"Yes," she spluttered.

"Oh, dear," he said. "You got a bit on your chin."

"You're the one wielding the spoon."

"Sit still." He leaned forward and licked a drop of sauce off her skin. "Mmm, delicious."

"Have some," she deadpanned. "There's plenty."

"Oh, but I wouldn't want to deprive you of valuable nutrients."

She snorted in response.

"Here is another bite—oh, dear, I seem to have missed your mouth again." His tongue flicked out and cleaned up the mess.

"You did that deliberately!" she accused.

"And purposefully waste food that could be feeding my pregnant wife?" He placed one affronted hand on his chest. "What a cur you must think me."

"Perhaps not a cur, but certainly a sneaky little—"

"Victory!"

She wagged her finger at him. "Mmph grmphng gtrmph."

"Don't talk with your mouth full. It's very bad manners."

She swallowed. "I said, I will have my vengeance, you—" She broke off when the spoon connected with her nose.

"Now look what you did," he said, shaking his head

in an exaggerated motion. "You were moving around so much I missed your mouth. Hold still now."

She pursed her lips but couldn't stop the barest hint of a smile from breaking through.

"That's a good girl," he murmured, leaning forward. He caught the tip of her nose in his mouth and gave it a little suck until all the gravy was gone.

"Turner!"

"The only woman in the world with a ticklish nose," he chuckled. "And I had the good sense to marry you."

"Stop, stop, stop."

"Putting gravy on your face, or kissing you?"

Her breath caught in her throat. "Putting gravy on my face. You don't need an excuse to kiss me."

He leaned forward. "I don't?"

"No."

"Imagine my relief." His nose touched hers.

"Turner?"

"Hmmm?"

"If you don't kiss me soon, I think I shall go mad."

He teased her with the most feathery light of kisses. "Will that do?"

She shook her head.

He deepened the kiss. "That?"

"I'm afraid not."

"What do you need?" he whispered, his voice hot against her lips.

"What do *you* need?" she countered. Her hands slid up his arms to his shoulders, and out of habit, she began to knead.

And apparently instantly diffused his ardor. "Oh, Lord, Miranda," he groaned, his body going limp, "that's wonderful. No, don't stop. Please don't stop."

"It's remarkable," she said with a faint smile. "You really are putty in my hands."

"Anything," he moaned. "Just don't stop."

"Why are you so tense?"

He opened his eyes and leveled a wry glance at her. "You know very well."

She blushed. Her physician had informed her during his last visit that it was time to stop marital relations. Turner hadn't stopped grumbling for a week.

"I refuse to believe," she said, lifting her fingers from his shoulders and then smiling when he moaned in protest, "that I am the sole cause of your horrid backaches."

"Stress from not being able to make love to you, physical exertion from carrying your now enormous body up the stairs . . ."

"You've never once had to carry me up the stairs!"

"Yes, well, I've thought about it, and that has certainly been enough to give me a backache. Right . . ." He twisted his arm around and pointed to a spot on his back. ". . . there."

Miranda pursed her lips but nonetheless started rubbing where he indicated. "You, my lord, are a big baby."

"Mmmm-hmmm," he agreed, his head practically lolling to the side. "Mind if I lie down? It'll make it easier for you."

How, Miranda wondered, had he managed to manipulate her into rubbing his back right there on the carpet? But she was enjoying herself, too. She loved touching him, loved memorizing the contours of his body. Smiling to herself, she pulled his shirt out of the waistband of his breeches and slipped her hands underneath so that she could touch his skin. It was warm and silky, and she could not help but run her hands lightly over it, just to feel the golden softness that was uniquely him.

"I wish you could rub my back," she heard herself say. It had been many weeks since she'd last been able to lie on her stomach.

He turned his head so that she could see his face, and he smiled. Then, with a little groan, he sat up. "Sit still," he said softly, turning her around so that he could massage her back.

It felt like heaven. "Oh, Turner," she sighed. "That feels so lovely."

He made a noise—a strange one, and she twisted as best she could so that she could see his face. "I'm sorry," she said, grimacing as she saw the desire and restraint at war in his eyes. "I miss you, too, if that's any consolation."

He crushed her to him, holding her as tightly as he was able without pressing too hard against her belly. "It's not your fault, puss."

"No, I know, but I'm still sorry. I miss you dreadfully." She lowered her voice. "Sometimes you're so deep inside of me, it feels like you're touching my heart. I miss that most of all."

"Don't talk like that," he rasped.

"I'm sorry."

"And for the love of God, stop apologizing."

She almost giggled. "I'm—no, I take that back. I'm not. But I *am* sorry that you, er, that you are in such a state. It doesn't seem fair."

"It's more than fair. I get a healthy wife and a beautiful baby. And all I have to do is restrain myself for a few months."

"But you shouldn't have to," she murmured suggestively, her hand straying to the buttons at the front of his breeches. "You shouldn't have to."

"Miranda, stop. I can't take it."

"You shouldn't have to," she repeated as she pushed his already untucked shirt up over his chest and kissed his flat stomach.

"What—oh, God, Miranda." He let out a ragged moan.

Her lips moved ever lower.

"Oh, God! Miranda!"

7 MAY 1820

I am shameless.
But my husband does not complain.

Chapter 18

The next morning, Turner dropped a gentle kiss on his wife's forehead. "You're certain you'll be all right without me?"

Miranda swallowed and nodded, blinking back tears that she had sworn she wouldn't shed. The sky was still dark, but Turner had wanted an early start to London. She was sitting up in bed, her hands resting atop her belly as she watched him get dressed. "Your valet is going to have an apoplectic fit," she said, trying to tease him. "You know he thinks you don't know how to dress yourself properly."

Clad only in breeches, Turner walked to her side and perched on the edge of the bed. "You're sure you don't mind my leaving?"

"Of course I mind. I'd much rather have you here." A wobbly smile touched her face. "But I will be just fine. And I'll most likely get a lot more work done without you here to distract me."

"Oh? And am I so very distracting?"

"Very. Although"—she smiled sheepishly—"I can't be 'distracted' very much lately."

"Mmmm. Sad, but true. I, unfortunately, am distracted all the time." He cupped her chin with his fingers and lowered his lips onto hers in a passionately tender kiss. "Every time I see you," he murmured.

"Every time?" she asked doubtfully.

He gave her a solemn nod.

"But I look like a cow."

"Mmm-hmm." His lips never left hers. "But a very attractive cow."

"You wretch!" She pulled away and punched him playfully on the shoulder.

He smiled devilishly in return. "It appears that this trip to London is going to be beneficial to my health. Or at least my body. It is fortunate I do not bruise easily."

She pouted and stuck out her tongue.

He clucked at her before standing up and crossing the room. "I see that motherhood has not brought maturity along with it."

Her pillow went sailing across the room.

Turner was back at her side in an instant, his body spreading out on the bed along the length of hers. "Maybe I should remain, if only to keep a firm rein on you."

"Maybe you should."

He kissed her again, this time with barely restrained passion and emotion. "Have I told you," he murmured as his lips explored the soft planes of her face, "how much I adore being married to you?"

"N-not today."

"It's early yet. Surely you can excuse my lapse." He caught her earlobe between his teeth. "I'm certain I told you yesterday."

And the day before, Miranda thought bittersweetly. And the day before that, too, but he'd never told her that he loved her. Why was it always "I love being with you" and "I love doing things with you" and never "I love *you*"? He couldn't even seem to bring himself to say, "I adore you." "I adore being married to you" was obviously much safer.

Turner caught the melancholy look in her eye. "Is something wrong, puss?"

"No, no," she lied. "Nothing. I just . . . I'm just going to miss you, that's all."

"I shall miss you, too." He kissed her one last time and then stood up to pull on his shirt.

Miranda watched him as he moved about the room, gathering his belongings. Her hands were clenched under the covers, twisting the sheets into angry spirals. He wasn't going to say anything unless she did first. And why should he? He was obviously perfectly content with matters as they were. She was going to have to force the issue, but she was so scared—so scared that he wouldn't pull her into his arms and tell her that he had only been waiting for her to tell him that she loved him again. But most of all, she was terrified that he'd swallow uncomfortably and say something that began with, "You know how much I *like* you, Miranda . . ."

That thought was sufficiently chilling that she shuddered, her breath catching in a fearful sigh.

"Are you certain you're feeling well?" Turner asked in a concerned voice.

How easy it would be to lie to him. Only a few words and he would remain by her side, holding her warmly at night and kissing her so tenderly that she could almost let herself believe that he loved her. But if there was one thing they needed between them, it was truth, so she just nodded. "I am well, Turner, truly. It was just a waking-up-in-the-morning sort of shiver. My body is still asleep, I think."

"As the rest of you should be. I don't want you overdoing it while I'm gone. You're due in less than two months."

She smiled wryly. "A fact I am unlikely to forget."

"Good. You've my baby in there, after all." Turner pulled on his coat and leaned over to kiss her good-bye.

"My baby, too."

"Mmmm, I know." He straightened, preparing to depart. "That's why I love her so much already."

"Turner!"

He turned around. Her voice sounded odd, almost fearful. "What is it, Miranda?"

"I just wanted to tell you . . . that is, I wanted you to know . . ."

"What is it, Miranda?"

"I just wanted you to know that I love you." The words burst from her mouth in a tumbling rush, as if she were afraid that if she slowed down she'd lose her courage altogether.

He froze, and it felt as if his body were not his own. He'd been waiting for this. Hadn't he? And wasn't it a *good* thing? Didn't he want her love?

His eyes met hers, and he could *hear* what she was thinking—

Don't break my heart, Turner. Please don't break my heart.

Turner's lips parted. He'd been telling himself over the last few months that he wanted her to say it again, but now that she had, he felt as if a noose were tightening around his throat. He couldn't breathe. He couldn't think. And he certainly couldn't see straight because all he could see were those big, brown eyes, and they looked so desperate.

"Miranda, I—" He choked on his words. Why couldn't he say it? Didn't he feel it? Why was it so hard?

"Don't, Turner," she said in a quavering voice. "Don't say anything. Just forget about it."

Something lurched in his throat, but he managed, "You know how much I care for you."

"Have a good time in London."

Her voice was flat, devastatingly so, and he knew he could not leave her this way. "Miranda, please."

"Don't talk to me!" she cried out. "I don't want to hear your excuses, and I don't want to hear your platitudes! I don't want to hear anything!"

Except I love you.

The unspoken words hung in the air between them. Turner could feel her slipping farther and farther away from him, and he felt powerless to stop this gulf that was opening up between them. He knew what he had to do, and it shouldn't have been hard. It was just three little words, for God's sake. And he wanted to say them. But he was standing at the edge of something, and he just could not take that last step forward.

It was not rational. It did not make sense. He did not know if he was scared to love her or scared that she loved him. He didn't know if he was scared at all. Maybe he was just dead inside, his heart too battered from his first marriage to behave in a logical, normal manner.

"Darling," he began, trying to think of something that would make her happy again. Or if that wasn't possible, at least wipe away some of the devastation in her eyes.

"Don't call me that," she said in a voice so low he could barely hear her. "Call me by my name."

He wanted to yell. He wanted to scream. He wanted to shake her by the shoulders and make her understand that *he* didn't understand. But he didn't know how to do any of those things, so he just nodded his head and said, "I will see you in a few weeks, then."

She nodded. Once. And then she looked away. "I expect you will."

"Good-bye," he said softly, and he shut the door behind him.

"There is a lot you can do with green," Olivia said as she fingered the fraying drapes in the west salon. "And you have always looked good in green."

"I'm not going to wear the drapes," Miranda replied.

"I know, but one wants to look one's best in one's drawing room, don't you think?"

"I suppose *one* does," Miranda returned, teasing Olivia for her affected speech.

"Oh, stop. If you didn't want my advice you shouldn't have invited me." Olivia's lips curved into an artless smile. "But I'm so glad you did. I've missed you dreadfully, Miranda. Haverbreaks is terribly dull in the winter. Fiona Bennet keeps calling on me."

"A hideous circumstance," Miranda agreed.

"I'm tempted to accept one of her invitations out of sheer boredom."

"Oh, don't do that."

"You're not still holding a grudge for the ribbon incident at my eleventh birthday party, are you?"

Miranda held her thumb and forefinger about a half inch apart. "Just a small one."

"Goodness, let it go. After all, you landed Turner. And right beneath all of our noses." Olivia was still slightly miffed that her brother and her best friend had been courting without her knowledge. "Although I must say, it is perfectly beastly of him to run off to London and leave you here alone."

Miranda smiled tightly as she fingered the fabric of her skirt. "It's not so bad," she murmured.

"But your time is so near," Olivia protested. "He shouldn't have left you alone."

"He didn't," Miranda said firmly, trying to change the subject. "You're here, aren't you?"

"Yes, yes, and I would stay for the birthing if I could, but Mama says it isn't proper for an unmarried lady."

"I can't think of anything more proper," Miranda retorted. "It's not as if you're not going to be in this very same situation in a few years."

"I do require a husband first," Olivia reminded her.

"I don't foresee any problem with that. How many offers did you receive this year? Six?"

"Eight."

"So no complaining, then."

"I'm not, I just . . . Oh, never mind, she says I may remain at Rosedale. I'm just not allowed to remain with *you.*"

"The drapes," Miranda reminded her.

"Yes, of course," Olivia said briskly, once again all business. "If we upholster in green, the drapes can be a contrasting color. Perhaps a secondary color from the upholstery fabric."

Miranda nodded and smiled when appropriate, but her mind was far away. London, to be exact. Her husband intruded on her thoughts every second of the day. She would be discussing a matter with the housekeeper when his smile would suddenly dance before her eyes. She couldn't finish the book she was reading because the sound of his laughter kept floating through her ears. And at night, when she was nearly asleep, the feather-light touch of his kiss teased her lips until she ached for his warm body next to hers.

"Miranda? Miranda!"

Miranda heard Olivia impatiently repeating her name. "What? Oh, I'm sorry, Livvy. My mind was miles away."

"I know. It rarely seems to reside at Rosedale these days."

Miranda faked a heartfelt sigh. "It's the baby, I imagine. It makes me maudlin." In another two months, she thought ruefully, she wasn't going to be able to blame her momentary lapses of reason on the baby, and then what would she do? She smiled blandly at Olivia. "What did you want to tell me?"

"I was merely going to say that if you don't like green, we might redo the room in a dusty rose color. You could call it the rose salon. Which would be so fitting for Rosedale."

"You don't think it would be too feminine?" Miranda asked. "Turner uses this room quite a bit, too."

"Hmmm. That *is* a problem."

Miranda didn't even realize that she was clenching her fists until her nails bit into her palms. Funny how even the mention of his name could set her off. "On the other hand," she said, her eyes narrowing dangerously. "I've always liked dusty rose. Let's do it."

"Are you sure?" Now Olivia was doubtful. "Turner—"

"Hang Turner," Miranda cut in with just enough vehemence to make Olivia raise her eyebrows. "If he wanted a say in the decor, he shouldn't have gone off to London."

"You shouldn't get snappy," Olivia said placatingly. "I'm certain he misses you very much."

"Nonsense. He probably hasn't thought of me at all."

She was haunting him.

Turner had thought, after four interminable days in a closed carriage, that he would be able to remove Miranda from his thoughts when he reached London and all its distractions.

But he was wrong.

Their last conversation played out in his mind, over and over and over again, but every time Turner attempted to change his lines, to pretend that he had said something else, that he had *thought* of something else to say, the whole thing disappeared. The memory dissolved and all he was left with was her eyes, big, and brown, and flat with pain.

It was an unfamiliar emotion, guilt. It burned, and it prickled, and it grabbed him by the throat. Anger had been much, much easier. Anger was clean. It was precise. And it was never about him.

It had been about Leticia. It had been about her many men. But it had never had to be about him.

But this—This was something else. And there was no way he could live like this. They could be happy again, couldn't they? He had certainly been happy before. She had been, too. She might complain about his failings, but he knew that she had been happy.

And she would be again, he vowed. Once Miranda accepted that he cared for her in every way he knew how, they could go back to the comfortable existence they'd carved out since their marriage. She would have the baby. They would be a family. He would make love to her with his hands and with his lips, with everything but words.

He had won her once before. He could do it again.

Two weeks later, Miranda was sitting in her new rose salon, trying to read a book but spending far more time staring out the window. Turner had sent word that he would be arriving within the next few days, and she couldn't stop her heart from racing every time she heard a noise that sounded like a carriage coming up the drive.

The sun had slipped down below the horizon before she realized that she hadn't yet turned a single page in her book. A concerned servant brought in the supper she had forgotten to request, and Miranda had barely finished her bowl of soup before she fell asleep on the sofa.

A few hours later, the carriage for which she'd been watching so diligently came to a halt in front of the house, and Turner, weary from travel yet still eager to see his wife, hopped down. He reached into one of his bags and withdrew a neatly wrapped package, leaving the rest of his luggage with the vehicle for the footmen to bring in. He looked up at the house and noted that no light was burning in their bedroom. He hoped that Miranda wasn't already asleep; he hadn't the heart to wake her, but he really wanted to speak with her that evening and try to make amends.

He stomped up the front steps, trying to dislodge some of the mud from his boots as he did so. The butler, who had been watching for him almost as long as Miranda, opened the door before Turner could knock.

"Good evening, Brearley," Turner said affably.

"May I be the first to welcome you home, my lord."

"Thank you. Is my wife still awake?"

"I believe she is in the rose salon, my lord. Reading, I think."

Turner shrugged off his coat. "She certainly likes to do that."

"We are fortunate to have such a well-read lady," Brearley added.

Turner blinked. "We don't have a rose salon, Brearley."

"We do now, my lord. In the former west salon."

"Oh? So she decorated. Well, good for her. I want her to think of this place as home."

"As do we all, my lord."

Turner smiled. Miranda had aroused a fierce loyalty among the household staff. The maids positively worshipped her. "I'll go surprise her now." He strode across the front hall, veering right until he reached what used to be the west salon. The door was slightly ajar, and Turner could see the flicker of a candle. Silly woman. She ought to know that she needed more than one candle to read.

He pushed the door open a few more inches and poked his head in. Miranda was lying back on the sofa, her mouth soft and slightly open as she slept. A book was lying across her belly, and a half-eaten meal sat on the table next to her. She looked so lovely and innocent, his heart ached. He had missed her on his journey—he had thought of her, and their inauspicious parting, nearly every minute of every day. But he did not think he'd realized just how deep and elemental his longing had been until this very moment, when he saw her again, her eyes closed, her chest rising and falling gently in slumber.

He'd told himself he would not wake her, but that, he reasoned, was when he'd thought she would be in their bedchamber. She was going to have to be awakened in order to go upstairs to bed, so he might as well be the one to do it.

He walked over to the sofa, pushed her dinner to the side, and perched on the table, letting his package rest on his lap. "Wake up, dar—" He broke off, belatedly remembering how she had ordered him not to use endearments any longer. He touched her shoulder. "Wake up, Miranda."

She blinked. "Turner?" Her voice was groggy.

"Hello, puss." Hang her if she didn't want him to call her that. If he wanted to use an endearment, he damned well would.

"I'd almost—" She yawned. "I'd almost given up on you."

"I told you I'd arrive today."

"But the roads . . ."

"They weren't so bad." He smiled down at her. Her sleepy mind hadn't yet remembered that it was mad at him, and he saw no reason to issue a reminder. He touched her cheek. "I missed you."

Miranda yawned again. "Did you?"

"Very much." He paused. "Did you miss me?"

"I . . . yes." Lying served no purpose, she realized. He already knew that she loved him. "Did you have a good time in London?" she asked politely.

"I'd rather you had been with me," he replied, and he sounded too measured, as if his sentences had been carefully balanced so as not to offend.

And then, in the same polite voice: "Did you have a good time while I was gone?"

"Olivia came for a few days."

"Did she?"

Miranda nodded. And then she said, "Other than that, however, I had a great deal of time to think."

There was a long silence, and then: "I see."

She watched as he set his package down, stood, and walked over to where the solitary candle was burning. "It's quite dark in here," he said, but there was something stilted about it, and she wished she could see his face as he picked up the candle and used it to light several more.

"I fell asleep while it was still twilight," she told him, because . . . well, because there seemed to be some sort of unspoken agreement between them to keep this all cordial and careful and civil and everything else that meant they avoided anything real.

"Really?" he replied. "It gets dark quite early now. You must have been very tired."

"It's wearying to carry an extra person around one's middle."

He smiled. Finally. "It won't be much longer."

"No, but I want this last month to be as pleasant as possible."

The words hung in the air. She had not meant them innocently, and he did not misinterpret. "What do you mean by that?" he asked, each word so soft and so precise that she could not miss his serious intent.

"I mean . . ." She swallowed nervously, wishing that she was standing up with her hands on her hips, or with her arms crossed, or anything but this utterly vulnerable position lying back on the sofa. "It means that I cannot go on as we were before."

"I thought we were happy," he said cautiously.

"We were. I was. I mean . . . but I wasn't."

"Either you were or you weren't, puss. One or the other."

"Both," she said, hating the low tone of finality in his voice. "Don't you understand?" And then she looked at him. "No, I can see you do not."

"I don't know what you want me to do," he said flatly. But they both knew he was lying.

"I need to know where I stand with you, Turner."

"Where you stand with me?" he asked in a disbelieving voice. "Where you stand with me? Bloody hell, woman. You're my wife. What else do you need to know?"

"I need to know that you love me!" she burst out, clumsily getting to her feet. He made no reply, just stood there with a muscle twitching in his cheek, so she added, "Or I need to know that you don't."

"What the hell does that mean?"

"It means I want to know what you feel, Turner. I need to know how you feel about me. If you don't—if you don't—" She squeezed her eyes shut and clenched her hands, trying to figure out just what it was she wanted to say. "It doesn't matter if you don't care," she finally said. "But I have to know."

"What the devil are you talking about?" He raked his fingers angrily through his hair. "Every minute of the day I tell you I adore you."

"You don't tell me you adore me. You tell me you adore being married to me."

"What is the difference?" he fairly yelled.

"Maybe you just adore being married."

"After Leticia?" he spat.

"I'm sorry," she said, because she was. For that. But not for the rest. "There is a difference," she said in a low voice. "A large one. I want to know if you care for *me*, not just for the way I make you feel."

He rested his hands on the windowsill, leaning heavily

on it as he stared out the window. She could see only his back, but she heard him clearly as he said, "I don't know what you're talking about."

"You don't want to know," she burst out. "You're *afraid* to think about it. You—"

Turner whirled around and silenced her with a look that was as hard as any she had ever seen. Even that night when he'd first kissed her, when he was sitting alone, getting drunk after burying Leticia—he had not looked like this.

He stepped toward her, his movements slow and seething with anger. "I am not a domineering husband, but my leniency does not extend to being called a coward. Choose your words with greater care, *wife*."

"And you may choose your attitudes with greater care," she countered, his snide tone raking along her spine. "I am not a silly little"—her entire body shook as she fought for words—"*confection* you can treat as if I lacked a brain."

"Oh, for Christ's sake, Miranda. When have I ever treated you like that? When? You tell me, because I am damned curious."

Miranda stammered, unable to meet his challenge. Finally she said, "I don't like being spoken to in supercilious tones, Turner."

"Then don't provoke me." His expression came dangerously close to a sneer.

"Don't provoke *you*?" she burst out incredulously, advancing toward him. "You don't provoke *me*!"

"I haven't done a damned thing, Miranda. One minute I thought we were blissfully happy and the next you've come at me like a fury, accusing me of God knows what awful crime, and—"

He stopped when he felt her frantic fingers biting into his upper arms. "You thought we were blissfully happy?" she whispered.

For a moment, when he looked at her, it was almost as if he were merely surprised. "Of course I did," he said. "I told you all the time." But then he gave himself a shake, and he rolled his eyes and pushed her away. "Oh, but I forgot. Everything I've done, everything I've said—none of it mattered. You don't *want* to know that I am happy with you. You don't care if I like to be with you. You just want to know how I feel."

And then, because she couldn't not say it, she whispered, "How *do* you feel about me?"

It was as if she'd popped him with a pin. He had been all movement and energy, the words spilling mockingly from his mouth, and now . . . Now he just stood there, not making a noise, just staring at her as if she had released Medusa into their sitting room.

"Miranda, I—I—"

"You what, Turner? You what?"

"I . . . Oh, Christ, Miranda, this isn't fair."

"You can't say it." Her eyes filled with horror. Until that moment she had held out hope that he would simply blurt it out, that maybe he was just thinking too hard about everything, and when the moment was right, and their passions were high, the words would spill from his lips, and he would realize that he loved her.

"My God," Miranda breathed. The little piece of her heart that had always believed that he would come to love her shriveled and died in the space of a second, tearing out most of her soul along with it. "My God," she said again. "You can't say it."

Turner saw the emptiness in her eyes and knew that he had lost her. "I don't want to hurt you," he said lamely.

"It's too late." Her words caught in her throat, and she walked slowly to the door.

"Wait!"

She stopped, turned.

He reached down and picked up the package he'd brought in with him. "Here," he said, his tone dull and flat. "I brought you this."

Miranda took the package from his hand, staring at his back as he strode from the room. With shaking hands, she unwrapped it. *Le Morte d'Arthur.* The very copy she had so coveted from the gentlemen's bookshop. "Oh, Turner," she whispered. "Why did you have to go and do something so sweet? Why can't you just let me hate you?"

Many hours later, as she wiped the book with a handkerchief, she found herself hoping that her salty tears had not permanently ruined the leather cover.

7 JUNE 1820

> *Lady Rudland and Olivia arrived today to await the birth of "the heir," as the entire Bevelstoke clan calls him. The physician does not seem to think that I will deliver for close to a*

month, but Lady Rudland said that she did not want to take any chances.

I am sure that they have noticed that Turner and I no longer share a bedroom. It is uncommon, of course, for married couples to share a bedroom, but last time they were here we did, and I am certain that they are wondering about our separation. It has been two weeks now since I moved my belongings.

My bed is drafty and cold. I hate it.

I am not even excited for the birth of the child.

Chapter 19

The next few weeks were hideous. Turner took to having his food sent up to his study; sitting across from Miranda for an hour each evening was more than he could bear. He had lost her this time, and it was agony to look into her eyes and see them so empty and devoid of emotion.

If Miranda was unable to feel anything any longer, then Turner felt too much.

He was furious with her for putting him on the spot and trying to force him to admit to emotions that he wasn't sure he felt.

He was enraged that she had decided to forsake their marriage after deciding that he had not passed some sort of test she'd set out for him.

He felt guilty that he had made her so miserable. He was confused as to how to treat her and terrified that he would never win her back.

He was angry with himself for being unable to just tell her that he loved her and felt somehow inadequate that he didn't even know how to determine if he was in love.

But most of all, he felt lonely. He was lonely for his wife. He missed her and all her funny little comments and quirky expressions. Every now and then he'd pass her in the hall, and he'd force himself to look into her face, trying to catch a glimpse of the woman he'd married. But she was gone. Miranda had become a different woman. She didn't seem to care anymore. About anything.

His mother, who had come to stay until the child was born, had sought him out to tell him that Miranda was barely picking at her food. He had sworn under his breath. She ought to realize that that was unhealthy. But he couldn't bring himself to seek her out and shake some sense into her. He merely instructed a few of the servants to keep a watchful eye on her.

They brought him daily reports, usually in the early evening, when he was sitting in his study, pondering alcohol and the obliterating effects thereof. This night was no different; he was on his third brandy when he heard a sharp rap at the door.

"Enter."

To his great surprise, his mother walked in.

He nodded politely. "You've come to chastise me, I imagine."

Lady Rudland crossed her arms. "And just what do you think you need chastising for?"

His smile lacked all humor. "Why don't you tell me? I'm sure you have an extensive list."

"Have you seen your wife in the past week?" she demanded.

"No, I don't believe I ha— Oh, wait a minute." He took a sip of brandy. "I passed her in the hall a few days ago. Tuesday, I think it was."

"She is over eight months' pregnant, Nigel."

"I assure you, I am aware."

"You are a cur to leave her alone in her time of need."

He took another swig. "Just to make things clear, she left me alone, not the other way around. And don't call me Nigel."

"I'll call you whatever I damned well please."

Turner raised his brows at the first use of profanity he'd ever heard escape his mother's lips. "Congratulations, you've sunk to my level."

"Give me that!" She lunged forward and grabbed the glass out of his hand. Amber liquid splashed out onto the desk. "I am appalled at you, Nigel. You're just as bad as when you were with Leticia. You're hateful, rude—" She broke off when his hand wrapped around her wrist.

"Don't ever make the mistake of comparing Miranda to Leticia," he said in a menacing voice.

"I didn't!" Her eyes widened in surprise. "I would never dream of it."

"Good." He let go of her suddenly and walked over to the window. The landscape was as bleak as his mood.

His mother remained silent for quite some time, but then she asked, "How do you intend to salvage your marriage, Turner?"

He let out a weary breath. "Why are you so certain that it is I who need to do the salvaging?"

"For the love of God, just look at the girl. She is obviously in love with you."

His fingers gripped the windowsill until his knuckles turned white. "I've seen no indication of that lately."

"How could you? You haven't seen her in weeks. For your sake, I hope you haven't killed whatever it was she felt for you."

Turner said nothing. He just wanted the conversation to end.

"She is not the same woman she was a few months ago," his mother continued. "She was so happy. She'd have done anything for you."

"Things change, Mother," he said tersely.

"And they can change back," Lady Rudland said, her voice soft yet insistent. "Come dine with us this evening. It's terribly awkward without you."

"It will be far more awkward with me, I assure you."

"Let me be the judge of that."

Turner stood straight, taking a long, shaky breath. Was his mother right? Could he and Miranda resolve their differences?

"Leticia is still in this house," his mother said softly. "Let her go. Let Miranda heal you. She will, you know, if you'd only give her the chance."

He felt his mother's hand on his shoulder but he did not turn around, too proud to let her see the face of his pain.

The first pain squeezed her belly about an hour before she was due to go down for dinner. Startled, Miranda put her hand on her stomach. The doctor had told her that she'd most likely deliver in two weeks. "Well, it looks like you're going to be early," she said softly. "Just stay in through supper, would you? I'm actually hungry. I haven't been for weeks, you know, and I need some food."

The baby kicked in response.

"So that's the way it's going to be, is it?" Miranda whispered, a smile touching her features for the first time in weeks. "I shall strike a bargain with you. You let me get through dinner in peace, and I promise not to give you a name like Iphigenia."

She felt another kick.

"If you're a girl, of course. If you're a boy, then I promise not to name you . . . Nigel!" She laughed, the sound unfamiliar and . . . nice. "I promise not to name you Nigel."

The baby was still.

"Good. Now, let's get ourselves dressed, shall we?"

Miranda rang for her maid, and an hour later, she descended the stairs to the dining room, holding the railing tightly all the way down. She wasn't sure why she didn't want to tell anyone that the baby was on its way—perhaps it was just her natural aversion to making a fuss. Besides, except for a pain every ten minutes or so, she was feeling fine. She certainly had no wish to be confined to her bed just yet. She just hoped the baby could manage to restrain itself through dinner. There was something vaguely embarrassing about childbirth, and she had no wish to learn why firsthand at the dining room table.

"Oh, there you are, Miranda," Olivia called out. "We were just having a drink in the rose salon. Join us?"

Miranda nodded and followed her friend.

"You look a little odd, Miranda," Olivia continued. "Are you feeling well?"

"Just large, thank you."

"Well, you'll be shrinking soon."

Sooner than anyone else realized, Miranda thought wryly.

Lady Rudland handed her a glass of lemonade.

"Thank you," Miranda said. "I'm suddenly very thirsty." Heedless of proper etiquette, Miranda downed it in one gulp. Lady Rudland didn't say a word as she refilled the glass. Miranda drank that one almost as quickly. "Do you think supper is ready?" she asked. "I'm dreadfully hungry." That was really only half of the story. She was going to deliver the baby at the dining room table if they tarried much longer.

"Certainly," Lady Rudland replied, slightly taken aback by Miranda's eagerness. "Lead on. It's your house after all, Miranda."

"So it is." She quirked her head, took hold of her stomach as if that might hold everything in, and stepped out into the hall.

She walked right into Turner.

"Good evening, Miranda."

His voice was rich and husky, and she felt something flutter deep in her heart.

"I trust you are well," he said.

She nodded, trying not to look at him. She'd spent the last month training herself not to melt into a pool of desire and longing every time she saw him. She'd learned to school her features into an impassive mask. They all knew he had devastated her; she did not need everyone to see it every time she walked into a room.

"Excuse me," she murmured, stepping past him toward the dining room.

Turner caught her arm. "Allow me to escort you, puss."

Miranda's lower lip began to quiver. What was he trying to do? Had she been feeling less confused—or less pregnant—she probably would have made an attempt to wrench herself from his grasp, but as it was, she acquiesced and let him lead her to the table.

Turner said nothing during the first few courses, which was just as well for Miranda, who was happy to avoid all conversation in favor of her food. Lady Rudland and Olivia tried to engage her in conversation, but Miranda always managed to have her mouth full. She was saved from responding by chewing, swallowing, and then murmuring, "I'm really quite hungry."

This worked for the first three courses, until the baby stopped cooperating. She'd thought she was getting quite good at not reacting to the pains, but she must have winced, because Turner looked sharply in her direction and asked, "Is something wrong?"

She smiled wanly, chewed, swallowed, and murmured, "Not at all. But I really am quite hungry."

"So we see," Olivia said dryly, earning herself a reproving stare from her mother.

Miranda took another bite of her chicken almondine and then winced again. This time Turner was certain he'd seen it. "You made a noise," he said firmly. "I heard you. What is wrong?"

She chewed and swallowed. "Nothing. Although I am quite hungry."

"Perhaps you are eating too quickly," Olivia suggested.

Miranda jumped on the excuse. "Yes, yes, that must be it. I shall slow down." Thankfully, the conversation changed directions when Lady Rudland drew Turner into a discussion of the bill he'd recently supported in Parliament. Miranda was grateful that his attention had been engaged elsewhere; he'd been watching her too closely, and it was getting difficult to keep her face serene when she felt a contraction.

Her belly clenched again, and this time she lost her patience. "Stop that," she whispered, looking down at her middle. "Or you will certainly be Iphigenia."

"Did you say something, Miranda?" Olivia asked.

"Oh, no, I don't think so."

Another few minutes went by, and she felt another squeeze. "Stop that, Nigel," she whispered. "We had a bargain."

"I'm certain you said something," Olivia said sharply.

"Did you just call me Nigel?" Turner asked.

Funny, Miranda thought, how calling him Nigel seemed to upset him more than her leaving the marriage bed. "Of course not. You're just imagining things. But I vow I am tired. I believe I shall retire, if none of you minds." She started to stand up, then felt a rush of liquid between her legs. She sat back down. "Perhaps I'll wait for dessert."

Lady Rudland excused herself, claiming that she was on a slimming regime and could not bear to watch the rest of them eat their pudding. Her departure made it more difficult for Miranda to avoid the conversation, but she did her best, pretending to be engrossed in her food and hoping no one would ask her a question. Finally, the meal was over. Turner stood and walked over to her side, offering his arm to her.

"No, I believe I'll sit here for a moment. A bit tired, you know." She could feel a flush creeping up along her neck. Good heavens, no one had ever written an etiquette book concerning what to do when one's baby wanted to be born in a formal dining room. Miranda was utterly mortified and so scared that she could not seem to pick herself up off the chair.

"Would you like another serving?" Turner's tone was dry.

"Yes, please," she replied, her voice cracking.

"Miranda, are you certain you're feeling well?" Olivia asked as Turner summoned a footman. "You look quite odd."

"Get your mother," Miranda croaked. "Now."

"Is it . . . ?"

Miranda nodded.

"Oh my," Olivia said with a gulp. "It's time."

"What time?" Turner asked irritably. Then he glimpsed Miranda's terrified expression. "Holy bloody hell. That time." He strode across the room and scooped his wife into his arms, oblivious to the way her sodden skirts were staining the fine fabric of his jacket.

Miranda clung to his powerful frame, forgetting all her vows to remain indifferent to him. She buried her face in the crook of his neck, letting his strength seep into her. She was going to need it in the hours ahead.

"You little fool," he murmured. "How long have you been sitting there in pain?"

She chose not to answer, knowing that the truth would only earn her a scolding.

Turner carried her up the stairs to a guest bedroom that had been prepared for the delivery. By the time he had laid her down on the bed, Lady Rudland had come rushing in. "Thank you so much, Turner," she said quickly. "Go summon the physician."

"Brearley has already taken care of it," he replied, looking down at Miranda with an anxious expression.

"Well, then, go keep yourself occupied. Have a drink."

"I'm not thirsty."

Lady Rudland sighed. "Do I need to spell it out for you, son? Go away."

"Why?" Turner looked incredulous.

"There is no place for men in childbirth."

"There was certainly place enough for me beforehand," he muttered.

Miranda blushed deep crimson. "Turner, please," she begged.

He looked down at her. "Do you want me to go?"

"Yes. No. I don't know."

He put his hands on his hips and faced his mother. "I think I should stay. It's my child, too."

"Oh, very well. Just go over to that corner and stay out of the way." Lady Rudland waved her arms, shooing him away.

Another contraction gripped Miranda. "Eeeengh," she moaned.

"What was that?" Turner shot over to her side in a flash. "Is this normal? Should she be—"

"Turner, hush!" Lady Rudland said. "You're going to worry her." She turned down to Miranda and pressed a damp cloth to her brow. "Pay him no mind, dear. It's perfectly normal."

"I know. I . . ." She paused to catch her breath. "Could I get out of this dress?"

"Oh, goodness, of course. I'm so sorry. I forgot all about it. You must be so uncomfortable. Turner, come here and give me a hand."

"No!" Miranda exclaimed sharply.

He stopped short, and his face went cold.

"I mean, either you do it or have him do it," Miranda told her mother-in-law. "But not both."

"That's the childbirth talking," Lady Rudland said soothingly. "You're not thinking clearly."

"No! He can do it if you want because he's . . . seen me before. Or you can do it because you're a woman. But I don't want you seeing me while he sees me. Don't you understand?" Miranda gripped the older woman's arm with uncharacteristic force.

Back in the corner, Turner suppressed a smile. "I'll let you do the honors, Mother," he said, keeping his voice flat so that he didn't burst out laughing. With a sharp nod, he left the room. He forced himself to walk halfway down the hall before letting laughter take over. What a funny little set of scruples his wife had.

Back in the bedroom, Miranda was gritting her teeth

against another contraction as Lady Rudland peeled off her ruined dress.

"Is he gone?" she asked. She did not trust him not to peek in.

Her mother-in-law nodded. "He won't bother us."

"It's not a bother," Miranda said, before she could think the better of it.

"Of course it is. Men have no place during childbirth. It's messy, and it's painful, and not a one of them knows how to be useful. Better to let them sit outside and ponder all the ways they should reward you for your hard work."

"He bought me a book," Miranda whispered.

"Did he? I was thinking of diamonds, myself."

"That would be nice, too," Miranda said weakly.

"I shall drop a hint in his ear." Lady Rudland finished getting Miranda into her nightgown and fluffed the pillows behind her. "There you are. Are you comfortable?"

Another pain gripped her belly. "Not. Really," she squeezed between her teeth.

"Was that another one?" Lady Rudland asked. "Goodness. They are coming very close together. This may be an uncommonly fast birth. I do hope Dr. Winters arrives soon."

Miranda held her breath as she rode through the wave of pain, nodding her agreement.

Lady Rudland took her hand and squeezed, her face scrunching in empathy. "If it makes you feel any better," she said, "it's much worse with twins."

"It doesn't," Miranda gasped.

"Make you feel any better?"

"No."

Lady Rudland sighed. "I didn't think it would, actually. But don't worry," she added, brightening a bit. "This will all be over soon."

Twenty-two hours later, Miranda wanted a new definition of the word *soon*. Her entire body was wracked with pain, her breath was coming in ragged gasps, and she felt as if she just couldn't get enough air into her body. And the contractions kept on coming, each one worse than the last. "I feel one coming," she whimpered.

Lady Rudland immediately mopped her brow with a cool cloth. "Just bear down, sweetheart."

"I can't . . . I'm too . . . Bloody hell!" she yelled, using her husband's favorite epithet.

Out in the hall, Turner stiffened as he heard her cry out. After getting Miranda changed out of her soiled dress, his mother had taken him out of earshot and convinced him that everyone would be better off if he stayed out in the hall. Olivia had brought two chairs out from a nearby sitting room and was diligently keeping him company, trying not to wince when Miranda yelled out in pain. "That sounded like a bad one," she said nervously, trying to make conversation.

He glared at her. Wrong thing to say.

"I'm sure it will all be over soon," Olivia said with more hope than certainty. "I don't think it could get much worse."

Miranda yelled out again, clearly in agony.

"At least I don't think so," Olivia added weakly.

Turner let his face fall into his hands. "I'm never going to touch her again," he moaned.

"He's never going to touch me again!" they heard Miranda roar.

"Well, it doesn't look like you'll have much argument from your wife on that point," Olivia chirped. She nudged his chin with her knuckles. "Buck up, big brother. You're about to become a father."

"Soon, I hope," he muttered. "I don't think I can take much more of this."

"If you think it's bad, just think how Miranda must feel."

He leveled a deadly stare at her. Wrong thing to say again. Olivia shut her mouth.

Back in the birthing room, Miranda was holding her mother-in-law's hand in a death grip. "Make it stop," she moaned. "Please make it stop."

"It will be over soon, I assure you."

Miranda yanked her down until they were nearly face to face. "You said that *yesterday*!"

"Excuse me, Lady Rudland?"

It was Dr. Winters, who had arrived an hour after the pains had started.

"If I could have a word with you?"

"Yes, yes, of course," Lady Rudland said, carefully extricating her hand from Miranda's. "I'll be right back. I promise."

Miranda nodded jerkily and grabbed hold of the sheets, needing something to squeeze when the pain overtook her body. Her head lolled from side to side as she tried to take a deep breath. Where was Turner? Didn't he realize that she needed him in here? She needed his warmth, his smile, but most of all, she needed his strength because she didn't think she had enough of her own to get her through this ordeal.

But she was stubborn, and she had her pride, and she could not bring herself to ask Lady Rudland where he was. Instead she gritted her teeth and tried not to cry out from the pain.

"Miranda?" Lady Rudland was looking down at her with a concerned expression. "Miranda, darling, the doctor says you have to push harder. The babe needs a little help coming out."

"I'm too tired," she whimpered. "I can't do it anymore." *I need Turner.* But she didn't know how to say the words.

"Yes, you can. If you just push a little harder now, it will be over much more quickly."

"I can't . . . I can't . . . I—ohhhh!"

"That's it, Lady Turner," Dr. Winters said briskly. "Push now."

"I . . . Oh, it hurts. It hurts."

"Push. I can see the head."

"You can?" Miranda tried to lift her head.

"Shhh, don't strain your neck," Lady Rudland said. "You won't be able to see anything, anyway. Trust me."

"Keep pushing," the doctor said.

"I'm trying. I'm trying." Miranda clamped her teeth together and squeezed. "Is it . . . Can you . . ." She took a few giant gulps of air. "What kind is it?"

"I can't tell yet," Dr. Winters replied. "Hold on. Wait a minute . . . There we are." Once the head had emerged, the tiny body slipped out quickly. "It's a girl."

"It is?" Miranda breathed. She sighed wearily. "Of course it is. Turner always gets what he wants."

Lady Rudland opened the door and poked her head into the hall while the doctor saw to the baby. "Turner?"

He looked up, his face haggard.

"It's over, Turner. It's a girl. You have a daughter."

"A girl?" Turner echoed. The long wait in the hall had worn him down, and after nearly a full day of listening to his wife cry out in pain, he could not quite believe that it was done, and he was a father.

"She's beautiful," his mother said. "Perfect in every way."

"A girl," he said again, shaking his head in wonder. He turned to his sister, who had remained at his side through-out the night. "A girl. Olivia, I have a girl!" And then, surprising them both, he threw his arms around her and hugged.

"I know, I know." Even Olivia had a hard time keeping the tears in her eyes.

Turner gave her one last squeeze, then looked back to his mother. "What color eyes does she have? Are they brown?"

An amused smile spread on Lady Rudland's face. "I don't know, darling. I didn't even look. But babies' eyes often change color while they're small. We probably won't know for certain for some time yet."

"They will be brown," Turner said firmly.

Olivia's eyes widened in sudden awareness. "You love her."

"Hmmm? What did you say, brat?"

"You love her. You love Miranda."

Funny, but that tightness in his throat he always felt at the mention of the L-word was gone. "I—" Turner stopped short, his mouth opening slightly in stunned surprise.

"You love her," Olivia repeated.

"I think I do," he said wonderingly. "I love her. I love Miranda."

"It's about time you realized it," his mother said pertly.

Turner sat slack-jawed, amazed at how *easy* it all felt now. Why had it taken him so long to realize it? It should have been clear as day. He loved Miranda. He loved everything about her, from her delicately arched eyebrows to her often sarcastic jibes and the way her head tilted when she was curious. He loved her wit, her warmth, her loyalty. He even loved the way her eyes were slightly too close together. And now she had given him a child. She had lain in that bed and labored for hours under tremendous pain, all to give him a child. Tears welled up in his eyes. "I want to see her." He almost choked on the words.

"The doctor will have the baby ready in a moment," his mother said.

"No. I want to see Miranda."

"Oh. Well, I don't see any harm in that. Hold on just a moment. Dr. Winters?"

They heard a hushed expletive, and then the baby was thrust into her grandmother's arms.

Turner flung the door open. "What's wrong?"

"She's losing far too much blood," the doctor said grimly.

Turner looked down at his wife and nearly stumbled in terror. There was blood everywhere; it seemed to be pouring from her, and her face was deathly pale. "Oh, God," he said in a strangled voice. "Oh, Miranda."

I gave you birth today. I don't know your name yet. They haven't even let me hold you. I thought I might name you after my mother. She was a lovely woman, and she always hugged me so tightly at bedtime. Her name was Caroline. I hope Turner likes it. We never discussed names.

Am I asleep? I can hear everyone around me, but I can't seem to say anything to them. I am trying to remember these words in my head so that I may write them down later.

I think I am asleep.

Chapter 20

The doctor managed to staunch the bleeding, but he was shaking his head as he washed his hands. "She's lost a lot of blood," he said grimly. "She's going to be weak."

"But she'll pull through?" Turner asked anxiously.

Dr. Winters raised his shoulders in a melancholy shrug. "We can only hope."

Not liking that answer, Turner pushed past the doctor and sat down in a chair by his wife's bed. He picked up her limp hand and held it in his. "She'll pull through," he said hoarsely. "She has to."

Lady Rudland cleared her throat. "Dr. Winters, do you have any idea what caused all of the bleeding?"

"It could be a tear in the uterus. Probably from when the afterbirth pulled away."

"Is this a common occurrence?"

The doctor nodded. "I'm afraid I must go. There is another woman in the area who is expecting, and I need to get some sleep if I'm to attend to her properly."

"But Miranda . . ." Lady Rudland's words trailed off as she looked at her daughter-in-law with dismay and fear.

"There is nothing more I can do for her. We must only hope and pray that her body heals the tear, and she does not bleed again."

"And if she does?" Turner asked flatly.

"If she does, press clean bandages up against her as I did. And send for me."

"And if we did, is there any chance in hell that you could get here in time?" Turner asked caustically, grief and terror ripping away all politeness.

The doctor chose not to reply. He nodded his head. "Lady Rudland. Lord Turner."

As the door closed, Lady Rudland crossed the room to her son's side. "Turner," she said soothingly. "You should get some rest. You've been up all night."

"So have you."

"Yes, but I . . ." Her words trailed off. If her husband were dying, she'd want to be with him. She dropped a kiss on the top of Turner's head. "I'll leave you alone with her."

He spun around, his eyes flashing dangerously. "Damn it all, Mother! I am not here to say my final good-byes. There is no need to talk like she is dying."

"Of course not." But her eyes, filled with pity and grief, told a different story. She quietly left the room.

Turner stared down at Miranda's pale face, a muscle working spasmodically in his throat. "I should have told you that I love you," he said hoarsely. "I should have told you. It's all you wanted to hear, wasn't it? And I was too stupid to realize it. I think I've loved you all along, sweetheart. All along. Every since that day in the carriage when you finally told me that you loved me. I was—"

He stopped, thinking he'd seen movement in her face. But it was just his own shadow, moving along her skin as he rocked back and forth.

"I was just so surprised," he said, once he found his voice again. "So surprised that someone could love me and not want any sort of power over me. So surprised that you could love me and not want to change me. And I . . . I didn't think I *could* love anymore. But I was wrong!" His hands flexed jerkily, and he had to resist the urge to take her by the shoulders and shake. "I was wrong, damn it, and it wasn't your fault. It wasn't your fault, puss. It was mine. Or maybe Leticia's, but definitely not yours."

He picked up her hand again and brought it to his lips. "It was never your fault, puss," he said entreatingly. "So come back to me. Please. I swear, you're scaring me. You don't want to scare me, do you? I assure you, it's not a pretty sight."

There was no response. He wished she'd cough, or restlessly shift position, or anything. But she just lay there, so still, so unmoving that a moment of sheer terror descended on him and he frantically turned her hand over to feel for her pulse on the inside of her wrist. Turner sighed in relief. It was there. It was soft, but it was there.

He let out a weary yawn. He was exhausted, and his eyelids were drooping, but he could not let himself sleep. He needed to *be* with her. He needed to see her, to hear her breathe, to simply watch the way the light played across her skin.

"It's too dark," he muttered, getting to his feet. "It's like a goddamned morgue in here. He searched the room, shuffling through drawers and closets until he found some more candles. He quickly lit them all and shoved them into holders. It was still too dark. He strode to the door, flung it open, and yelled out, "Brearley! Mother! Olivia!"

Eight people immediately answered his summons, all fearing the worst.

"I need more candles," Turner said, his voice belying his terror and exhaustion. A few maids immediately scurried off.

"But it's already so bright in here," Olivia said, poking her head into the room. Her breath caught when she saw Miranda, her best friend since infancy, lying so still. "Is she going to be all right?" she whispered.

"She's going to be just fine," Turner snapped. "Provided that we can get some light in here."

Olivia cleared her throat. "I should like to go in and say something to her."

"She isn't going to die!" Turner exploded. "Do you hear me? She isn't going to die. There is no need to talk that way. You don't have to say good-bye."

"But if she did," Olivia persisted, tears rolling down her cheeks. "I should feel—"

Turner's control snapped, and he shoved his sister up against the wall. "She isn't going to die," he said in a low, deadly voice. "I would appreciate it if you would stop acting otherwise."

Olivia nodded jerkily.

Turner suddenly let her go and then stared at his hands as if they were foreign objects. "My God," he said raggedly. "What is happening to me?"

"It's all right, Turner," Olivia said soothingly, cautiously touching his shoulder. "You have every right to be overwrought."

"No I don't. Not when she needs me to be strong for her." He strode back into the room and sat back down next to his wife. "I don't matter right now," he muttered, swallowing convulsively. "Nothing matters but Miranda."

A bleary-eyed housemaid entered the room with some candles.

"Light them all," Turner ordered. "I want it bright as day in here. Do you hear me? Bright as day." He turned back to Miranda and smoothed his hand over her brow. "She always did love sunny days." He caught himself in horror and looked frantically at his sister. "I mean—she *loves* sunny days."

Olivia, unable to watch her brother in such a grief-stricken state, nodded and quietly departed.

A few hours later, Lady Rudland entered the room carrying a small bundle wrapped in a soft pink blanket. "I brought your daughter," she said softly.

Turner looked up, shocked to realize that he had completely forgotten about the existence of this tiny person. He stared at her in disbelief. "She's so small."

His mother smiled. "Babies usually come that way."

"I know but . . . look at her." He reached out his index finger to her hand. Tiny fingers grasped it with surprising firmness. Turner looked up at his mother, amazement at this new life clearly written on his bleak face. "Can I hold her?"

"Of course." Lady Rudland settled the bundle in his arms. "She's yours, you know."

"She is, isn't she?" He looked down at the pink face and touched her nose. "How do you do? Welcome to the world, puss."

"Puss?" Lady Rudland said in an amused tone. "What a funny nickname."

Turner shook his head. "No, it's not funny. It's absolutely perfect." He looked back up at his mother. "How long will she be this small?"

"Oh, I don't know. For a little while, at least." She crossed over to the window and pulled the drapes halfway back. "The sun is starting to come up. Olivia told me that you wanted some light in the room."

He nodded, unable to take his eyes off his daughter.

She finished fussing at the window and turned back to him. "Oh, Turner . . . she has brown eyes."

"She does?" He looked back down at the baby. Her eyes were closed in sleep. "I knew she would."

"Well, she wouldn't want to disappoint her papa on her first day out, would she?"

"Or her mother." Turner looked over at Miranda, still deathly pale, then hugged this new bundle of life closer to him.

Lady Rudland glanced at her son's blue eyes, so like her own, and said, "I daresay Miranda was hoping for blue eyes."

Turner swallowed uncomfortably. Miranda had loved him so long and so well, and he had spurned her. Now he might lose her, and she'd never know that he realized what a stupid ass he'd been. She'd never know that he loved her. "I daresay she would," he said in a choked voice. "She'll just have to wait until the next one."

Lady Rudland caught her lip between her teeth. "Of course, dear," she said consolingly. "Have you given any thought as to names?"

He looked up in surprise, as if the idea of a name had never occurred to him. "I . . . No. I forgot," he admitted.

"Olivia and I thought of some pretty names. What do you think of Julianna? Or Claire. I suggested Fiona, but Olivia didn't like it."

"Miranda would never allow her daughter to be named Fiona," he said dully. "She always hated Fiona Bennet."

"That little girl who lives near Haverbreaks? I never knew."

"It's a moot point, Mother. I'm not naming her without consulting Miranda."

Lady Rudland swallowed again. "Of course, dear. I'll just . . . I'll just leave you now. Give you some time alone with your family."

Turner looked at his wife and then at his daughter. "That's your mama," he whispered. "She's very tired. It took a lot of her strength to get you out. I can't imagine why. You're not very big." To demonstrate his point, he touched one of her tiny fingers. "I don't think she's even seen you yet. I know she would want to. She would hold you and hug you and kiss you. Do you know why?" He awkwardly brushed away a tear. "Because she loves you, that's why. I'd wager she loves you even more than she loves me. And I think she must love me quite a bit because I haven't always behaved as I should."

He stole a glance at Miranda to make sure she hadn't woken up before he added, "Men can be asses. We're silly and we're stupid and we rarely open our eyes wide enough to see the blessings that are right in front of our faces. But I see you," he added, smiling down at his daughter. "And I see your mother, and I hope her heart is big enough to forgive me this last time. I think it is, though. Your mama has a very big heart."

The baby gurgled, causing Turner to smile with delight. "I can see that you agree with me. You're very clever for being just a day old. But then again, I don't see why I should be surprised. Your mama is very clever, too."

The baby cooed.

"You flatter me, puss. But for the time being, I'll let you think I'm clever, too." He looked over at Miranda and whispered, "Only the two of us need to know just how stupid I've been."

The baby made another baby noise, leading Turner to believe that his daughter must be the most intelligent child in the British Isles. "Do you want to meet your mother, puss? Here, why don't we introduce the two of you." His movements were awkward, for he had never held a baby before, but somehow he managed to settle his daughter in the crook of Miranda's arm. "There you go. Mmmm, it's warm there, isn't it? I'd like to trade places with you. Your mama has very soft skin." He reached out and touched the baby's cheek. "Not as soft as yours, however. You, little one, are quite astonishingly perfect."

The baby began to fidget and after a few moments let out a lusty wail. "Oh, dear," Turner muttered, completely at a loss. He picked her up and cradled her against his shoulder, taking great care to support her head as he had seen his mother do. "There, there, now. Shhh. Be quiet now. That's right."

His entreaties obviously weren't working because she bellowed in his ear.

A knock sounded on the door, and Lady Rudland looked inside. "Do you want me to take her, Turner?"

He shook his head, loath to part with his daughter.

"I think she's hungry, Turner. The wet nurse is in the next room."

"Oh. Of course." He looked vaguely embarrassed as he handed the baby to his mother. "Here you are."

He was alone again with Miranda. She hadn't moved at all during his vigil, save for the shallow rise and fall of her chest. "It's morning, Miranda," he said, taking her hand in his again and trying to cajole her into consciousness. "Time to wake up. Will you? If not for yourself, then for me. I'm frightfully tired, but you know I can't go to sleep until you wake up."

But she did not move. She did not turn in her sleep, and she did not snore, and she was terrifying him. "Miranda," he said, hearing the panic in his voice, "this is enough. Do you hear me? It's enough. You need to—"

He broke off, unable to go on any longer. He gave her hand a squeeze and looked away. Tears blurred his vision.

How was he going to go on without her? How would he raise their daughter all on his own? How would he even know what to name her? And worst of all, how could he live with himself if she died without ever hearing him say that he loved her?

With fresh determination, he wiped away his tears and turned back to her. "I love you, Miranda," he said loudly, hoping that he could penetrate her haze, even if she never woke up. His voice grew urgent. "I love you. You. Not what you do for me or the way you make me feel. Just you."

A slight sound escaped her lips, so soft that Turner initially thought he had imagined it. "Did you say something?" His eyes searched her face frantically, looking for any sign of movement. Her lips quivered again, and his heart leaped with joy. "What was that, Miranda? Please, just say it once again. I didn't hear you the first time." He put his ear down to her lips.

Her voice was weak, but the word came through loud and clear: "Good."

Turner began to laugh. He couldn't help it. How like Miranda to have a smart mouth while on her supposed deathbed. "You're going to be all right, aren't you?"

Her chin moved only a fraction of an inch, but it was definitely a nod.

Wild with happiness and relief, he ran to the door and yelled out the good news for the rest of the house to hear. Not surprisingly, his mother, Olivia, and much of the household staff came running into the hall.

"She's all right," he gasped, not even caring that his face was wet with tears. "She's all right."

"Turner." The word came like a croak from the bed.

"What is it, my love?" He rushed to her side.

"Caroline," she said softly, using all her strength to curve her lips into a smile. "Call her Caroline."

He lifted her hand to his in a courtly kiss. "Caroline it is. You gave me a perfect little girl."

"You always get what you want," she whispered.

He gazed down at her lovingly, suddenly realizing the extent of the miracle that had brought her back from the dead. "Yes," he said hoarsely. "It seems that I do."

A few days later, Miranda was feeling much improved. At her request, she had been moved to the bedroom she and Turner had shared during the first months of their marriage. The surroundings comforted her, and she wanted to show her husband that she wanted a real marriage. They belonged together. It was that simple.

She was still confined to her bed, but she'd regained much of her strength, and her cheeks were tinged with a healthy pink glow. Although that might just have been love. Miranda had never felt so much of it before. Turner couldn't seem to say two sentences without blurting it out, and Caroline brought out such love in both of them, it was indescribable.

Olivia and Lady Rudland fussed over her, too, but Turner tried to keep their interference at a minimum, wanting his wife wholly to himself. He was sitting by her side one day as she woke up from a nap.

"Good afternoon," he murmured.

"Afternoon? Is it really?" She let out a giant yawn.

"Past noon, at least."

"Goodness. I've never felt this lazy before."

"You deserve it," he assured her, his blue eyes glowing warm with love. "Every minute of it."

"How is the baby?"

Turner smiled. She managed to ask that question within the first minute of any conversation. "Very well. She's got quite a set of lungs, I must say."

"She's very sweet, isn't she?"

He nodded. "Just like her mother."

"Oh, I'm not so sweet."

He dropped a kiss on her nose. "Under that temper of yours, you're very sweet. Trust me. I've tasted you."

She blushed. "You're incorrigible."

"I'm *happy*," he corrected. "Really, truly, happy."

"Turner?"

He looked down at her intently, hearing the hesitation in her voice. "What, my love?"

"What happened?"

"I'm not sure I understand what you mean."

She opened her mouth and then closed it, obviously trying to find the right words. "Why did you . . . suddenly realize . . ."

"That I loved you?"

She nodded mutely.

"I don't know. I think it was inside of me all along. I was just too blind to see it."

She swallowed nervously. "Was it when I almost died?"

She didn't know why, but the idea that he couldn't realize his love until she was snatched away from him didn't sit well with her.

He shook his head. "It was when you gave me Caroline. I heard her cry out, and the sound was so . . . so . . . I can't describe it, but I loved her instantly. Oh, Miranda, fatherhood is an awesome thing. When I hold her in my arms . . . I wish you knew what it was like."

"Rather like motherhood, I imagine," she said smartly.

He touched her lips with his forefinger. "Such a mouth on you. Let me finish my story. I have friends who have had children, and they have told me how remarkable it is to have a new life that is a piece of your own flesh and blood. But I—" He cleared his throat. "I realized that I didn't love her because she was a piece of me, I loved her because she was a piece of you."

Miranda's eyes filled with tears. "Oh, Turner."

"No, let me finish. I don't know what I did or said to deserve you, Miranda, but now that I have you, I'm not letting go. I love you so much." He swallowed, choking on his words. "So much."

"Oh, Turner, I love you, too. You know that, don't you?"

He nodded. "I thank you for that. It's the most precious gift I have ever received."

"We're going to be really happy, aren't we?" She gave him a wobbly smile.

"Beyond words, love, beyond words."

"And we'll have more children?"

His expression turned stern. "Provided that you don't give me another scare like this one. Besides, the best way to avoid children is abstinence, and I don't think I'm going to be able to accomplish that."

She blushed, but she also said, "Good."

He leaned down and gave her as passionate a kiss as he dared. "I should let you get some rest," he said, reluctantly tearing himself away from her.

"No, no. Please don't go. I'm not tired."

"Are you sure?"

What bliss it was to have someone care for her so deeply. "Yes, I'm sure. But I want you to get me something. Would you mind?"

"Of course not. What is it?"

She pointed out her finger. "There is a silk-covered box on my desk in the sitting room. Inside it is a key."

Turner raised his brows questioningly but followed her summons. "The green box?" he called out.

"Yes."

"Here you are." He walked back into the bedroom, holding up the key.

"Good. Now if you go back to my desk, you'll find a large wooden box in the bottom drawer."

He walked back into the sitting room. "Here we are. Lord, it's heavy. What do you have in here? Rocks?"

"Books."

"Books? What kind of books are so precious they need to be locked up?"

"They're my journals."

He reappeared, carrying the wooden box in both arms. "You keep a journal? I never knew."

"It was at your suggestion."

He turned. "It was not."

"It was. The day we first met. I told you about Fiona Bennet and how horrid she was, and you told me to keep a journal."

"I did?"

"Mmm-hmm. And I remember exactly what you said to me. I asked you why I should keep a journal and you said, 'Because someday you're going to grow into yourself, and you will be as beautiful as you already are smart. And then you can look back into your diary and realize just how silly little girls like Fiona Bennet are. And you'll laugh when you remember that your mother said your legs started at your shoulders. And maybe you'll save a little smile for me when you remember the nice chat we had today.'"

He stared at her in awe, wisps of the memory starting to come back to him. "And you said you'd save a *big* smile for me."

She nodded. "I memorized what you said word for word. It was the nicest thing anyone had ever said to me."

"My God, Miranda," he breathed reverently. "You really love me, don't you?"

She nodded. "Since that day. Here, bring me the box."

He set the box on the bed and handed her the key. She opened it and pulled out several books. Some were leather-bound, and some were covered with girlish floral fabric, but she reached for the simplest one, a small notebook reminiscent of the sort he'd used while a student. "This was the first," she said, turning the cover with reverent fingers. "I really have loved you all along. See?"

He looked down at the first entry.

2 MARCH 1810

Today I fell in love.

A tear welled up in his eye. "Me too, my love. Me too."